She Belongs To Me

Southern Romantic Suspense

(Charlotte ~ Book One)

Carmen DeSousa

She Belongs to Me
A Southern Romantic-Suspense Novel
(Charlotte ~ Book One)
Copyright© 2014 by Carmen DeSousa

www.CarmenDeSousaBooks.com
PO Box 253
Delmont, PA 15626
U.S.A.

ISBN-10: 1-945143-17-7
ISBN-13: 9781945143175

Cover Design by Viola Estrella: www.estrellacoverart.com

"If I'm honest I have to tell you I still read fairy-tales and I like them best of all." — Audrey Hepburn

Prologue

Three Days Ago ...

A loud crack startled Jordan from his sleep. His hand flew to his pounding head as he looked around the room for the source of the noise.

It sounded like a gunshot, or perhaps he was just having another nightmare. Sometimes he couldn't tell the difference.

Years in the military and working as a cop had unquestionably done a number on his psyche, so he always investigated. Often it was his dog chasing a squirrel in his sleep or the cat moving through the wood shutters as she stalked a lizard from behind her prison of glass and brick. These sounds he knew. A gunshot, though also familiar, didn't encroach on his daily routine anymore. Nowadays, most of his police work comprised of slaving behind a desk.

The room was pitch-black, and his alarm hadn't gone off, so it was still early. He patted his wife's side of the bed. Empty. Though, that wasn't unusual. She'd been staying up later than he did, using studying as an excuse, and had been falling asleep on the sofa for weeks. He didn't buy it. Things between them hadn't been the same for months.

But tonight he thought they'd resolved whatever her problem was. He was willing to take some of the blame. But as she'd pointed out with the age-old *it wasn't him, it was her* line, she'd admitted something was wrong, just not what that something was.

Fuming, he disentangled himself from the blankets that had already twisted around his feet as he thought about their conversation earlier. He'd given her an ultimatum when he came home. He didn't understand what was happening, but things had to change. Dejectedly, he'd informed her if she wanted to leave, fine, just do it and get it over with so he could move on with his life. She hadn't accepted his offer; instead, she started kissing him.

She hadn't come near him in almost two months. Every time he broached the subject, she complained about her school deadlines or she didn't feel well. Tonight was different; she was different. The old passion was there as if it had never left, which it hadn't for him. She was the one who had withdrawn. She was the one who didn't want to be close to him. God how he missed her.

Jordan now wondered if everything earlier had been a performance to distract him. Had she wanted to leave, but wasn't prepared? She would graduate within a few months, something she'd been focusing on the last five years of their marriage. Would she not need him anymore? He hated feeling this way, but what else could explain her aloof manner lately?

His anger almost at the brink, he rolled out of bed, pulling on his boxers and a t-shirt. If she'd fallen asleep on the sofa again, he'd wake her and demand answers. He wouldn't let her sidetrack him by acting as if she wanted him. He loved her, but he couldn't continue like this. He wouldn't. It was too painful.

As he stood, the pounding in his head from the excessive amount of alcohol he'd consumed earlier nearly sent him to his knees. Tonight was the first time in years he'd drank, one of the reasons it'd been so easy for her to persuade him that she wanted him too.

Jordan felt his way out of their master bedroom, opening the door without a sound, unsure if he really wanted to argue in the middle of the night. He shot a quick glance at the clock radio's glowing red numbers: just shy of midnight. It hadn't even been an hour since he'd fallen asleep.

She must have gotten up almost immediately after they'd made love. *No*, he amended, after they'd had sex as that was all it must have meant to her. He must have been sleeping deeply to already be dreaming of gun battles. His posttraumatic stress disorder rarely allowed him a night without nightmares.

No lights were on in their office, so he padded his way into the hallway and down the staircase to the kitchen and family room.

Sometimes when she left their bed, she'd feign insomnia and go downstairs to watch TV. But he didn't hear any chatter or see the familiar flickering light; in fact, the house was eerily quiet.

Remembering the ill-omened sound that had awakened him, his heart started racing in his chest, and his stomach felt like an empty pit as he entered their family room.

A greenish glow from the electronic equipment cast eerie shadows across the living area, and as his vision adjusted, he could see she wasn't on the sofa either.

Had she left their house in the middle of the night? Had his friends been right? Was Jaynee having an affair? Resentment welled in his heart that she would do that to him after all these years, after everything he'd provided.

A breeze emanated from the back porch. He squinted, realizing the patio door stood wide open. She must have left, but why would she leave without closing the door?

Jordan made his way to the French doors and attempted to pull the door shut, but something blocked its track. He switched on the overhead light, and she was there ...

He dropped to his knees, his hands fluttering to her face in horror. "Oh, my God ... Jaynee ... What have you done?" He barely recognized the peal of words that had escaped his throat.

Blood dripped from his wife's forehead and pooled onto the planks of their wood deck. Her arm was draped across the threshold. Beside her lay the .38 caliber revolver he'd given her for protection when they first married.

Jordan's first instinct was disbelief, and he wanted to inspect the gun to ensure it was hers. But his police training snapped into gear. Instead, he knelt over her to confirm she was still breathing. Thank God, she was, but it was faint, and she was unconscious.

Scrambling to his feet, his vision blurred by tears, he searched for the cordless phone. Jaynee never kept the phone in the same place, and she never kept the ringer on. Hunting from room to room, he finally found it in the spare bathroom.

Punching in the three numbers, Jordan staggered back to his fading wife.

"Emergency!" he answered the automated question, waiting until a woman's voice came on the line. "My wife has been shot! She's breathing, but barely. I need an ambulance!" His voice emerged hysterical, a combination of pain and pleading, but he knew he needed to remain composed so she'd understand him.

The dispatcher asked a torrent of questions to keep him talking.

"Listen, ma'am," Jordan interrupted the woman's queries, racing to the front of the house, "I'm a cop. I know crime-scene protocol. I'll leave the front entrance open for the officers and medics. My wife is unconscious from a gunshot wound to the head. The firearm is beside her. I need to get back to her."

Jordan disconnected the phone as he returned to Jaynee, slumping down next to her, hoping she could still hear him.

"Jaynee, can you hear me? I love you. I'm so sorry. I didn't mean those terrible words. Please don't leave me like this. Please come back ... I don't want you to leave. I promise whatever is going on, we'll work it out, but please don't leave me."

Inhaling a mouthful of air, he positioned his fingers against her carotid artery to confirm she was still breathing. She was, but her pulse felt weak. He needed her to comprehend how much his life counted on her survival.

"Jaynee, you need to fight. You've always been a fighter, so I want you to fight to live. Fight for us," he commanded, his tone beseeching and demanding. Once again, tears fell unrestricted down his face. He never cried, not before tonight. But at this moment, he knew more than ever how much his wife meant to him and how he could never subsist without her.

"Dear God," Jordan pleaded in a quiet prayer. "Please save her. Give me another opportunity. I don't want anything without her. Please, take everything from me, but not Jaynee."

The wail of a siren snatched him from his invocations, but he didn't move; he couldn't leave her.

After a few minutes, the telltale sound of an officer's heavy boots indicated that the police had arrived.

"Stand up slowly with your hands up, and step away from the gun," the officer commanded in a loud authoritative tone. The bellow of the officer's voice sounded hollow in Jordan's ears as if he were still in his nightmare. "Hands where I can see them!" he repeated.

Jordan didn't want to leave Jaynee's side, but lifting his arms, he backed away from his wife. He understood procedure, knew they needed to cordon off the area, but he couldn't fathom the suggestion of leaving her side.

The officer focused his eyes on Jordan while he kept both hands gripped on his unholstered gun. "You made the 911 call? You're a cop?"

"Yeah. Charlotte-Meck." Jordan glanced down at Jaynee. "She's my wife; her name is Jaynee. I was sleeping when I heard the gunshot. I came down to look for her and found her like this. She's still breathing, but it's labored." Jordan glanced over the officer's shoulder toward the entry. "Where's the ambulance?" he asked, uninterested in anything but saving his wife.

"They're just a couple of minutes away," the cop muttered, tone distracted, obvious concern penetrating his voice. The man knelt near Jaynee's head, checked her pulse, then stood up, his eyes grave.

No matter what the situation, cops didn't like to see other cops in peril. The officer's chin pressed against the mouthpiece clipped to his shoulder strap, spewing words into the radio, all the while keeping his eyes and gun trained on Jordan.

Jordan's mind was a fog, only deciphering fragments of what the officer muttered, something about the house being secure. Of course, he realized after a few seconds;

paramedics would confirm it was safe before entering the house of a gunshot victim. The cop obviously thought that he could have shot his wife.

Domestic disturbances were one of the most perilous of all police calls. Scorned lovers were notorious for turning the gun on others and then themselves after realizing they'd murdered their loved ones in a moment of distraught passion.

Finally, the ambulance arrived.

Jordan watched as two medics poured through the door and rushed over to his dying wife. The older of the two shouted orders to the younger while a third and fourth paramedic carried a stretcher into the room. Jordan backed out of their way, knowing he could do nothing but watch as they struggled to save her life.

***

Outside, hidden in the vegetation at the back of the property, he watched in frustration.

He should have made his escape when her husband found her. He hated seeing him with her, but couldn't bear to leave. So he waited and watched, questioning her intentions, wondering why she had a gun.

Now he would have to stay and watch, sit by as her husband wept over her. As if *he* cared about her. Her so-called husband could never love her the way he could. He wasn't supposed to be her husband. It was all a mistake. A mistake he intended on rectifying as soon as possible.

He would wait now, as he had for years. He had plenty of practice with waiting. She would survive, of course she would. She belonged to him, forever.

***

The gun had been unexpected, why did she have a gun? Was she still alive? If so, would she remember the conversation? Would the police suspect foul play? And if so, would there be any evidence to suggest the shooting as anything other than her attempted suicide?

These and a hundred other questions swarmed unabated as the vehicle crawled down the gravel road, the driver watching carefully so as not to be recognized by the officers or paramedics.

***

Jordan followed the ambulance in his wife's Altima. He understood they wouldn't permit him in the back with Jaynee, and he would be helpless in the front. He knew he could maintain their speed, probably even arrive at the hospital faster than they could.

As a patrolman, he'd always been the first on a crime scene. He decided to stay behind the ambulance, attempting to remain collected.

His heart pounded in his chest as his mind agonized over the "what ifs." What if he hadn't gotten drunk? What if he hadn't fallen asleep? What if he hadn't accepted her reassurances that everything was okay? He should have insisted she tell him the truth.

But why would Jaynee attempt to commit suicide?

She'd been struggling to finish college for five years and was now within a few months of graduating. They'd repeatedly discussed having children afterward. She intended on working out of their residence so it would have been perfect. It was what she'd said she wanted.

Had he pushed her to extremes? Maybe he only thought she wanted what he wanted.

She'd always been adept at suppressing unpleasant situations. Hadn't she done that her entire life? Jaynee had seemed content when she moved here after they got married five years ago. Jordan thought he'd shown her the love she needed to forget her past. Now he wondered if he'd ever understood her.

He promised himself he would — he wouldn't assume everything was okay any longer. He'd find out what was wrong. But for now, he'd do whatever necessary to get her healthy again. She was going to survive. She was a fighter.

Tears stung his eyes as he realized she'd now have to fight for her life. He wiped them away as he pulled into the parking area for the hospital emergency room. Jaynee needed him. She needed to hear his voice, understand he was here for her, comprehend that he still loved her ... that he would always love her.

Racing through the entrance of the ER to the receptionist, Jordan introduced himself as Caycee Jaynee Monroe's husband.

The crotchety older woman told him to have a seat. Someone would attend to him. Her personality was cold, as the hospital itself.

Jordan couldn't sit. He paced the hard tile floor, stopping and looking at the locked double doors every few seconds.

Fifteen minutes later, a nurse finally approached, directing him to an alcove, away from the main area. "Your wife is in surgery, Mr. Monroe."

"How is she?" He wanted to rush the doors and find out if Jaynee was okay, but he knew he had to stay calm.

"I'm sorry. All I know is that she's in surgery."

"But ... she's alive ... so ... she'll live, right?"

"Again, I'm sorry. I don't have any additional information. The doctor will be with you as soon as he can." She patted his arm, then hurried away.

The hours passed slowly, even with officers interrogating him and finally accepting an affidavit of his account. They assured him, however, that they would return in the morning or when his wife woke up.

When he thought he couldn't bear the agony of waiting one second longer, a familiar person stepped into the waiting room. The older man nodded toward the locked doors, a silent request for Jordan to accompany him to a separate area. Jordan had spoken to Dr. McMullen many times over the years. He rarely came to the emergency room, though. Normally a nurse updated a loved one on the patient's status — unless it was bad news.

This wasn't good; this was never an encouraging sign, but he followed obediently. The tears that had never come before this evening flowed again.

He'd lost the only woman he ever loved. Had he done something to cause this? How would he survive without Jaynee? She was his entire life. She couldn't be gone; he'd feel it, wouldn't he?

His chest felt tight, and his stomach lurched at the same time a chill traveled down his spine. He followed the doctor into his office and sat down on the sofa. His head fell into his hands; he couldn't handle this.

Jordan looked up as Dr. John McMullen sat beside him, his face unreadable. Although he looked like he wanted to comfort him, Jordan knew Dr. McMullen wouldn't offer him any artificial expectations.

McMullen had always been honest, but unlike some physicians Jordan had met in his career, he'd also been sympathetic, especially when it came to the lives of first responders — or their relatives. Jordan had witnessed his compassion for years.

Having been the bearer of dreadful news to countless spouses and parents after their tragic loss, Jordan had tried to emulate his demeanor. Now he was on the receiving end of McMullen's sympathetic stare, and it wasn't any more comforting.

Preparing for the blow, Jordan clenched his hands into fists and pressed them against his face.

"Caycee is in ICU now," Dr. McMullen began. "The bullet entered the left side of her skull below her temple and exited through the frontal bone. She survived the operation..."

Jordan dropped his hands to his side as his eyes connected with the doctor's gaze. Thank God! Jaynee was alive. He let out the breath he'd been holding as he awaited the rest of the doctor's summation.

"But, Jordan," his tone softened, "we can't be certain she'll make it. Even if she does, there's no way to distinguish what damage the bullet inflicted until she awakes."

Jordan swallowed hard. "But she survived the surgery," he repeated, as if to hear it again.

"Yes, she did. We have her in a drug-induced coma, and we won't attempt to revive her until the cranial pressure decreases. She wouldn't be able to tolerate the pain if we did." The doctor patted Jordan's arm. "You can see Caycee now, Jordan, and you need to talk to her. Studies indicate numerous coma patients respond to a loved one's voice."

"Jaynee ..." Jordan said emphatically, drawing in a breath and shaking his head in disbelief. "Please call her Jaynee. She doesn't like Caycee, so she goes by her middle name. Please inform the nurses." The doctor nodded, and Jordan stood. "I'd like to see my wife now."

Dr. McMullen led him down the hall and stopped in front of one of the ICU rooms. Jordan felt the man's cool hands on his forearm, but couldn't see his face through his tears. With a final squeeze of consolation, the doctor turned and left him alone.

Jordan stepped into the cold antiseptic-scented room. His legs felt as though they'd vanished from beneath him, and he'd collapse to the floor at any moment. He couldn't move.

Jaynee lay motionless on the hospital bed. Numerous wires leading from her body connected to several machines that created an ominous cacophony and an eerie yellowish glow in the small room. It looked like a scene from a soap opera.

Under the fluorescent lights, her skin was pallid, except around her eyes, which had splotches of crimson and were swollen and puffy. And worse, where her long, beautiful curls should be was nothing but white gauze.

He forced his legs to move to her bedside. His tears fell without restraint as he touched her cheek.

Talk to her.

He lowered his head to his wife's ear, hoping she could hear through the bandages ... and while unconscious. "I love you, Jaynee. No matter what's happened, I love you, and I know you love me too."

Jordan believed the words, wanted the words to be true. But he couldn't help but wonder what was so awful that his wife would attempt to take her life.

Unless ... was there something he didn't know about her?

Chapter One

Five years ago …

C.J. tapped her foot while a kid sitting in the front row attempted to sidetrack Professor Rawlings with his incessant questions about the life of Hemingway.

Everyone knew the professor would go off on a tangent and run out of time, then end up dismissing the class. The plan had backfired, though. It was time to leave, and here she still sat as the teacher droned on about his favorite author.

She rarely minded. She enjoyed listening to the professor. But today was Wednesday, which meant she had an early shift at the steakhouse where she worked. She checked the time on her cell phone for the tenth time in five minutes. She couldn't be late.

Tim, the general manager, scheduled her for as many early shifts as possible, because she was one of the few employees who always showed up on time and was willing to close if he needed her to.

Because of this, she also received the largest stations. The way she figured ... if she had to be there ... might as well make as much money as possible. As a college student, she was able to pay her bills working only three days a week. If she picked up extra shifts, the money was gravy and went toward her savings. And more importantly, the extra shifts didn't affect her studying anymore because, in the last year, she'd stopped dating altogether.

The lecture ended, and the teacher excused the class, calling out, "Don't forget your novella is due next week. Make sure it's not tedious. I *loathe* boring stories. And if it makes me laugh, you'll receive extra points. Also, drinking and fishing are always excellent subjects." He finished his montage as the students hurriedly exited the classroom.

Yep, he loved Hemingway and wanted to be just like him. Well, he'd have to make do with her paper. It was everything he'd said not to write. It was very sad; it was real life. It entailed drinking and fishing, but not what he was referring to, she was pretty sure.

Since she had a few minutes to spare, C.J. stopped by the post office on the way to work. Her twenty-second birthday was a little over a week away, and although she and her mother weren't close, her mother always sent her a hundred bucks for her birthday. And her best friend, Rainey, always sent a funny card. They'd been friends since third grade — until C.J. moved from South Florida, that is.

They'd managed to visit each other a couple of times over the last four years, but mostly they just kept in touch by email. It hadn't been the same, and she missed her friend terribly. She was the only person who knew what she'd been through in her life. But Rainey had been preoccupied with finishing college, and C.J. had been busy wasting her time. When she thought about the wasted years, she felt sick. Why had she been such a fool?

Determined not to squander away any more of her youth, and resolute to change her life for the better, she'd started back to college last month.

Parking alongside the building, she sprinted from the car, ran inside, grabbed a handful of envelopes, jumped back in her car, and was on her way to work in seconds.

It was ridiculous she still used a post office box, but old habits were hard to break. After high school, she'd moved around a lot and had always used her grandmother's address. It would be easy enough to use her home address now that she had her own place, but after some issues with her ex-boyfriend, she decided it was for the best.

She chanced a sideways glance at the bills and letters on the passenger seat as she sped down the road. The extra-large pink envelope was certainly from her mother. As if sending her a card a couple of times a year would change the past.

She looked down at the seat again, and another envelope stopped her heart. She recognized the handwriting. She'd made herself clear in her last letter that she didn't want him to write or contact her again. They were over.

Nervous, as though he could see her, she stuffed the letter in her work apron. It was going straight into the dumpster, where she wouldn't even be tempted to read his response to her rejection.

She didn't understand her luck with dating. For that matter, she didn't understand the trouble she'd had with all the men in her life. Clenching the steering wheel, she sucked in a breath to calm herself. She refused to let any man ever bring her down again. She was a *good* person. She didn't smoke or do drugs and rarely drank. Still, she'd suffered two horrific relationships in high school, and then after moving to the Tampa Bay area four years earlier, had dated several delinquents before finding herself in a real predicament.

What had she done to deserve the cards life had handed her? The more she thought about it, the madder she got. She didn't perceive herself as wild-looking. But every time she went out with what looked to be a decent guy — a guy who had a vehicle and an occupation anyway — they'd go out and end up at some party. The next thing she knew, her date would drop down and do a line of coke or light up a joint.

God and C.J. had always been on friendly terms, but now even He was ticking her off. She prayed to Him nightly for a decent man. Maybe He was irritated because she hadn't been to church in forever. It wasn't anything personal with Him; she just couldn't contend with the charlatans. And the last thing she wanted to do was be a hypocrite herself. So for the past year, since He hadn't been answering her prayers, she decided the best path was to abstain from dating altogether.

She drove swiftly into the restaurant parking lot in her Ford Focus, parked in the rear, and trotted into the restaurant.

After she punched her timecard, she set out to do her prep work. She had ice tea duty today, so all she had to do was make a few back-ups of sweet tea, and then set up for the rest of the night. Then she'd just have to roll silverware until her first customer arrived. Usually one of her regular retirees would show up for the early-bird dinner and save her from the monotonous task.

Amy, the hostess, meandered through the service doors minutes after the restaurant opened. "You have a table, C.J."

C.J. glanced up and saw a wide grin lift Amy's round cheeks. Amy didn't usually inform the wait staff when they had a customer. Management expected servers to pay attention.

Happy to have a customer, she grabbed her apron to leave but noticed Amy still standing there with that silly grin ... now accompanied by lifted eyebrows.

"What?" She looked herself over to make sure she wasn't wearing flip-flops or something abnormal. "Did I forget something?"

"Nope. Just wanted to let you know you have a guest. A one-top in booth six," Amy replied in a droll manner.

Oh great, she must have ticked her off. Amy knew servers hated single diners. Typically she sat them in the lounge area. Single diners were a waste of table space, as she only made half a normal tip. She needed money, and single diners wouldn't bring in enough to pay her bills.

She glowered at Amy, whose smile hadn't diminished.

"What?" she asked, raising her hands in frustration. The night wasn't starting well. "Why are you smiling?"

"Just want to see your reaction." Amy smirked, then turned to walk away, but paused at the doorway. "I'll be nearby if you need any help," she called over her shoulder, finally leaving the kitchen with C.J. staring after her.

"Why would I need help?" C.J. muttered, rolling her eyes at Amy's retreating backside.

Content that she didn't have to continue rolling silverware, though, she ventured off to greet her guest. She dug in her apron for a pen, trying not to think about the crumpled letter that she'd forgotten to toss in the dumpster. Why couldn't he just leave her alone?

Distracted, she didn't bother to look at her patron as she rattled off her standard greeting. "Hi, my name is C.J. I'll be your server this evening. Can I start you off with something to drink?" Finally finding her pen, she raised her eyes from her ticket book as she awaited an answer.

At that precise moment, the man sitting in her booth looked up from his menu, acknowledging her presence.

Wow! Now she understood Amy's grin and offer to assist. The man at her table was a real looker. Not in a generic Hollywood way. He was a genuine all-American, but striking, male. The man's face, chiseled and sculpted to perfection, stared back: square chin, high cheekbones, and angular nose, all framed by a neatly trimmed beard trailing up his jaw that only added to his rugged look. His hair was a deep brown, almost black, and cropped short, military-style. His build resembled an officer of some sort. His shoulders were broad and held back in perfect posture, and based on their width, she now understood the need for a larger booth.

His eyes were the best, though. He had a lightly tanned complexion with dark brows, and beneath thick eyelashes were a set of arresting steel-blue eyes. They were beautiful. The shock of electricity that shot through her, though, was incapacitating. She couldn't think; *wow* wasn't quite enough to describe what she felt. Her feet felt as though they were rooted to the wood floor below her, and she couldn't remember the last time she'd just gawked at a complete stranger.

A flash of blond hair caught her eye, pulling her out of her daze. Amy was peering around the corner, her grin still wide, apparently pleased with her reaction. Then she winked and turned away, leaving C.J. to her own devices.

The man's eyes held contact with hers for a few seconds before speaking, as though he were dumbstruck too. "Yes, ma'am, do you have sweet tea?" His strong southern accent sent another shock through her.

"Call me C.J., please. I'm too young to be a *ma'am*. And yes, we do. I made it myself," she answered too quickly, not contemplating her words. Why had she felt the need to offer that tidbit? As if it mattered who brewed the tea.

A slow smile lifted his cheeks. "Sounds good, C.J. I'll take that then." His cute southern drawl made her initials sound like two words the way he drew them out, and the heartbreaking smile sent a shiver down her spine. Fine tan lines feathered from the corners of his eyes, similar to her father. Her dad had been the only man who'd ever made her laugh. A pang of longing hit her hard.

"I'll give you a couple of minutes and be right back with your tea." Her voice cracked, and she turned away from him to retreat to the safety of the kitchen.

Entering the kitchen, she whooshed out the breath she'd been holding. What the heck was happening? Why was her stomach doing loop-de-loops? Why did this guy have to stride in here, all-masculine looking, and start her heart pounding? It felt as if she'd been shocked with one of those *heart-thingies*, and her heart was beating for the first time in years. She gripped the letter in her apron she hadn't discarded yet. It was a significant reminder not to let a man's cute smile influence her.

Get a hold of yourself, she thought. He's just a guy. So he was good looking. What difference did that make? The men she dated were always attractive. Maybe that was the problem.

Pulling in a deep relaxing breath through her nose, she held it a couple of seconds and then blew it out in a slow exhale. "There," she said aloud. "That's better."

She busied herself with getting his drink. What was she worried about anyway? He looked like a nice guy, not at all her variety of man. It wasn't as if he'd even be interested. Guys like him were never attracted to her. She only managed to be a magnet for trouble, men who looked good on the outside, but were horrible inside.

***

Disorientated, Jordan wilted into his booth. He'd just gaped at the waitress when she'd requested his drink order.

He didn't understand what had happened, but he'd felt the electricity ignite. He'd read about it, seen it in movies, and heard his grandmother's accounts, but he'd never experienced it. The strike had been instantaneous. What had Nanna called it? The thunderbolt, or was it lightning bolt? He may not remember the name, but it had happened. The second his eyes had connected with C.J.'s he felt the charge. It was as if his entire being had been struck, and everything he wanted or ever desired was wrapped up in this moment, in this girl.

He should leave. This couldn't be happening. Not here. She was pretty, but it wasn't that. There was something about her. He felt drawn to her. He knew he wouldn't be able to leave even if he wanted to escape this emotion. It was too powerful.

C.J. placed his beverage on the coaster and smiled. "Are you ready to order?"

"Um ... yes, ma'am, I'll take the sirloin, medium-well, please." Shoot, he reprimanded himself. She'd requested he call her C.J., but he couldn't help it. That was how a respectful southerner spoke; his father would have had his head if he'd addressed a woman any other way.

"Sir, could I recommend either ordering your steak medium or switching to the strip steak? Or, we could butterfly it. Our steaks are thick, and sirloin can be tough if overcooked."

He smiled up at her, unable to contain the pleasure that rushed through his body at this simple gesture. As though she wanted to take care of him. Of course, she probably offered this to all her customers. "Butterflying it will be fine, thank you." He tipped his head in a respectful manner.

She wrote down his order, then sauntered away. His heart pounded faster than normal, and a warm feeling rushed his veins. He had to make her his.

Never having asked a waitress out before, he wondered how he would go about it. Men probably hit on her all the time. She was pretty, a natural beauty, even without makeup. Her dark hair was up in a ponytail, but a few strands had escaped. He felt the urge to tuck them behind her ear just to touch her hair.

But her eyes were her most incredible feature. They were a deep hazel, like cat's eyes, standing out in contrast to her olive skin. Her body was also perfect, not like all the bony, thin girls he'd seen around here. She was petite, but shapely, about five-three he guessed. He liked that too. She was perfect for his six-foot frame.

Where was his imagination going already? Perfect for what ... dancing? He chastised himself, but knew he couldn't let her escape without at least attempting to see if there was anything under her cover, as his mother had always put it. Was she just a simple-minded waitress? She didn't sound unintelligent. No matter the looks, he could never deal with ignorance. He needed someone with whom he could relate.

Again, his thoughts were uncontainable. He'd only just met this girl and was already sizing up whether she was worthy. She'd probably think he was an ignorant hick anyway. Women loved his southern accent, but were always surprised when there was more behind his drawl than just a country boy.

She stopped by the table with a pitcher of tea. He looked up at her and couldn't have prevented the smile on his face, even if he'd tried. "What does C.J. stand for?"

She refilled his glass, then leaned toward him. "I never tell anyone. It's a secret." She smiled, then turned and strolled off again, as if she had no clue what her whispered words had done to his insides.

Secret? What did that mean? She'd smiled sweetly, but she'd also dismissed his query.

His eyes followed her as she approached an older couple. She sat down beside the man as if she knew him. A protective instinct crept up out of nowhere.

Seriously, man, get a grip. He's like seventy-something.

Jordan wasn't jealous of the man, he realized. He was envious she wasn't sitting, talking, and laughing with him. At this moment, he wanted nothing more than just that.

C.J. disappeared into the kitchen again, returning a few minutes later with drinks for the couple and a salad, which must be his. He was proficient at reading people. What she did next would determine if he would act on his feelings.

If she delivered the drinks before his salad, she might be interested. But if she dropped off his salad first so she could go back and talk to the couple instead of him, then he'd know just to forget about trying to approach her and always wonder ... what if?

Passing right by him, she walked to the couple's table and dropped off their drinks. He smiled, pleased with this simple outcome.

Watching the effortless sway of her walk as she returned to him, he almost let out a whoo-hoo. But then, she set down his salad and bread and turned to walk off again.

"Excuse me, C.J.?" he spoke in a rushed panic, a pathetic endeavor to keep her near him.

"Yes?" She turned back, her dazzling eyes bright and beautiful. "Did you need something?"

He stifled a chuckle. How juvenile. He was acting as if he were seventeen not twenty-seven.

"Why is it a secret?" he blurted out the first question that popped into his head.

She shook her head and chuckled out a breath. "My name?"

"Yes, why won't you tell me your real name?"

"Well," she said, taking a seat across from him, "I just don't like it. Besides, no one forgets C.J. It's easy to remember, which brings my customers back to me."

Her eyes narrowed, showing a little crinkle between them. She looked up and flicked her gaze around the room as if expecting someone to charge through the door. He'd seen this look before — in victims.

"I can't imagine anyone forgetting your name, even if it was eight syllables," he offered. *What kind of corny line was that?* He wanted to slap himself.

But instead of rushing off again, she smiled. "Where are you from?" she asked. "You're not from Florida, are you?"

"Now why would you think that?" he teased, smiling. Maybe he could get her to let down her guard.

"Well, your accent obviously. Plenty of Floridians have southern accents, just not in Pinellas County. Even so, there's something else I can't quite place, but I know it's not a Floridian trait." She relaxed deeper in the booth, crossing her arms, awaiting his response.

Wondering what she was getting at but deciding to engage her until he got what he wanted, he offered a compromise. "I'll make you a deal," he hedged, staring into her eyes a fraction longer than necessary, watching as her eyes grew wide. "You tell me your real name and I'll tell you mine ... and where I'm from."

She sprang from the table.

Oops, guess I lost that standoff, he thought wryly.

"I have to get their salads," she stammered, shaking her head as if trying to dislodge something. "I'll be right back."

Relief washed over him. For a second he thought he'd been too assertive, which he tended to be sometimes.

***

Even though she knew she had plenty of time, C.J. rushed to the kitchen. The Smiths enjoyed sipping their cocktails before they ate. But she had to escape.

Could he really be interested, or was he just having fun? Thinking about his piercing blue eyes that seemed to read her, she tightened her hand around the envelope concealed in her apron. She couldn't trust herself. She made disastrous decisions when it came to men. She couldn't continue flirting with disaster, even if he looked like fun.

She stood in the kitchen, pulling on her bottom lip, and took deep breaths. Slowly, her pulse returned to normal.

After calming herself down again, she ordered the Smiths' dinner and waited for their salads. She ambled her way to her regulars' table, brandishing a fresh iced tea for the man who was upsetting her world just by asking what her initials stood for. And what was with his ridiculous comment about never forgetting her name?

Quickly trading out his drink, not giving him a chance to speak, she retreated to the Smiths, deciding to chat with them before she'd have to pick up his dinner. She could allow someone else to deliver his meal. But she wanted to see him again, even for a few seconds. Stupid, stupid, stupid. Would she always be so dense? If she were being honest with herself, she'd initiated the flirting. People asked what C.J. stood for all the time. For some dim-witted reason, though, she'd decided to taunt him by withholding the answer. He'd turned her teasing around on her, however, and now she felt nauseated.

***

C.J. managed to ignore him, yet continued to perform her job flawlessly. She permitted him only the time needed to replace his beverage, then headed to her other table.

Did it mean she wasn't interested? Did he care?

He watched her laugh with the couple. They looked happy, as if they'd been married for fifty years, as his grandparents had been. He was seven years older than his grandparents had been when they married. He hadn't been thinking about marriage these last few years; it hadn't even been a thought. It was this girl, and this blasted thunderbolt his grandmother had cursed him with that had him thinking crazy thoughts about a woman who wouldn't even tell him her name.

His grandmother had explained how she and his grandfather had met in an apple orchard when she was nineteen and he was twenty, and how she'd known he was the one. His grandfather must have known too because he'd asked her to marry him within weeks of their initial meeting. Nanna assured Jordan it would happen to him also, just as it had with his father and his father before him. Jordan had listened to her anecdotes but had all but given up on something spectacular happening to him — until now.

Jordan's gaze followed C.J. as she left the table and disappeared into the kitchen. He was probably creeping her out, but he couldn't stop watching her. He saw her glance his way a couple of times. Of course, she was his waitress; she could have just been checking his drink levels.

C.J. walked out of the kitchen with his dinner in one hand, a new sweet tea in the other, and a bottle of something tucked in her apron. She set down his dinner and a fresh glass of sweet tea but didn't leave right away.

"Do you use steak sauce?" she asked in a cool professional manner.

"Yes, please," he replied as smoothly as possible. She was going to play hard-to-get, something he wasn't accustomed to. Not that he had a lot of experience dating. He didn't. But he'd never had to try hard. Women seemed more than willing to approach him, or his sisters were always ready to set him up.

"That's what I thought." A warm smile flashed across her face as she set down a bottle of A.1. and settled into the booth again, sighing. "My name is Caycee Jaynee Evans, both spelled with *ay* and both ending in *ee*. Caycee is a boy's name, and Jaynee should have been Jayne. It would flow better. Try explaining how to spell Caycee Jaynee long enough, and you end up with C.J.," she babbled.

Maybe a date wouldn't be so difficult after all. "I understand. I like them both, especially Jaynee. Can I call you Jaynee?"

A small huff escaped as she shook her head in confusion. "Why would you want to do that? You'll probably never even see me again. And by the way, it's your turn. What's your name, and where *exactly* are you from?"

Her eyes were impatient, and Jordan knew as before, he had only mere seconds to talk before she darted off.

"My name is Jordan Monroe, and I'm from a little town in North Carolina called Stanfield. It's about forty-five minutes southeast of Charlotte."

"Figures," she huffed again, sounding displeased with this revelation, "a real southern gentleman. And I was right. You'll never see me again. So why does it matter what my name is?" She jumped up, scurrying away before he could respond.

Okay, so it was going to be difficult to ask her out.

C.J. stopped by a few minutes later to check on his steak but left swiftly so as not to allow any time for additional questions or conversation.

The dinner was delicious, but the overwhelming desire to break through her shield was frustrating. What had compelled him to ask a complete stranger if he could call her by her middle name? It was personal. He wanted it to be personal. He'd seen the disappointment when she sighed at his response. She'd called him a southern gentleman. Not a redneck, a country boy, or a hick. References he'd become familiar with over the years, particularly in the

Army. He'd even referred to himself by those disparaging names on occasion.

C.J. had two more groups of customers sit down in her section, and he knew he couldn't keep bugging her.

She walked back to his table, a cool look in her eyes. "Have a nice evening," she said, then laid the check on the table.

He had a couple bills ready. He stuffed the two twenties inside the folder and jumped up beside her. "Thank you, C.J. You can keep the change. I hope it makes up for me irritating you."

Staring at his hands, she accepted the folder without a word and then looked up at him.

"Would you meet me for coffee after you finish work?" The words left his mouth before he even considered why he was asking her. They lived six hundred miles apart. What was he thinking?

Surprising him, her eyes filled with so much passion that he was positive she was going to say *yes*. But with a sudden look of resolve, she shoved her hands in her pockets. He could hear her wrinkling up a piece of paper. She was just nervous.

After a couple seconds, though, she stared up at him, those gorgeous eyes growing a shade deeper. "I don't date," she said in a soft but determined voice. Her brows narrowed as though she had something else to say, but she turned to greet her next table.

Her words hit him like a steel bat, but something about her eyes told him he shouldn't give up. There had been something about the way she'd dismissed him that said she'd regretted telling him *no*.

He walked toward the exit, but at the last second altered his course and headed to the bar and ordered a beer he wouldn't drink.

Chapter Two

C.J. watched as Jordan walked out of her life. She was angry with herself for saying *no*, but angrier that she'd wanted to say *yes*. Her stomach was in knots, and she didn't even know him. She'd been smart to say *no*.

He'd return to Charlotte, or wherever he was from in North Carolina, and never consider her again. She couldn't withdraw her eyes from him as he walked toward the door. She wanted to dart after him, tell him she'd changed her mind and decided she would meet him. Then, to her amazement, he turned and headed for the bar. She averted her eyes when he turned his head and looked back at her. She didn't want him to catch her gawking.

She turned away and let out a breath. He was offering her another chance she didn't want. At least that's what she kept telling herself, even if she knew she was lying.

C.J. approached her next table, two young couples in their early thirties. She knew how to up the check, and at the same time, give herself a reason to visit the bar.

"Ladies," she said, speaking only to the women. "We have a special creation tonight, a raspberry margarita. We take our famous frozen lime margaritas and add a swirl of Chambord liquor. If you like margaritas, you must try this one." The women giggled and looked at their partners who encouraged them to go ahead. "And may I recommend a couple of our signature draft beers for you, gentlemen?"

Order in hand, she was off to the service bar, which was at the far end of the customers' area. Across from the service station sat Jordan.

He smiled as she approached, a brilliant smile exposing a perfect set of white teeth. He was an ideal specimen of a man, and obviously he didn't know how to take no for an answer. Of course, he could have just decided to have a beer, but she doubted that. Most guys would have scampered off with their tail between their legs, but here Jordan sat, smiling at her.

He lifted his glass as if offering her a salute, then took a sip and set his mug back on the bar.

Unable to control herself, she smiled and then scooped up her drink order, returning to her customers. Adrenaline coursed through her veins as if she'd just run a marathon. The cocktails she carried nearly toppled over as her hands quivered beneath the tray. How could a man she didn't even know affect her in such a way?

As the night progressed, she made excuses to walk by the bar. Every time she saw a food order for the bar, she'd snatch it up and personally deliver it to the bartender. All her tables were against the window, so her back was always to the bar, but she could swear she felt Jordan's eyes following her.

She wondered if she should be worried, but somehow, *worried* wasn't the word coming to mind, flattered was more like it.

As soon as she saw the bartender in the kitchen, she darted over to him. "Billy, hey, gotta sec?"

The bartender was grabbing a dinner plate, but he stopped to listen. Some bartenders could be cocky, but Billy had always been nice. Of course, the extra tip she threw him at the end of her shift probably helped.

"Sure, but I'm in the weeds. Whacha need, C.J.?"

"I was just wondering about the guy at the far end of the bar? The —"

Billy cut her off by rolling his eyes. "You're the tenth server who's asked me about him. The military-looking guy, right?" C.J. nodded sheepishly. "Name's Jordan. Seems like an interesting guy … great tipper by the way. I think he said he's a contractor. Makes sense, he looks like a construction worker. It's weird, though. He's ordered several beers, but he only takes a sip or two, then pushes them away."

"So … has he asked about me —"

"Gotta go, C.J. We'll talk later." Billy turned and darted off.

Was Jordan waiting for her, she wondered.

Business was slow, and Tim informed C.J. he'd closed her section. Under normal circumstances, this news would disappoint her. Typically, she'd offer to close for another server, but tonight she felt otherwise inclined.

She walked up behind the gentleman playing havoc with her perfect strategy of not dating while finishing college. What could it hurt? He didn't even live here.

"Jordan," she said in the boldest tone she could muster, leaning up against the counter alongside his barstool. "Are you stalking me? I already told you I don't date."

***

Jordan felt a buzz rush through him when she said his name.

He lifted his eyes to meet hers, inclining his head slightly. "I didn't ask you on a date. I asked you to coffee." He concentrated on keeping his voice confident. It wasn't easy. She made him feel a little shaky inside. Something he wasn't accustomed to ... with women or anyone else for that matter. He was used to being in control, taking command of every situation.

"Even if I did date, I can't go out like this. I smell like a restaurant," she protested.

It sounded like a pout from a child. But if she weren't interested, she wouldn't have come over to remind him she didn't date. He almost laughed, but restrained himself, realizing he was going to get his wish. He wanted this more than anything he'd ever wanted. Something about this woman had his insides bubbling.

He moved his head closer, keeping his eyes indifferent. "You smell fine to me. Besides, I've been sitting here for hours, so I don't think I'd notice anyway."

"I look terrible. My hair's a mess. I don't have on any makeup, and ..." she glanced down at her uniform "Look at the way I'm dressed."

Following her gaze to her restaurant-issued shirt and khaki shorts, Jordan grinned. She was surrendering, and he was reveling in his victory. Now to seize control. "It's just coffee, Jaynee. If you want to get gussied-up when I invite you on a real date, that'd be awesome. But right now, I just want to talk to you for a while. I saw a Starbucks a couple of blocks up the street; I'll see you when you finish work."

Smiling, he turned away, focusing his attention elsewhere. He'd paid as he ordered so he wouldn't have to wait to pay his tab. He gave the bartender a friendly nod. "Nice meetin' ya, Billy. See ya 'round."

He hoped it would work. He hoped she wouldn't leave him sitting there like a dope. Perhaps he'd offended her by calling her Jaynee. How presumptuous he was behaving. He'd never pressed a girl to go out with him. But he needed at least one chance to survey these unbridled emotions running rampant through his mind.

He left the restaurant with one fleeting glance in her direction. Her mouth was all but hanging open as she watched him walk away. Yes, it would work; she'd be there. He ambled off, grinning ear to ear.

***

C.J. stood there speechless, her jaw open in a catatonic stupor, baffled by her reaction.

She thought she'd been in control. She'd just wanted to tease him, never considering for a second that he'd be able to turn the tables on her. But he had, and now she felt all warm and fuzzy inside. He'd called her Jaynee again. She liked the way he said her middle name with that drawl. Would she go to meet him? Did she have a choice?

No man had ever affected her in this manner. Not even the one whose letter she'd repeatedly crumbled in her pocket, and she'd spent years with him. Wasted was a more accurate depiction. Would Jordan be the same? He didn't even live in Florida. Where could this possibly lead? That was the thought confirming her resolution. It was just coffee, nothing more as he'd suggested. If she didn't go, she'd always wonder.

***

Jordan waited patiently. It was only eight thirty, and he figured it would take her until at least nine to finish up at work and walk through the door at Starbucks.

She'd only had one table left. He'd wanted to offer to pay their bill if they'd leave, but he couldn't. She would think he was insane. She probably already thought he was controlling, but he knew she just needed a push. Why would anyone as pretty as her not date?

His eyes focused on the door every time it opened. He sat at a small table in the corner where she would sit across from him. She would come. He was certain. He saw something in her eyes. No doubt, she felt the instant attraction, too.

He glanced at his phone. Nine o'clock. How long would he wait? Until they closed ... and if she didn't show ... what then? Would he return to the restaurant tomorrow and allow her to reject him again? Yes, without a moment's hesitation.

The door opened again. He glanced up, and she was there ...

Unable to masquerade his elation, he smiled wide and stood as she walked toward him. He pulled out a chair for her to sit. She was more reserved than he was, but she offered him a warm smile in return.

Jaynee had removed her barrette, and her hair fell around her shoulders and down her back in light curls. Her full lips glistened, beckoning a kiss. He'd been wrong. She wasn't just pretty; she was beautiful. How had he not noticed how breathtaking she was?

Jordan sat back down in his chair. "Thank you for not standing me up. I don't think my self-esteem could have taken it," he admitted.

"Well, you didn't leave me any choice. I didn't want you to wait here all night, and it didn't look as if you were going to accept no for an answer. Why is that?" She chuckled, shaking her head, clearly mystified by his insistence. It was nice to hear her laugh. She'd been so serious earlier.

"I honestly don't know." He smiled. "What would you like to drink?"

"A ... vanilla latte ..."

Her answer was immediate, but sounded more like a question, uncomfortable, as though she weren't accustomed to men buying things for her.

Jordan walked to the counter to order her drink. He liked that she knew what she wanted. He hated when women couldn't make simple decisions. Her selection had been uncomplicated, too, not a total frou-frou drink. He drank his coffee black. Years in the military warranted that practice. What some women consumed could hardly be called coffee.

He watched Jaynee while waiting for her drink. Why hadn't he accepted no for an answer? It wasn't his first rejection. That wasn't his motivation. It hadn't bothered him that she'd said *no*. What troubled him was the thought of never seeing her again. He wanted to open her cover. He wanted to discover everything about her.

He couldn't just tell her that. However, he'd try to be as straightforward as possible and could only hope he wouldn't frighten her away.

He offered the lady behind the counter a thankful nod when she set down the drink, then picked up Jaynee's coffee and headed back to her, unable to ignore the bounce in his step. For the first time in a while, he was excited about getting to know a woman. It'd been years since he'd done anything other than go out with a woman because his sister or best friend had forced a date on him.

As he placed her steaming latte in front of her, Jordan couldn't contain a chuckle when he thought about what he was doing. "Now I'm waiting on you," he said, leaning closer, so close he could smell her. She smelled incredible. He detected a slight grin, but then she gnawed on her bottom lip. Something made her apprehensive.

"Thank you, and thank you for being such a gentleman. Men don't stand when women enter the room, pull out chairs for them to sit, or insist they have coffee with them anymore, do they? Though ... I'm not sure that last aspect constitutes gentlemanly behavior."

He took a seat across from her and just smiled at her comment. Her eyes flicked toward the door, then down at her coffee. Was she afraid of someone walking in and seeing her with him? She didn't have a ring. That was the first thing he'd looked for before asking her out.

Her eyes returned to him. "Why did you want to have coffee with me when you don't even live here?" She flashed a half-hearted attempt at a smile.

"I honestly don't know." He paused for an instant and gave some thought to what he wanted to tell her. "I don't want to scare you, but I felt something from the moment our eyes met." She didn't rocket from her chair again ... a positive indication. So he continued, "It didn't matter that we didn't know each other or if I lived in another country. I just couldn't walk away, always wondering, *What if?* Does that make sense?"

She gave him a real smile this time but then fiddled with her stirrer stick, swirling her coffee. "Sort of, but it doesn't make sense. Those things don't happen in reality, only in movies. Real life is harsh; there are no fairy tales." She flashed a glance at the door again, as if it were her escape, he guessed, but she remained seated. She took a sip from her coffee. "This will keep me up all night you know."

"I'm sorry," he said, shaking his head and sighing. "So you don't believe people can have an instant attraction to each other?"

"Sure I do," she said through a chuckle, "a physical one. But then after the initial attraction wears off, they'll show their true stripes." Her eyes returned to her cup.

Just when he thought he'd broken through her guard, she'd thrown him a curve ball. "Wow ... sounds as though someone did a number on you." She shrugged, and he knew he'd stumbled onto something. "And since you'll be up all night," he grinned when her eyes grew wide, "I'd be happy to stay up with you and listen if you want to talk."

Jaynee sucked in a deep breath, then exhaled sharply, shaking her head. "I'm damaged goods, trust me. I'm not worth staying up all night." She took another deep breath. He was sure she wanted to say more, but she turned her head and gazed at the door.

She probably expected him to charge the exit. Maybe she wanted him to retreat. Perhaps most men would, but he couldn't force himself to budge. He wanted to know more.

"Jaynee ... can I call you Jaynee?" He kept his voice low and soft.

"Yes ... I suppose. I actually like it." She returned her eyes to his. They were misty. He decided to change the subject.

"Perfect. I do too." He kept his expression light, hoping he hadn't pushed her. He really wanted to connect with her. "What do you like to do for fun, Jaynee?"

She shrugged. "Not much. I work and go to college. Spend my free days at the beach or with my grandmother. She's the only positive thing in my life." She smiled at the mention of her grandmother. So they had at least one thing in common. They were both close with their grandmothers.

***

Jaynee felt herself relax as Jordan fired questions at her. He hadn't run away when she tried to frighten him off. He seemed generally interested in her boring existence.

He asked her about her favorite movies, books, and music. He asked about her major in college, her family — but that was a short subject — where she'd visited, and where she wanted to go.

Jordan's life was much more interesting. He'd been an Army brat, so he'd lived all over the world as a kid, and then joined the service himself when he was nineteen. He liked scuba diving, camping, hiking, kayaking, and countless of other activities she'd never dreamed of but now found herself wanting to learn.

The most impressive quality about Jordan, though, was why he was in Clearwater.

Several hurricanes had struck Florida in the last couple of months. Jordan had been working in South West Florida, doing construction work. He'd been on his way home when another class-four storm came through this area. There wasn't too much destruction, but he stopped by a local church to see if he could offer assistance before he left town. According to Jordan, he'd spent the last two days cleaning up and making small repairs.

Who was this man, and how had he turned up in her booth? He seemed genuinely good, but she'd thought that before. None of the guys she'd dated had been *good*. If he really was a good man, what did he see in her? If he knew everything, would he still be interested?

"So, Jaynee," Jordan drawled after they'd talked for hours. "Will you honor me with a real date?" His accent and smile sent another shock through her. How could she resist? She couldn't help but notice the erratic beating of her heart every time he smiled.

"I'm not off again until Saturday. Will you still be around?" She hoped, but then wondered if seeing Jordan again would be smart.

"I don't think I have a choice. I would like to finish the book."

"What does that mean?" Her look of confusion must have humored him. His smile broadened.

"It's just something I learned from my mother." He ignored her question and continued, "Can I see you before Saturday ... breakfast, lunch, or coffee again?" His voice was low and intense, his eyes persuasive.

Her heartbeat quickened again without warning. This wasn't good. If she felt like this now, she could only imagine how she would feel on a real date, and then he would leave.

"I have school tomorrow and work again tomorrow night." The words flowed out of her mouth, seemingly of their own accord, as if she had no control over her lips. "But I'll meet you for coffee again tomorrow after work if that's all right. I'll try to be here by nine. It depends on how busy we are."

Suddenly, she was thrilled at the thought of him wanting to see her again but managed to keep her emotions intact. She couldn't mistake desire for something else. He was a stranger from out of town. Where could this possibly lead?

She gathered up her purse and keys. It was late. They had talked for hours and time had slipped away from her.

Jordan stood and held the chair for her again. They walked out of the coffee shop, and he escorted her across the parking lot. He held his arm behind the small of her back, barely touching her. The act was more of a protective action than a romantic gesture, but a rush of warmth soared through her at his touch.

She paused at her vehicle before opening the door. *Would he kiss her?* she wondered. She licked her lips in anticipation.

Jordan inhaled deeply as he lowered his head. He brushed his fingertips under her chin, lifting her head so that her lips were within inches of his. "You are lovelier than words, Jaynee, and you don't smell like a restaurant ... actually, you smell like vanilla. I'll be waiting to see you tomorrow." He took a step backward.

She opened the car door and climbed in, sighing. Jordan shut the door and gave her a little wave. Jaynee stared at him in her rearview mirror. He stood there watching her as she drove away.

Embarrassed at her reaction to his words and touch, she felt her cheeks burn. She'd wanted him to kiss her. Her entire body felt as if it were on fire. This is bad. *This is not smart, Jaynee*, she thought to herself. Now in the privacy of her car, she giggled at the name he'd bestowed.

"Jaynee," she repeated, aloud this time, liking the way it sounded but then proceeded to rebuke herself swiftly, "What have you gotten yourself into this time?"

***

Jordan jumped into his truck and followed Jaynee home, careful to keep his distance. He hated the idea of following her. No doubt what she would think if she detected his shadowing. But he couldn't bear for her to drive home alone, unprotected.

What was he thinking? She drove herself home every night. Why did he feel this overwhelming need to protect her? He couldn't explain it, but there was something about her, and he wasn't about to leave without having a chance to finish the book. He just hoped there'd be an opportunity to write himself into her story.

He'd wanted to kiss her something fierce. His entire being longed for her, and he could see she was attracted to him as well, but he'd restrained himself. Something told him this might be his last first kiss. So it should be special, not standing in a parking lot. Still, the emotions were powerful.

He wanted to sprint up to her once she pulled in her driveway, but he couldn't. She'd run in terror. She would definitely think he was stalking her. He would have to be patient. But he didn't know if he could. Jaynee had gotten under his skin, unlike no women ever had. Letting her go wasn't an option.

Chapter Three

Jaynee spent extra time getting ready the next morning. She tossed a change of clothes, a little makeup, and her vanilla-scented body spray and lotion in her bag. It had surprised her that Jordan noticed the fragrance.

For not wanting to see him again, she was certainly going through a lot of trouble. She blow-dried and straightened her hair, an undertaking that took an extra twenty minutes, only to end up pulling it back for work and school. The Florida humidity would have it curling up by this evening, but at least the curls would be soft, not wild looking.

The day at school dragged. She found herself checking the time every five minutes. She wanted to call in sick to work but needed the money. Besides, he hadn't given her his number. So he could have already left town, and she may never see him again. She couldn't blame him if he stood her up. After all, she'd tried to warn him off.

Her words hadn't seemed to bother him, though. He'd even tried to make her feel better when he saw her eyes water up. He couldn't have missed her reaction, and yet, he remained seated, even managed to turn the conversation to a more pleasant topic.

Could Jordan be everything he seemed? How disappointed would she be when he returned to North Carolina? Her insides burned at the thought. The appropriate action was to put those ideas aside. Tomorrow wasn't important. She would enjoy the moment, live for today, and not worry about tomorrow.

From school, she drove to work in a daze, already resigned to forget about him. If he showed tonight, great, if not, oh well. She would just have to stumble through the next few hours and accept whatever happened.

She had just finished her prep work and had started to roll silverware when Amy poked her head around the corner, an impish grin spilling across her face again.

Powerless to stop herself, Jaynee smiled wide in response. "No ... don't tell me ... he's here, isn't he?" She couldn't contain the excitement in her voice.

"Sure ..." Amy sneered. "As if you didn't already know. You haven't worn makeup since you started here. You lucky dog, he's a hunk. And did you see his pickup?" Jealousy seeped through her words, but deep down, she knew Amy was thrilled to see her interested in someone. She'd been trying to set her up for months.

"No," Jaynee answered honestly. She'd never cared about trivial things like vehicles. Moreover, she was too enthralled with him to notice what he'd been driving.

She held her breath as she stepped out of the kitchen. Rounding the corner, she caught Jordan's gaze, and a glorious smile spread across his face. Was it possible it was for her? She couldn't contain her smile either, but a nondescript "Hi" was all she could choke out. Her mouth suddenly felt parched. Her heart also started acting up, thumping so loudly she was sure he would hear it.

"Hello, Jaynee," he drawled, his voice seductive. Whether that was his intention, she couldn't be certain. "I needed to eat, and the food here is good, and the service is incredible, so why experiment with something new?" He folded up the menu and returned it to the end of the table as carefree as could be as if they were old friends. "What do you recommend?"

Jaynee looked around the restaurant and then back at Jordan, shrugging. "Um ... the grilled chicken and shrimp over fettuccine is my favorite," she said in a casual tone, trying to imitate his relaxed behavior. It wasn't working.

"I'll take that with a salad and sweet tea, please. Did I liberate you from rolling silverware again?" His eyes brightened at the notion.

Her heart fluttered, trying to resume its normal rhythm. "Yes, you did. Thank you for that. I'll order your dinner and be right back."

She placed the order, waited for his salad while she retrieved his beverage, and then grabbed a loaf of bread. She wouldn't have to dart off until another customer arrived. Jordan was watching as she rounded the corner again. How could he be looking at her like that? He made her feel wanted. No one had ever looked at her the way Jordan did. As though he cared about her thoughts and dreams. The way he'd listened to her last night as she rambled on about her pathetic life had made her believe he had a real interest in her as a person, not just an object to possess.

After placing his drink and food on the table, she took a seat opposite him again.

He smiled in response, clearly pleased that they didn't have to go through the back-and-forth banter that they had yesterday. "It's nice you can sit down with your customers.

I only wish you were staying and eating with me. I hate eating alone."

His words rang with sincerity, something she wasn't used to with men. But she needed to keep the personal talk to a minimum. Nothing could come of this, she reminded herself.

"Management actually encourages us to sit with our customers, although not the eating part." She giggled at the thought but then leaned across the table. "Why are you really here?" She peered up at his face, narrowing her eyebrows. "Did you think I'd stand you up and you needed to pressure me?" She smiled, hoping the words didn't emerge too harshly. She didn't think Jordan was the stalker type, and she didn't mind him pursuing her; actually, it was rather flattering. But she'd never allow a man to control her again.

"Not exactly. I just couldn't wait to see you. I had to make sure I didn't dream you up. And now I see you're even more beautiful than I remembered yesterday." His eyes smoldered, and she felt her emotions spiraling inside again. "Are you okay with me coming here?"

Again, his honesty surprised her, sparking something within. Why should she conceal her interest? She only hoped he wasn't pretending attraction in expectation of a vacation fling.

She sighed deeply. "It was a long day for me."

He smiled, obviously pleased with her admission. He pushed the tomatoes onto his bread plate, then speared a perfect forkful of salad. "I won't hold up your table, but I did need to eat."

Jaynee stood. She couldn't remain with one customer without getting into trouble.

"Well, it's not as if you don't tip well. Do you always tip like that, or was that just for me?" The hostess trailed two older couples behind her, heading toward one of her tables. "Sorry, I have to move around, and Amy's getting ready to seat me."

"Of course." Jordan gestured his hand for her to proceed. "As long as you regard me as your number one priority ... that's all I ask."

His eyes were intense, and Jaynee couldn't suppress a laugh at his request. "Number one priority? Well, okay, if that's all ..." What was he asking, and why was she okay with it? Two states separated them. Where did he intend for this to go? Was this just an affair to remember, or worse — to forget? He seemed sincere, and she didn't want to destroy what little enjoyment she could have by broaching the subject.

"And yes, I always double the tip when I eat alone. It doesn't seem fair otherwise."

She smiled at him and shook her head, letting out a small *humph*. "So it wasn't just me," she teased but then walked away before he could comment. He was too cute and too sweet, which meant he was too good to be true.

Jaynee waited on her other tables, but always kept her attention on Jordan — she didn't want him to think he wasn't her number one priority. She made sure she was in the kitchen when his dinner was ready, then grabbed another fresh mug of tea, and headed to his table.

After he had finished his meal, she left the check and checked on her other customers.

As yesterday, he stood as she returned to him. "Will I distract you if I sit at the bar?" His fingers grazed hers as he handed her the folder with the dinner check inside. She could see two bills sticking out. He'd obviously given her way too much of a tip again.

Her heart thudded uncontrollably at his slight touch. "Yes ..." she admitted, gulping, but hoped he would.

"Good." He flashed a wicked grin, then strolled toward the bar.

Jaynee decided to do something unprecedented. "Tim..." Hesitantly, she walked up to the general manager. It was too early for him to cut a server, but other waitresses had asked this early. She knew this, of course, because she always picked up their slack. "I know it's early, but could you close my station."

He cocked his head and narrowed his eyes. "Seriously? You never ask me to cut you early, C.J. Don't tell me you're going to start acting like the rest of the college kids?"

She waved him off. "No, no, it's nothing like that. Actually, I have a paper due, and I need to work on it," she told a half-truth. She did need to work on her novella; though, she had no plans to do that tonight.

"Fine. I'll tell Amy not to seat you again." She turned to walk off, hoping he wouldn't press her. "But, C.J ..." She turned to look back at him. "Please don't make this a habit. I like the fact I can count on you. The reason I give you the best stations." He lowered his gaze and smiled, assuring her of this fact.

She completed her closing duties, so when her last table finished, she was ready to leave. She rushed to the employees' lounge, changed clothes, freshened up, and then headed to meet Jordan at the bar. It was only eight.

Bounding up behind him, she startled him. He turned around quickly when she touched his arm, shielding his body. She cringed at the suddenness of his movements. He reacted as she'd seen men do in thriller movies, as if they were gearing up for an attack.

Not wanting to ruin their night, she passed it off as nothing. Jordan was a big man, but he wasn't dangerous. He was sweet. "How 'bout ice cream instead of coffee? I know a great little place off the causeway where we can pick some up and then drive to the beach. Also, if it's okay with you, we can drop off my car on the way." She usually wouldn't allow that. But if he intended to try something, he wouldn't have hung around where everyone could identify him, or he would have attempted something last night. He hadn't even tried to kiss her.

Jordan smiled wildly again, sending her blood coursing through her veins. "I always wanted a woman to say that."

She scrunched up her nose in confusion. "Say what?"

"'I know a great little place,' like they always say in the movies. It's rather romantic, don't you think?" His cheeks lifted, revealing a dimple she hadn't noticed.

Romantic? Jordan wasn't effeminate in the least, and yet, he wasn't afraid to verbalize something as romantic.

Jordan stood and directed her toward the exit. His hand rested lightly against her lower back again. Amy's eyes were wide as were a couple of the girls who'd stopped bussing tables. Jaynee had heard their whispers earlier as they'd checked out Jordan. They too had noticed him two evenings in a row, but she'd kept her mouth shut.

Jordan escorted her to her vehicle as he had the previous night, closed her inside, and then without a word, walked to his truck. Amy had been right. It was an eye-catching pickup. It was a brand new F-150, a mammoth of a truck with its customized lift-kit and chrome wheels, the paint a pristine solid black. A true country boy's truck — it fit him.

Why hadn't they discussed what he did for a living? Billy had mentioned construction, but she'd never thought to ask. She now wondered. Although, she was positive it wasn't anything like how her ex had made money, but then, she hadn't discovered what he did for income until it was too late.

After pulling into her driveway, Jaynee shifted her car in park and sprinted around to Jordan's F-150. He'd already jumped down and had opened the passenger door.

He chuckled lightly as he helped her up. "I guess I need to install running boards."

"Hey ... is that a *short* joke?" she asked as he climbed into the driver's seat. Truly though, she reveled at the idea of Jordan wanting to install running boards — for her?

"Not at all ... your height is perfect. I'm not into tall and skinny girls." He crinkled his nose, as though frowning at the notion.

She put her hands on her hips and jutted out her bottom lip, pretending to be offended. "So, I'm not skinny either?"

"Thank God, no!" he offered, laughing. "Jaynee, so far ... you are perfect in every way."

"So far ..." Remembering the analogy he'd cited yesterday, she turned it on him. "Are you sure you want to finish the book?"

Jordan turned in his seat, lowering his head so their eyes were level with each other. He held her gaze for a moment, then said, "I do."

Just two little innocent words, and yet the implication in his tone sent shivers down her spine.

"What if you don't like what you find?" Wishing she could take back her ridiculous words, she gave him directions before he could respond. "Take a right on

Curlew Road at the light which will take us directly to the Dunedin Causeway."

He stopped at the intersection but didn't turn right on red. Instead, he looked at her. "Jaynee," his tone was solemn ... serious, "are you doing anything illegal or immoral, or have you committed a crime against someone?"

"Of course not!" she retorted.

He smiled, shrugging. He looked to the left, then started moving again, turning right. "Then it doesn't matter. Whatever your life was up to now doesn't matter to me. When you trust me enough to tell me why you don't believe in happiness, I'll listen. Otherwise, as long as it doesn't fit into one of those categories, it doesn't matter."

She remained silent as they drove toward the causeway. His question and then comment that it didn't matter made it sound as if he wanted more than a couple of days. How was that possible? Did whatever company he worked for have a location here. That would be nice.

"That's it up ahead." Jaynee pointed to a yellow house-like structure with a front porch, its appearance similar to eateries located in the Florida Keys. She'd been so excited when they built it. Beforehand, there wasn't any place to get ice cream or dine on the causeway after sunset. "There are tables or we can take it with us," she offered, appreciating the sound of *us* a little too much, and it was only their second non-date.

Jordan parked, then made his way around his truck to help her down. Placing his hands on either side of her waist, he lifted her, holding her up a second longer than necessary. His gaze locked with hers for a brief second, and Jaynee saw something she'd never seen in a man's eyes. It was more than passion; there was hope. He set her down after a moment, not acting on the natural impulses they clearly both felt. Instead, he led her across the parking lot, his arm tighter around her waist. She already felt comfortable with his protective touch, something foreign to her.

As they walked through the breezeway, he glanced down at her. "Are you hungry?"

She suppressed a laugh by covering her mouth. Immature thoughts ran rampantly. She was hungry all right but guessed that wasn't what he was referring to. "Ice cream will be fine. I'm a big fan of ice cream."

"What's funny?" He smiled at her, probably thinking she was crazy for bursting into laughter over a simple question.

"Nothing. I was just being silly. I'll have mint chocolate chip in a cup, please," she said, attempting to change the subject.

Jordan paid for their dessert, and they returned to his truck. They drove over the draw bridge, approaching the dual line of palm trees bordering the beaches of Hurricane Pass. The sun, having dipped below the horizon within the last half-hour, shot brilliant bursts of brushstrokes in every spectrum from pink to red across the sky, saturating the heavens with warmth. But what made the display even more breathtaking, was sharing it for the first time with someone special. Someone she could never have. But she had tonight.

"Caladesi and Honeymoon Island are voted in the top ten beaches in America, but they close at twilight. The causeway is great to relax and watch the sunset; though unfortunately, we're a little late for that, too. Just pull into whichever section looks good," she babbled, wondering if

Jordan thought she was insane because of her giggling and then rambling.

"It's beautiful," Jordan said with meaning. "It looks like a postcard."

Driving onto the beach, he backed his truck close to the water's edge. Jaynee waited while he walked around the back of his truck, dropped the tailgate, and then opened her door. After handing her his cup, he scooped her up into his arms before she could object. He carried her around to the truck bed and placed her gently on the tailgate. Tears actually formed in her eyes ... she'd never been treated so well. She'd never met such a tender man

Jordan jumped up beside her in one agile move, but then immediately noticed her tears. "What's wrong? Did I hurt you?" His eyes searched her face.

She felt like a moron. She never cried — not lately anyway — and twice her eyes had glazed over in his presence. "Just the opposite. Why are you treating me like this?" The ridiculous tears snaked aimlessly down her cheeks.

"Like what? What did I do?" Grief filled his face as he reached to brush the tears away with his fingertips.

"Why are you being so chivalrous, Jordan? If you just a want a vacation fling before leaving, why would you exert such effort? It'll only hurt more when you disappear in a few days." She felt like such an imbecile. Why was she doing this? Why couldn't she enjoy this moment? She didn't want a relationship, she reminded herself futilely. Why did she keep trying to lie to herself? She wanted him more than she'd ever wanted any man.

***

Jordan set down his dessert, sighed, and then gently cupped Jaynee's face with both hands. She sucked in a mouthful of air as if preparing for impact. What did she think he was going to do? Someone had hurt her badly. He planned to find out, but first he needed to assure her he wasn't some schmuck who only wanted to take advantage of her.

"Jaynee, I don't know how to say this without scaring the heck out of you, or myself for that matter, but I'm not pretending anything. And I'm definitely not interested in a one-night stand. I don't know how this is going to work, but I ... all I know is I want —"

He pulled her face to his, kissing her softly once, twice, a third. As she parted her lips, inviting him in, he kissed her deeper, passionately. They fit together perfectly, and his body ached to have her closer. Not in a sexual way, he wanted all of her, mind and soul. He wanted to know everything. He released only her lips but continued holding onto her face. All he knew was he wanted that to be his last first kiss.

"I don't know how to explain this, Jaynee, but I assure you I don't want a *fling*. I'm not pretending anything. Can we just sit a minute, eat our ice cream, and then we can talk. Okay?"

He wanted to bask in this moment. The feelings soaring through him were powerful, like nothing he'd ever experienced. He wanted to kiss her again, taste her lips, breathe in her scent, but he didn't want to alarm her.

They ate without talking while staring out at the waves crashing against the beach. *How* was *this going to work?* He'd told her the truth. He didn't want a one-night stand, but he did want her.

When he finished eating, he draped his arm around her shoulders. God, he loved this.

It felt so natural. The evening was warm, but the ice cream made it feel cooler. Jaynee shivered, so he pulled her closer. She made no objection, which he was thankful for. He didn't want to release her. He truly enjoyed her company.

"Tell me more about you," she said suddenly, breaking the silence.

Not wanting to talk about himself, he sighed lightly in response. But then realizing it was the best way for her to trust him, he decided to share more than just the basics, as he'd done last night. "Well ... I told you I left the military after my initial tour — because my dad was dying and my mom needed me — but it's a little more entailed than that. I didn't want to end up like my father. A career in the military ... it's rough on the family. So ... I returned to the only place that ever felt like home. Where my grandparents had always lived and my mother and sisters now live." He hadn't discussed his jobs, but since it was a major part of who he was, he figured he needed to tell her what he did for a living too. Some women freaked, wanting nothing to do with a cop and others thrilled at the idea. "I'd always wanted to be a police officer, and it's an easy transition from the military, so I became a cop. Now you probably understand why I asked you those questions earlier." She nodded, but didn't comment, so he continued, "I also started helping folks remodel their houses. Before I knew it, people were paying me to build things for them. In the last few years, my small handyman operation has grown to a full-scale construction company. I have a beautiful house in Stanfield. It's far enough from my mother and grandmother to discourage daily visits, but close enough to watch over them. I like being a cop, but I don't have to anymore. My company pays the bills with enough left over that I can take the time to help in emergencies like these hurricanes."

Jordan paused. He felt as though he were telling her his life story, and still, he didn't know enough about her. He wanted to know everything. He felt like an addict who needed a fix.

He shrugged. "What else would you like to know?" He lowered his head to look at her eyes. She just stared at him. She probably thought he was ridiculous and simple-minded the way he prattled.

"Are you sure you're real? Why aren't you married or have a girlfriend?" Jaynee's eyes flashed with panic, then she pulled back from him. "You don't, do you?"

"Jaynee, how many times are you going to insult me tonight? First you accuse me of trying to seduce you for a one-night stand, and now you think I could be sitting here, spilling out my guts if I were married. What in the world happened to you, girl?"

This time, she kissed him. He felt a hungry need in her embrace. She wrapped her arms around his neck, pulling closer. He gave in to her, drawing her entire body onto his lap, holding her as close as possible.

Pulling back, he whispered, "Can we go back to your house? I promise nothing will happen, but I feel a little uncomfortable out here in the open and really want to talk to you tonight." He saw the apprehension in her eyes. "You can trust me. I swear I'll never ask anything of you emotionally or physically you're unable to give, and I'll never hurt you. But you need to give me a chance to prove myself." He jumped down from the truck bed with her still in his arms and carried her back to the cab. "We can stay here if you want, inside the truck. I just don't like being open to the elements of society with my attention otherwise diverted. Cop, remember?"

"Yes, I remember. Do you remember the way to my house?"

"*I do.*" Did she notice the inference in his words? For the first time in his life, he actually imagined saying them for real. Imagined what it would feel like to have one woman forever.

After climbing into the driver's seat, he lifted the center console and slid her next to him. He draped his arm over her shoulders. He could get used to this, he thought with utter contentment. If he could just shatter her barriers, he believed they could make this work. He would lay everything on the line and see where it led.

Chapter Four

As Jaynee slipped the key into the lock of her front door, she glanced over her shoulder at Jordan. Her eyes then shifted to the empty street beyond. Nothing was out of the ordinary, except that she was about to let the first man into her home in over a year.

She was fragile and therefore needed to be careful. She'd made too many mistakes with men. However, she didn't want to be so cautious that she missed something great. Her refusing-to-date stance wasn't making sense. Jordan represented everything she'd ever wanted in a man. How or why he was attracted to her, she couldn't comprehend, but for some reason, he seemed interested.

Although she wanted to, she couldn't deny the strong emotions she felt for him. It scared her. She'd been hurt in the past. But hadn't she prayed incessantly for God to send her a man like Jordan? Still, she needed to be sure that what she felt was real. Her heart couldn't handle another pummeling.

Once inside, Jordan locked the deadbolt behind them. The latch clicked loudly into place, making her jump. What had she done? Could she really trust him?

Jordan took her hand and led her to the sofa, pulling her down beside him. Her heart started beating out an uncontrollable rhythm. *Dear God*, she prayed silently, *please don't let him hurt me.* She knew he wouldn't hurt her physically; it was the mental agony she couldn't handle.

Gathering her other hand in his, he gazed into her eyes. "Jaynee," he started, then stopped, his lips curving up, "Jaynee and Jordan, it sounds like characters in a story, doesn't it?"

His smile was wonderful, too good to be true. He didn't sound like a Marine or a cop. He looked every bit the tough guy, but was a hundred percent gentleman and romantic simultaneously. Although her heart continued to race in her chest, it wasn't out of nervousness anymore, but anticipation.

Warmth crawled over her cheeks. "Yes, it does." She glanced at her hands clasped between his.

He released her hands and brushed away the bangs draping over her eyes, then lowered his hands to her waist and pulled her closer.

"Where were we?" he drawled. His mouth moved back over hers, soft, warm, inviting.

She melted under his touch, wondering how this man had escaped every other woman. His tongue slid across her lips, parting them, then slowly circled her tongue. Electricity soared through her under his embrace. She wrapped her arms around his neck, pulling her body closer. His lips were urgent, making her want more. She lowered her hands to his chest and began to unbutton his shirt.

Unexpectedly, he moved his hands from around her waist and gathered both of her wrists. He pulled her hands to his chest, effectively stopping her progress.

Her mind raced. Had she done something wrong?

Jordan's lips slowed as his mouth progressed the line of her jaw to her ear. "Not tonight, my love," he whispered through delicate kisses. "Not until you can give me all of you, heart and soul." He pulled her closer and caressed her hair. His warm breath saturated her neck, sending chills down her spine.

The emotions that raged through her were terrifying. Giving away her body was easy; she couldn't give up her heart. Never again. Why was he doing this to her?

"Jaynee, I don't want to scare you, but I have feelings for you. I don't know how this could happen so fast; it certainly hasn't ever happened before. But I'm willing to follow through if you will open up."

What was he implying? He'd mentioned feelings, but had also said "my love." Warmth overflowed her veins again, and she was positive her heart would pound through her chest. For the first time in years, she wanted to trust someone, wanted to believe. What if she succumbed and he shattered what was left of her sanity? She didn't possess the strength to resist nor did she want to. But would he get up and leave the moment she disclosed her past?

She gulped. "I don't know ..." Her throat was so dry; her words came out in a raspy murmur as if she hadn't spoken all day. "How much do you want to know?"

"Everything." He leaned back against the arm of the couch and stared into her eyes again. "You'll have to give up all your demons; I have too much to give. You will have to empty yourself completely to make room for my love." Jaynee looked down at her lap, and once again, Jordan lifted her chin, forcing her to look at his steel-blue eyes. "I've waited for you practically my entire life. I didn't believe it was possible, but I believe now." He took her face between both hands as if to give testament to his words. "I have been struck, Jaynee. Not by the proverbial love-at-first-sight or Cupid's arrow, but by something more powerful." He took a deep breath and continued, "From the second our eyes met, electricity soared through me, and somehow you became the center of my universe. Nothing else seemed to matter. I wasn't looking for this. I tried to get up and leave the restaurant the moment it happened, but I couldn't, even when you turned me down. But the funny thing is ... I saw it in your eyes yesterday, and I see it now. You felt it too, didn't you?"

Not believing his words, she slowly moved her head back and forth. This couldn't be real, but how could she deny that she'd felt it too? She was hesitant, but she needed to be truthful. "Yes, but ... it's not possible —"

He grasped her shoulders and pulled her closer, cutting off her words with a kiss that demanded everything. His mouth enveloped hers, making her want to cry out for more. Once again, though, he pulled back too soon.

"You did experience it?" Jaynee nodded, her mind spinning from the kiss he'd planted on her. He sighed. "Thank God, and you're not going to dismiss me as if I'm some kind of maniac?"

"No ..." She gulped again, knowing he meant well, but positive he'd leave. "But you still want to hear my story?"

He nodded with a slight tilt of his head. "Yes. I want to take it from you, but only if you're ready." He brushed her hair away from her face again and rested his hand against her cheek. "Who hurt you, Jaynee?"

She shook her head. "I'm frightened, Jordan." She couldn't reveal her secrets. Acid churned in her stomach at the thought of exposing her skeletons. "I've never opened up before and don't know if I can. I just want to finish college and not have to worry about anything but myself. What if I give you everything inside of me, and then you turn around and hurt me? I can't handle more heartbreak." She chewed on her bottom lip, trying to resist, knowing a relationship with him was impossible. "You live in another state for heaven's sake."

Jordan waited without saying a word. His eyes looked sincere ... as if he really cared about her. Why? Why did he care?

She heaved a sigh. "It wasn't just one person. Everyone in my life has hurt me except my grandmother. My parents, family members, so-called friends, my ex-boyfriend, everyone has destroyed a piece of me. I was born a mistake and continue to make horrible decisions." Tears began to fall again. She dropped her head to shield herself.

He nudged up her chin. "You don't have to hide from me, Jaynee." His tone was gentle, reassuring. "And you don't have to talk now. But I promise I'll be here when you're ready." He stretched out the length of the couch and pulled her down with him. His arm encircled her neck. After wiping away her tears, he grazed his fingertips across her cheekbones and down her jaw. "You're so beautiful," he crooned, his words just above a whisper.

She released a nervous chuckle. "Hardly. I'm a blubbering fool." Her voice was barely audible from the ridiculous tears.

"Will you be my fool then?" He brushed his lips across her forehead. "You don't have to explain anything. We can start with a clean slate."

It didn't seem possible, but he pulled her even closer, and all she could think was that she wasn't close enough. Maybe if she could bare her soul, she would be closer.

"Why aren't you taken?" she asked again, the question in her mind that didn't compute.

He exhaled as he contemplated his answer. "Honestly ... I haven't found anyone I was interested in." He tilted up her chin, softly kissed her lips, then pulled back, smiling. "Until now ..."

She couldn't help but smile, though it was a half-hearted attempt. Could she trust him? His arms felt so wonderful wrapped around her. She wanted to trust him. She wanted to believe he was sincere.

He moved his hand to the back of her head. His hand trailed down her hair and finally rested on her hip. His touch caused her mind to rocket. Feelings she hadn't considered in ages invaded her senses.

He inhaled deeply before speaking again. "But, I *do* date ... I just don't usually make it to a second date. Women I've gone out with expect a dumb hick, I suppose, and my interests run deeper than most girls can keep pace. But not you ... You held my attention from the first few seconds. And then, when we talked for hours yesterday and there was so much more I wanted to know ... I didn't want to let you go and hated I didn't get your phone number. I counted the minutes until the restaurant opened for dinner. Here I go rambling again. I want to hear about you, and I keep doing all the talking."

***

Jaynee let out what sounded like a contented sigh — it was a wonderful sound — then she nestled her head farther against his chest. He couldn't help but notice how wonderful it felt to have her in his arms.

"Too good to be true." Her words muffled against his shirt, and Jordan wasn't sure he'd heard correctly.

He pulled the afghan off the back of the sofa and wrapped it around her. Pressing his lips to her forehead again, he breathed in the unique vanilla scent. She smelled incredible, and he wanted her more than he'd ever wanted any woman. It had taken every ounce of self-control he possessed to impede her hands. It had been too long, and Jaynee was sexy, warm, and delicate. The thought of making love to her sent his mind and body soaring with desire. More than the physical want, though, was for her to trust and love him. Yes, that's what he wanted. He wanted to take her home. He wanted her to be his wife. It didn't matter that he didn't know her secrets; it didn't matter that they'd only met yesterday. Nothing mattered other than he couldn't accept to live without her from this moment. He felt an all-consuming need not only to love her, but also to protect her.

Jaynee's body went limp with sleep, and her quiet breaths grew soft and even. He wondered if he should leave. She'd mentioned her grandmother lived across the street. What would she think of a strange truck in the driveway?

She'd said that she didn't date, so he was sure she didn't make a habit of bringing men home. She was a consenting adult and did have an ex-boyfriend; though, she'd said it singularly, as if there had only been one. He shifted his thoughts. He didn't want to think about her with another man. The immediate fury that welled up inside of him at just the thought — he cut off the image.

Instead, he looked at the woman in his arms. She would be his, and he didn't need to worry. He'd never lose control again.

He'd learned to subdue his anger after the last time. The idea of someone he loved looking at him as if he couldn't be trusted ensured that. It was the main reason he didn't drink much.

He wasn't an alcoholic. But when he drank too much, he became either amorous or antagonistic depending on the situation. Either of which could land a man in a heap of trouble. He liked to keep his thoughts clear, and right now, he was thinking crystal clear. Jaynee would be his.

Closing his eyes, he decided to stay. It felt too good holding her. Moreover, maybe he could attain some morning time with her. Tomorrow was a school day, but maybe she'd skip and they could return to the beach she'd mentioned. What had she called it? Honeymoon Island ... how apropos.

***

Kenny's car crawled through Caycee's neighborhood for the third time this evening. The truck in her driveway was still there, and it was late. She had an overnight guest.

Brian wouldn't be happy about that when he called, collect as usual. He'd been furious when he heard about her just having coffee with the guy.

Brian had asked Kenny if she'd received his letter. *How the hell am I supposed to know if she got a letter or not?* he'd asked him. Stalking his buddy's ex-girlfriend wasn't something he particularly enjoyed. If he got caught, he'd end up in jail, right alongside Brian.

It was ridiculous that Brian insisted he drive by the restaurant and her house every night. But he'd agreed to do it. It was the least he could do for his friend who had not given him up as an accomplice. But he knew Brian would turn on him in a heartbeat if Kenny didn't do what he wanted.

In truth, he didn't understand Brian's infatuation. Caycee was good looking, sure, but Brian was obsessed with her. Always saying how "she was his" and "she belonged to him." It was downright creepy.

It wasn't as if Kenny was the best dude in the world. He had his share of relationships, but he never carried on so much about one woman. He'd use them and let them go.

But Caycee held some kind of spell over Brian. Not enough to make him stop doing what he wanted, but he'd go crazy if anyone even looked at her.

He remembered one dude who was sitting beside Brian and Kenny at the bar where she used to work. He'd merely commented to his buddy, "I'd like to hit that."

Any warm-blooded male would. 'Course Kenny knew better than to say it aloud. Brian didn't say a word to the dude. Instead, he waited until it appeared as though he were leaving. When the man went to the bathroom, Brian dragged Kenny outside.

After getting a tire iron from his car, Brian waited around the side of the building, telling Kenny to keep a lookout. When the dude rounded the corner, Brian grabbed him and beat the crap out of him. He never hit him on the head, but the dude sure wasn't going to be able to walk or write for a while. Brian hadn't uttered a word or stolen the man's wallet, and it was too dark to ID him, so the crime had gone down as a hate crime. Kenny knew better. It was a crime of passion; Brian was obsessed.

As Kenny drove away from Caycee's house, he scrolled through his playlist on his iPod for Korn. He needed to clear his mind. The guitar solo in *Did my Time* stole his cares away for a few minutes, but then he thought about what Brian would ask of him.

Brian wouldn't be happy about Caycee's new beau. He wondered what he would expect him to do. Kenny couldn't beat down someone with a tire iron. He was a petty thief, nothing more, just enough to survive. All he needed was enough money to smoke a little weed, get drunk, and skim and surf when the waves were up.

Brian was the big-money guy. Always wanting more, always needing more. Intelligent too ... smarter than Kenny could ever be, but he'd gotten busted and would be away for five years. He expected Caycee to wait, even though she'd broken off their relationship almost six months before his arrest. Kenny knew Brian wouldn't accept the idea of her dating again. He was fine as long as she didn't date anyone else, and she hadn't, until now.

Chapter Five

Three days ago ...

Jaynee heard Jordan's whispered words, but they sounded distant. He wanted her to wake up. She attempted to open her eyes, but they were heavy, as if a massive wool blanket was smothering her.

She tried to roll over, but she couldn't feel her hands, her feet ... or any other part of her body for that matter. Muffled sounds filled the air, but they were difficult to discern. They sounded far away, as though they were outside her wool cocoon.

Where was she? How did she get here? She tried to call for Jordan, but her lips wouldn't respond either. Would he even rescue her from her prison? She vaguely recalled that he was angry, but she couldn't remember why.

Her entire body felt numb. The only thing she felt was her head and it started pounding uncontrollably. Without warning, the throbbing increased, and she cried out in the darkness for relief. The voices were closer now, but they weren't helping. The pain was unbearable. It felt as if something were crushing her head in a vice. Her screams echoed inside this fleeced darkness, making the pain worse.

***

"What's happening?" Jordan wailed as several nurses rounded the corner when the alarms pierced the silent space.

The first nurse who entered, pushed by him, flashing a penlight in Jaynee's eyes. Another nurse checked the wires connected to Jaynee's head, but then suddenly whipped around to look at the screen. The P.A. who'd been attending to Jaynee earlier ran into the room.

Jordan stood up, staring in horror as they bustled around his wife, rearranging wires as if they were going to take her away from him.

Jaynee was hurting. She hadn't moved, but her features creased as if she were in pain. He stepped forward. "Is she —"

"Sit down, sir!" The male P.A. demanded, then started shouting orders to the nurses as they wheeled her out of the room and down the corridor.

Jordan jumped up from the chair and sped toward the door, following his wife at a distance, but then the hospital staff charged through the double doors of the O.R. Jaynee was going back to surgery again? What had gone wrong?

He had been talking to her, holding her hand just minutes ago. The machines had maintained a steady rhythm, lulling him into a near slumber. It had been almost seven hours since her surgery when her eyes had started darting under her lids. He had begged her to wake up ... apologized for pushing her to this extreme. He'd been sure she was coming around until the alarm had sounded.

Unwilling to bear her empty room, he made his way to the private waiting area and dropped into one of the chairs. *Dear God, I can't lose her*, he prayed silently. He hadn't stopped praying all night, but he wasn't sure God was listening. After all, he'd been the one who had gotten drunk and told her to leave.

After pacing the floor of the waiting room for three torturously long hours, Jordan got frustrated and searched for someone who could give him information.

"Michelle!" He spotted the nurse who'd been in Jaynee's room earlier. He'd spoken with her in the past. She'd always been rather flirtatious. Maybe he could glean some information from her. "Is there anything new? Is Jaynee out of surgery yet?" Not wanting to cry in front of the hospital staff, he blinked to dry his eyes. He had to keep himself together. He had to remain strong for Jaynee.

"I'm sorry, Mr. Monroe. There's nothing new I can tell you. Dr. McMullen will notify you the moment your wife is out of surgery. Please go back to the waiting room." The nurse's eyes were kind, but demanding. She wouldn't share any information even if she had any.

Jordan felt alone. His sisters had come earlier, but had to return to their families. His mother had stayed beside him, but she had to check on his grandmother who was too sick to leave the house. He'd informed Jaynee's family of the *accident*, but then begged them not to come. The hospital would only allow two people at a time in her room, and he couldn't imagine having to deal with his mother-in-law's drama. Certainly, she would make everything about her.

The one person he wouldn't have minded coming was her grandmother, but she'd just had surgery and wasn't able to walk yet. Jordan assured them he would call if there was any change, but now he didn't feel like talking to any of them. They were just as much responsible for Jaynee's situation as he was.

He recognized the same people who had been in the small waiting area designated for ICU that he'd seen earlier. The one couple had come, left, and returned. But one visitor, like him, seemed to be a fixture. As if in a trance, the man kept his eyes lowered. He'd stared at the same page of a magazine for untold minutes, as though he weren't actually reading it. He wasn't wearing a ring, so maybe he was waiting for news of a friend or relative.

Jordan glanced up at the TV, willing it to break, since he hadn't been able to find the remote. If he had to endure one more loop of the news broadcasting on the local channel, he would go insane. It was the identical transmission over and over. At least they hadn't picked up Jaynee's story yet. Reporters would have a field day with that tidbit of information. He could hear it now, *Cop's wife suspiciously found shot in their home after an argument.*

Jordan was about to lose his sanity, when finally, Dr. McMullen stepped into the handkerchief-sized waiting area. The other man looked up in anticipation too. He'd been waiting as long as Jordan had for information.

"Jordan, you can come with me now." The doctor's tone was solemn. Jordan was unable to read if the news was good or bad.

Dr. McMullen walked in silence alongside Jordan as they headed toward Jaynee's room. As much as Jordan wanted to bombard him with questions, he held his tongue. If Jaynee had died, the doctor would be walking toward his office, not her room, he assured himself.

"Jaynee is stable now, Jordan. You can go inside."

Jordan searched the doctor's eyes for the truth, fearful he might discover it. "What happened? All the monitors were normal. Her eyes were moving under her lids, and she looked as though she were coming around." He spat out the questions, hoping the doctor would give him some assurance.

"Jaynee's ICP, short for intracranial pressure, shot up. To give you an example, a normal ICP reading for someone who has a bad headache is around four to five. The worst headache you've ever experienced is around eight to nine. After surgery, Jaynee's ICP had been hovering around twelve to fourteen. The reason we've kept her in an induced coma. The alarms sounded because the pressure on her brain increased to over forty."

Jordan dropped his head, shaking it, hoping he was still in his nightmare. He looked back up at the doctor who hadn't continued. The doctor had more bad news. Jordan could sense it in his eyes. "What does that mean?"

McMullen took a breath before continuing, "We had to remove a piece of her skull and some fluid to lower the pressure, Jordan. She's stable now. Not where we would prefer, but we'll take it, considering the alternative."

The alternative ... Dead. He couldn't imagine it. Jaynee couldn't die. He dropped his head in his hands. This couldn't be happening. These things happened to other people. Not them. Was the doctor hiding something else?

He looked back at his eyes. He was proficient in reading people. His job demanded the skill. "What's going to happen now? Will she wake up, or will you keep her in a comatose state? Will she be okay?" Desperate for any positive information, the words rushed from his lips.

"If the pressure remains normal, we'll wean her off the medication in slow increments. Then we'll have to wait and observe." The doctor turned and walked away, leaving Jordan with his reason for living wrapped up in additional wires and covered by thick hospital blankets.

Jaynee hated her feet covered. He reached down and untucked the blanket and sheet from the bottom of the bed before sitting beside his wife.

Resting his head against the side of her bed, he felt the tears track noiselessly down his face again. He'd assumed she was through the worst and was returning to him. He felt uncomfortable talking aloud, but they'd insisted he needed to talk to her. Did she want to hear his voice? Maybe *he* was upsetting her.

"Jaynee, love, I'm here for you, as always, as I promised from the start. You don't have to explain anything; just return to me, please. I told you before, nothing else matters but you. I love you. I don't care what happened. I only want you back in my arms, and I know you want me too. I know you still love me." He ran his fingertips over her skin, caressing her arm. There was nothing else to say.

"Would you like me to sing to you? I heard a country song the other day. It's sad in the beginning, but it has a happy ending. It reminded me of us. It's about a husband who's asking his wife if he still gives her everything she needs and does he get another chance."

In a low whisper, Jordan sang the words in Jaynee's ear. He didn't like his voice, but she'd always commented how much she enjoyed it and how she thought he sounded like Garth Brooks. He reflected back on all the occasions they'd sang together driving to the mountains. She loved singing, and he loved listening to her ... it meant she was happy, even when she was singing sad songs.

He tried to remember the words to other songs; mostly he only recalled the choruses. Jaynee had always laughed when he filled in whatever words sounded right or his incessant singing to the pets.

He now wondered if everything had bugged her. Had all his quirks she laughed at actually annoyed her? He shook the thoughts from his head. No ... not his Jaynee. She wasn't phony. Her honesty was one of the first characteristics he'd liked about her.

It was something entirely different. Something from her past ... it was the only logical explanation. Nothing else made sense. He knew she loved him; they'd been destined from the moment they'd met.

***

Jaynee struggled with the immense blanket smothering her, wondering why she couldn't just throw it off.

She hated feeling trapped. She didn't even like her feet covered in bed. Jordan was the opposite. He'd have his side of the bed sheets and blankets tucked in tightly, while she kicked them off as soon as she climbed into bed, no matter how cold it was. And they always kept it cool inside the house; she couldn't breathe with electric heat.

The pain had subsided somewhat, and she could hear murmurs again, or was it singing? Was Jordan here? Why couldn't she see him? Didn't he see her smothered by this awful blanket? He knew she was claustrophobic, knew she hated feeling trapped.

She listened to the surrounding sounds. Yes, it was definitely Jordan singing in a hushed whisper, but also something else, an annoying buzzing and beeping.

Then it hit her. She was in the hospital.

The reason he was beside her ... why he wasn't uncovering her. Was she dying? Did they assume she wasn't alive?

Jaynee tried to recall the last thing that happened, but there was nothing except Jordan. All she remembered was Jordan. He was angry, but she couldn't remember why, and then he wasn't. He'd kissed her, and they'd made love. Their bodies entangled together afterward as they always did, his arms wrapped around her. He was her strong tower. She felt safe in his arms, but there was something else.

She was afraid, but she couldn't remember why.

Chapter Six

Five years ago ...

Jaynee awoke in Jordan's arms, surprised that she didn't feel uncomfortable physically or mentally. He'd stayed overnight and hadn't attempted anything. She peeked through half-opened lids to see if he was awake.

He was staring out the window, but obviously sensing her stir, he turned his gaze to her. "Mornin', darlin'," he drawled, his baritone voice deep and raspy from not speaking yet. A glorious smile spread across his face as if he'd won some incredible honor.

She smiled up at him, astounded he hadn't altered his position overnight. She assumed he would have come to his senses and realized what a basket case she was.

She cleared her throat. "Good Morning. Did you sleep well?" She knew he couldn't have.

"Never better. I thought we fit perfectly together." He pulled her closer to demonstrate, slid his arm underneath her, and sat up with her in his arms. "However, I do need to brush my teeth. I feel rough. I don't suppose you have an extra toothbrush?"

Realizing she may have morning breath too, Jaynee inched her way out of his arms and stood up before speaking. "Actually, I do. Would you like to take a shower, too?"

Jordan stood up beside her and pulled her back into his arms, brushing her hair off her neck. "You don't mind? I could just go to the hotel." He looked down at her, his eyes forlorn. Hoping, she assumed, she wouldn't ask him to leave.

"Don't be silly ... my grandmother and neighbors have already seen your truck. It's not as if you can sneak away. You might as well get cleaned up." She pulled away from him, then walked toward the bathroom. "Just let me grab my toothbrush and anything else I'd rather you not see." She giggled at the thought. She didn't want him to see any panties hanging on the shower rod or some other embarrassing female paraphernalia. She wasn't accustomed to having company. "Would you mind walking across the street to meet my grandmother for breakfast?" she called from the bathroom.

Jordan stepped inside the doorframe of the small room, startling her. "You want to introduce me to your grandmother?"

She shook her head and let out a small laugh. "Well, yeah, naturally ... I told you she's the most important person in my life."

He grabbed her waist and pulled her to his body. He buried his head against the nape of her neck. Chills ran down her spine as he worked his way up her throat with small kisses. He pushed back her hair so he could continue kissing the line of her jaw up to her ear. His breaths quickened. "Thank you, Jaynee, for giving me a chance.

You won't be sorry. I'm going to love you like no one has ever loved you."

She sucked in a ragged breath, feeling as if she would collapse any second. Jordan was rocking apart her world. *Love?* She pulled back to look at him, certain he would decipher the trepidation in her eyes.

He touched her cheek with his large palm. "I'm scaring you, aren't I? Do you want me to stop?" His eyes, filled with nothing but sincerity, searched hers for an answer.

"Yes ... No..." She rested her head against his broad chest. "I mean, yes, you're scaring me. But, no, I don't want you to stop." She stepped back from his embrace. "Get ready, Jordan. I'll call my grandmother and tell her we're coming over for breakfast." Her vision blurred as she tried to focus on the wall behind him. If she looked at his face, she was positive she would break down again. *Love her like no one has ever loved her* ... That wouldn't be too hard; no one had ever loved her.

Jaynee picked up her toothbrush and paste, pulled out a toothbrush and some other new travel-sized items from her toiletry bag for him, and then left the room. Walking into the kitchen dazed, she picked up the phone and dialed the only number she knew by heart.

Her grandmother's gravelly voice answered after the first ring.

"Hi, Gram. I'm bringing company over for breakfast ... Yes, he belongs to the gigantic truck outside, but before you ask ... No, nothing happened it was just late ... I know ... I remember. Listen ... Gram, please listen to me. This is serious. I think I just met the man I'm going to marry —" Jaynee stopped her words dead in their tracks, but it was too late.

His strong arms encircled her waist. "You didn't leave me any toothpaste." His voice was a low whisper in her ear. He smiled down at her as his arm reached around her shoulder to the tube of paste still clutched in her hand. Squirting some out on his brush, he kissed her neck and walked away without uttering another word.

Oh, dear God. I can't believe he heard me. He had to have heard me.

"Gram, are you there? I'm sorry ... No, not *him*. I already told you he's out of my life forever. We'll be over in a little while. Please don't mention anything about *him*."

Jaynee hung up the phone and stood at the kitchen sink, just staring out the window. Had he heard what she'd said? Of course, he'd heard her. Oh heavens, what would he think? Now he'd definitely run for the hills of North Carolina.

Did she believe what she'd said, though? Was Jordan the One? She'd never believed that about any man, even the one she'd dated for several years.

Those same muscular arms circled around her again. He brushed the hair off her neck and buried his face between her jaw and shoulder.

Maybe he hadn't heard her ridiculous proclamation. She turned in his arms, ready for a fresh kiss. Her insides were still churning from the ones he'd given her last night, and she was ready for more.

Leaning back from her lips, though, he narrowed his eyes. "So ... who is he, and where can I find him? This man you're going to marry." His voice was lighthearted.

He *had* heard her, but he wasn't running. She tried to act casually, as if that were even possible. "Oh, just a guy I met who seems perfect in every way. Except for the minor detail that he eavesdropped on a private conversation." She brushed nonexistent dust off his shirt, then raised her eyebrows.

"Did you mean it?" His voice was deep and earnest as he stared intently into her eyes.

No doubt, she was crazy about him. Only apprehension that he'd hurt her made her cautious. She gulped down the lump of fear lodged in her throat. "I think so." She did mean it, as crazy as it sounded.

Jordan pulled her closer. His mouth covered hers. She already knew his kiss. How his tongue would part her lips and gently circle around hers. He was incredible. His mouth, his body, his heart. And for some reason, he wanted her.

He scooped her up and carried her back to the sofa. She longed to feel his skin on hers. It had been too long since she'd felt wanted. She began unbuttoning his shirt, and again he stopped her. This time by smoothly moving her hands around his neck.

"We're expected across the street," he chided with a chuckle.

Attempting to unravel him, she batted her eyelashes. "We have thirty minutes."

A smile flashed across his face. "I don't know what you're familiar with, darlin', but half an hour won't even be a warm-up."

Jaynee caught her breath. Again, like the first night, he'd turned her flirting around on her. "Umm ..." She was speechless as fire burned through her.

He ran his fingers along her jaw, coaxing her to him. "I want you too, but not like this. Just kiss me again," he insisted, but then kissed her, his arms tightening around her waist.

Her body burned with pleasure. Never had she wanted a man so much, and twice he'd told her *no*. It didn't offend her, though; she knew he wanted her too. She could feel that need in his kiss and hear it in the low groan escaping his throat.

He pulled back after they'd gotten lost in the kiss. "Go take a shower before I lose my willpower and we stand up your grandmother. That wouldn't make for a good first impression."

He pushed her away, but held onto her hand, kissing it, and then let it fall after a few seconds.

Jaynee hurried through her shower.

She toweled off, sprayed on body mist and deodorant, dabbed on a hint of mascara, fluffed her hair with her hairdryer, and she was ready.

Easing her way out of the bathroom, covered only by a towel, she glanced toward the living room. She should have remembered a robe. Jordan smiled, but remained on the couch as she made her way to the bedroom.

Did she want him to follow her into her bedroom? Yes, but conversely, no. She liked the idea of waiting. That half an hour warm-up comment got her blood racing. Undoubtedly, he knew what he was doing.

Slipping into her favorite white dress, she glanced at herself in the mirror. It was a little late in the year for a sundress. But it was unseasonably warm, and she liked the way it looked on her. Her Portuguese heritage gave her a natural glow that contrasted with the white dress and showed off her tan the best. She hoped Jordan would appreciate the dress also.

She opened the bedroom door and found him standing in the hallway, waiting patiently.

"May I?" he asked as he stepped past her and into her bedroom. He gave a quick glance around the room. "You're clean, but not a freak about it. I like that." He sat down sinuously on the edge of her bed, pulling her with him so that she was standing between his legs, his hands resting on her hips. "Are you skipping school today?"

"It appears I am," she said.

"How 'bout work ... do you *have* to work this evening?"

"At five." She heard the disappointment in her own voice and knew he wouldn't miss it. "I need the money. Friday night is big bucks."

"So, should I show up and distract you again?" He flashed that same devilishly handsome grin he had yesterday. The man made her blood boil just by smiling.

"Not tonight," she said, smiling despite herself. "That's the late shift, so I'll be busy from the moment I clock in. But if you like, I'll meet you at the Starbucks around ten o'clock." He nodded, and she moved in closer. "And then, we'll have all day Saturday and Sunday if you still want an actual date. I'll even get *gussied-up* for you," she said, quoting his words from the first night.

"Better than this?" He flipped the ruffles on her dress. "I can't imagine. Maybe you shouldn't. We might not make it out the door. Speaking of which ... let's go. I have a grandmother to impress, and I don't want to be late."

Jaynee let them into her grandmother's house. It was normal for her to walk right in, but never with a guest. The aroma of Linguica permeated the air as soon as she opened the door. Jaynee glanced back at Jordan for his reaction.

An intrigued and delighted look lit up his face. "What is that?"

She laughed. Jordan liked to eat, she noticed. "That delectable smell is Linguica. It's a Portuguese sausage. My grandmother's specialty."

Gram leaned over the stove, flipping over pieces of Linguica. After leveling a large splatter screen over the pan, she placed several slices of fresh bread on top to steam the flavor of the sausage into the bread.

Jaynee grinned when she looked at her grandmother. Normally she walked around in her duster, as she called it, but no matter what the age, she always tried to look good when company called. And she did. She'd even put on a little lipstick. You'd never know she was seventy-nine. She looked and acted closer to sixty. She still worked in her garden daily. Grampy, on the other hand, just hung around and slept. He'd been dying for as long as Jaynee could remember, but he was wonderful. She loved them both with all her heart.

"Good morning, Cay." Gram looked up at her. "Breakfast's almost finished. Come and give your Grammie a kiss." It was as if she was twelve all over again, but Jaynee complied. "And, who's this?" Gram asked with a smirk.

"Gram, this is Jordan – Jordan, this is Gram. Everyone calls her Gram."

They shook hands, and Jordan gave Gram one of his breathtaking smiles. It wasn't lost on her; Jaynee could see it in her eyes. Gram had always been a sucker for a military-looking man, and Jordan certainly looked the part.

Grampy had been in the Navy, and Jaynee was positive Gram had married him because of the way he looked in his uniform. Grampy had been on leave when he noticed her at the community pond. And according to Gramp's story, his friend had dared him to go up and kiss Gram. Jaynee had been shocked when she heard it the first time. Who would have thought they did those things back then? But it was love at first sight. He asked her to marry him thirteen days later. They were married within a month and had been married for over fifty years. Jaynee couldn't help but wonder if the magic would repeat itself with Jordan and her.

Jordan ate everything on his plate, then looked up for more, which Jaynee knew thrilled her grandmother.

"Cay ..." Her grandmother looked at her with disapproval in her eyes. "Get Jordan seconds."

Jaynee stood up with his plate and refilled it.

"Thanks," he said, offering her a sheepish grin. Then he looked to her grandmother. "And thanks for the breakfast, Gram. It's wonderful."

Jaynee removed her plate and started cleaning up the kitchen.

"So, Jordan, tell me about yourself. Where are you from, what do you do for a living? How long do you plan to stay in Florida —"

Jaynee whirled around. "Gram!"

"It's okay." Jordan turned to look at Jaynee and shrugged. "I don't mind."

"Never mind, Jordan. Cay will tell me later. She tells me everything." Her grandmother winked at her. Gram wouldn't have cared if he had three eyes. Her single concern was he wasn't Jaynee's ex and that Jaynee was happy.

Gram got up from the table and walked to the living room. Jordan followed, throwing Jaynee a quick smile, and it looked as if he might have blushed from her grandmother's statement.

Jaynee decided it was safe to stay in the kitchen area and finish the dishes. Only the breakfast bar separated them, so she could see and hear them. She could only hope her grandmother wouldn't get too energetic with Jordan and start telling him her life story.

Gram, thankfully, took a seat in her recliner while Jordan strode from picture to picture along the living room wall. "Is this you, Jaynee?"

Gram looked up and stared between the two of them obviously taken aback by him referring to her by her middle name. She was just Caycee or Cay to the family. But undaunted by an opportunity to gloat over her granddaughter's photos, Gram got back up and walked over to the wall, pointing out different pictures of Jaynee around the room.

"Would you like to see some baby pictures of Caycee, Jordan? I have tons of albums."

Jaynee dropped the towel she was using and ran into the living room. "We'll pass this time, Gram," Jaynee interrupted before Jordan agreed to pore over old photo albums. He had no idea what he was getting himself into. "I want to take Jordan up to Tarpon Springs before work tonight."

Jordan glanced at Jaynee with understanding and acceptance, but also a look of sadness as if he really wanted to spend the day perusing old photographs of her.

"Okay then ... have fun, kids. Jordan, it was nice to meet you. You're welcome back anytime," Gram said. And she'd meant it. Gram didn't say anything she didn't mean.

As they walked out the door, Jordan hugged Gram. Jaynee was thrilled. Of course, she knew Gram would like Jordan. She just wanted Jaynee to be happy. It was all she'd ever wanted. Her grandmother had spent the majority of her retirement taking care of her. Jaynee was the daughter she'd never had. Gram had raised four boys and always wanted a little girl. Fortunately, her boys had turned around and had almost all daughters. Jaynee ended up being like her daughter, though, when her mother abandoned her.

Jaynee glanced over her shoulder and waved at her grandmother. Gram had a huge grin on her face as she watched them walk away.

Jordan waved too, then took her hand in his and brought it to his lips. "I really like your grandmother," Jordan confessed while they walked across the street. "She reminds me of my grandmother. She's a firecracker, isn't she?"

"You have no idea." And he didn't. No one other than Jaynee understood what tragedies Gram had dealt with in her life. Even her own children and grandchildren weren't privy to the stories she'd shared with Jaynee. They'd always had an intimate relationship because of their similar backgrounds, even if they were fifty-seven years apart.

"I'm glad she was there for you," he murmured, his voice filled with compassion. He really did care about her. "So, what's Tarpon Springs, or was that just an excuse to get me alone?" He nuzzled her neck playfully as they approached his truck.

Jordan had changed the subject again, just as he'd done the last time he'd sensed her getting upset. Could he already read her emotions?

She plastered a smile on her face, refusing to think about her family and all the troubles they'd caused her. Jordan made her happy, something she hadn't felt in a long time. "The Tarpon Spring's Sponge Docks are where the Greek sponge divers — to this day — continue to go out diving.

It's interesting. And there are several pleasant spots to get lunch on the water. I think you'll enjoy it."

"As long as I'm with you ... I'll love it." As they approached his truck, he put his arm around her waist and pulled her to his side. He leaned back against the side of the truck and moved her in front of him. "And you're positive I can't convince you to call in sick tonight?" His eyes bore into hers, an attempt to persuade her no doubt. It almost worked.

"Nope. I'm too responsible, and I really can't afford for my manager to take away my good shifts and stations. Besides, I'm off tomorrow. I wouldn't want you to get tired of me."

Jordan opened the passenger door and helped her into the cab. His hands lingered a little too leisurely on her waist just to be helpful. He was enjoying his work.

"That's not gonna happen, darlin'," he said in the most seductive drawl she'd heard yet and then closed the door.

Jaynee sighed and smiled as she watched him stroll around the front of the truck. Jordan was real, and her grandmother approved. Maybe this really could work. Maybe if she told him everything, he'd understand.

Chapter Seven

The night was going to drag along for Jordan. He had five hours to fill, and all he could think about was when he would see Jaynee again.

He'd dropped her off at her house at four thirty to change and go to work. He'd wanted to take her to the restaurant and wait, but she'd insisted she didn't want him hanging around. Instead, she said she'd call him before she left and tell him what time she'd meet him.

He knew she left work after dark every night, but he'd sworn he'd seen the same car outside the restaurant two nights in a row, in the parking lot of the coffee house, and then again parked on the street two houses down from hers. The old navy blue Ford Taurus was a common car, but he didn't believe in coincidences. Unlike North Carolina, Florida allowed window tint that was so dark he couldn't see the driver, and that really had him nervous. Then again, it was probably just the cop in him. He saw bad guys everywhere.

Instead of dwelling on *what ifs*, he focused his thoughts on their day together. The Sponge Docks were quaint. He enjoyed strolling down the street, their fingers intertwined. Although he had to admit, he hadn't been paying much attention to his surroundings. His mind was on Jaynee and the conversation he'd overheard this morning. She'd said, "The man I'm going to marry." When he asked if she meant it, she'd said, "I think so."

He'd already decided he wasn't leaving Florida without her, and unfortunately, he did have to return home. He could stay another week; he had plenty of vacation time. But his business would start falling behind. His brothers-in-law and partner were doing an okay job, but they didn't have his business sense. He'd given them all jobs and made them and his sisters in turn well off, but he continued to run his construction business.

It drove him crazy that Jaynee was worried about missing a night at work. He'd led her to believe he was doing okay — actually, he'd downplayed his business — when in fact, his company built million-dollar homes. Not that she seemed to mind. She seemed fine with the fact he was just a cop. Another thing he appreciated about her.

Plenty of girls back home were attracted to him physically, his money, and his possessions, but weren't interested in the depth of him as a person. And he hadn't found one he was even remotely interested in making his wife. When he did date, it was usually out of boredom or because one of his sisters had set him up with a friend.

He hadn't noticed anyone in the last couple of years anyway. He'd been too busy with his business. He didn't even have to continue working on the force; his company brought in plenty of money. But he loved being a cop, and he'd hoped that soon they'd transfer him to the detective division. Working on the street every day was starting to wear on him. However, those dreams now took a back burner; there was only one thing he wanted now. He'd found the one person he needed more than anything. He just had to figure out how to secure her affections without scaring her off in the process. Her confession this morning had given him cause to hope.

Jordan decided to take a chance. In the likelihood she felt the same way about him, and wasn't terrified of making a commitment, he'd be ready.

He'd been heading to the movies to squander some time when he made the decision. So he made a U-turn and headed back to a jewelry shop he'd seen earlier that looked promising.

He would find something extraordinary and unique, not just a bauble from a national jewelry store other women might possess. She was too important. He wanted to wow her, convince her that she could trust him, make her feel as crazy about him as he was her.

It wasn't about which stone was the most expensive or the biggest. He wanted the prettiest diamond, and he found it in the small store. It was a beautiful custom-made ring. Exquisite, just like Jaynee.

He locked the engagement ring in the glove compartment of his truck and went about killing time before Jaynee got off work.

His mind wandered. Now he just had to find the precise moment to ask her to marry him. He was thankful he'd overheard her declaration; otherwise, he might not have had the courage to buy the ring.

Jordan headed back to the movie theater to waste a few hours. Absolutely nothing good was playing, so he opted for a non-thinking, sci-fi alien movie. It would definitely take his mind off the hours until he could be with her again. Then, they'd have the entire weekend, and afterward, hopefully forever.

The movie didn't keep his interest. No matter how hard he concentrated, he couldn't follow it. His mind was elsewhere. He checked his watch every five minutes. She hadn't expected to be out before ten, and it wasn't even nine. He needed to relax.

Finally, the movie was nearing the end. They were sharing a moment, the human girl and the alien predator — was she supposed to like him? It was a face only a mother could love. Jordan must have missed an important part because the scene wasn't making any sense.

His cell phone vibrated. He glanced at the number and sighed in relief. It wasn't even nine yet.

He bolted out of his seat and clicked *answer*. "Hang on a sec, Jaynee." He literally ran to the corridor. "Hey ... you're early," he finally said when he exited the theater.

"Are you still at the movies? You can meet me at Starbucks when it's over." Jaynee spoke the words nonchalantly as if she couldn't fathom the notion he'd been waiting all night to see her.

"Are you kidding?" he burst out. "I hardly even know what I was watching. I'll meet you at the restaurant. You haven't left yet, right?"

"I have about fifteen minutes. I have a couple —"

"Good." He cut off her words. "I'll come and get you." He hung up the phone before she could argue. He didn't like the idea of her walking out to her car alone. He couldn't discount seeing that old beat-up Taurus several times. As a cop, he'd been trained to trust his instincts. She was strong willed and probably never asked for an escort.

As a cop, he'd received plenty of calls where a waitress had been attacked leaving work. Real-life predators knew tipped employees walked out with cash money. It frustrated him that restaurant owners and managers mandated their staff park in the furthest regions of the parking lots and rarely provided women escorts to their vehicles. With Jaynee, it was doubly tempting, as she looked appealing too.

Jordan sprinted to his truck. After disarming the alarm, he jumped inside, turned the key, and threw the shifter into drive, stomping on the gas. The wheels squealed in protest. The restaurant was only fifteen minutes away, and Jaynee had said she had closing work to do. But the thought of something happening to her — he squelched the idea, reminding himself she did this nightly. He really needed to loosen up before he frightened her by being overbearing.

***

Jaynee stared at the blank screen on her phone. "What was that all about?" she growled, unconcerned with eyes all around watching her. "I told him I'd meet him at Starbucks. Men! They're so pushy." She was glad he wanted to see her, but ... she waved away her frustration so she could get out of there.

She finished her closing duties, freshened herself up, then headed out the side door toward her car at the rear of the parking lot. She realized now she'd have to wait for Jordan. She'd call him back and tell him not to come ... remind him that she said she'd meet him. She fished through her purse for her phone.

When she finally found her phone, she realized it wouldn't work. Jordan was chivalrous. He held open doors, helped her into his truck, and even pulled out chairs.

Despite her earlier irritation, she smiled as she walked through the parking lot. She was thinking about Jordan when she felt hands grab her from behind, pick her up, and shove her against her vehicle. The impact with the door knocked the wind out of her, and she gasped for a breath. She couldn't see her attacker, but smelled his rancid breath. He reeked of cheap booze. In her peripherals, she caught a glimpse of two men flanking him, but they held their distance. Her heart pounded. What would they do to her? She couldn't live through this again.

"Did you get the letter, Caycee?" The man pressing her to the car kept his voice muted and guttural, but it sounded vaguely familiar.

"What letter?" She attempted to twist out of his grip, but he wrenched her arm against her back, shoving her harder into her car. Tears flooded her eyes. Brian had sent someone to follow her again. Why wouldn't he just let her go?

"Consider this your warning." He let go of her, and she fell to the ground. He hovered over her. He wore his hat drawn low over his eyes. In the shadows of the parking lot, it was hard to make out his features, but she thought she recognized him. "He made it clear what will happen if you date other men. Maybe we should give you an illustration tonight," he snickered, lowering his body over her.

Tires screeched from behind him. Her perpetrator turned to look, but it was too late. Jordan had already jumped out of the truck, holding something small and black in his hand. He made a beeline for the man hovering over her. Jordan pulled her attacker off her and smashed the cylinder object into the man's gut. The fiend doubled over, choking. Faster than she could discern how, the second man was on the ground, his leg in an unnatural position under his own body. The third coward ran off the moment his friends collapsed. The first man, still lurched over, started vomiting when the second man's screams filled the air.

Jordan scooped her up and carried her back to his truck, lifting her inside. After slamming the door behind her, he watched that the would-be assailants remained on the ground.

Jaynee was in a panic. Should she call 911 to report the attack or request an ambulance? Deciding Jordan would do what he thought was best, she remained motionless inside the cab. Adrenaline rushed through her veins. Her heart nearly pounded through her chest.

Jordan climbed into the truck and turned to her, eyes wide. His look terrified her for a moment. But he was her savior; she had no reason to worry. He'd said he'd never hurt her. "Are you okay?" his normal serene voice roared louder than she'd ever heard. His tone seethed with raw emotion.

"Y ... yes ... I think so," she stuttered. She wasn't. Her body shivered uncontrollably, and she could barely speak.

"Did they hurt you?" The words came out in a growl.

"I'm just a little shaken." Although her arm did hurt from him yanking it behind her, and her tailbone ached from hitting the concrete, she thought it better not to mention that, or he might go back after the thugs. She definitely couldn't mention the reason they'd attacked her. No telling what he would do with that information.

Kenny, it dawned on her ... Brian's best friend. She knew it would happen eventually; she just hadn't expected him to find out so quickly. It had been a year, and Brian simply couldn't accept the fact it was over between them. Panic paralyzed her. What if they'd hurt Jordan?

Jordan threw the truck into drive and peeled out of the parking lot in the opposite direction of Starbucks. She didn't utter a word as he drove down Highway 19 entirely too fast. Instead, she buckled up. He was furious. Why? Was he mad at her?

Jordan flashed a glance in the mirror, then changed lanes. He turned his fiery gaze back to her. "You can't go back there."

She flinched away from his hostile expression. "My ... car ..." she stammered. She didn't understand. What was he implying?

"We'll get your vehicle tomorrow, but you can't return to work there. They'll come back, Jaynee. It's what dirt bags like them do. They're like sharks ... once they've tasted blood —" He clenched his jaw as his hands tightened on the steering wheel.

She could see he was having a difficult time staying composed, but still... "I can't quit my job!" Who the heck did he think he was? She glowered at him in the darkness.

***

Jordan ignored her response; obviously, she didn't understand. She couldn't fathom how much he already cared about her.

This wasn't how the night was supposed to go. He didn't want to make her angry. How could he explain she didn't need to work ... that he'd take care of her forever. He couldn't. This wasn't how he wanted to go about this.

He pulled into the parking area of his hotel. Without saying a word, he jumped out and walked around to Jaynee's side of the truck. Instead of opening the door, she just sat there, waiting — for what he wasn't sure.

Irritated, he pulled the remote out of his pocket, clicked unlock, and then opened the door. He offered her his hand. "Please, Jaynee," he pleaded, "I apologize if I scared you. And I was too upset to go anywhere, so I figured I'd just come here." He worked to keep his tone light. It wasn't easy. Fire radiated through his veins. He could have killed those thugs. He wanted to, but he was a cop. And cops were supposed to uphold the law. For the first time in his life, he wished he wasn't an officer.

She glared down from the truck at his waiting arms, but made no effort to move.

A crinkle appeared between her eyes, something she did when she was confused or frustrated. He wondered which it was. "You didn't frighten me. Why would you think I was afraid of you? I'm mad at you. There's a difference." She crossed her arms over her chest.

"I'm sorry. Let me help you down from the cab, please."

She turned toward him muttering something about, "ridiculously high truck," but allowed him to help her.

Jordan reached into the glove box and pulled out the plastic bag with the discreet little box. Tonight may not be the right time, but he didn't want to leave the ring in the truck for some thief to abscond with it. Jaynee didn't seem to pay him any attention or wasn't curious in the least at what was in the sack.

He wrapped his arm around her waist, directing her across the parking lot. She shrugged off his touch, but continued walking forward. She didn't appear uneasy about coming to his room, but she *was* clearly irritated by his remark.

They walked through the lobby in silence. After entering the elevator, he pressed the button for the fourth floor.

"Sorry it's not fancier," he said, breaking the silence when the elevator door shut. "I wasn't anticipating company." She said nothing, so he continued, "On business trips I just pick a popular hotel chain close to my area of work." She looked up at him then. He could see she was still angry, but a hint of a smile lifted just the corner of her mouth.

***

Jaynee tried to remain indignant, but found this small revelation pleasant. The majority of men she met came to Florida only to party. Jordan hadn't even picked a hotel on the beach. He really was here just to help.

"I'm glad ... I mean ... I'm happy you weren't expecting *company*," she confessed.

Jordan led her out of the elevator and down the hall. He held open the hotel door, and she entered the room, wondering what the hell she was thinking.

Although she'd wanted Jordan last night and this morning, her home had felt safer. The thought of entering his hotel room, on the other hand, had her feeling a little anxious. What would she do if he became aggressive? She closed her eyes, pondering how she always got herself into these predicaments. No matter how much her brain screamed for her to run, though, her heart wouldn't listen. Something told her Jordan was different. She couldn't leave.

As soon as he walked into the room, he went to the tiny refrigerator and pulled out two sodas and a couple packets of crackers. "Did you eat? You should eat something. I can order a pizza or something else. What do you like?" He rattled off the words as if he were in a rush, then walked over to the dresser and pulled out a large t-shirt. "Your shirt is ripped. I'd rather you not go back to your place if that's okay with you. Those scumbags have been stalking you, and they know where you live. Feel free to use whatever you want in the bathroom if you want to fix those scrapes on your arm." He tossed the shirt on the bed and turned away from her, walking toward the window.

He was agitated and evidently needed to relax too. Why did he think they were stalking her? Why wouldn't he have thought that it was a random act? She decided not to ask. Jaynee just stared at him, not sure what to say. She felt completely comfortable with Jordan but couldn't help but be cautious about the situation. He hadn't pressured her with anything; he was simply offering her something she didn't understand. She was so accustomed to people taking from her. She didn't know what to do when someone was willing to give without expectation of anything in return.

"I'm not hungry," she finally said, then picked up his shirt and headed off toward the bathroom before he could respond.

Once inside the bathroom, she decided to take a shower. Steaming hot water poured over her body, dissolving the grime and filth she felt from those degenerates' attack. He'd called her Caycee and had asked about the letter she'd discarded. Brian had obviously sent Kenny to intimidate her.

They wouldn't have hurt her ... she knew indisputably. Brian was many things, but he'd never laid a hand on her, and she was sure he'd kill whoever did. Those barbarians were only there to frighten her. She now wondered what was in the letter. No, she decided immediately ... she didn't care.

She would let go of her past. She would never open another letter or cry another tear over her ex, her mother, or even her father for that matter. She would tell Jordan everything. If he still wanted her, great. If not, she'd still let it go. She was tired of shouldering her past. It felt like a horse collar weighing her down.

She hadn't had feelings for Brian in years anyway. He'd destroyed everything the first time she discovered he'd cheated. Tolerating drugs and alcohol had been stupid enough, but she'd never stay with a man who didn't care enough to be faithful.

***

Jordan stared out the window, attempting to control his emotions.

He contemplated having a drink to settle his nerves. It'd been so long since he'd had more than a few sips of alcohol, though, so he wasn't sure how he'd react. The last thing he wanted was to be undisciplined around Jaynee. He wanted her to trust him. He needed her to believe in love.

As he thought about Jaynee, he realized she was the only drug he needed. Already his adrenaline had slowed, replaced by a different sensation. He envisioned her walking out of the bathroom in his t-shirt, hair wet, smelling fresh and clean, and then she would lie in his arms all night. He imagined they were already married, and it was just another night. How he hoped it could turn out that way. What he wouldn't do to have her in his arms every night for the rest of his life. Yes, he definitely felt better.

He quickly changed out of his jeans into shorts. He reached for a t-shirt, but then realized he'd given Jaynee his last one, his favorite one, his Van Halen concert shirt. The band wasn't expected to tour again for a while; he hoped he wouldn't lose it. It would look ridiculous if he dressed in a polo or oxford shirt, so he opted for nothing. He'd stopped her last night and this morning when she'd tried to unbutton his shirt, so he hoped she wouldn't think he was being forward. But an even larger desire was that she would appreciate what she would see.

Jordan stretched back on the bed, staring up at the ceiling, waiting for her return, not knowing what would happen when she came out of the bathroom. Naturally, he knew what he wanted to occur; he was a man after all. The question was...*What was the right thing to do?* He'd turned his life around a few years ago and had not been with a woman since. It hadn't been an issue. He'd never wanted a woman the way he yearned for Jaynee.

No doubt, he wanted to make love to her, but he would be the gentleman she needed tonight and let her set the pace.

Chapter Eight

Jaynee stepped out of the bathroom. The shower had definitely helped her feel better.

Jordan was lying on the bed, his hands folded behind his head. He'd changed his clothes and was wearing just a pair of cargo-style shorts. His chest was broad and muscular, and she could see the outline of his abdominal muscles. Not only was he beautiful on the inside, but he also had an awesome body, and she felt warm inside just looking at him. He was just staring at the ceiling, not even watching TV. He looked over at her as she started across the room. His eyes widened, and his mouth lifted into a heart throbbing smile. His good mood had definitely returned.

"Well, that shirt has never looked better, and without a doubt, you're more beautiful every time I see you. Why do you even bother putting on makeup when you look so incredible coming out of the shower?"

Her cheeks warmed, and she wondered if he'd notice or if he'd assume that she'd taken too hot a shower.

He held out his arms for her to come to him, an irresistible request. Her feelings seemed to change directly in response to his. No longer angry about his earlier demand that she shouldn't return to work, she walked over to the bed and allowed him to pull her into his warm embrace.

"And you smell ... Mmm ... good enough to eat." He groaned lightly, quickly rolling her onto her back, supporting his weight above her. He pressed his lips against hers with more fervor than the last time they'd kissed, and she felt the burning need in him as his breaths quickened.

She pulled him down on top of her, letting the weight of his body overtake her as she ran her hands over his shoulders and down his back. He was strong; she liked that.

He pulled back a few inches from her face and locked his steel-blue eyes with hers. "Are you ready to give me all of you, or just your body?" His velvety voice stroked her soul as if he'd reached in and brushed the very essence of her being.

She wasn't sure exactly what he asking, but at the moment, she didn't care. She wanted him ... all of him. "I'm ... ready," she whispered, breathless. Her heart was tapping out such a vicious rhythm in her chest that she found it difficult to speak.

He continued to drill his gaze ... as though he could read her thoughts. "Are you positive? Heart and soul, nothing less. I won't accept anything less than everything. You don't have to *tell* me all that has happened, but you can't keep anything from me from this moment forward. You will have to submit everything and be willing to be loved completely, and I promise you, I'll do the same."

Submit everything? The thought scared her, but she wanted him in her life — *somehow.* "I'm willing," she gasped. Her heart swelled in her chest. She wanted to believe she could trust him and truly wanted to feel loved by Jordan.

He lowered his head, and his warm breath caressed her neck. "Tell me, Jaynee. Tell me what you want."

"You ..." Her blood raced through her veins as he trailed a line of kisses up her throat, continuing along her jaw.

"I need more, Jaynee. Everything, heart and soul, remember? Tell me." His whispered words sounded like pleas. He wanted her too.

"Please, Jordan, I want you." The words rushed out of her. He *was* what she wanted. It had been too long since she'd felt anything.

His mouth was hot over her lips again, kissing off her words. His kisses moved up her jaw to her ear again. "I love you, Jaynee. Are you ready for my love? There's no turning back."

His breathing increased as his lips moved back and forth along the line of her jaw, waiting and anticipating.

Her hands smoothed over his broad shoulders and traced the lines of his biceps. Dear heavens she wanted him. Why was he toying with her? "Yes, Jordan, I want all of you." She did, more than she'd ever imagined was possible. She needed to feel again, and he was doing just that. He was opening up a well she'd thought had run dry.

He trailed kisses up her throat again as his fingers grazed her neck. "Open your eyes, Jaynee." She did, and she witnessed the burning in his. "Don't you know what I want?"

She slowly moved her head back and forth, unable to form a coherent response. He teased her with his tongue as he moved his mouth back over hers, his lips moving on hers as he spoke between his kisses.

"Tell me, Jaynee. I want to know what you're feeling. I need to hear you say it aloud."

She tried to pull him closer, but he was stronger and held himself suspended over her. "Make love to me, Jordan. Now, please."

His breathing was ragged, but he pulled back abruptly. "That's not what I need to hear. I love you, Jaynee, but you're not ready to make love to me."

He rolled onto his back, pulling her with him. His fingertips caressed her lips, then brushed lightly over her cheekbones. Excitement burned in his eyes, but she could tell he wouldn't continue. He wasn't going to make love to her. What happened? How could he stop so easily?

"I *am* ready, Jordan. Why did you stop?"

He brushed her hair over her shoulder. "Jaynee ... did you hear me? Did you hear me even once? I love you, and I want you, but I don't want to *just* have sex. I want all of you. Don't you understand?"

She lowered her gaze, shaking her head. She didn't understand. If he loved her, why didn't he want to make love to her? Suddenly, she felt like a harlot.

He nudged up her chin and kissed her softly. "I'm sorry, love. It's not that I don't want you. Believe me, I do. But, there's no turning back for me. When we make love, it'll be because you love me firstly, and then because you want me. Not the opposite. I know it's soon, and I'm sorry if I'm scaring you." He sighed. "It's just — from the little bit you've told me ... that everyone has hurt you ... I don't want to be on that list. I don't want to take advantage of you like everyone else in your life. I want all of you. Can't you see that, Jaynee?" His eyes melted into hers as if trying to prove his words.

She gazed back astonished, not certain how to respond. She'd heard him say it, but wasn't sure he'd really meant it.

Hadn't she heard in all the songs and in movies where men said they loved a girl just to get her in the sack? Did she love Jordan? She believed so, but couldn't say it now, just to get him to sleep with her. How ironic. She'd worried that he would attempt to sleep with her, when repeatedly it was her endeavoring to seduce him.

"Jordan, I —"

He shushed her gently with his fingertips. "You don't have to say anything, Jaynee. It's enough to have you here in my arms. You will fall in love with me. I promise." He embraced her tightly, and she knew he was right. How could she not be in love with Jordan? He was the most incredible man she'd ever met. If she could only release herself, let go of the past. Maybe she could believe.

***

Jordan watched Jaynee as she slept in his arms. She was beautiful, kind, smart ... everything he'd ever sought after and more. And she loved him; he could see it in her eyes. He was confident she would be his bride, but first she had to admit she was in love with him.

Would she be okay moving to North Carolina, changing colleges, and the hardest part, leaving her grandmother? It was the logical choice. He had a career, business, and home to return to in Charlotte.

He stroked her silky-smooth curls and exposed arms. Her skin had a natural glow, the epitome of a native Floridian. Would she miss her state?

It wasn't as though she was happy here. She'd hinted numerous times the only thing positive in her life was her grandmother. He wondered how he was going to get her to confess her troubled past. He'd been honest when he said he didn't care. She didn't have to tell him, but he ached to take away the pain. He drifted off to sleep holding her securely in his arms, hoping she would recognize her feelings and tell him what he needed to hear.

Sudden movement and muffled groans woke him up. The soft light of the alarm clock cast a red hue on Jaynee's face, and he could see her eyes dart under her lids. She was dreaming.

"No! Please don't!" Jaynee's cries broke the silent air, and then desperate mumblings with more pleadings emerged from her lips, but her eyes remained closed.

Jordan shook her gently. "Jaynee, wake up." He hated that she was in pain, even in her dream. "Jaynee, love ... you're having a nightmare." She continued to plead for something to stop. "Caycee!" he said louder, watching gratefully as her eyes popped open. "It's okay ... I'm here. You're okay." He caressed her hair and arms to calm her. She didn't utter another word and drifted right back asleep.

It was quiet again; only the whir of the air conditioner filled the room. It didn't matter how peaceful it was; he wouldn't be able to fall back asleep. The nightmare and scream had been unexpected. What had she lived through that frightened her so much? He wondered if she'd remember the dream. He'd wanted to ask her about it, but perhaps that would startle her just as much. She certainly wasn't accustomed to a man in her bed.

Since he wouldn't be able to fall back asleep, he lay there pondering how he would ask her to marry him and whether he could really deal with not knowing her past. He couldn't come up with anything original because he wasn't familiar with the area and didn't know what she would like.

But more than anything ... he didn't have time. He needed to get back home. And he didn't want to start a long-distance relationship. It wasn't that he couldn't remain faithful. No doubt there. But he didn't think he could leave her without it killing him. He had to convince her that they belonged together. But how do you accomplish that with someone who doesn't believe in happiness?

***

Jaynee awoke to strong arms embracing her for the second morning. "Mmm, I could get used to this," she mumbled sleepily as she attempted to burrow herself deeper into the crux of Jordan's arms.

Jordan squeezed her shoulders. "That's a very good thing, because I don't want to let you go."

She sighed but didn't look at his face to see his expression. He'd made his position on what he'd wanted clear last night. The ball was entirely in her court. She had to decide if she could trust her instincts. It wasn't an easy thing to do when you've made errors in judgment your entire life.

"Are you awake now, darlin'?" he asked, a playful lilt in his tone.

"Uh-uh. It's Saturday. I don't have to be anywhere. I don't want to get up."

"Who said anything about getting out of bed?" he drawled.

He lifted her chin so he could look into her eyes, then kissed her head, her cheekbones. He brushed the hair off her neck, continuing to plant kisses down her neck and under her ear.

Chills ran down her body as he grazed his fingers down the length of her side. He trailed his hand farther, down her waist, her thigh, then wrapped his large hand behind her knee and hitched her leg over his.

Her body shivered with anticipation.

His hands were like magic as they caressed her exposed skin. Every square inch of her body reacted to his touches, and she couldn't keep herself from moaning with satisfaction. Something she'd never done in the past. She'd never felt comfortable with a man before Jordan. The thought of someone touching her had always made her uneasy.

With Jordan, everything felt different. She hungered for his touch, the intimacy of his embrace, to feel loved. That was it ... She felt his love right through his fingertips.

"Jaynee," he said on a sigh.

Her body quivered when he whispered her name. But as before, he stopped short of anything sexual. He gathered her tightly against his body. There was no mistake that he was as aroused as she was.

"Please don't stop, Jordan. Your touch is incredible." She groaned in exasperation.

He gripped her tighter, releasing another sigh. He was serious. He wasn't going to make love to her until she admitted she loved him.

Why couldn't she just say it? She did love him. She knew she'd be happy with him forever. Hadn't she admitted to her grandmother that he was the man she was going to marry?

"I can't, Jaynee. I'm sorry." His voice was raspy as if he were holding back some emotion. "Not until you realize you love me, too."

"Jordan, you have ... I mean ... you have made love before, right?" What on earth made her ask such a question? He was twenty-seven years old and too incredible not to have made love to a woman before.

***

Jordan looked at Jaynee solemnly as he thought about his answer. "I've had sex, yes. But I can honestly say now that I've never made love. I've never cared before I met you. I don't understand either, but I just can't." He stared into her eyes. "And you? I know you have, but —" He couldn't form the words to ask the question he didn't want to hear the answer to. The thought of her with someone else angered him. What was wrong with him?

"Only with one person," she said through a whisper, apparently still hesitant to reveal anything from her past. "I thought it was love, but now I realize it never was. I wish I'd never met him. I wish it had been you, Jordan. I never felt about him the way I already feel about you, and we were together almost three years."

Now we're getting somewhere, he thought.

He didn't want to hear about her former lover but was thankful to hear she'd only had one. And even better, she was opening up and admitting she had feelings for him.

He took a deep breath. He had to ask, and he knew he was going to hate hearing about her former relationship, since he was pretty sure that something had happened to her, but it was the only way to get her to open up. "What happened?"

Chapter Nine

Jaynee sighed heavily in response to Jordan wanting to know about her past. Was it time? He'd said he didn't care, but would he leave when he found out she was damaged merchandise ... that she'd never be able to escape her demons?

Decision made, she pulled herself upright. "It's a long story."

"I have all day." He sat up, pulled her back into his arms, and rested his back against the headboard.

She pulled away slightly so that her back was also touching the headboard, but she wasn't looking him in the eyes. She braced herself for what she was about to do.

"Okay, from the beginning, but I'll have to edit. I'll fill in the pieces later if you decide to keep me." Why was she doing this? He said it didn't matter, but she knew it did ... it was the only way to free herself. If he wanted her after she told him her past, she'd be able to trust him. "You're right, though. We can't start a relationship without you knowing what you're getting yourself into." She glanced at his face.

He closed his eyes and shook his head. "If you were mine, I'd definitely *keep you*."

"Okay ..." Jaynee let out a long breath. "I told you my mother left when I was three, but I didn't explain why." She looked at his face to gauge his reaction. Was he really ready for her story? "Let me back up a tad, so I can fit my dad in, which will help you understand the choices of both my parents.

"When my dad was nineteen, he married a beautiful, tall model-type woman. My dad was only five seven, but he was attractive in a rugged, country boy way. He was always the life of the party, and women loved him. Anyway, his first wife had a baby, a boy. Come to find out, she'd been having an affair with his boss, and it was his baby. He moved away and never looked back.

"Three months later, he met my mother. Two months later at only eighteen, she got pregnant. She was beautiful. She loved to laugh and fish — which was his favorite pastime. Life was perfect until I came along." Jaynee shut her eyes as she remembered the turmoil she went through as a child. "You know how children always blame themselves for their parents' separation."

"Oh, Jaynee," Jordan interrupted. "It wasn't your fault; you were a baby." His eyes were instantly concerned.

"I know it wasn't my fault. I didn't ask to be born. But, I *was* the cause of their troubles. My mother went crazy afterward. Dad had to work, but she constantly harassed him. She accused him of drinking and cheating and not holding down a job. He worked as a mechanic for his older brother and ran a part-time business installing security systems.

"My grandmother and aunt noticed the change in her first. My grandmother said that every time we'd visit, I'd stay near her and cry when my mother tried to come near me. My aunt told me a story about a birthday party at her house. My mother sat me on the couch but wouldn't let me move, said she was punishing me. When my aunt brought me cake and ice cream, she grabbed them and threw them away.

"But the only time my mother slipped was in front of my uncle. I had dropped something I was playing with, and it broke. She ran over, hand drawn back to slap me across the face when my uncle grabbed her and told her firmly, 'You will never hit that child in my house!' She gathered me up and left."

Jordan reached out to Jaynee as if he wanted to comfort her, but then he dropped his hand back on the bed.

"No one said anything. Like my dad's first marriage, they had suspicions, but didn't think it was their place to interfere. My dad never talked derogatory about my mother, but he did reveal a story years later about the day he left.

"He said she'd been in a rotten mood all morning, yelling about everything I did. Apparently, I was sick and had thrown up on the floor. My father had to work but promised he would be home early to watch me so she could have a break.

"He explained something didn't feel right, so he turned around and returned home. When he opened the door, she had me lifted in the air, shaking me violently, screaming at the top of her lungs. She hadn't heard him enter. He told her to put me down immediately."

Jaynee paused and took a breath. It wasn't the worst story in her life, but it still sent chills down her spine when she thought about what her mother did next. Jordan hadn't said a word the entire time, but his eyes were expectant. She hoped he was really going to be able to handle this.

"She didn't put me down. Instead, she threw me across the room ... I had just turned three."

Jaynee looked up at Jordan and saw the horror in his eyes. He just shook his head and sighed. The idea of someone throwing a child across the room like a rag doll evidently upset him, too. Of course, as a cop, he must be accustomed to these accounts.

She took another breath and continued. "When my dad bent over to pick me up, she crouched over top of him and banged on his back. Instinctively, he knocked her to the floor. He confessed he'd never hit a woman in his life, but had no choice. It was an automatic impulse, as it all had happened so quickly. As if he should be sorry for his actions," she said almost in a growl.

Jaynee pulled her legs underneath her and continued, "He put me on the front of his motorcycle, placed his too-large helmet on my head, and drove me to my aunt's house. My aunt said the sight of my father pulling onto her driveway with me on his motorcycle was the saddest sight she'd ever seen. She went on to say she'd never seen my dad cry before or ever again after that day.

"My mom left town after that incident, but returned when I was five. My dad loved her, but she couldn't handle raising a child according to a child psychiatrist assigned to my case. My father had to choose, so he chose me. Luckily, the judge agreed; he gave my dad full custody. If he'd stayed with my mom, she probably would have killed me. I don't remember much. But for years, I woke up with nightmares, feeling as though something was crushing me. I'd wake up screaming, pleading that the pain would stop.

"My mother wriggled back into my life when I was twelve but only for a week every other year until I was eighteen. I've seen her only once as an adult, and we got into a terrible fight. My mom is a troubled woman. More times than I know of, she has attempted suicide by slashing her wrist or overdosing on drugs."

Jaynee didn't look up to see Jordan's reaction this time; instead, she moved on to finish her father's story.

"My dad remarried my evil stepmother, his third wife, who also abused me. Mostly mental abuse, though. But I do remember one time when she kept coming into my room after I'd done something wrong. Gram was visiting for the weekend and said to my father, 'Didn't you divorce her mother for abusing her?' My father stepped in on that incident, but the abuse continued. When I was fourteen, I actually fought back and won. She never touched me again.

"Before he married her, though, I was sent to live with one of my other uncles. Not the one who saved me from my mom — Uncle Adam's the best. At my other uncle's house, I witnessed sexual abuse against my cousins. He molested me too, but never intercourse, thank God for that. It's been hard enough dealing with the other memories."

Jaynee paused long enough to look at Jordan and gauge his response. His lips were in a straight line; his pallor had turned bright red. He was struggling with this revelation. His eyes burned as they did last night when it looked as if he might turn around and kill her attackers. She had to let him know this man could no longer hurt anyone.

"He died five years ago, Jordan, before I felt old enough to confront him. I found out after his death that the family knew he had issues, but thought they were resolved when he married and had children. I also found out he'd molested my father — his younger brother by ten years — when he was a boy. Why my dad ever allowed me to live with him ... I'll never know." She shook her head in confusion.

"Oh, Jaynee ... I'm so sorry," Jordan whispered.

Jaynee felt the tears well up and struggled to control her sobs. "Jordan," she cried softly, closing her eyes and shaking her head. "Let me finish. Unbelievable as it may seem that wasn't the worst situation in my life. My father did the worst thing I ever had to contend with."

Wiping her eyes, she continued. "At seventeen, I already lived on my own, because my father was a newlywed again. We saw each other constantly, though. We met for lunch, went to arcades, and once went to Busch Gardens, just the two of us." *It was an awesome day*, she thought to herself. He'd even allowed her to sample the beer they gave away. She didn't like it, but it was just the two of them, and it felt special.

She gulped before continuing.

"My father was unhappy when his last marriage failed and deeply troubled by his past. I tried to get others to see what I saw, but no one recognized it because he was always so outwardly happy. He took his life a few years ago. I was the last person he'd spoken with. The bad thing is ... I think I could have stopped it. The night before his death, I sent my uncle and aunt to see him. My father assured them he was fine. I should have shown up or Baker Acted him. Of course, as a cop, I'm sure you know what that means."

Jordan merely nodded again, allowing her to continue.

"The next morning, my father woke up, walked into the backyard in his bathrobe, and shot himself with a shotgun. I know there's nothing I could've done, but I will always have to live with the fact that I didn't go to him myself."

Jordan shook his head, allowing a long breath to escape his lungs. "It wasn't your fault —"

"I'll never know ..." Jaynee cut him off, brushing away a tear. "I have to finish, or I'll lose my nerve. I made more stupid decisions after he died." She looked up at the ceiling, thinking she should just stop now. Jordan didn't need to hear her life.

"Please continue, Jaynee," he said, resting his hand on hers.

She sniffed and continued, "Devastated, I moved from South Florida to live with my grandmother, the only person who'd never hurt me. A few months after I moved here, I met a guy ... a great guy." She looked up when Jordan winced. He didn't need to hear this part, but really, her past with her dysfunctional family was over ... This part of her past wasn't over. As much as she didn't want to talk about the men she'd dated, he had to know about this one.

She squeezed his hand. "Jordan, I want you to know I wasn't just an ignorant young girl, so I had to say that. When we first met, he seemed okay. After a few months of dating, though, he confessed that he previously had a drug problem and had been in jail before we met. We had a good relationship for about six months, and then one day he just disappeared for days. I couldn't reach him anywhere, so I knew more than likely, he'd gone on a binge.

"Unfortunately, I was right. I felt it was my duty to help him. He agreed to go to rehab, so I saw him through it. I stayed with him through two other drug rehabs over the next two and a half years. When I discovered his infidelity, it was the final straw. I severed all ties a year ago, told him not to call or write me again, told him we were through. He never accepted my leaving and would harass any man I tried to date, so I stopped dating entirely. They incarcerated him about six months ago, and he is supposed to serve a minimum of five years.

"The day you and I met ... I received a letter from him ..." Again Jaynee looked up, measuring his reaction. His face appeared composed, but his eyes were grave.

"I didn't open his letter. I threw it in the dumpster on my way to see you." Pausing, she took a deep breath and looked him deep in the eyes. This was the part that would anger him. More than someone molesting her or two suicidal parents, she'd withheld information. Something he'd asked her not to do. Though, he'd said, "Up to this point" she wasn't to keep anything from him.

"Those guys last night — the dirtbags — they knew my ex. The leader called me Caycee and asked if I'd read his letter."

"What?" His face was incredulous. He leaned in, his eyes narrowed. "Why didn't you tell me?" he spat the question. She knew she should have left out that part.

"You said it didn't matter up to this moment. You said that last night, Jordan." Tears formed in her eyes. She knew if she told him the truth, he'd leave her. "You said it didn't matter, as long as I told you everything from now on, but I knew you'd despise me. I knew you couldn't want me. That's why I couldn't tell you what you wanted to hear last night. Because I couldn't tell you how much I already loved you without telling you everything first, and I was afraid. Afraid you'd think I was damaged and stupid." The words tumbled out of her mouth, muffled by her sobs. The tears flowed freely. She couldn't find any way to impede them. She dropped her head into her hands, shielding her face. She wanted to crawl across the floor and disappear. "You're a cop ... You certainly wouldn't want anything to do with me ... a woman who stupidly stayed with a convict. A

convict who won't stop stalking me ... even from prison —
"

Jordan pulled her into his arms. He rocked her and pressed his lips to her forehead. "Jaynee, nothing has changed. I just wish you had told me, so I could have taken care of them." He sounded angry with the men but thrilled by her words. She just realized ... through all her pain, she'd admitted she loved him too. "I'm sorry, Jaynee. I'm sorry for everything. My God, what you've been through, and that was the *edited* version. God, I wish I could take it all away. Please let me. Let me take care of you forever. No one will ever hurt you again. I promise."

He looked at her solemnly as if deciding on a course of action. "You had a nightmare last night. I understand it now. The attack probably triggered it. And the way your eyes darted around the first time you sat down with me. You've been living in an atmosphere of fear your entire life. I'll never allow that again."

He continued to rock her. Her sobs slowed. She was happy to be in his arms. He wasn't running away. "You still want me?" she asked in total disbelief. How could he want any part of her?

"Jaynee, none of this has been your fault. And I told you ... it doesn't matter. I love you."

She could see he really meant it. "But what if those jerks try to hurt you next time ... because of me?"

"Are you serious?" He pretended to be offended. "Do you honestly believe those guys are competition? That's insulting." Humor danced in his eyes.

"No, not really. You were amazing. What was that thing you were using?"

"A kubotan, a martial arts weapon I conveniently use as a keychain. It's an effective method of knocking the wind out of someone or disabling other body parts. If I'd known —" He sucked in a breath, closed his eyes, and released the breath as he shook his head. "He'd be absent a working vital organ."

"And the kick to the other guy?" she asked enthusiastically.

"Sorry you saw that." He looked a little sheepish. But she couldn't help but notice he looked a little pleased she'd witnessed him take on three men, displaying he could protect her. He continued smiling slightly. "I'm a black belt in Isshinryu karate, a defensive tactics trainer, and a firing range instructor — because I'm the best shot," he said with a wink. He wasn't gloating; he just couldn't stop himself from trying to prove his worth.

His face took on a severe look. "Jaynee, I didn't say this right last night, so I'd like to try again. I don't want you to go back there or anywhere else for that matter where you have to walk into a dark parking lot. It's not safe, especially for someone who looks like you." His eyes pleaded with her, attempting to make her understand.

"But I have to work, Jordan, and it's the best money for the amount of time I put in while I finish college." She appreciated the fact that he was worried about her, but she couldn't just quit her job.

Jordan released a heavy breath. "Jaynee, can't you hear what I'm saying? For such a bright girl, you're rather obtuse." He smiled to lighten the insult.

Not sure whether to be offended or flattered, she tilted her head.

"Can you honestly sit there and not see how madly in love I am? Can you truthfully admit you don't feel it too?"

"No," she admitted.

"No you can't see, or no you can't admit you feel something too?" he asked, exasperated. He smiled, but it didn't reach the feather-light strokes of tanlines at the corners of his eyes, the ones that came from him smiling all the time. Except now, since she was clearly frustrating him with her lack of belief. He still wanted her, but he refused to accept anything but everything.

"You're right ... I *can't* deny it. I do love you, Jordan, as irrational as it sounds to fall in love with someone after only a few days. But I know I do."

"How 'bout after the first evening?" he offered. "I loved you from the first night, and every second thereafter it has only gotten stronger, and I can't deny it. I know what I want; I know what I need."

Jordan jumped up without warning and moved off the bed, pulling her with him. "Jaynee, I know this is fast, and sorry if I'm scaring you, or if you would have preferred an elaborate production. But I hope this will prove to you how serious I am and compensate for the lack of showmanship on my part."

He reached into the drawer of the nightstand, pulled out a tiny box, and fell to one knee. His fingers deftly removed the ring from the box while she watched in disbelief.

Jaynee gasped, then blinked her eyes feverishly.

Steadfast, Jordan continued with his objective. "Jaynee, my love, will you marry me?" He held her left hand, ring ready, gazing into her eyes expectantly. "Will you accept this as a promise from me to love you and take care of you for the rest of our lives?"

She couldn't speak. Tears rolled down her face. She stared into his eyes for untold seconds while he waited patiently, ring ready. He didn't seem burdened by her pause. He understood this was sudden.

When she finally found her breath, she asked, "Jordan...can I have a minute?"

He dropped her hand and stood back up, but didn't look upset by her request. "Of course, take as long as necessary. I know this is sudden, but I do love you, Jaynee, something fierce."

She could see the fire in his eyes. He really did love her. He wasn't playing some kind of joke; he didn't want to take advantage of her and leave her, as everyone else had. And the most surprising thing of all, she loved him too.

Jordan took a step forward and rested his hands on her shoulders. "You don't have to give me an answer now; there's no rush. I'll fly back every weekend until you're ready. I *won't* give up on you, Jaynee."

She walked into the bathroom and stared at herself in the mirror. This was all she'd ever wanted, someone to love her and accept her as she was. She'd told him almost everything. A couple of details she could never admit. Two secrets would go to her grave. Jordan didn't ask to know everything, though, he accepted her as she was.

The frightened girl inside of her struggled for her to listen ... whispered to her that Jordan would only hurt her as everyone else had. When she walked out of this bathroom, there was a decision to make. Either she would accept Jordan's proposal or she would move away from this state, from everything she'd ever known. She would start a new life, move to California. From there, she wasn't sure what she'd do, but she would leave everything behind. Bury the frightened, abused girl forever. She made her decision right then, and when she stepped out of the bathroom, she felt as if she'd left a part of her closed in that little room.

She would leave behind her past, but she would do it with Jordan. Once again, she would offer up her heart and pray he didn't trample on it as everyone else in her life had.

Chapter Ten

Jaynee inhaled deeply as she stepped over the threshold into her new life. Jordan was sitting on the edge of the bed, eyes expectant. When she stopped a few feet away from him, he bounded toward her, but stopped short of reaching her.

He lowered his face in front of hers, but said nothing, just waited, as he'd said he would.

She smiled. "I love you, Jordan Monroe, with all my heart and soul. Yes, I'll marry you."

He wrapped his arms around her waist and pulled her to him. "That's all I needed to hear, Jaynee." Jordan burned a trail of kisses over her collarbone and up her neck, burying his head under her hair. He pulled her back to the bed and held her as he kissed her. Her entire body quivered.

He pulled back. "Open your eyes, Jaynee. I want to see your eyes." He lifted her left hand and gently slid the ring onto her ring finger, then softly laid her on her back.

She was completely comfortable with her decision. They lay entangled as one on the bed, but he didn't attempt to make love to her. Instead, he just stroked her hair as she lay with her head on his chest.

Completely content in his embrace, she didn't want to get out of bed, but she heard his stomach grumble and knew he was probably famished.

She chuckled quietly. "What's for breakfast?"

"You caught that? Maybe I should run down to the buffet and pick up some breakfast to hold us over. What do you think? Then, we'll decide what we want to do today."

"Sounds perfect."

He kissed her again, then got off the bed. She curled her body into a ball as she watched him grab some clothes, and then he disappeared into the bathroom.

She let out a long sigh. He was gorgeous, loving, and kind. How had she gotten so fortunate all of the sudden? Was it possible all the awful circumstances that had happened were so she could appreciate him when he came into her life, or was Jordan an answer to her daily prayer to God?

The moment he left, Jaynee bounded out of bed and ran to the bathroom. She brushed her hair and teeth, splashed water on her face, then jumped back under the sheet in minutes.

Jordan returned carrying several plates: one with fresh fruit, another with different varieties of muffins and sweet rolls, and still another piled with waffles and eggs. "Sorry, no Linguica ... but I got a little bit of everything else." He chuckled as he set out his smorgasbord.

After pulling the table next to the bed, he sat down beside her and offered her a grape. How could she resist?

He picked up a mini muffin and swallowed it in one bite. "So, what do you want to do today?"

"Um ... I'm not sure. Did you want to go to the beach?" She really just wanted to remain here with him. But not being from Florida, she figured he might want to see the beach in daylight.

"I have a suggestion, but you need to answer a question first." He took her hand in his, kissing it. "Do you like the ring? That's not the question ... just wondering. I wanted the most beautiful and unique, like you, not just the biggest diamond; however, you could choose a different one."

"No!" she shrieked. "I mean, no, I don't want to exchange it. I love it! It's exquisite. It would be exactly what I would have chosen if I had a choice of any ring in the world. It's a princess cut, right?"

"Yes," he said, flashing another beautiful smile, pleased by her acceptance, it seemed.

She shook her head. "You shouldn't have done that. I would never have wanted something so expensive."

"But you like it?"

She nodded.

"Then don't worry. Now, the question I meant to ask. Do you want a big wedding?"

"No." She shook her head again. "I hardly have anyone to invite."

"Would your grandmother or family be upset if you didn't?" Instant concern filled his voice.

"My grandmother wants only what makes me happy, and I really don't care what my mother thinks. No, I don't want a large wedding."

How strange to be discussing this over breakfast, in a t-shirt, with a man she'd only met barely four days ago. Her heart fluttered at the insanity that, amazingly, felt right.

"Then, would you like to fly to Vegas and get married today?"

Jaynee choked on the bite of fruit she'd just popped into her mouth. "What?"

He rubbed her back. "Hear me out. Not a tacky Elvis wedding. There's a romantic resort I've heard of where we can get married, and then we can continue the honeymoon right there. Plus, Las Vegas has great hiking. Not to mention shows, dancing, boating, horseback riding, whatever you want. What do you think?" His eyes were bright. This sudden thought had apparently energized him.

She covered her mouth so she could speak. "You're serious?"

"Of course, I'm serious." He tilted his head. "Why would I want to wait? Unless you wanted a grand wedding and reception, then I would give you that instead."

"What about your family? Won't they be offended?" Unlike her, Jordan had a very close family. He'd told her about his two sisters and their husbands, even his mother and grandmother lived nearby.

"Nah." He waved his hand in dismissal. "They learned eons ago to let me have my way."

She narrowed her eyes. "Do you always get your way?"

"Usually. I got you, didn't I?" He tilted his head to the side and gave her a penetrating gaze.

Unable to resist, she smiled. "Yes, you did." He definitely had her.

"So ... what do you think?" His eyes were intense staring into hers, awaiting her response.

"Do I have a choice?" she asked, not surprised he always got his way.

"Of course you do. You can have a full-scale wedding or Vegas. Those are your choices." He grinned, then raised his eyebrows in anticipation.

She noticed he hadn't offered her the choice of saying *no*, only how to go about marrying him.

"Isn't the bride supposed to pay for the wedding?" Unfortunately, no one in her family would be able to foot the bill.

"Jaynee, I assure you ... you don't have to worry about money. I have plenty. I've been a cop for almost five years, and I've been running my own company almost as long." He smiled, happy to share this inconsequential tidbit of information. He pushed the table back and stood. "You have a couple of calls to make. You need to quit your job and let your grandmother know we're coming over. I'll make the arrangements immediately." He was already walking across the room to his laptop. He really was accustomed to getting his way. Just like the first night when he asked her, no, insisted she go out with him.

She stood up and just stared at him. "What about college? I have a paper due next week."

Jordan didn't even turn around as he continued across the room, taking a seat in front of his laptop. "The semester just started. You can drop your classes without affecting your grade, and I'll pay for you to enroll in Charlotte."

Jaynee sank to the floor as the blood rushed from her head. "Oh ..."

Jordan darted out of the chair, dropping down in front of her, taking both of her hands in his. "Jaynee, are you okay?"

"I don't know ... I forgot ... I mean ... I don't know what I was thinking. I forgot you lived in North Carolina. I assumed you'd stay here." Her eyes fell away.

He turned her face back to his. "Jaynee, I already thought about this. The only thing in Florida is your grandmother, and I'm sure she'll understand. I have a home, career, and business in North Carolina. I know you'll love it there. I'm sorry. What I meant to say is *we* have a home. And I know you'll love it. If not, we'll get a new one. But you *will* love it, I'm certain."

Jaynee thought about what Jordan was offering her besides love. He was offering her a fresh start. Wasn't that what she'd decided she needed? She was just nervous. Would her grandmother understand? Would she realize it would be healthy for her to move away from this area, especially after last night? She would. Gram wanted what was best for her little girl, as she'd always put it.

Jordan still kneeled in front of her, holding her hands, his eyes anxious.

Her heart swelled as she thought about what she was preparing to say and do. She wasn't just agreeing to marry Jordan; she was giving up her entire life. Although she'd had it rough, it was still her life.

Steeling herself, she nodded. "I love you too, Jordan. Yes, I'll marry you in Vegas, and I'll follow you to North Carolina."

Without warning, he lifted her off the floor and swung her around. "Now I really am the happiest man alive. I'd been worried about the specifics. But now ... Jaynee, I promise you, I'm going to make you the happiest woman alive!" He kissed her. "I have a hotel and flight to book. Make your calls ... then we'll go get you some clothes. You'll need some cold-weather gear and a wedding dress, naturally." He set her back down, then walked over to the desk, and flopped into the chair. His fingers flew across the keyboard.

Jaynee didn't know what to feel ... overwhelmed came to mind. But, she *was* happy. It felt like a fairy tale. She'd fallen asleep, and the prince had shown up to wake her from her nightmare. He even wanted to buy her a dress ... and her ring. She gazed at the sparkling diamond on her hand as a quiver swept through her body. It must have cost over ten thousand, heck maybe even twenty.

She'd seen those types of rings when she went shopping with her girlfriend. Rainey had chosen her own ring and told her fiancé where to buy it. They had a long engagement too, over three years. Jordan had also said if she didn't like *their* house, he'd purchase a new one. He'd obviously downplayed his little construction business. Well, at least she'd fallen for him, admitted she loved him, and agreed to marry him before she knew he was well off. Maybe that was the reason he hadn't told her. Perhaps he had issues with people using him, too.

Jaynee picked up the phone, making the easiest call first to her boss. She didn't explain why she was quitting, and she wasn't on the schedule again until Wednesday, so he had plenty of time to replace her shifts. Still, he sounded displeased. She considered telling him about the assault but knew the attack had been against her, not just a random act.

Now for the difficult task — telling Gram. They should do it together — in person. Hadn't she already hinted yesterday, not believing for a minute Jordan would have felt the same way and ask her? Gram would be content as long as Jaynee was happy.

She called her grandmother and told her they would be stopping by.

Jaynee glanced up at Jordan working on the computer and was unable to keep from smiling. Sensing her gaze, he grinned. He was beautiful, even if he was spoiled. She wondered if they'd have a little time before leaving, and the thought surprised her. The desire to make love consumed her. Never had she wanted a man so much; her body yearned for him.

What the heck, she thought, *I'll be his wife shortly*. It sounded bizarre. She'd never wanted to marry anyone, but now her entire life was changing for this incredible man she'd only just met.

She ambled up behind Jordan, draping her arms around his shoulders and resting her hands on his chest. She nuzzled her face into his neck and started kissing him — a move she'd picked up from him. He leaned back into her kisses, then reached back with his arms and pulled her onto his lap.

"I thought you'd never come over here. We have about an hour before we have to get ready ... we can shop in Vegas."

He stood up with her in his arms, carried her back to the bed, and continued to kiss her but nothing more.

"Jordan, you're driving me crazy," she finally breathed out when he stopped kissing her long enough for her to catch her breath.

"I figured it was only fair..." His voice was breathless too. "You've been driving me crazy for days."

"Why won't you make love to me then?" Her frustration surprised her.

"Jaynee —" He stopped short, brushing her hair away from her face but keeping his hand against her cheek. "I want to, believe me, but not yet. You're going to marry me, right?"

She nodded, answering him at the same time, "Yes."

"Then we'll be married tonight, so this is our last chance at a first time. Wouldn't it be nice to wait, to not be rushed?

Right now, we don't have enough time. But tonight...I promise I'll make it worth the wait."

How could she argue with his pure logic? "I guess you're right," she conceded, falling back into his embrace. "I just never wanted anyone as much as I want you at this moment."

"Me neither ..." he said, crushing her tighter to him. But all she could think was she wanted him to hold her even closer. He brushed his lips over her cheek. "Every part of you, heart and soul."

They flew first-class to Las Vegas. Somewhere Jaynee had never been or ever desired to go; she wasn't a gambler. They were going because Las Vegas was the fastest and most popular place in the world to get married. Then again, she was taking the biggest gamble of her life. Before, when something didn't work out, she could walk away. She wouldn't walk away from a marriage.

Jordan had made all the arrangements. She'd heard him on the phone while she got ready.

She knew he had a head for business by the way he talked on the phone. He'd said, "I won't settle for that," at least three times while making hotel reservations. He never raised his voice, and she could only hear part of what he was saying, but then his smile indicated he must have gotten his way, because he informed her they would be married this evening in the gardens of the Venetian.

Jaynee found that Jordan easily took control of most situations, including the discussion with her grandmother of their intention to get married. He told Gram how much he loved Jaynee and would take care of her and provide her every need. He apologized she had to move to North Carolina but promised she could return as often as she wanted. Even Gram had easily succumbed to his charm, just as Jaynee had.

He left his F-150 along with her Focus in her driveway and then locked both keys in his truck. Right on schedule, a livery vehicle whisked them off to the airport.

In the air, Jaynee lifted the armrest and scooted next to Jordan. He was so comfortable to snuggle with, not one protruding bone. Lean muscle enclosed every inch of his body.

"So, what were all those calls concerning?" She peered up at him while resting her head on his shoulder. "I've hardly had an opportunity to talk to you in the last couple hours."

"I was making arrangements," he said. "I have a flatbed truck delivering my pickup to North Carolina, and they're moving your car to your grandmother's so you'll have something to drive when you visit. I scheduled a moving company to pack your house. Everything will be in Stanfield when we arrive on Thursday. I booked us for five nights in Vegas. I have to go back to work on Monday, so I figured we'd want a few days at home together alone." He let out a chuckle, but continued before she could comment. "We're having a cookout with just immediate family on Friday night at *our* house. My mother and sisters will prepare dinner so you won't have to worry about entertaining in a house you aren't familiar with. And then, Saturday, we're having a wedding reception. I don't know where yet, but my secretary Lorraine will take care of all the arrangements." He smiled widely, visibly proud of his achievements.

Jaynee's mouth dropped open, but words escaped her. He put his finger under her chin, pulled her mouth back up, and kissed her.

His brow furrowed. "You okay, love?" he asked when she didn't respond.

"Uh, Jordan ... you *are* quite controlling, aren't you?" Her lips pursed together in an attempt to hold back the sudden swell of anger. What had seemed great earlier suddenly concerned her. How much of her life would he try to control?

His shoulders sagged, and his eyes took on a look of an adolescent scolded for a wrongdoing.

She quickly continued, "I'm sorry. That was rude. Thank you for everything. However, will you promise me something?" He nodded and waited for her request. "I know you want to take care of me, but I've been on my own since I was seventeen. I've made mistakes, but I'm hardly incapable of making decisions. If we're going to be married, we need to discuss what *we* are going to do in the future. Not that I don't enjoy surprises, but would it have hurt to consult with me about a wedding reception and dinner with family members I've never met, not to mention moving my house —" She broke off, struggling to keep her voice level. She had a bit of a temper, and with the stress of everything, she was feeling a bit overwhelmed.

Jordan bolted upright and stared into her eyes. "I'm sorry. I just wanted to make everything effortless. I won't do it again. I suppose I am a bit controlling, but not in a bad way, I swear. I've just been in charge of my business and family so long that it's become ingrained." His voice was compliant and apologetic.

She couldn't stay mad at him, looking at the way his eyes melted into hers.

Jaynee took a deep calming breath. "I'm not upset, Jordan, merely taken by surprise. I'm not used to people taking care of me or making decisions. Can we just agree to discuss everything from here on out?" She rested her head back on his shoulder again. "With the exception of surprises, of course, I don't mind that you don't want me to see the pictures of where we're going. I understand that the fiancé ..." She paused and smiled at the word. Jordan liked it too, it seemed; his face lit up at her reference. "... is supposed to arrange the honeymoon and keep it a secret."

He rested his head on hers. "I am, but I'll be more considerate in the future."

"My Prince Charming," she said, sighing softly, latching her arm around his again.

"Not even close," he offered, chuckling, obviously amused by her comparison. "But, thank you."

***

Lorraine Condrey gently set the phone back in the cradle. She wanted to launch it across her desk at the empty office next to her. But as always, she kept her feelings locked away for nobody to witness.

How dare he? How could Jordan leave on business, meet someone, and abruptly decide to marry her? Was he utterly insane? No ... he wasn't. He was the most thoughtful, caring, loving, smartest, gorgeous, and gentlest man she'd ever known. He belonged to her. From the time they were teenagers, she'd always known he was the One. Why hadn't she told him?

She knew why. Because he would never regard her any other way than the girl down the street, with whom he and his sisters spent their summers. She'd seen all the girls who'd pursued him when he'd moved here permanently. Some, she knew, would even purposely speed through his section of town, hoping he'd pull them over.

Now, she was responsible for organizing his wedding reception. She heard correctly. He was getting married tonight, and nothing would stop Jordan. When he set his mind to something, he never surrendered. All she could do was do the best for her boss. *Make it beautiful,* he'd said. *Spare nothing. Anything you can think of to make it special. I trust you.* So, she would. Then, when his impromptu marriage failed, she'd be there to shoulder his burden. She wouldn't hesitate again. She'd comfort him the way she'd always wanted to.

The door flew open, jolting Lorraine from her thoughts. All three partners, both of his brothers-in-law — Robert Brooks and Ronald Duncan — and Detective John Ramos stormed into the office.

"Is it true, Lorraine? Did Jordan call you with the news?" Bobby's booming voice rang out before he barely entered the office. "Sissy just called and said Jordan is getting married?"

Ronny narrowed his eyes and interjected, "Rachael said the same thing. Said he met a girl and they flew to Vegas this morning. Is it true?"

Detective Ramos said nothing, just had a questioning look that said without words, *Certainly his best friend and partner would call him before making such a drastic decision,* but Lorraine had thought the same thing.

Of course, they were all working on Saturday. It was the only day the entire team could get together and discuss their current projects. And naturally, they'd come to her for answers. Jordan rarely made a move without checking with her — she was his walking-daily-planner. But he had this time. It was too late to tell him he couldn't fit a marriage into his schedule ... that he was booked for that role for the rest of his life. Too late.

Lorraine shook her head in disbelief as the three men stared at her as if she held the answer to some mysterious equation. They knew Jordan made quick decisions. A quality they'd come to admire about him, what gave every one of them an opportunity to work for him. He'd been the one not fearful to venture on his own into the construction business and had brought them in with him in his enterprises, making them all wealthy in the process.

Lorraine pasted on a smile. "It's true, called me a few minutes ago. I have to find a suitable location for a wedding reception before Saturday. 'Magine that. Jordan gettin' married."

She hoped the despair hadn't seeped into her voice. But Bobby high-fived Ronny and John, then let out a hoot and a holler, so she figured he hadn't noticed her reaction. Ronny, she wasn't so sure; he didn't seem as excited. She wondered why. John said nothing, just stood there with his mouth hung open, probably jealous. Jordan and John had competed with each other since they were teenagers. Although it wasn't Jordan's fault, John just always wanted whatever Jordan had.

Bobby slammed his hand on the table, causing Lorraine to jump. "Gone off and found him a Florida beach bunny. That dog! And he said he had no intention of settlin' down anytime soon, hardly even dated from what I'd seen." Bobby's loud voice rang through Lorraine's system. She couldn't take it any longer; she had to get out of this office — Jordan's office.

"Bobby?" Lorraine interrupted his pace around the office. "I know we leave early on Saturday, but I have a few things to organize. Can y'all manage without me today?" The calm tone of her voice amazed her. She felt nothing but sorrow and heartbreak and wanted to scream and hit something — rather, someone.

Bobby waved her off. "Sure thing, Lorraine. See ya Monday." He turned his attention back to Ronny and John as she gathered up her purse and car keys. "She's probably tall with long platinum hair," Bobby rambled.

"From Florida, yeah ... that and she's most likely tanned with baby blue eyes," Ronny added, wiggling his eyebrows.

John smacked Ronny on the back. "Every time I went to Florida for spring break, the babes all had rockin' bodies. I'm sure she's hot," John completed the appraisal.

Ugh! Men! Lorraine seethed under her breath. Jordan wouldn't have done that. He wouldn't talk about another man's wife-to-be. Tears streamed down her face. She probably wasn't a witch at all. Jordan wouldn't have fallen for fraudulence. She was, however, undoubtedly, prettier than words. Lorraine charged out of the construction trailer, jumped into her car, and raced out of the parking lot entirely too fast. Clumps of the North Carolina red clay splattered against the undercarriage of her car, but she didn't care. She just wanted to escape.

***

Jaynee held onto Jordan's hand as he trailed her through the luggage pickup and to the rental counter.

He had a rental car waiting and drove them to the front entrance of the lavish resort. After handing the keys to the valet, Jordan escorted Jaynee to the front desk.

Every square inch of the lobby had decorative, ornate moldings and marble, along with aged stone sculptures and re-creations of Italian artwork as far as she could see. A potent scent, reminiscent of jasmine and lavender, filled the air. It was very relaxing. Jaynee felt it working on her senses, even as butterflies swarmed her stomach.

It was rather busy, but the female clerk accepted papers from Jordan with a smile. "Welcome to the Venetian," the woman said in a singsong voice. "You'll be staying in a Venetian Luxury View. The suite has a king-size bed, is non-smoking, and you have a lovely view of the Venetian's Private Pool and Gardens."

Embarrassed by the gleam in the woman's eyes, Jaynee looked down shyly as she handed them card-keys and various pamphlets of information.

"Isn't this incredible?" Jordan paused in the lobby, admiring the overflowing archways and painted ceilings. They lingered around the shops and leaned against the railing, watching lovers in Venice-style gondolas get serenaded by the gondoliers.

When they finally made it to their suite, he held open the door, allowing her to enter first.

"Do you like it?" were his first words.

Jaynee was in awe. "It's beautiful, Jordan." She opened the first door after walking through a short hall. The bathroom — four times larger than hers, larger than most homes she'd been in — held a gigantic garden tub surrounded by marble, and then there were double vanities, a separate shower, and a water closet.

She walked farther into the room, taking in the enormous bed with a canopy that sat flush against the ceiling and draped down the back of the bed — it filled half the room. Across from the bed was a sunken sitting room with an L-shaped sofa, dinette, and a large window overlooking the pool and gardens.

"So ..." Jordan came up behind her and wrapped his arms around her. "How 'bout we go find you a dress?"

She exhaled in relief at the feel of his arms and his words. He wasn't upset about what she'd said on the plane. He'd been so quiet on the ride to the hotel that she'd worried she'd upset him. Maybe he was just as nervous as she was. "Can I pick out my dress?" she teased, turning around in his arms.

"As long as you promise not to worry about the price, but agree to select the loveliest dress since you have to choose one off-the-rack."

She rolled her eyes. "What do you know about off-the-rack?"

"I have two sisters, remember? Believe me ... I've seen all the drama when it comes to women. My one sister — never mind ... I don't want to scare you. Let's just say she's a prima donna." He kissed her on the top of the head. "Let's clean up and go shopping."

After they'd freshened up, they drove to a promising-looking boutique the front desk had recommended. Jordan handed her a credit card as she stepped out of the car. "I ordered one with your name on it. They shipped it overnight, so it'll be here Monday."

Again, Jaynee was speechless. Did the man think of everything? She leaned back into the car at his expectant look and kissed him. "You'll be back in an hour, right?"

"You sure that's long enough?"

Jaynee backed away and stood upright. "Yes, I'm a fast shopper."

He smiled at her comment then waited until she entered the shop before he drove away.

She had no lack of assistance finding the perfect dress. The sales ladies selected several gowns another woman assured her would look magnificent. When she finally chose a favorite, they measured her and guaranteed her they'd have the dress altered and shipped back to her suite immediately.

Jaynee had never heard of such a thing. She thought for sure she would have to just deal with the fit. Several more women followed up with an assortment of different shoes, lingerie, garter belts, and veils while the other woman watched over them.

She stared incredulously at the woman whom she could only assume was the owner or manager. The woman had made sure Jaynee received more attention than she'd ever received in any store. Her standard attire of jeans and a t-shirt rarely got her waited on, often overlooked many times before she would march up to the counter and demand service. But here, the ladies were falling over her. She made eye contact with the woman, summoning her with a crook of her finger.

"He called you, didn't he?" Jaynee questioned the woman in wild disbelief, trying to sound casual.

The manager couldn't disguise her sheepish grin. "Yes, and you're not to leave until you have everything."

The woman smiled with delight, obviously a romantic and a woman who appreciated men like Jordan. Jaynee wondered if it was the amount of the purchase or had he promised a large tip as well. She smiled in spite of herself. "*Thank you, Lord,*" she whispered. "*Thank you for finding what I couldn't and throwing him in front of me.*"

A man walked in carrying a note and a single red rose, looking for one Jaynee Evans. She asked for her purse to give him a tip, but he put up his hands. "Already handled, ma'am," the man said, grinning.

The ladies swooned as she opened the letter, insisting she read it to them while they poked, maneuvered, and prodded her in different directions.

> *Jaynee, it's a surprise so it should be all right. I arranged for a return ride to the hotel and made an appointment at the spa. It's your wedding day after all, so it should be extraordinary. I'll meet you in the gardens at 7:00 PM sharp. I'll be the one in black and white with the largest smile on his face, waiting for his bride.*
> *Love, Jordan*

Jaynee laughed softly. He was going to take the *surprise* comment to his own level. The man was incredible. Again, she couldn't comprehend how she'd managed to be so fortunate after so many years of pain.

Jordan had booked a spa package called *Euphoria*; a treatment intended to indulge every sense in a luxurious ritual, consisting of an aromatic scalp massage and a warm botanical body mask, later washed away in an exquisitely prepared bath. Then she would receive a soothing massage using herb-infused oils.

Next stop facial. She selected the Total Elegant Facial, knowing how some excessive treatments could leave her face blotchy, and she just wanted to look radiant. Jordan had ordered food too. But since she could feel the butterflies already swarming in her stomach, she just nibbled at a few pieces.

He'd also booked her a hair appointment, apparently anything she wanted according to the spa coordinator. Although the stylist tried to talk her into highlights, Jaynee settled for a shampoo, trim, and style, not wanting to change her appearance.

Lastly, a manicure and spa pedicure, which was one of Jaynee's ultimate ideas of relaxing. The manicurist attempted to convince her into painting her nails, but as always, she just requested a buff and shine. However, appreciating the way it made her feet look so dainty and clean, she did opt for a French pedicure.

It was almost seven when she was finished.

She had just enough time to return to the room, throw on her dress, and meet Jordan in the gardens — wherever they were. She gawked at the mirror, barely recognizing her face; it was blushed and glowing from the treatments, but there was something else. She was happy, and she could see the light in her eyes.

A knock on the door startled her. She looked through the peephole and saw a steward dressed in a tuxedo. "Yes?" she asked, opening the door cautiously, hoping nothing had happened to Jordan.

"Per your groom's request, I'm here to escort you to the gardens, Miss."

Had he read her mind? He wouldn't even allow her to get lost in the hotel. Amazing. "Thank you. I'll be right out." She inhaled deeply and took one final look at herself before leaving the room for the last time as a single woman.

Chapter Eleven

The area, designed to look like a small chapel set in the midst of a summer garden, overflowed with lush greenery and flowering plants.

Jaynee thought she might have missed a large wedding with family and friends, but she didn't.

It was just God, Jordan, and her. The staff provided her with a beautiful bouquet, and the garden smelled of roses and freesia.

Jaynee looked up as she started her walk toward Jordan. He inhaled deeply, and then his eyes were wide with delight as a brilliant smile spread across his face. He was so extraordinarily handsome in his tuxedo, and amazingly, he wanted her. Forever.

***

Jordan marveled as Jaynee advanced the small path while violins and a harp played a soft rendition of Wagner's Wedding March.

She took his breath away. Not only was she stunning, but she was his — forever. He'd wanted to give her a large wedding, but at the same time, the thought of making her his wife today exhilarated him.

He hadn't wanted to wait months to prepare a wedding. The thought of leaving Florida without her had terrified him. What if those thugs had come back and hurt her?

As Jaynee approached, her grandmother's comments from earlier invaded his thoughts. She'd walked over to talk to him while Jaynee was inside packing. Gram understood why Jaynee didn't want a big wedding, but she'd assured Jordan that even though Jaynee had felt abandoned by her parents, her remaining family had taken her in as their own.

Jordan assured her grandmother that he would do what he could to make everything right. Gram had hugged him then, requesting he take care of Jaynee, explaining that no matter how tough she acted, a hurt little girl hid beneath her bravado. He promised a solemn vow that no one would ever hurt Jaynee again.

When the preacher announced, "You may kiss the bride," Jordan felt triumphant. He held Jaynee securely in his arms as he kissed her with everything in him, then pulled back to look at her face. He wasn't surprised to see tears, but was happy they were tears of joy. He was amazed, however, that his eyes too had watered up, just a light glaze giving away his emotions.

Jordan escorted Jaynee toward the exit as the soft melody settled into the triumphant ending of the wedding march. He walked her to the front of the hotel where a white Hummer limousine waited for them.

"Aren't we going back to the room, Jordan?" Jaynee looked puzzled as the chauffeur opened the door.

"Not yet ... This is my night to spoil you." He nuzzled his face into her neck as he helped her up into the vehicle.

The Hummer headed to a restaurant called *Michael Mina Bellagio*, supposedly the most romantic restaurant in Vegas, according to his research.

Once they arrived, they strolled through the botanical gardens as they awaited their table. It was incredibly difficult to keep his eyes, let alone his hands, to himself. All he could think was that this magnificent woman was his. He wanted to proclaim it loudly for all to hear. His joy was so overpowering he was sure Jaynee would think him insane; surely, she could see his elation. He wanted nothing more than to carry her to the room, but he needed this evening to be exceptional. She'd given up everything for him; he needed her to believe in happiness.

After dinner, he whisked her back to the waiting limo, and they were off to Vegas' version of the Eiffel Tower. There, they had a wonderful view of the water show at the Bellagio.

He produced a bottle of champagne from inside his jacket that he'd hidden when they got out of the limo. "I wasn't sure if you drank, but I thought it was appropriate."

"I don't drink much, but I do enjoy champagne. Just don't let me drink too much; I get frisky."

"Oh ..." he mused, wagging his eyebrows, "well then, I guess I just won't let you out of my sight. Not that I was planning on that anyway, my bride." He poured them both a glass but set his down after only a few sips. He brushed her hair off her neck then cupped her face with his palm, pulling her lips to his. "I love you, Jaynee. Thank you for marrying me."

She leaned her head into his palm and sighed. "I love you too, Jordan. Thank you for asking."

***

Jaynee rested back against Jordan, thankful when he draped his jacket over her shoulders and wrapped his arms around her, as it was getting chilly.

When the water show ended, he lowered his lips to her ear. "Would you like a gondola ride, or is there something else you want to do?" His honey-sweet accent was smooth and seductive, sending chills down her entire body.

She tilted her head up to look at him. "We can do that tomorrow, I suppose. I'd like to go to the room ... with my husband."

"I thought you'd never ask." His warm breath caressed her neck. His teeth grazed her lobe as his lips eagerly moved their way down the line of her jaw. He turned her toward him, finding her lips. He pulled back after only a moment. "Let's go."

Back at the Venetian, Jordan led Jaynee back to the room, trailing them around the shops and gardens. Characters dressed in Renaissance-era clothing roamed the streets, occasionally breaking into opera-style singing Jaynee wasn't too fond of, but it was interesting.

A mime approached, clearly recognizing them as newlyweds. He swayed his hips as if they should dance.

"Shall we?" The question was rhetorical. Instead of waiting for an answer, Jordan twirled her out once then pulled her back into his arms as he lowered her gracefully into a dip, his strong arms secured around her.

The mime jumped up and down, clapping his hands noiselessly, then proceeded to make a mock display as if tapping on a glass, beckoning them to kiss. Jordan obliged, and a cheer emerged from the surrounding crowd Jaynee hadn't noticed had gathered. Jordan stepped back and bowed, pulling her with him.

"Jordan, you're crazy." She let out a laugh. "And a ham! Can we go?" she pleaded. Not accustomed to the spotlight, she felt heat spread across her cheeks.

"If you insist, my lady." He waved off the crowd and pulled her to his side again.

Finally, they made their way to the room. Although it shouldn't have taken her by surprise, the wind rushed out of her when he swung her up into his arms and carried her over the threshold of their room. She hadn't even noticed him open the door.

He carried her down the hall, but then just stood there holding her, gazing into her eyes. "Welcome to the wedding suite, my bride." His eyes were bright and excited.

Jordan held her close and kissed her passionately now that they were in private. She couldn't help but wonder if he wasn't able to decide what to do with her now that he had her exactly where he wanted.

"Are you happy?" she asked, breathless from their kiss.

His warm smile was confirmation enough, but he answered anyway, "Exceedingly so, and you, my love?"

"Extremely. Kiss me again, Jordan."

His lips were exultant, his breath heavy. She could feel his heart thundering in his chest as he carried her to the bed, sitting her upright, his lips never leaving hers.

"Ah, traditions," he groaned, pulling back slightly. He lifted her dress just high enough to expose the garter wrapped around her thigh.

"How did you know that was there ..." She giggled as he tickled the area beneath her knee.

He grinned up at her. "I didn't, but I'd hoped. I did tell that woman at the store ... everything."

Ever so gently, his strong hands moved up her thigh. His fingers lingered under the lace, tracing a circle around her thigh; then slowly, he pulled the garter lower. Her heart pounded in her chest, her thoughts wild as his hands traced the exposed skin down her leg. Her flesh tingled with anticipation.

He lifted her onto the middle of the bed and proceeded to remove his jacket, never withdrawing his eyes from hers as he laid it on a nearby chair. He slid in beside her, his head perched on his arm. With unhurried movements, he used his other hand to trace her collarbone and bare shoulders, lowering his lips to her neck. His kisses were persuasive as he nudged up her head with his nose and buried his mouth deeper under the thick tresses of her hair.

"Jaynee." He let out a feral gasp as a whoosh of air escaped his lungs. "No man could possibly want his wife this much."

He pulled her up so she was also on her side. His arm slipped under her head, supporting her as his other hand pulled her face to his, his lips finding hers. His tongue glided over her lips, exploring. She parted her mouth, an invitation.

Without hesitation, his mouth was hard on hers. His hand gripped the back of her head as his fingers intertwined in her hair. Her body thrilled with delight; his kissing alone was enough to take her being to another dimension. She breathed in his warmth as he reacted to every thought she had ... as if he could read what she wanted next, where she wanted him to touch her.

His hand slid down from her hair to her back, trailing across her bare skin, searching and wanting. Slowly, his eyes searching hers, he placed his fingers on the zipper at the back of her dress.

"May I?" he whispered, subdued, breathless. He didn't have to ask, but she assumed he wanted her verbal consent, the perfect gentleman.

"Please ..." was all she could murmur before his lips returned to hers.

"Jaynee," he whispered her name again, his breathing as ragged as hers. "I want to make love to you more than anything I've ever wanted."

He unzipped her dress completely, pulling it off her shoulders and over her waist. She wriggled out the rest of the way. His hand trailed over her waist, tracing a pattern across her stomach, leaving a track of fire everywhere he touched.

She reached up and began unbuttoning his shirt; he didn't stop her this time. Instead, when she finished, he returned her to her back as he freed his arms from his shirt and tossed it on the floor.

Jordan crawled over top of her, suspending his body over hers. "God, you're beautiful."

Self-conscious, she lowered her eyes and took the opportunity to outline his chest with her fingers, following a path to his abs. She looked back up and searched his eyes, a silent request. He plunged his mouth back on hers, an affirmation. She moved her hands to his belt, removing all restraints.

It seemed as if it would never end, and she didn't know if she ever wanted it to, but when it finally did, the room spun, her mind exploded, a pleasure she never knew possible washed over her entire body, and a groan of undiluted gratification escaped her lips.

"Wow!" was all she could manage to utter when they finished making love.

"That's an understatement!" He bent his head down once more to kiss her under her jaw, then fell back down alongside her and scooped her up into his embrace.

They lay there without moving for an immeasurable length of time.

"How are you feeling, my love?" His tone was blissful.

She looked up at him. "You have to ask?" Her face flushed so heavily she could feel the warmth in her cheeks.

"Not really. Not if it was half as good for you as it was for me." He nuzzled the side of her face as he pulled her closer so he could reach her neck.

"Probably twice as good is more accurate," she countered. "You're amazing." He pulled back to look at her as if what she'd said shocked him. He might have even blushed, or the hint of pink on his cheeks could have been from the lovemaking, she guessed.

He huffed lightly, but she could see the hint of a smile. She'd embarrassed him? She didn't think that was possible. He always seemed so self-assured.

"So, it's early," he said, obviously changing the subject, "what else would you like to do? Do you want dessert?"

"No," she sulked, "because then we'd have to get dressed, and I don't want to move." She jutted out her lower lip, the pout southern girls learn early in life. He must have noticed, because he touched his fingertips to her lower lip, effectively pushing it back, causing her to smile instead.

"Room service then?" he suggested. "I worked up quite an appetite and need to build up my energy for later." His smile was devious; a low growl escaping his lips made her body shiver in pleasant ways.

"In that case, order up whatever you want." She kissed him on the forehead then bounded from the bed, wrapping herself in an afghan. Aware of his ever-watching eyes, she sauntered her way around the edge of the bed. She rounded the corner to the bathroom then poked her head back around to see if he was still watching. He was. "I'm going to take a bubble bath." She closed the door but then opened it slightly, calling out, "You're welcome to join me."

"I'll be there in two minutes. Make it hot!" His laugh came out in an exuberant burst.

Chapter Twelve

Jaynee awoke with Jordan's arms still wrapped around her. She slowly raised her head, expecting him to be asleep.

He pressed his lips to her forehead. "Good morning, Mrs. Monroe." His eyes sparkled in the dim light filtering through the edges of the drawn curtains.

"Good morning," she crooned. "Are you sure you sleep?"

He grinned devilishly as he moved her to her back. "Yes, but I had an incredible dream that woke me. I'd complain, but I know reality is even better." His eyes smoldered as his fingers traced her lips.

She blinked at his penetrating gaze. "What was your dream about?" The events of their wedding night pelted her senses, and her body yearned with anticipation, hoping his dream had involved her.

"How 'bout I show you?" His words dripped with seduction.

The question was rhetorical; he didn't give her an opportunity to answer. Once again, he took her to a place she'd be happy if she never returned. She wondered how any woman could ever tire of this; she couldn't see herself ever not wanting him. Desire burned through her entire body. When their lovemaking ended, a triumphant smile spread across his face.

"Show off," she murmured, touching the tip of his nose with her finger.

He pulled her face to his for a quick kiss. "Just taking care of my husbandly duties."

"Well, you're doing a marvelous job," she offered. "Not that I have a lot of expertise in this area, but I can't imagine it getting any better."

"A challenge ..." he mused, drawing the word out with a southern version of a French accent.

Embarrassed again, she buried her head against his chest. "And just *how* did you get so experienced?"

He'd said he'd been with women, but had never made love. He never elaborated on *how* many women, though. She hoped that she'd been good enough, hoped he couldn't tell how inexperienced she was.

He sighed. "I'm not experienced, Jaynee." He rolled his eyes at her comment; clearly, he didn't want to talk about it. "You're embarrassing me." Jordan pushed her up gently. "I'm hungry. Get dressed before I attack you again." He shooed her off with a swat on her butt. "Dress in jeans and a long-sleeved t-shirt today," he added as she walked away. "We'll be outdoors all day."

Traffic on the road was light, and within minutes, they were already off the main strip heading for the highway.

They drove in silence for about fifteen minutes when Jordan leaned over and brushed her cheek. "What are you thinking about?"

She turned in her seat and faced him. "I wasn't thinking about anything really. Just wondering where we're going, but didn't want to ask in case it was a surprise."

He lifted her hand from her lap and laced his fingers with hers. "It's not really a surprise, just a place I looked up online that was fairly close. I told you outdoors. Do you like being outdoors?"

"I love it! My dad took me to the White Mountains in New Hampshire a few times when I was young, along with my stepbrothers and stepsister. It was his favorite place in the world," she babbled on, happy to share a happier part of her life with Jordan.

He smiled, and his eyes were bright with fresh enthusiasm, evidently grateful to hear everything in her life wasn't tragic, and perhaps he was happy they shared a passion for the outdoors.

They made one stop, an outdoor store. Jordan picked up a daypack, hiking boots for both of them, and a jacket for her. He also grabbed some type of blanket, tossed in a few snacks from the counter and a couple of water bottles, and they were back on the road in minutes.

"This is a rather strenuous hike," Jordan cautioned her. "But from what I read, it is worth the climb. It will take six hours round trip at a regular pace. But if you get tired, I could always carry you," he added with a grin.

She smacked him on the arm, then gestured that they should be on their way. "I assure you I'm not a sissy. I'm plenty used to exercise."

The hike *was* difficult at first. It climbed steeply, and with the sudden rise in altitude, the scenery changed drastically from where they'd started. As they climbed higher, the trail weaved its way through an Alpine forest, something Jaynee hadn't expected in the middle of the desert. It was cool too, about fifty degrees, so she was grateful for the long-sleeved shirt and jacket.

Jordan pointed out different trees they passed, Juniper, White Fir, Ponderosa, Limber, and Bristlecone Pines. They traveled through what looked to be a meadow, but the flowers had all gone to sleep for the fall. She wondered what it would be like in the spring.

Lost in daydreams of coming back over the years to visit their honeymoon spot, she smiled. Not sure what she was thinking, but obviously content with her happiness, Jordan smiled too and gently squeezed her hand in his.

They walked onto several expansive vistas to take in the surrounding peaks. Jordan pointed in the direction of the tallest. "That's Mount Charleston, and over there is McFarland Peak."

"They're beautiful, Jordan." Both of the peaks were snowcapped, and Jaynee couldn't help but marvel at the majesty.

Because of the strenuous hike, the trail was secluded, and they saw only one other hiker who trekked by them swiftly with his dog — a chow-chow — following obediently by his side. She was sure there was a leash law, but it didn't bother her. She could see he looked to be a skilled hiker and was sure it wasn't the man's first time either.

After a couple of hours hiking, Jordan led them to an isolated piece of ground obscured by the trees from the trail they'd just traversed, but which still overlooked the desert floor below. He spread out the blanket, allowing them both to sit, and then handed her one of the protein bars and a bottle of water. They ate in silence, absorbing the solitude of the surrounding Toiyabe National Forest. It was so serene and quiet.

Jordan trailed his hand down her back. "I selected this trail because it was supposed to be the most private. Are you enjoying it?"

"It's beautiful, so serene and quiet," she said, voicing the words she'd just contemplated.

He reclined back on the blanket, pulling her down beside him. Out of the breeze, the sun felt warmer as it caressed her face. She removed her jacket, making a pillow for under his head. She had his arm, which was perfectly comfortable.

Birds chirped, and she heard a few squirrels scurry through the wood.

Jordan pulled up on his side, but secured her head with his arm. His other hand moved over her stomach and tenderly moved her t-shirt up just above her navel. He trailed his fingers with slow motions over the soft area there. Her body quivered under his touch as chills ran rampant down her arms.

"Jaynee ..." he started, but then stopped.

She waited a second, but he didn't continue. "Yes?"

He ran a finger over his eyebrow, smoothing it, in what looked to be a nervous gesture. "Do you want children?"

The question startled her; she hadn't expected him to ask about children of all things. She shouldn't want kids after everything she'd been through, but she knew someday she did. "Yes, I do," was all she could think to say, wondering if he wanted to have children. It was probably something they should have discussed before jumping into a marriage, but love made you do silly things sometimes.

"Do you think it's possible you could be pregnant right now?"

"What? No!" she blurted out a little too loudly, sitting up immediately. "Why in the world would you assume that?" She definitely wasn't expecting this conversation.

He shrugged. "Well, we didn't use protection, so ... wouldn't it be possible?"

"You sound as if that would be a good thing." She couldn't keep the shock out of her voice. Would he really want her to be pregnant?

"And you don't? I thought you said you wanted to have kids." He narrowed his brows. "But I'm confused, why do you think it wouldn't be possible?" He sat up swiftly, his gaze now boring into hers.

His sudden distress surprised her. He *did* want her to be pregnant. What could he be thinking? She was still in college. *Pregnant* ... was he insane?

"I'm on the pill, Jordan, that's why. Do you honestly think I wouldn't have taken precaution these last two days if there'd been any chance of becoming pregnant?"

"But why ... why would you be taking birth control? I thought you didn't date." His eyes, narrowing in confusion again, quickly turned to dark suspicion.

Jaynee fought to control her emotions. She wanted to be furious at his conjecture, tell him it was none of his business why she was on the pill.

"It's not what you're insinuating, Jordan. I had no intention of having sex anytime soon." She huffed out a breath and shook her head. She didn't really want to talk about her womanly issues. "My doctor prescribed the pill to regulate my periods. As it turns out, I'm glad he did." As though mortified by his insinuation, his head lowered, and she inclined hers in response. "What are you thinking, though? You'd want me to be *pregnant*?" The last word came out as an oath.

His eyes softened, and immediately his features were apologetic. "That makes sense. I apologize. That was rude for me to insinuate such a thing, and it's clearly none of my business what you did before we met." His eyes were truly regretful and obliging as he pulled her back into his arms. "But *yes*, I would like that. I'm twenty-seven, and I'm ready for children. You're right, though; you'll want to continue your college. But I promise you, even if you didn't, I'll provide a good home for us and a family.

Jaynee couldn't help but relax at his comments, knowing he was a hopeless romantic at heart, obviously. "We have time, Jordan. There's no rush. Besides, I like the idea of having you all to myself for a while," she murmured, touching his cheek with her fingertips.

"I understand. I'm just excited about our life and ready to move ahead." He rubbed tiny circles on her back.

"You're the most wonderful man." She leaned in to kiss him. "It's just hard for me to comprehend that you want things that most men don't. I always hear about men being afraid to make a commitment. How did I get so lucky?"

He huffed out a laugh and shook his head. "I think you deserve a little good fortune, Jaynee. And I'm happy to be your Prince Charming if that's how you view me ... even if I don't always act charming." He laughed at his comment then pulled her back into his arms.

They were quiet again. Was that their first argument? No, it was a misunderstanding. Children ... she wasn't even twenty-two. What could he be thinking? Her mother had her when she was nineteen; of course, she wasn't a good representation of what was normal. She would never be like her. Maybe that worried Jordan. No ... he couldn't possibly think she'd be anything like her mother. But maybe he thought she wouldn't want children after her experiences.

She didn't want to voice her concerns. It was too comfortable sitting in silence. She realized one of the situations of marrying quickly — you discover secrets after it's too late. All the quirks were hers, though; she couldn't find fault in him. Not that she was trying, but there certainly must be something. She giggled at the notion, trying to find fault in her husband. He did like to be in control of everything, as he'd already admitted. But in a good way, she amended.

A rustle in the trees pulled her from her mental wanderings. She looked up at Jordan; his eyes were already there.

He placed his finger to his lips. "Shh, be very still. Maybe they'll come closer."

Did she want whatever it was to come closer? If he wasn't troubled, she surely had no reason to feel nervous. He pulled her farther to his side of the blanket so she could see what he was looking at.

"What is it?" she asked in a hushed tone.

"I'd hoped we'd see some, but didn't want to mention it in the event we didn't. They're wild horses."

"Really?" she asked too loudly, excited by the prospect. Three majestic heads popped up from the grass they'd been eating. "Wild horses," she whispered. "How cool." One had a chestnut-colored mane cropped to his neck, but the other two had long ebony-black manes that swayed down their necks.

When the horses finally moved along, they were able to speak again. They hadn't tried to make contact; instead, they simply enjoyed the opportunity to watch the magnificent creatures in their natural state.

"Jordan, do you have horses?" she asked abruptly.

He laughed. "No, but we can if you want; our property is plenty large enough."

"Really, we can?"

"Whatever you wish, my love. Let's start heading back; there's something else I want to show you."

They descended the path faster than their ascent. She had to move fast to keep his tempo, but finally he slowed his pace. Could they have made it back to the start already? That's when she heard it — a waterfall.

"Jordan!" she exclaimed. "I love waterfalls!"

He stood behind her, his arms wrapped around her waist as they stared at the magnificence and splendor. Something about a waterfall entranced her, especially in the desert. The breeze created as the cascading falls pounded the river below caressed her body like a cool embrace. And the sound of the crashing water drowned out all other noises as it beat the rocks beneath the waiting river's surface, lulling her into a trance. The natural beauty was simply breathtaking and therapeutic.

Her eyes glazed over just a tad at the thoughtfulness that Jordan had put into their week. "Thank you," she whispered.

He bent his head over her shoulder, kissing her neck. "I love them too."

***

Kenny had driven by Caycee's house several times yesterday, throughout the night, and again today. Neither

her Focus nor the dude's F-150 had moved. No wonder Brian was infatuated; she must be a nympho.

He'd stopped by Caycee's work late Saturday, assuming she would be working on a weekend. She wasn't. That was all the information he'd gotten from the witch upfront. Amy, the girl's nametag read, refused to tell him anything.

Now, Kenny just stared at Caycee's grandmother's house. Brian had told him she lived across the street. The older woman had come out a couple of times. Once to get the mail, another to putter around in her garden for a few minutes pulling weeds. Maybe he could offer his services, do some chores around the house. He could be pleasant when he wanted. Whatever he did, he had to do it quickly. He'd promised to meet Brian during visiting hours today, and Brian would be upset if he didn't have information.

Kenny pulled into the driveway of her grandmother's house. He saw her scrutinize him through the blinds with concern, evidently not used to company as with so many old folks. Maybe he should visit his grandma; she and his baby sister had been the only family members that had been kind to him growing up. The only ones he'd loved back.

The old woman opened the main door but kept the storm door closed between them. Sad, he thought. If he'd meant her harm, that certainly wouldn't stop him.

"Hello, ma'am, I was doing some work for the Johnsons ..." he started. He'd seen her neighbor's name on their mailbox. How convenient, how stupid. All some people needed was association to make them feel comfortable. "... and was wondering if you needed any odd jobs done around your house? I'm sure they would provide you a good reference."

"That's polite to offer, young man, but my son handles all my upkeep." She smiled sweetly, just like his grandmother.

"How 'bout the lady 'cross the street? The Johnsons mentioned she was single and may need help around her house?"

"Oh, that's Caycee, she was only renting. No, she won't need any help. She left yesterday ... she's getting married and moving away." Her face looked a little concerned, but she smiled anyway.

Kenny worked to control the distress that surged up inside him. "Wow, that's something ... where'd she move to?" he asked offhandedly, as if it weren't important, just making conversation. Surely, this old woman didn't get many visitors and would love to talk about her granddaughter.

The expression on Caycee's grandmother's face changed. She may be old, but she wasn't ignorant. Just like his grandma. "I couldn't tell you even if I knew. She asked me not to tell anyone. Goodbye, son, have a good day." She shut the door in his face. Just like his family.

Crap! Brian was gonna be furious. Kenny drove to the jail, fearful the entire trip. Would Brian give him up now? Would he break his end of the bargain because he'd failed?

Kenny waited in silence in the pale-gray slathered room. Claustrophobia washed over him as his eyes darted around the concrete-block visiting area that had no windows and only a single exit leading to freedom. He could never come here. He could never let them incarcerate him. It would kill him. The thought of being in a cell was no different from what his father had done to him — the beatings, the darkness, and worse, the screams from his sister. He could never handle it.

He sat stock-still as Brian stepped to the window and picked up the phone. "So, what d'ya have for me? Who is he? Did you talk to her?" He wasted no time in chitchat.

"Not quite, but I did what you said. I waited for her to leave work, then asked her if she'd read the letter. She acted as if she didn't know what I was talking about, so I got a little persuasive, roughed her up a bit. You know?"

"You did what?" Brian lurched to his feet, pressing his fists to his temples as if he were able to come through the glass but then regained his composure. His mouth twisted. "Don't you *ever* put a hand on her again, do you hear me?" He was calmer, but his words still came out in a rush of anger. "No one touches Caycee but me. Do you understand? That's all you were supposed to get across." Brian continued to seethe, but he pulled himself together, sinking down in his chair before officers intervened on Kenny's behalf.

Kenny wasn't sure what to do. If he told Brian that Caycee was getting married, would he forget about her and move on with his life? Not much of a life it was behind bars. If he didn't tell him, he wouldn't know ... at least until they released him; then he'd come after Kenny.

"Brian ..." Kenny started with trepidation. "I'm sorry, man ... it's over ... it's too late."

"What do you mean?" He bristled. "What's over? What's too late?" His tone was demanding ... frightening, even behind the glass separating them.

"Her ... Caycee, she's gone. She's moving away and ..." Kenny gulped. " ... look, man, don't shoot the messenger. I've kept tabs on her for almost six months. The only thing she did was work and go to school. Now all of the sudden, she's having coffee with some schmo, and then he's with her every minute for four days and now —"

"Now ... what?" Brian barked into the mouthpiece. "What happened?" he repeated, enraged. "Say it! What happened to Caycee?" Brian slammed the phone against the partition separating him from freedom. The guards started toward him, clubs drawn, ready to inflict pain.

Kenny winced at the scene, deciding to assuage Brian's concerns. "Nothing happened to Caycee, Brian, she's okay, but ... she's married, dude."

The conversation halted as Brian slammed the phone against the glass again. The waiting guards had had enough and dragged Brian from the room, each man latching onto one of his arms.

"No!" Brian's tortured peal pierced the air as if Kenny had thrust a knife into his heart.

Kenny knew without a doubt Brian would call tonight, tell him he would turn him over as his accomplice. He should leave town. But where would he go? He left the jailhouse distraught, his head lowered, hoping no one recognized him. All he wanted was to seep into the ground, disappear, and start a new life.

Chapter Thirteen

After returning from their hike, Jaynee decided to take a nap before dinner, but awoke to a dark and quiet hotel room.

Only the soft blue lights of the Venetian's gardens shone through the cracks in the curtains. Her hand patted the space next to her, searching for her husband, but came up empty. Instead, she heard crinkling as her hand stumbled on a piece of paper. She flicked on the lamp, her heart skipping fearfully. Had he left her? Had he decided it was too much? Oh, God, please, no. Her breath caught in her throat as she unfolded the hotel stationary.

My Beautiful Wife,
I made reservations for seven at Emeril's, which I hear is quite delicious. I anxiously await your presence downstairs. I thought of waiting, but I knew we would never make it out of the suite. I hope you don't mind, I purchased you a gift. I couldn't resist. The dress will look fabulous on you. It will bring out the green in your eyes, and oh how I anticipate removing each button to reveal what's

underneath afterward. My heart longs for your
arrival. Please hurry!
Yours forever,
Jordan
P.S. Too formal? Just trying to be the Prince
Charming you think I am.
:)

Instantaneous relief melted through her. How could she have considered for a second that he'd left her? And how cute he was.

She saw the dress hanging on the back of the door. When did he ...? How had he had time to shop? She must have slept longer than she thought, or maybe yesterday ... the woman at the boutique.

The evening gown was an elegant deep emerald green. It had a plunging neckline with delicate gold buttons all the way down where they met the bottom of the dress, which was cut in an upside down V, and then the rest of the gown angled to floor length. Next to the dress were other accompaniments. A box she assumed held shoes and another she wasn't sure of its contents. She reached for the package and lifted the top. It contained an entire ensemble of what she could only imagine she was to wear under the dress, also in deep green.

Blood coursed through her veins; she felt as if her heart would crash through her chest. Everything seemed surreal but beautiful. She thought of Jordan waiting, and her mind soared.

Her hands shook in anticipation, making it difficult to apply her makeup. She really didn't need any; her face was still glowing from the facial and the sun today. She applied a little eye shadow, just enough to bring out the green ... as he'd suggested. She opted for a neutral peach slightly brighter than her skin tone, lined the rims of her eyes with a darker bronze color, and lastly applied a layer of mascara.

The lingerie fit flawlessly, which somehow she never doubted. The dress followed every curve of her body without clinging. The V-neck plunged enough to be sexy without showing excess cleavage, and the cut at the bottom opened high enough to see the front outline of the lower half of her legs. The shoes were black velvet with straps around the ankles and an attractive high heel.

She looked in the mirror and wondered if it *was* too much. She sucked in a breath and wondered if her new husband found her as sexy as she felt.

When she arrived at the restaurant, Jordan was leaning against a wall, arms folded across his chest, legs crossed at the ankles. She couldn't help but think he looked like a 007 agent and anticipated an English accent to emerge from his lips, with a little country twang, naturally.

He wore a dark suit with a crisp white shirt and a tie clearly selected to complement her gown. His smile lit up his entire face when he saw her. She wondered how many women had already attempted to proposition him, but his smile was for her, and it was clear he liked what he saw.

"*Wow* ..." he drew out the word. Warmth filled her cheeks, a normal occurrence anymore. He reached his hand out to brush it across her cheek. "You look amazing. Not that you don't always, but I was right, that green on you is breathtaking, and your skin is radiant, my little Florida girl."

Over dinner, Jaynee learned more about Jordan, more than she'd ever known about her previous boyfriend in their three years together.

Any minute, she was certain that her alarm would detonate, waking her up from her dream, and it would be time for college, then work, and that cycle would repeat daily. But for now, she was inside a gondola, traversing the waters around the hotel in this magical place he'd chosen.

Her thoughts drifted while leaning back in Jordan's embrace. She was nervous about meeting his family. What would they think? Would they accept her? Would they think she was crazy? That thought calmed her a bit. They couldn't think she was crazy without thinking Jordan was insane too. Luckily, they couldn't accuse her of being pregnant after only a few days, even though she knew some would ... why else would anyone marry so quickly? *Love* ... she giggled to herself.

Jordan nuzzled her neck, squeezing her tight against his chest. "What's funny?"

"Nothing ... I was just thinking how crazy this all feels." She peered up at him. "Good crazy," she amended.

He nodded in understanding and rested his chin on her head, relaxing with her in his arms while the gondolier did the work.

Her thoughts returned to their whirlwind romance. Did anyone believe in true love or love-at-first-sight? Jordan had alleged it was something more powerful, and she'd felt it too. The electricity that soared through her and still did every time he touched her, but would it be enough to make them last? Jordan had a dog and cat. What would they think? Okay, she'd lost her senses ... she was worrying about animals for Pete's sake!

She nestled into him farther. She wouldn't agonize over the inconsequential. She would just breathe in his affection, accepting he knew best.

The next morning when she awoke in Jordan's arms again, he was already awake as usual, just lying back staring at the ceiling.

"What are you thinking about?" she asked when he looked down at her.

He pulled her chin up to kiss her. "You, mostly, how fortunate I feel ... but also how I'm going to get you to wake up earlier?" His mouth turned up in a sideways grin.

"What time is it?"

"Seven."

Her eyes shot up. "That's late?"

"Seven ... *Pacific Time* ... and when you have to be ready by eight, it is. I'm an early riser, Jaynee, usually between three and four."

She scowled. "So, you've just been lying here these mornings," she paused as she counted the days ... had it been three mornings, no, four, she thought, "waiting for me to wake?" She rather liked that, but it still embarrassed her.

He tightened his grip around her. "Actually, yes, I enjoy watching you wake up in my arms."

Once again, his charm curbed any frustration.

She traced circles on his bare chest. "So, what are we doing today?" she asked, knowing he wouldn't divulge his plans.

He flashed an enormous smile. "Nope. It's a surprise ... you said surprises were acceptable."

"Okay, then ... what should I wear?"

"Jeans and a shirt will be fine, but bring a jacket."

She attempted to roll out of his arms, and he stopped her. "Where do you think you're going?"

"But you said ..."

"We have a few minutes to play around." He rolled her over on her back and nuzzled her neck while moving his hands across her body. "Just a taster of later ... unless you could get ready in fifteen minutes."

"I think I can manage." She shivered as his hand trailed down her neck and sides, not from cold, but from the goosebumps his fingers raised on her flesh.

It was fifty-five minutes later. She'd finished her shower, had just pulled on a pair of jeans and a t-shirt, and was stepping into her flip-flops as he nudged her out the door. "Hey, mister, it's your fault we're running late. Stop being so pushy."

He pulled the door closed behind them. "I didn't hear any disagreements from you," he teased.

"How could you? You seemed completely, otherwise absorbed," she offered, giggling.

"I'll rephrase. It didn't feel as if you had any complaints."

"I didn't." She latched onto his arm and let him drag her down the hall.

He grabbed the elevator door before it closed, pulled her in, and pressed the button for the lobby. When it landed, he led her through the atrium to the entryway. Once outside, he spotted a limo and walked toward it, pulling her in his wake.

"A limo again?" Would he ever cease to amaze her? The night of their wedding, she'd expected as much, but what had he planned today that warranted a limousine.

He scooted next to her in the back seat of the stretched Lincoln. "Yep, but that's not the surprise." He turned to the driver. "Don't suppose you could find a coffee shop drive-through, could you? My wife gets irritable without her latte and muffin in the morning."

He reached his hand through the opening, handing the driver what surely must have been a generous tip, because he smiled, saying, "Whatever you want, sir. We have plenty of time."

Jordan turned back to Jaynee with a Cheshire grin and a wink. Yep, he was accustomed to getting his way.

Fifteen minutes later, the driver pulled into the parking lot of an airport. The chauffeur parked alongside other limos and cars, next to a metal building advertising Helicopter Flights over the Grand Canyon. Scores of people milled around, awaiting instruction.

"We're going in a helicopter?" It was impossible to contain the excitement in her voice.

His eyes brightened at her enthusiasm. "Yes, will you like that?"

"Heck yeah, I will!" She practically jumped up and down. "My dad was a pilot, amongst other things. When I was fifteen, he taught me to fly his Cessna. But I always wanted to go up in a helicopter," she shrieked, unable to contain her overwhelming delight.

A gentleman approached, directing them to the front office where they needed to review their itinerary and supply copies of their drivers' licenses. In no time, they were boarding a chopper. The pilot, Jonathan, went over safety information, putting everyone at ease — but mostly the other couples who looked as if they might get sick.

Jonathan was comforting, assuring everyone the weather was perfect for a flight, and it should be smooth sailing.

As the helicopter took flight, Jaynee squeezed Jordan's hand. He rubbed small circles into the back of her hand, reassuring her of his presence. The sensual action soothed her, and soon she forgot about the flight. Heck, she almost forgot to look at the scenery.

The pilot was entertaining and informative, taking every opportunity to break into the prerecorded information, inserting his own personal anecdotes about Nevada's history and his personal experiences of the region. He remembered everyone's name, and when there was a point of interest on that person's corresponding side, he used their name as he pointed it out.

Forty-five minutes into the flight, Jaynee felt them drop. She winced, and Jordan was quick to notice and explain. "We are descending into the canyon. It's about a three-thousand-foot drop, and we'll be able to get out, have lunch, and look around."

She never thought for a second that she'd be able to walk on the canyon floor. But then again, Jordan continually managed to surprise her.

For lunch, they sat under Native American structures evidently built just for such purpose and ate from individual picnic baskets. Each lunch included champagne to toast the adventure. Jordan took a sip of his, then slid his glass in front of her.

Chapter Fourteen

Jaynee rested her hands on her hips. "Dare I ask?" she mused as they arrived back at the hotel four hours later.

"What do you mean?" Jordan said innocently, wrapping his arms around her waist and leading her into the lobby.

"What you have planned next," she teased, "dining in Paris, skiing in the Swiss Alps?"

His eyebrows shot up. "Would you like that? I'm sure that could be arranged."

She burst out in a laugh. "No, I would not! It was meant to be funny, Jordan. I just meant you're so chock-full of surprises as if you're going off some menu in a book, how to make a girl fall in love with you in ten days or less."

"Ah, but that was *How to Lose a Guy*." He chuckled. "I won a girl, and I believe I did it in three."

"Uh —" she started to speak, but he held up his finger for her to hold that thought as he motioned for the valet to retrieve their car.

Then he continued before she had the opportunity to voice her opinion. "Actually, it was instantaneous ... it just took three days for you to acknowledge your feelings," he said, a smile in his voice.

She sighed, exasperated, it was no use. He was right; he was always right. "So ... where are we going, since you clearly just requested the car?" she asked again.

"Shopping, we need to get you some cold-weather clothes. Not that I don't love the cute little sundresses, shorts, and flip-flops, but they're not practical in North Carolina year-round. It gets rather cold in the winter." He pulled her closer while they waited for their car.

She leaned back so she could look at his face. "Jordan, really ... I can purchase my own clothing; I do have money. We don't have to squander time shopping."

"You're right, you do ... half of everything I have, and I expect you to use it. But, I *want* to go shopping with you, and I'm afraid it won't be as simple when we return home." His brow furrowed as though he were contemplating the situation.

She didn't like the sound of that. "Won't we have time together?"

His expression turned worried as if she'd run away from him in that instant. How could he not perceive the hold he already had over her?

"Yes," he said, smoothing his hand down her hair. "I didn't mean we wouldn't see each other. It's just...I've been gone so long. I know there'll be a lot of catching up."

She leaned into his side. The last thing she wanted him to think was that she was needy. "I understand." Clearly, Jordan was an extremely busy man, and yet, he was taking additional time off work. "Well, you don't return until Monday. So we better enjoy the remainder of our week, don't you agree?" She reached up on her tippy toes and pecked him on the cheek.

The look in his eyes warmed up. "I do. And we need to get you another dress. We're going dancing tonight."

The valet pulled their car up in front of the building, and Jordan nudged her through the exit to their rental. As he held the passenger door for her to enter, he exchanged a tip for the keys. The young valet's eyes beamed with appreciation. Jaynee shook her head. He wasn't just like this with her; he was like this with everyone. He seemed to brighten up the room wherever he went with his smile. She wondered again how he'd escaped the clutches of some prettier, richer girl than herself. She'd done nothing to entice him to fall in love with her.

"*Dancing?*" she asked as he buckled his seatbelt. "Wouldn't I just need jeans and cowboy boots?"

He shook his head. "Not the kind of dancing I'm thinking. I envisioned something mid-calf, flowing, and red. Although ... I do like the idea of just jeans and boots. We'll have to purchase those too, but that'll have to be a private dance." He flashed a wicked smile, wiggling his eyebrows at her as he shifted the car into drive.

Ignoring his private dance comment, she asked, "What in the world type of dancing are you planning, Jordan?"

He glanced in the rearview mirror before pulling out of the drive, then back at her. "*Salsa* ..." His tone was seductive as he enunciated the word.

"You, *Salsa* dance?"

He huffed at her reaction. "Baby ... it's not my fault you think I'm a dumb country boy because of my accent, which, by the way, I can suppress if I want." He did so instantaneously, demonstrating his ability. "I told you my interests run deeper ... I thought you'd like —"

She sucked in a breath, interrupting him, at the endearment *baby*; she hated anyone to call her *baby*. But she addressed his accusation first. "I have never thought you a *dumb country boy*, Jordan. Country, yes, but never dumb!" Her face flushed with anger that he would even imply such a thing.

He reached across the seat and stroked her arm. "I know, darlin'. I didn't mean you literally thought I was dumb." He sighed. "I've just been accustomed to people making assumptions about my heritage and intellect my entire life." His accent was back to normal; she liked it better that way. "My parents were from North Carolina, and as you know, my sisters and I spent all our summers with my grandparents there, so I did pick up the accent. But I've traveled all over the world and have lived in many different cultures with my parents and then again on my own in the military. I enjoy every variety of music imaginable and think a good night out doesn't just consist of getting drunk and going muddin'. Although, muddin' can be fun." He pulled her hand to his lips. "So what do you say … wanna go dancing with me tonight?"

Her heart fluttered at the feel of his lips on her hand. "I say yes, and I love your accent, Jordan. Don't turn it off again, please."

"Anything you say, love." And he drew out the words even slower in that seductive southern drawl, sending chills down her spine. He was such a charmer.

"Jordan," she started to speak, not knowing how to introduce the subject without introducing an entire discussion, but she had to say something. "I love it when you call me *love* and *darling*, and even *babe* is okay, but please don't call me *baby*. I'm sorry … I just don't like it. It sounds demeaning." She hoped that would be enough explanation.

Jordan's head cocked just slightly as he glanced at her. His eyes took on a suspicious look, but then it looked as if he'd shaken off her bizarre request. "I guess it does sound somewhat demeaning; though my mother still calls me baby when she thinks I'm upset," he said, chuckling. "It's just the southern way. We don't mean anything by it; it just seems to flow naturally."

His smile was repentant, and she wished she'd never mentioned it. It wasn't that important. He wasn't her ex, and he was never condescending. She wrapped her arms around his biceps, laying her head on his shoulder, hoping to end the conversation. It worked.

The mall beneath Caesar's Palace was remarkable. Jaynee couldn't get over how everything was underground, but felt as if it were outside. The ceiling, painted to resemble the sky, was amazingly realistic, and there were scores of fountains and statues as well as many areas of cobblestone walkways and a winding escalator. She wasn't sure how she could possibly shop, as she wanted nothing else but to absorb all the sights, but Jordan had other plans.

He pulled her through Diesel, Lucky You, Guess, and other stores where previously she'd only window-shopped. She shouldn't have been surprised based on the way he always dressed. Although it was usually just jeans and a shirt, they were always top-of-the-line and fit perfectly. He suggested different things he thought would look awesome.

"Why don't you try them on?" He gave her a slow smile, and she couldn't resist.

When they stepped in front of Victoria's Secret, he whispered, "Surprise me. I'll return in about half an hour."

After handing her a credit card with her married name, he loped off. Her eyes followed him as he walked away, waiting for him to turn and glance back in her direction. He didn't disappoint. He turned, smiled, made a gesture that she should carry on, and then strolled off again.

Jaynee stood in the doorway, not sure where to begin. *Surprise him?* She thought about the lingerie he'd purchased yesterday that matched the emerald dress. He'd said red tonight, so that's where she'd start.

She decided on a lacy red number she hoped would work under the dress she hadn't found yet. She was apprehensive about purchasing anything else, even though he kept pushing the issue. She didn't have any lingerie and was really in the need of some essentials anyway, so she went to work. She found a beautifully adorned white eyelet nightie and decided to find more attractive undergarments than the plain cotton ones she always wore. He should appreciate that, she thought. It didn't take her half an hour to finish; she'd always been a speedy shopper, so she waited outside the store, gazing around, fascinated by all the detail that went into designing the mall.

Jordan returned thirty minutes later, carrying a dress bag and a second sack with a box she assumed held another pair of shoes. "I hope you don't mind ... I bought you a dress. I knew you'd grumble about the price, so I just bought it. Do you want to try it on? Not that you need to, I'm quite confident it will fit your curves."

Her jaw dropped again.

Jordan nudged up her chin with the tip of his finger. "You can help me select a suit and tie to match ... how's that?" he suggested, a smile flashing across his face.

"I'm sure I don't need to try it on. I'm sure it's perfect, just like everything you do," she said, shaking her head in disbelief.

Jordan laughed in relief. "Whew! I thought you were gonna give me a difficult time again."

Jaynee narrowed her eyes. "Do I give you a hard time? I'm sorry; I don't mean to. I just don't want you to assume you have to spend money on me to make me happy. I was just as content drinking coffee, window shopping, and climbing a mountain with you."

"I know, Jaynee, and I'm grateful. I know you didn't know I had money, but I have plenty, I assure you. I've had no one to spend it on these last few years, so allow me to have a little fun, okay?"

Jordan took the pink bag from her, acting as though he were going to peek, so she attempted to grab it back as he held it out of her reach.

"You said you wanted to be surprised," she reprimanded.

"That I did," he conceded, relinquishing the bag.

He slipped his arm around her waist, pulling her safely to his side. She always felt so protected with Jordan as if nothing could ever touch her. It seemed he was always looking for danger, as if someone was going to swoop in at any second and carry her off. It must be the cop mentality, since they were underground, how could it get any safer?

***

This wasn't good; this couldn't be happening. Jordan was going to ruin everything by getting married. If something happened to him now, everything would go to his wife.

Who gets married after only a few days? Admittedly, most of the things Jordan had done had been crazy, but everything had always worked out for him. Jordan got everything; he had the Midas touch. Everything Jordan bought and sold always paid off. He never made a mistake — until now. No way would this marriage succeed, and when it didn't, when it fell apart, his *bride* would get everything. That couldn't happen; it had been too long for everything to fall apart now. There had to be somehow to make this work, some way to benefit from this added inconvenience. Maybe it could, maybe this woman would be worth something too.

It would take time to formulate a new plan, something executed perfectly so there would be no suspicions. Time, it was a precious commodity, but in the end, everything would have its payoff. It would all be worth it in the end.

***

Jordan suggested eating at the Cheesecake Factory for dinner so they could watch the Fall of Atlantis.

Jaynee watched the show in awe, feeling a little melancholy that siblings would fight over money, since she didn't have any brothers or sisters.

The story told of King Atlas deciding which of his children would rule Atlantis. The siblings' greed ended up poisoning the kingdom — and eventually, one another. The gods determined to destroy Atlantis with fire and flood as a gigantic winged beast watched from its perch while moving statues of fire and ice appeared.

Jordan never ceased to amaze her. She found herself enthralled with stories of his military service, family, and his construction company, but she noticed he never mentioned police work.

After dinner, they strolled by an aquarium containing sharks, rays, and other sea life vying for food fed to them by a diver. Jaynee stood mesmerized. Such uncomplicated gestures on Jordan's part, simple things like this made her feel special. He must spend all his time thinking about what he'll show her next.

Her life had been so boring before him. As she reflected back on her day-to-day life, it was a wonder she hadn't died from boredom. With Jordan, everything seemed to be an adventure. When the feeding frenzy ended, Jordan took her hand and led her toward the exit.

Overall, it was a spectacular day, and she was exhausted. She wanted nothing more than to retreat to their hotel, relax around the pool, and then retire early to their room, but Jordan wanted to go dancing.

***

Jordan pressed his lips to Jaynee's hair. She smelled incredible, the familiar vanilla scent that was uniquely Jaynee. He'd always appreciated perfume, but her simple, fresh smell was warm and seductive.

He'd told her dancing, but now all he wanted was to relax with her in his arms. Soon, he'd be back to the pressures of everyday life.

"Jaynee ..." he whispered her name, appreciating the way it sounded on his lips, knowing he was the only man ever to call her by her middle name. He liked that.

"Mmm?" she asked, barely a murmur from her sensuous lips.

He didn't want to disappoint her, but he really had no desire to leave the room all night. He wanted to lie in bed with her snuggled against him, even if they did nothing.

Simply holding her would be fulfilling. She sounded drained anyway.

"Are you still up for dancing tonight, or are you too exhausted?" he asked tentatively.

She lifted her head, and her eyes caught his, those beautiful cat-like eyes. "Jordan, I'll be content with whatever you want."

She clearly didn't want to disappoint him. Did that mean she didn't want to go, or she did want to? That's what happened when he didn't just make decisions, something he'd learned his entire life. Make a decision … see it through. He was a man of action, and it had served him well. He wasn't going to change. He'd always followed his gut feelings in business — and life. He'd certainly done that where Jaynee was concerned.

"Then we'll stay in this evening," he said. "We can go dancing tomorrow. I'd rather just hold you the entire evening — in private." There. That was his M.O. Make a decision, stick to it. She'd get used to it … he hoped.

Jaynee smiled her sweet smile. He loved to see her smile; she didn't do it often enough. "That sounds wonderful. I was contemplating the same thing. Maybe a little time around the pool to get heated up, and then we can go back to the room?"

He kissed the top of her head again. "That's my girl. We're thinking more and more alike every minute."

Chapter Fifteen

Yesterday ...

Patricia Monroe peered into the hospital room, hating the grief she saw on her son's face. He hadn't eaten or left Jaynee's bedside, and it showed in the deep dark circles under his eyes.

She ran her fingers through her son's hair as she'd done when he was a child. "Jordan, honey, you need to eat something and try to get some rest. It's been almost two days. You can't continue without food or sleep." Her voice echoed in the cold room. She hated the hospital. If it wasn't an emergency, her kids would have to hog tie her and drag her here.

Exhausted physically and mentally, her son leaned into her hand. "I know, Mom, I just can't leave. What if she wakes up and I'm not here for her? What then?" he fretted, his head falling into his hands. "She'll think I don't care ... that I don't love her ..." Obviously not wanting to say more, he shook his head.

She'd asked him, but he refused to talk about it. The only thing she knew was that Jaynee was here because she'd been shot ... presumably self-inflicted. For the life of her, she couldn't imagine why Jaynee would have shot herself.

She despised seeing her son like this. He'd always been strong. He'd taken care of the family after his daddy had died, providing for them all, even gave her daughters' husbands jobs. He was her baby, a man, she knew, but always her baby. She loved Jaynee too, like a daughter, but now she felt resentment and betrayal at what Jaynee was doing to her son.

"I spoke with the doctor, Jordan. They won't bring Jaynee outta the coma for a while, not 'til the swelling is under control. Just take a break for a few minutes, for me, please. Just long enough to get something to eat and clear your head. It'll be good for you. That way you *can* be here when she wakes up."

If she wakes up, Pat thought, but she wouldn't dare utter the words to Jordan. He was madly in love with Jaynee. Even though things seemed rough lately, his feelings would never alter. She'd noticed the difference at Thanksgiving. Jaynee had appeared normal, but Jordan had been withdrawn and angry. He'd sat on the sofa most of the day brooding, and then he'd been rude when *he* was ready to leave. She'd never seen him act like that, especially around Jaynee. But she knew his feelings would never change; he'd love Jaynee until the day he died.

It was the same when she'd met Jordan's daddy and his grandfather before him had met his wife. The Monroe men seemed destined for *love at first sight* or as Pat's mother-in-law had alleged, *the thunderbolt*. Pat had never believed in the old Italian folklore. But it had happened three times, so there must be something to that darned curse.

Now look where it had landed Jordan. He was thirty-two, with a wife dying in the hospital, and no children, which meant no grandchildren for her. She had her grandbabies from Melissa, and she loved them, but they needed another Monroe. And she couldn't wait to hold her boy's babies, knowing they'd be just as loveable as Jordan had been. Never gave her a lick of trouble. 'Course, he and his daddy were something else. She knew it was because they were so similar, but neither of them wanted to hear nothing 'bout that.

Jordan stood up beside her, his head lowered, his eyes rimmed with red. She draped her arms around him in understanding.

He massaged his temples. "I love her so much, Mom. I don't know what I'll do if anything happens to her."

She stroked his back lovingly. "I know, baby. I'm sorry." She closed her eyes, knowing she was preparing to lie. "It'll be all right, Jordan. We just need to keep praying."

Taking Jordan's hand, she escorted him out of the room to the elevator. "Let's get you something to eat and fresh air, then you can come right back. It's too late in the day; they won't do anything now. Maybe they'll bring her out of the coma tomorrow morning?" she offered, stepping into the elevator, her hand latched around his arm.

***

Brian had been waiting around the corner, listening to their conversation. He'd waited almost two days to see Caycee.

Mostly he waited in the primary waiting area so he wouldn't be accused of loitering, and more importantly, not be seen by Caycee's husband, Jordan Monroe. Brian seethed over the man's name and the thought that he'd been with Caycee all these years while Brian had been in jail.

Jordan had made eye contact with him yesterday, and Brian had been sure he connected him to Caycee. But he'd been so distraught when they rushed her back into surgery that he'd waited in the ICU area alongside her husband.

When he saw Jordan's mother enter the hospital today, he knew it was his chance, so he'd followed on the next elevator. He'd figured she would pull Jordan away from Caycee ... or *Jaynee* as she was calling herself. What a load of crap. These hicks couldn't even pronounce her middle name correctly.

As soon as the elevator doors closed and Jordan was out of sight, Brian moved to Caycee's bedside. He probably had fifteen minutes at best, then Jordan would return, standing where he should be ... would be soon. He wanted to kill him, but knew he couldn't, not now while Caycee needed him.

"Can you hear me, baby? I'm here. Everything is going to be okay. We can continue where we left off. I've changed, baby. I'm here, as I told you I'd be." He stroked her hand. She was just as beautiful as she'd always been. Why did he have to destroy everything? "I'll protect you, Caycee. No one will ever hurt you again."

"Sir, what are you doing? I don't recognize you as immediate family." The nurse's voice broke through Brian's thoughts. She glared at him, brows furrowed, ready to strike. He needed to put on his charisma.

"I'm ... *not* family," he said, glancing at her badge. "Michelle," he crooned, looking up at her from under his eyelashes, the look that had worked on every woman he'd ever encountered. He hadn't practiced in a while, so he hoped it would still work. After all, he was almost six years older than the boy he was before going to prison. He would have gotten out a year ago if it weren't for the fighting. "I'm an old friend. I've driven on my Harley for almost two days to get here as soon as I heard. Didn't even bother checking with anyone when I arrived, just showed up and found her all alone."

"Oh," she said, swallowing hard.

Like a charm, he thought. "I'd rather if you didn't mention my being here. Her husband doesn't like me, but me and Cay — Jaynee — have remained friends for years, and I couldn't stand not seeing her. You understand, don't you?"

"Of course ... it's just that procedure —"

He cut her off. "Oh, I understand ... I'll just be a few minutes. I'm exhausted from riding forty-eight hours straight anyway."

He stood fluidly, approaching her. She was pretty, a little too lanky, though, not his normal type. But appealing enough and it had been a long time.

"I don't suppose there's an empty room where I could lie down a little bit?" he asked, his eyes boring into hers. He knew how to get what he wanted. He was good looking and knew how to manipulate women. He'd spent the last six years doing nothing but working out, so not only was he tall and handsome, he was buff, and the ladies liked that.

"I'm not sure," she said, her voice low and quiet, bemused.

He winked. "No one will know ... you manage the floor, right?" he asked, keeping his voice low and seductive the way he knew women appreciated.

"Well, I guess," she said, her eyes darting around the room, unable to maintain eye contact.

He still had it. "Show me," he said, raising his voice a fraction higher, but still deep and domineering.

Michelle walked out of the room, leading him down the corridor. Several rooms at the end were dark, as though no one occupied them. She strolled into the last one and Brian followed.

***

Jaynee could hear voices again. Although muffled and distant, she thought she could discern most of them.

She recognized Jordan's; his was the clearest. And then she'd heard his mother's voice. Her mother-in-law had pleaded with Jordan about something. She wasn't sure what, but she sounded upset.

Then it was quiet. Just the incessant beeping noise, coupled with the darkness.

She heard another voice, familiar, but not quite decipherable. He called her *baby*; Jordan never called her *baby*. She hated it. Why was he calling her baby? Only it wasn't Jordan's voice, and yet, it sounded familiar, though distant.

Jaynee struggled with her memory, realizing she recognized the voice. *Baby* ... Oh, God, he called her baby. It wasn't possible. What happened? Where was Jordan? Was he okay? Brian! He'd found her. What would he do to Jordan? Why couldn't she remove this blanket? It was smothering her, holding her back from Jordan. He needed her.

***

Jordan and Pat sat in the cafeteria eating wordlessly. A few minutes passed before his mother couldn't tolerate it anymore. She wasn't comfortable with silence.

"Do you think she did it purposely, Jordan?" his mother asked in her normal blunt manner. Subtlety was never his mother's strong point either.

He grimaced at her candid words, not wanting to have this discussion. Not now, not ever. "No, I don't. Why would she?" His breath hitched in his throat at the remote possibility.

His mother picked at her sandwich without making eye contact with him. "Well, I noticed conversation has been strained —"

"But kill herself," he interrupted her, suddenly angry. "You've known her almost as long as I have, for Pete's sake!" He glowered at his mother. "Do you think she's capable of committing suicide?"

Why was he having this discussion? He should be with Jaynee. He didn't need fresh air or food. He needed Jaynee. Tomorrow they'd bring her up, and she'd explain to everyone, to him, that she hadn't tried to commit suicide. She wouldn't. She wasn't selfish, and she wouldn't hurt him.

A tiny voice reminded him her father had killed himself, and her mother had attempted suicide on several occasions. He shook his head. *No … not Jaynee.* She wouldn't do this to him. He had to believe.

Nauseated, Jordan pushed away his food. "If she'd been trying to kill herself, she would have done it correctly. She's a cop's wife. She'd know how to kill herself."

All of the sudden, the words made sense. She hadn't tried to commit suicide. Even the police had said it had been an accidental shooting. That based on the entry point, the gun had been at a distance of about where her hip was. She hadn't tried to shoot herself. She was afraid. But, of what? Or whom?

Jordan jumped up, shoving the chair against the table. It went underneath the lip and fell backward. He looked at it numbly then stormed off, ignoring his mother as she called after him. He had to hurry.

Jaynee was frightened. Why? As long as he'd known her, she'd never been afraid. Even when those hoodlums had attacked, the ones passing along information from her ex-loser, she hadn't been scared. She'd been afraid for him, though. It'd been over five years, and even though he'd gotten her a gun for protection — because they lived so far out in the country — he'd never seen her fearful of anything. The only thing she'd ever fretted about was his safety as a cop, his construction work, and back then that her ex would send his goons after him.

That was it! Jordan sprinted toward the opened elevator doors, anxious to return to Jaynee. He ignored the person running for the elevator as he hit the button to close the doors. There was no time. It had been over five years since his incarceration. Was Brian here? Had he threatened Jordan's life, or worse, Jaynee's?

Jordan would kill him. He'd destroy him, tear him apart limb from limb. No one would ever unearth him. One of the things a cop was proficient at, they knew how to perpetrate a crime, any crime, even murder if necessary. Brian would never terrorize Jaynee again.

He paced the elevator in frantic movements. It was ridiculously slow; he should have taken the stairs.

***

The man Jaynee was with Friday stood beside her bed. It was just a matter of time before she left Jordan, but this was better.

How much easier it would be if she died now. Not uncommon in these types of situations: she'd been in a coma for almost two days.

The man followed a nurse down the hall. By the look in his eyes, he'd be gone for a while. Jordan had left with Pat to get something to eat, so they'd be gone about fifteen minutes.

It would only take a few seconds to inject an air bubble into her veins, a simple method that would cause an aneurysm and go undetected if done carefully ... 50cc's was all it would take.

Jordan's death would be easy. Police officers ended up murdered all the time from wayward bullets, potential gang members attempting to prove their worth. Or, a construction job gone wrong could get him killed.

Simply a matter of time, and then everything would be right again. The elevator chimed, indicating its arrival. Not today, but soon. It was how it had to end.

***

Jordan waited for the elevator doors to open, practically climbing over an older couple entering.

He rushed down the hallway toward Jaynee's room, only stopping for a breath once he was in her doorway. She was all right ... thank God. He wouldn't leave again until she was out of this coma. His mother would just have to deliver food. He gently pulled loose the covers someone had tucked in again before he sat down next to her.

"I'm here, Jaynee," he whispered in her ear. "I know why you were upset, but you don't need to worry anymore. I'll protect you, I swear. No one will ever come near you again. I failed the first time, but I won't fail twice. I promise. I love you, Jaynee — forever."

***

Jaynee could hear Jordan's voice, soft and deep, sensual as always. He loved her; he'd always loved her.

She had to tell him about Brian. Why couldn't she open her eyes so she could see his face? Her mind launched back into pitch darkness, unable to remain with him.

Chapter Sixteen

Five years ago ...

The last two days of their honeymoon passed swiftly, and now Jaynee was boarding a plane with Jordan, heading toward her new residence.

She felt comfortable with Jordan, as if she'd already known him for years, not days. She'd discovered some of his likes, anything outdoors. His dislikes, such as his passionate hatred for innocent tomatoes. And his quirks, the strange noise he made when he brushed his teeth. She thought it might annoy her at first, but she found herself laughing every time she heard him.

And though they didn't allow much time for television, several times when she was in the bathroom, he'd clicked it on. She could hear him from the other room laughing all by himself, with no one to share in the humor.

Jaynee loved to watch funny shows, movies, and comedians but realized she rarely laughed aloud. Her father had made her laugh. He'd made everyone laugh. He'd be in a roomful of strangers and could have them laughing within minutes, forever the comedian. His wives had never

laughed at him, though. She remembered telling his last
wife, if you like him the way he is now, fishing, playing, and
humor, you'll succeed, if not, your marriage will never last.
The woman had told Jaynee she loved all of those things.
Afterward, Jaynee had learned otherwise. Not only did she
despise fishing, she couldn't even swim; she was terrified of
the water. Her dad had longed for retirement, so he could
move onto a houseboat and become a charter fishing boat
captain. When he realized his dream would never come to
fruition, shackled by a woman who didn't love him,
knowing if he divorced her, she'd take half his money and
retirement, he took his own life.

Jaynee found all the characteristics in Jordan that she'd
loved about her father. He was funny, charming, and above
all, giving. Jordan was the kind of man who would give the
shirt off his back to a stranger on the street if he needed it.

It had terrified her when she'd learned that her father
had killed himself, especially after growing up with the
knowledge that her mother had been suicidal.

She'd questioned her aunt about her concerns. How did
she stand a chance of being normal when both her parents
were crazy? Her aunt had chastised her lovingly, reminding
her that Gram was her mentor and telling her that she
thought she was the sweetest and strongest young lady
she'd ever known, and that she was proud she hadn't used
her past as a crutch.

Jaynee was thankful for her aunt and grandmother and
even her three older cousins who had all treated her like a
daughter. But it would never be the same; she would always
wonder what it would be like to have a real mother — a
family. An alive father and a mother who wasn't always one
step away from committing suicide.

She felt reprehensible for not allowing them the opportunity to participate in her wedding. She just hadn't wanted to burden them. Gram would have notified everyone. She would have to call her family next week and explain her actions, but right now, she was with Jordan.

And on Jordan's arm, she felt as though she were finally going home.

She wasn't sure if she even knew what home was supposed to feel like. She'd been unloved and abused most of her adolescence and had never felt wanted.

Living on her own this past year had been as close to a home as she'd ever known, but she was lonely. She did the same thing every day, ate the same foods, read the same things, and went to the same places. It wasn't a life; it was an existence.

Jordan was her home now. He was offering her love and a life. As they stood to board the plane, she wrapped her hands tightly around his arm.

Jordan looked down into her eyes, kissed her on the forehead, and draped his other arm across the front of her, pulling her closer. He didn't say anything but seemed to comprehend.

Jaynee reached up on her tippy toes. He tilted his head to kiss her gently on the lips. Not a long kiss, but it was warm and loving as his lips parted and melted into hers.

He pulled back to look at her face, searching her eyes, seemingly trying to discern her thoughts. "Are you nervous?"

"Not really. I was just thinking about how much I love you," she said, resting her head against his upper arm.

"I love you too." He pulled in a deep breath, then let it out, as if her words had provided him life-sustaining oxygen. She knew just his presence ... the warmth of his love filled her senses. "We'll be home soon. Are you ready to see your new house?"

"I am …" The truth of her statement hit her hard. She was ready to begin her new life with Jordan. "Won't you tell me anything about the house or the pets?"

"Nope," he said, directing her to their seat on the plane. He stored their luggage in the overhead compartment before continuing. "You know how I like my surprises. And since I can't make any alterations without consulting you first, I'll enjoy this final opportunity to surprise you."

She playfully slapped his arm. "Jordan, you know that's not what I meant, and you *have* managed to drop many surprises on me anyway." She looked at him under her lashes, an attempt to be seductive, whispering, "Besides, I rather like your surprises."

***

Melissa showed up early to ready Jordan's house for his return. Rachael too, but she hadn't stopped moaning since they'd arrived.

Jordan had asked Melissa to bring home Boomer, his boxer, who had been staying with her and Bobby while he was away. Melissa never minded. Boomer was like one of the family; everyone loved him. Boomer had seemed despondent the last couple of days, though. Even playing with the kids, he'd looked depressed. He kept looking toward the front door, anticipating Jordan to walk in, she suspected.

When she loaded him in the truck this morning, he was as happy as she'd seen him in weeks.

Jordan had requested Melissa and Rachael freshen up his residence. And if it wasn't too much trouble, to purchase two dozen red roses and have them sitting in the foyer so his new wife would see them when they arrived.

Rachael, as always, had complained. She grumbled about everything. Melissa had never understood why. Jordan was a fantastic brother. He was five years younger than Melissa and two years younger than Rachael, but he'd never been a nuisance as some of her girlfriends' little brothers had been. She'd loved taking him places when he was little. Everyone loved Jordan, especially her husband, Bobby.

Melissa had missed Jordan when he'd enlisted. That time of their life had been difficult for everyone. They all had returned to their parents' hometown when Daddy retired for medical reasons, but Daddy and Jordan always argued. It wasn't Jordan's fault; Daddy just never let up on him. He'd tried to push him toward a career that Jordan had never wanted. Jordan had always wanted to be a cop and had been extremely talented with his hands. He hadn't wanted the life Daddy had made for their family. Jordan had never had the desire to live in a different city every two years or be away from his family six months at a time. Even when he was young, Jordan had wanted a real family. He'd wanted a wife and kids, something unusual to hear from a teenage boy. And he'd always been great with her children. So it hadn't surprised Melissa when he called and said he was getting married and asked her to freshen up the house and prepare a cookout tomorrow.

She owed him big, and so did Rachael. If it weren't for Jordan, neither of them would be enjoying their current lifestyle. Jordan had started his business modestly, doing odd jobs at night and on weekends, and then larger opportunities had started pouring in, so he offered employment to both of their husbands. Next thing they knew, the three of them were building mansions on Lake Norman.

Of course, Jordan was the sole proprietor of the company, but both Bobby and Ronny did extremely well working with him. Ronny had attempted to venture out on his own, but when that failed, Jordan had welcomed him back, no hard feelings. Rachael could just get over herself. She always wanted more than she had ... was always afraid she'd mess up her perfect manicure.

It wasn't as though there was anything to clean anyway. Jordan never left junk around, always picked up after himself. More than she could say about Bobby, but Bobby was a wonderful husband. He worked hard, and when he finished, he was home with her and their children.

Melissa wondered what Jaynee would look like. Always one for surprises, Jordan had refused to divulge anything. Bobby thought she'd look like a beach bunny with long platinum hair and dark tanned skin. But that didn't sound like Jordan; he'd always preferred brunettes. She didn't care what Jaynee looked like, providing she treated her baby brother well; that was all that mattered to Melissa.

While Rachael finished vacuuming, Melissa pulled out the chocolate-chip cookies she'd baked and brewed a pot of vanilla coffee. The weather was perfect, a beautiful autumn day, so she opened the windows to allow the fragrance of the fallen leaves and cut grass to drift through the house.

After flipping on the water-heater fuse, she locked Boomer in the garage with his stuffed animal. The toy was missing both of its eyes and nose, had only three legs, and its tail was barely hanging on, but he lunged for it, happily throwing it in the air, and then proceeded to pounce on it once it landed. He loved his lion, and every year Jordan purchased him a new one for Christmas. It was a good thing Christmas was close, as Simba was looking rather ragged.

"So, tomorrow night around six," Melissa reminded Rachael as they exited the front door, locking it behind them. They all had keys to one another's houses in case any of them needed help. One big happy family, or at least Melissa had always thought so. "I'll prepare the barbecue, Mom's bringing dessert, and you'll make all the side dishes, right?"

"Sure, Sissy," Rachael grumbled. "Anything for our baby brother ..."

"Rachael, why are you always so negative?" Melissa asked, suppressing a growl. "You of all people should be thankful to Jordan for everything he's done for you and Ronny."

Rachael dropped her shoulders in surrender. "I know, and I am," she admitted. "I just think this is irresponsible of Jordan, marrying without the family knowing her, don't you agree?"

Melissa shook her head, suppressing a laugh at her sister's ridiculous comment. "When has Jordan ever done anything irresponsible? He's one of the most responsible men I know. We need to support him and make her feel welcome. Do you hear me? You need to be pleasant. Jordan deserves that." Melissa walked off, leaving Rachael standing on the porch.

***

Melissa was right, Rachael realized, but it still irritated her. Really, it was her husband who had her worried, since she knew he was incapable of supporting her current lifestyle.

Ronny had been such a bear Saturday and had been worried sick all week that this woman would change everything. She was probably after his money, Ronny had said. She'd ruin Jordan and his business ... maybe even fire his brothers.

But now that Rachael had considered his concerns, they did sound juvenile. Why had Ronny been so upset? Why was he worried? Even when they had lost almost everything, Jordan had helped them get back on their feet. He'd given Ronny his position back and an advance to catch-up on their mortgage payments.

Rachael would demonstrate southern hospitality to Jordan's bride. She could pretend to be sweet.

***

Lorraine watched from a driveway down the street as the two women left Jordan's house. She wondered what his sisters were doing, but then again, knowing Jordan, she could imagine.

She'd left work early in the pretense she was working on the reception for Jordan, but instead had decided to come here. She needed to see them when they arrived; she needed to witness with her own eyes that Jordan had really married someone else. Maybe his bride-to-be had developed cold feet and changed her mind after taking advantage of Jordan and his complimentary vacation to Vegas.

Jordan had called only once since Saturday. The conversation had lasted mere minutes, long enough to double-check that all arrangements for the reception were going smoothly and that she'd invited everyone from his precinct along with his other friends, neighbors, and associates they did regular business with.

He hadn't even inquired about their latest project. Would he allow the business to suffer because of this woman? Lorraine held a stake in the company too. When the company did well, she received her share of compensation. She couldn't afford to relinquish that part of Jordan too.

Chapter Seventeen

Jordan's vehicle was in the airport parking area, ticket on the dash. After unlocking the door with the keypad on the door, he reached under the seat and pulled out the keys. It dumbfounded Jaynee how much he could accomplish with just a few phone calls.

Who was this man? she wondered silently. Every time she thought she knew, something caused her to question her sanity of marrying so quickly. Would the love she felt for him conquer any issue that might creep up?

Evidently, it was a long drive from the airport to Jordan's home — their home. Jordan pointed out Charlotte in the distance but then headed in the opposite direction, traveling the outer loop of Charlotte's 485 beltway. The city was enormous. Jaynee could travel from one side of Pinellas County to the other in about half an hour depending on traffic, but Mecklenburg would take twice as long, and that was if a thruway crossed the county; it didn't look as if one did. The roads didn't run straight north and south and east and west as Florida's roads did. Instead, they seemed to ramble whichever direction they wanted.

They drove for forty-five minutes before Jordan exited the highway. She attempted to catalog the surrounding businesses, hoping to become familiar with the area. Jordan traveled along two more stretches of road before he finally turned onto one that had a no-outlet sign.

This had to be it. Her heart thumped loudly, nerves and excitement beating like one loud, rapid drum. The road turned to gravel, and they passed several large homes before a line of trees indicated that it was a dead-end. Jordan finally pulled into a driveway with brick pillars on each side and a white split-rail fence that seemed to go on forever.

The house was a two-story Victorian home. The front porch wrapped around the left side of the home, continuing its path around the back, separated by a small gate on the deck. A three-car attached garage was on the opposite side, and she noticed a large structure set off in the distance with four stalls.

Jaynee waited as Jordan walked around to her side of the pickup. This was really happening. She was a new bride, entering her new home ... her new life.

She bit down on her lip as he opened her door.

He held his arms out for her. "I'll install running boards this week."

Jaynee sucked in a deep breath and happily scooted into his waiting arms. "I already told you, I don't have a problem with our current arrangement."

He smiled and pulled her to his chest as he lifted her out of the truck but didn't set her down. Instead, he carried her up the front steps to an impressive entryway of solid-wood doors, approximately eight-foot tall.

Jordan unlocked the door while still carrying her, then pulled it open so he could enter sideways while kissing her as he stepped over the threshold. "Welcome home, Jaynee."

She looked around, attempting to absorb everything. He held her in what looked like a formal area with a stone fireplace off to the left. "It's amazing, Jordan!"

The room, decorated with such warm style and grace, was nothing like she'd imagined. The furniture was soft tan leather. The pictures on the wall were western motifs with ranches, horses, and sunsets over rolling hills. In the middle of the room, a coffee table held a vase overflowing with a couple dozen long-stemmed red roses, and in the air, she smelled fresh baked cookies and coffee.

Jordan continued to carry her through a short hall with a formal dining room off to the side, and at the end, an enormous kitchen with soaring maple cabinets and contrasting dark granite countertops waited. In the middle of the kitchen sat an island that would seat at least eight people. At the rear of the room, the sink was inlaid into a deep counter with a pass-through to the wraparound porch. A dinette area off the kitchen transitioned into a family room.

The entire rear portion of that room, completely enclosed with French doors, led out to the deck. Jordan set her down in the kitchen, but held his arms around her waist.

He inhaled a deep breath. "Ahh ... Melissa, she never fails to amaze me," he said, breathing in the delectable scent. "She makes delicious cookies, and I could go for coffee. How 'bout you?"

"Sure ..." Jaynee had just assumed a cleaning lady had readied the house and prepared the coffee and cookies. "Melissa ... your older sister, right? She did this?"

He dropped his arms from around her waist and walked toward the coffee pot. "Yes, I asked her for the roses and to freshen up the house, but she always goes overboard. I'm sure Rachael helped, but she probably complained the entire time." He laughed as he poured two cups of coffee, so it must not bother him.

A low groan, almost a howl, but not quite, emitted from a door off the kitchen. The strange wail sounded like the creature on Star Wars, Chewy or Chewbacca something.

Jordan set the cups on the counter, then motioned for her to join him. "Come on, Jaynee; let me introduce you to Boomer. He must be going insane about now." Jordan headed through a utility room off the kitchen that held a washer and dryer. He reached for the handle of the door on the other side of the area. "Step back, Jaynee. He'll come charging through, and it can hurt if he steps on you. He weighs about a hundred pounds."

As soon as Jordan opened the door, a brindle-colored boxer came barreling through, sliding across the tile floor. He looked like a cartoon character trying to obtain traction as he made a beeline toward Jordan, his entire body bending in what looked like an unnatural state as he wiggled and wagged his way around Jordan's feet. The sound she'd heard previously flowed freely from the beast's throat, resonating through the kitchen. Boomer moaned and yowled with delight, and then, he detected Jaynee. He charged in her direction. She thought he would jump, so she shrieked backward, but he came to a grinding halt in front of her. She bent over to ruffle his floppy ears; he was adorable. He sniffed and wiggled around her too, overjoyed to make her acquaintance, it seemed.

Jordan squatted down next to the pup and smoothed his fur under his neck. "He likes you. He's always had superior taste."

"It appears he does." She grinned and cupped the boxer under his chin, careful to avoid the bubbles forming at the sides of his mouth. "I like you too, Boomer."

Jordan stood up in front of her and rested his hands on her hips. "Would you like to see the backyard or the upstairs first?"

Jaynee peered up into his eyes. "I think maybe we should start with the backyard while it's still daylight. We may get sidetracked in the bedroom."

"Good point." He took her by the hand and led her out the patio door. Boomer followed behind them, but then darted off as soon as they stepped outside, clearing the porch steps in one leap.

Jordan led Jaynee across the expanse of the backyard then through a gate in the fence. From there, it was all downhill, literally. From the top, she could see a river below.

Jordan offered her his arm. "That's the Rocky River, and at certain times of the year it's great kayaking."

With a firm grip on Jordan's arm, she descended the knoll, careful not to slip on the red clay mashing under her sandals. When they made it to the bottom, Jaynee thrilled at the beautiful rushing water. Right outside her backyard. She never would have imagined. Beside the riverbank sat a miniature wooden cabin.

Jordan pointed to the shack. "That's our clubhouse. It contains all our kayak gear, fishing equipment, lawn chairs, and other outdoor items. I enjoy coming here when the weather's nice. It's always been my own private beach, but now it will be ours." He layered his hand over hers, and she felt a rush of warmth travel through her system.

"It's beautiful, and here I thought I was going to miss my beach," Jaynee said, silently reveling in the fact that he referred to everything as *ours*.

After they'd made their way back up the hill, Jordan approached the structure she'd seen from the driveway, which she now realized was a stable. "We don't have horses, but I've always wanted them. We can decide what we would like together. How does that sound?"

"Jordan, without a doubt you're the most incredible husband in the world. *Everything* sounds wonderful!" She wrapped her arms around his waist, but he swung her up into his arms, then twirled her around before setting her down.

The day was drawing to a close, and it was spectacular. The faint changing of the leaves and the smell of the surrounding woods was enchanting, and best of all ... it was quiet. She'd never lived anywhere so secluded from all the hustle and bustle of the city. No sirens, no construction noises, and no semi-trucks whizzed down the road. All she heard were birds singing.

"Jaynee, I have at least one more promise to keep, and I didn't know whether you would rather it be a surprise, or if you'd prefer to choose?" He stopped where they were walking and looked at her face, gauging her response. She hated him spending money on her; she'd made that clear, but he couldn't seem to stop trying to spoil her. She needed to convince him that she didn't need anything but him. She opened her mouth to protest, but he put his fingers over her mouth. "What kind of vehicle would you like?" he asked, quickly adding as her face turned down in embarrassment, "think of it as a wedding gift." He lowered his hand to her shoulder.

"Jordan, you've already given me everything —" Again, he raised his hand to her mouth, shushing her. She swatted away his hand with a laugh. "Stop that! I'm serious. I've given you nothing. You can't keep doing this."

"Well, that's not exactly accurate. You uprooted your entire life ... gave me your heart; that's a pretty big gift. You didn't throw me out as though I were a maniac. That was a good thing. And you love me for me, no pretenses. You actually fell in love with me before you knew what I had to offer other than love. But ... you need a car. You don't want to be cooped up here all day." His steel-blue eyes were intense as he gazed into her eyes, awaiting an answer.

Cooped up? Actually, this was like a vacation. *What the heck,* she thought. *I do need a vehicle.* "You know, Jordan, I've always wanted a Jeep ... a topless, off-road Jeep."

"*Okay,*" he hedged. "It's great to see you enthusiastic about something I can give you," he started walking toward the barn again, "but those are only practical for half the year here. What else? Something stylish and elegant, a Volvo, an Acura, or a Bimmer, what do you say?" He stopped and waited for her answer.

Jaynee knew one vehicle she'd always wanted but could never afford, even older. Diffidently, she said, "How about an Altima? I've always liked those."

He nodded, flashing her a bright smile. "What color?"

"Pearl!" she said in a matter-of-fact tone, grinning from ear to ear. "I like that multi-color white."

"That's better. I'll spoil you yet, Mrs. Monroe." His face beamed with pleasure at the notion. "Now, follow me ... I have something else to show you before I sweep you into the house."

Jaynee loved the sound of her new name coming off his lips, and the threat to sweep her away sent a thrill through her, heating her insides.

Jordan opened one of the stable doors, and inside wasn't a horse, but it was one of her dreams. An off-road ready CJ7 Jeep sat in the stall, topless, bright yellow, with humongous tires ... bigger than on his truck. She wondered how she'd ever climb into it. "What do you think? I've been working on it for years, but it's operational. I just tinker around with it adding accessories and such. Is it what you were thinking?"

"Oh, my God! It's exactly what I was imagining! How cool is that?" She felt exultant, like a little kid on Christmas day.

Jordan smiled at her elation. "It's not practical for everyday use, but it *is* fun on the weekends. I enjoy taking it when I go hiking, sort of starts the adventure. We can drive it next weekend; I have a special place I want to show you." His mouth turned up in her favorite smile. She was just going to have to get used to Jordan and all his surprises. At least this one didn't sound as if it would cost anything; it sounded like one of his hiking trips he'd mentioned.

Jaynee rested her hands on his chest. "Sounds awesome, Jordan. Are you going to sweep me back to the house now so I can see my new bedroom?"

"I thought you'd never ask. Maybe we should run. It'd be faster than me carrying you across the lawn and upstairs ... I may lose my strength." A wicked grin lit up his face as he reached down and grabbed her hand, sprinting across the lawn toward the house with her in tow.

Jaynee stopped about halfway to the house. "Jordan, where's my stuff? You said they packed my house?"

"It's all in the garage. We can go through everything later and get you unpacked, and I still need to bring our suitcases in from the truck. But first things first, we need to break-in our bed."

Following Jordan's lead, Jaynee kicked off her shoes at the entry and then followed him upstairs. He didn't bother giving her a tour of the second floor. Instead, he turned to the right and walked into an enormous master suite.

A king-sized sleigh bed, adorned with the same neutral gold and tan colors used throughout the house, sat center stage. The surrounding furniture, again light oak, matched the bed. And then a sitting area over to the far right side of the room contained a small loveseat and two wingback chairs. Pictures hanging on the walls were the same motif as downstairs, various outdoor scenes that lent warmth to the area.

Jaynee assumed the master bath was on the opposite side of the sitting area but didn't think she was going to get a chance to see it. Because Jordan decided right then and there that it was time to sweep her off her feet. It was so sudden it knocked the wind out of her, then his mouth was on hers, taking whatever breath she had left.

He removed his lips from hers as he swung her onto the middle of the bed, laying her down gently. She gasped at the chance for air, then proceeded to pull him down on top of her. His hands were frenzied over her body as he unbuttoned and removed her clothes.

"Welcome home, Mrs. Monroe," he whispered breathlessly. "It's so wonderful to finally have you here."

"It's good to be home, Mr. Monroe."

His mouth returned to hers, and her body arched in succession to his hands moving over her skin. She was in no mindset to wait this time while he teased her. Unbuttoning his jeans, she pushed them as low as she could with her hands. When that didn't do the trick, she used her feet to finish removing them. He helped her at the end, effectively kicking them off. She grabbed him again, pulling him down on top of her.

"Are you in a hurry, love?" he murmured into her ear, his warm breath sending a thrill through her entire being.

Oh, how he loved to tease her. She'd swear he liked foreplay more than she did. "Yes!" she blurted out. "You can take your time later; I want you now!"

Jordan obliged.

Jaynee was pretty sure a bomb must have exploded outside, not that she would have cared or noticed, but the pounding in her ears from her blood pumping and the fact that the room had literally gone black for a moment made her believe something had detonated. If not outside, certainly something had gone off inside of her body. The feelings soaring through her were so powerful, so overwhelming. Her entire body ached for more and more of him until she couldn't take any more. She finally collapsed in a heap — entirely spent — her head spinning from the sheer pleasure.

"Holy cow, Jordan." She whooshed out a breath as her body melted into the bed, feeling as though all her joints had disconnected, and she was just a pile of jelly.

"Wow yourself, Jaynee. You were like an animal. I'm out of breath, love." He fell down beside her, pulling her into an embrace. "I enjoyed it thoroughly though."

She nuzzled up to him, not ever wanting him to leave. She only had a few more days with him all to herself before they had to return to reality. They curled up together, only the sounds of their breaths filling the air; it was comforting.

He lifted her chin to look into her eyes. "Jaynee, I want you to know you're the first woman I've brought here."

She hadn't thought about it before, but now she understood his earlier comment about breaking in their bed and was pleased. Not sure how to respond, she just nodded, offering him a small smile.

He propped himself up on his arm. "A few years ago ... I was living a life I'm not proud of, but I turned my life around and haven't been with a woman since. I've thrown myself into my work to keep my mind occupied. I've dated a few women here and there, but mostly, I've just been waiting ... until I found my wife. Not that I was looking. I didn't intend to go to Florida and fall madly in love."

"Thank you for waiting for me, Jordan. I'm sure glad I was the one."

His eyes took on a solemn look. "I have a question, and I should have already asked, but I was hoping you were ... based on our conversations. I couldn't find a way to ask before ... but it's important."

"Yes ..." she asked, attempting to keep her face impassive. Last time he'd broached a subject like this, it was about children. "What is it, Jordan? You can ask me anything."

"Are you a Christian?" he blurted out.

"Oh," she whispered, understanding. "You're right; you should have asked." She was teasing him, but noticed his face grew serious, worried at once. She quickly assuaged his concern. "'Do not be unequally yoked' I think Paul said, right?"

He released the breath he was holding. "Yes, exactly. It would have been the first question my mother and grandmother asked, as they know that can cause friction in a marriage. Since you obviously are ... weren't you worried? I mean, because of your past issues with your ex."

She shook her head. "No. I prayed nightly for God to send you to me, since I obviously made lousy choices on my own."

He pulled her into an embrace. "I'll love you forever, Jaynee."

"I'll let you," she said, reaching up and kissing him, smiling so he knew she was playing ... sort of. It wasn't easy letting someone really love you. To trust another person with your heart and soul, but she'd decided she would. "I promise to love you forever too." She tapped his nose. "I would like to take a shower, wanna help?"

"Sure, but I need to get our things." He pulled her up from the bed and walked her into the master bath, taking his time to show her where everything was located. He traced patterns on her bare back as he pointed to the various closets and doors. "I'll be back in a couple of minutes." He kissed her on the lips before turning to leave.

The bathroom was just as impressive as the rest of the house. A large whirlpool tub and separate shower, large enough for two if not more, filled the majority of the area. The toilet was in a private water closet, and a double vanity spanned the entire opposite wall. Jaynee also took notice that the entire house was immaculate; nothing was out of place. She didn't think his sisters had cleaned; the house appeared as if it were always this way.

She stepped into the glassed-in shower, feeling exposed. But he'd seen and explored every inch of her body over the last few days ... and hadn't seemed displeased, so she brushed off the feelings.

Jordan strolled in a few minutes later, and the sound of his jeans hitting the floor made her smile. She didn't turn around, but waited earnestly. The door opened behind her, and in seconds, his arms enveloped her. The hot water poured over them, and she felt absolutely, totally loved.

When the hot water began to wane, they stepped out, and Jordan wrapped her in a fluffy cream-colored towel.

She found her suitcase opened on the bedroom floor and searched for the white lacy nightie she hadn't worn yet. She followed it up with a cotton robe. He liked surprises. *He can unwrap me*, she giggled to herself. She may not be able to give him a gift, but she could do her best to give all of herself, heart and soul, as he'd requested.

"Jaynee," Jordan called, stepping out of the cavernous closet dressed in comfortable-looking cotton pants and no shirt. Her heart skipped a beat; he was gorgeous. As many times as she'd seen him undressed, she couldn't get accustomed to his perfection. "We need new bedroom furniture. This isn't quite right for newlyweds. What do you think? Could you pick out something for us tomorrow?"

"Uh, sure ... but I think it looks wonderful." She didn't know how to select furniture; all she owned were hand-me-downs.

"I was thinking something from the islands ... something to bring in your Florida warmth. Dark wood with a canopy, framed images of palm trees and such." He crossed the room and stood in front of her, his hands immediately playing with the belt of her robe.

She stopped his hands. "Sounds as though you already know what you want ..." she trailed off, grinning.

"I usually do," he said, arching a brow, returning her smile. "What's underneath this?" He pushed back at the collar, exposing her shoulder.

"A surprise." She pulled away, leaving the bedroom to venture through the remaining upstairs.

Jordan followed, pointing out the room beside theirs. It was an entertainment room with built-in speakers and a flat-screen TV. The sofa was U-shaped and enormous; it would accommodate nine to ten people easily.

The next two rooms on the opposite side of the hall were identical and had nothing in them, future kids' rooms, she assumed. The final room at the end of the hallway was again massive with an entire wall of windows overlooking the backyard. It was set up as an office, but also held an elliptical machine and some type of weight training contraption. One of the top-of-the-line devices advertised on television.

He looked at her expectantly, as though waiting for her approval. "So that's it. What do you think?"

"I think it's magnificent, Jordan, but so enormous for one person. Why did you buy such an extravagant house?"

"Oh, I didn't buy it; I built it. It's the house I've always wanted." He beamed. "It has just enough room to grow."

"You built this?" She'd known that he owned a construction company, but the news shocked her. "Wow! It *is* wonderful."

"Well, I didn't do everything. I designed it and did work on it, but so did a lot of other workers at my business."

"Still ... to be able to do this ... *wow* ..." she said again, dragging out the word, truly impressed.

He wrapped his arms around her again, pleased by her acceptance. He'd meant what he'd said; he would have built her another house if she'd wanted him to.

"I'm so delighted you like it." Jordan took her hand, leading her downstairs to the kitchen. "Are you hungry? Want to order in?"

"Starving!" They hadn't eaten since that morning. She walked into the pantry and then rummaged through the fridge. "I can find something to make, though. What would you like to eat?"

"Umm ... I'm not sure ... what can you make?" he asked, an inquisitive look on his face.

"Well, I don't know what you have, but I can prepare just about darn near anything."

His eyes widened. "You can cook?"

"Of course, I can cook," she said indignantly. "I'm an excellent cook. I've worked in restaurants for the last five years, and my father was an incredible cook."

He grabbed her up in a hug. "Whoo-hoo! I was afraid to ask ... I just figured it was too good to be true; you couldn't possibly know how to cook too. Yes!"

"She's a Christian, and she can cook," she mocked, moving out from under his arms. "Maybe your mother won't give you a hard time." He looked embarrassed. She couldn't help but laugh at his assumption. Typical man ... the only thing better than a pretty woman was a woman who could cook.

He leaned back against the island, watching every step she took, as if intrigued by her very steps. "It wouldn't matter if she did."

She rummaged through the freezer, finding some frozen chicken patties. In the pantry, she pulled out a box of pasta and jarred spaghetti sauce. It wouldn't be as tasty as homemade chicken Parmesan, but it would work in a fix. "You didn't leave me much in the way of fresh ingredients, but I can throw something together. Just remember it's not homemade. I'll do better, I promise. We'll go shopping tomorrow for food too. Okay?"

He wrapped his arms around her, kissing the side of her neck. "I love you, Jaynee." She saw a light glaze in his eyes, but ignored it, not wanting to embarrass him.

"Go sit down, Jordan. This will take all of fifteen minutes." She shoved him off with a kiss on the cheek and a slap on his cute butt.

A wide smile lifted his face. "Then after dinner, I get my surprise?"

"Yes," she agreed, satisfied with this simple gift she could offer. He liked surprises, and she *could* cook. She would do everything possible to make him happy so he wouldn't toss her aside as everyone else had done her entire life.

Chapter Eighteen

Jaynee felt warm lips on her head. She opened her eyes, immediately darting her gaze to the clock. "Six forty-five," she groaned.

She never woke up before seven ... usually not even before eight. Years in the restaurant business had made her a late riser. And after staying in Vegas for five days, it felt like the middle of the night.

Jordan brushed the hair off her face and kissed her again. "Come on, sleepyhead, we have to be out of the house by eight-fifteen."

She rolled over and resituated herself. "I can get ready in half an hour." She did the mental math. "Wake me at seven forty-five."

Not thwarted by her protest, he scooted up behind her. "That gives us an hour. Are you sure I can't persuade you to wake up now?" He nuzzled his face into her neck and pulled the blanket off her waist. It didn't cover much of her anyway; she only covered her midriff when she slept. Otherwise, she felt claustrophobic.

His hands made their slow way over her hips and ended up latched around her, pulling her against his body.

She sighed in acquiescence, forgiving him promptly for waking her so early.

Their first stop of the day was a Nissan dealership on Independence Boulevard. Jaynee watched as Jordan strolled by the salesmen lurking around the front door, heading directly to the receptionist.

Within minutes, they were seated and signing papers. The salesman, Keith, escorted them around the building, showing them their new car, pointing out options and describing in detail the aspects of the new Altima.

Jordan stepped back and gestured to Jaynee. "Don't tell me; it's her car."

"I'm sorry," Keith apologized, starting over, paying attention to her.

After the salesman had finished his presentation, Jordan pulled him to the side. "Just deliver the car to the address on the paperwork." He took her arm and started to walk away.

"Uh, sir." Keith ran up behind them. "Um, I have to check with my manager."

Jordan gave him a stern nod. "Go ahead."

Jaynee watched the exchange in reverence. Jordan was like a different person when he put on his — she assumed — cop persona. He stood perfectly still while he waited for the salesman to process his request.

The salesman left them for a few minutes and then returned with a smile. "Whenever you would like it, sir," he offered, seemingly embarrassed he'd even had to ask.

Jordan's mouth lifted on one side. He loved getting his way. "Today, whenever, just drop it off at our home address and leave the keys inside. It'll be fine." And with that, Jordan directed her from the dealership and helped her into his truck.

"Do you like it?" he asked, after he climbed in and started the truck.

She nodded, but furrowed her brows. "Of course, but how ..." she trailed off, not surprised. He seemed to conduct business quite well over the phone and via his laptop.

"I have a woman named J.T. She locates all my commercial vehicles. She does all the footwork. All I do is sign. I never even have to go to the dealership; she brings them to my business. This was a special occasion, though." He turned the radio on but kept the volume low. "So, it's what you wanted?"

"It's perfect." Jaynee narrowed her eyes at him as a thought occurred to her. "So, what does the J.T. stand for?"

"I never asked," he replied without hesitation.

"Really?" She found that hard to accept. "Is she not attractive?"

He shrugged. "I suppose so, never thought about her that way. She's married."

"I just assumed since the way you bugged me about calling myself C.J., not accepting no for an answer until I admitted my entire name —"

He interrupted her with a boisterous laugh. "Oh, is that what you're getting at?" Her comment obviously caught him off guard. "Jaynee, your name had nothing to do with my persistence. I just wanted an excuse to talk to you, and to be quite honest, know everything about you, including why you called yourself C.J." He tore his eyes off the road for a quick glance at her, seemingly amused. "You're so silly. If I didn't know better, I'd think you're jealous of someone you've never met."

"I guess when you said, 'you have a woman,' well, I suppose I am," she retorted, serious.

He reached for her hand. "You don't have to be, love. There's no way any other woman will ever catch my eye. It's not possible. You've changed me completely from the moment we met. It was the same with my father and my grandfather." He curled his hand around hers, bringing it to his lips. "So, it's your dream car?" he asked, changing the subject.

"Yes, I love it! I can't wait to drive it. But, I prefer being with you than driving alone."

He smiled, seeming to appreciate her honesty.

Their next stop was a furniture store. It was as if Jordan already knew what he'd described would be there. They found the bedroom set he'd envisioned; though, he made her feel as if she'd discovered it. It was perfect. She could feel the island breezes already. He ordered the complete set, which they agreed to deliver by tomorrow. Again, part of his persuasion and the fact he must be a regular customer.

Their last stop was Harris Teeter. It was strange, grocery shopping together. It made their impromptu marriage suddenly authentic. Jaynee made her way down every aisle as she'd always done at home, the way her grandmother had taught her. Jordan continually checked the time on his phone, as if he were in a hurry. He probably only came into a grocery store on the rare occasion he was going to cook, and even then just for that night.

When they hit the third aisle and he sighed, she smiled up at him. "Are you in a hurry, Mr. Monroe?"

"I'm always in a hurry, but right now, I just want to make sure we're home before the family arrives."

She kept her expression blank; she'd almost forgotten about the cookout. "I thought country boys were supposed to be laid back. We have plenty of time," she glanced at her phone, "it's only one o'clock. If you want to eat, I need groceries." Then a thought occurred to her. "What do we need for tonight?"

"Nothing but drinks. My sisters are taking care of everything ... their gift to us. And I told you ... I'm not your typical country boy." He grinned and made an effort to throw something in the cart.

"I'll hurry," she assured him.

She grabbed a few of her favorite staples, then headed to the produce section to select fresh salad fixings. She mostly bought frozen vegetables, her favorite other than planting her own like Gram always had. She'd have to try her luck at a garden now that she was in a real home. She sighed in contentment at the thought.

Jordan looked down, touching her arm. "Is everything okay?" he asked. "I'm not in a hurry really, just impatient, but I'm better now ... this *is* kinda fun." He'd grabbed a few items he liked.

"That was good sighing, Jordan ... this *is* fun." She gestured her hand indicating the two of them. "I was picturing a garden, if you can imagine. A week ago, I had no idea I wanted to be married. Now I'm daydreaming of gardens. Who would have thought?"

He wrapped his arm around her waist, pulling her closer. "Me." Then he looked at her and winked. "I'll eventually learn your sounds, Jaynee. I'm very good at reading people. Cop, remember?"

"How could I forget? You always look as if you're on the lookout for some threat." She sighed again to keep him guessing and then walked toward the checkout.

They headed back to the house, about a thirty-five minute drive. Living in Stanfield would take some adjusting. She was accustomed to everything being five to ten minutes away from her home in Florida.

Jaynee put everything away, then darted upstairs to freshen up before her in-laws arrived.

Jordan walked up a few minutes later, carrying her personal boxes from Florida. "It's a beautiful night, so I'm going to prepare the backyard for company. Dinners always seem less formal outside, don't you think?"

She nodded, feeling relieved he wanted to make her comfortable. After all, he couldn't be nervous; they were his family and were evidently familiar with his history of making quick-second decisions in life-altering situations, according to him.

She unpacked all her clothes, but unfortunately, the movers must have missed some items. She'd known the exact sundress she'd wanted to wear ... now she had no idea what would look good. Everything Jordan had bought for her felt too dressy.

Frustrated, she decided a shower would help her relax, and she could do her hair and makeup from scratch so that she'd look refreshed.

Thirty minutes later, she was just staring at her face in the mirror, debating on which color shadow to use.

"Are you okay, Jaynee?" Jordan whispered as he walked into the bathroom.

She jumped for no reason; he hadn't even spoken loud.

She attempted a smile. "Yes, I'm just trying to look presentable."

"You're undeniably the most beautiful woman I've ever seen, and I know my family is going to love you as much as I do." He wrapped his arms around her and stared at her in the mirror. "But I'd like it if you could be downstairs before they arrive."

"I won't be long," she insisted.

He kissed her neck and turned to leave.

"Oh, by the way ... Jordan?" He looked back in her direction. "Did you unpack all my stuff?"

"Yeah ... all the boxes marked clothes, bedroom, and bath. Why?"

"I'm missing bits and pieces of clothes and stuff, and I knew exactly what outfit I wanted to wear."

"I'll look again, and if not, I'll call the movers in the morning to check if they left anything behind." He paused at the door. "Please hurry, Jaynee."

She sighed. "I won't be late. I promise."

Jaynee chose neutral colors, nothing flashy. She'd wear jeans and a long-sleeved t-shirt, similar to what Jordan was wearing.

She decided to style her hair. She had thick, unruly hair that could be curled or straightened, but it needed to be one or the other. She opted for straight, no reason to look wild. She followed the hairdryer with a flatiron; she wanted it to be impeccably straight and shiny tonight. Maybe it wouldn't curl up as it did in the Florida humidity.

She took one last look at herself. She didn't see what Jordan saw, but she'd always thought she looked good enough.

It was a quarter to six when she started downstairs. The scent of charcoal wafted through the house; it smelled homey, like all the cookouts at her uncle's house growing up. She'd always envied their family. She loved her cousins, but it wasn't the same as having siblings. Though she loved them, she never felt as if she'd belonged.

Jordan sprinted from the sofa to meet her at the bottom of the stairs. He looked up at her. "You look sensational. How is it possible you look better every time I see you?"

Feeling the warmth spread across her cheeks, she smiled. "I think you're biased."

"I don't think so." He stopped her two steps from the landing, kissing her and then pulling back to look at her. "I'm not sure this was a good idea. I don't think I want to share you tonight or any other night for that matter. Your eyes are incredible, do you know that?" He smoothed his palms down her hair. "And your hair, it's beautiful. I like it the other way, but this is different. It's so soft." He abruptly exhaled. "Oh well, too late, I hear my mom. I knew she'd be the first to arrive and early as always. Let's go, Mrs. Monroe."

He afforded her one more kiss, then lifted her by her waist and set her on the floor. She realized she'd been holding her breath; she hadn't even responded to his comments.

"Thank you, Jordan." She looked up at him. "For everything."

He squeezed her hand and opened the front door, leading her out to the porch to greet his family.

She inhaled a deep breath. Everything would be fine. What's the worst that could happen? It wasn't as if any of them would try to kill her.

Chapter Nineteen

Her mother-in-law had just stepped out of the car and was already walking around to the passenger side of her Crown Victoria to help Jordan's grandmother when Jaynee followed Jordan outside.

Jordan kissed her on the cheek. "Wait here." He darted down the steps to assist his grandmother before his mother could. Jaynee waited, feeling self-conscious, not knowing what to do or say. Pat ascended the porch in quick steps while Jordan took them slowly, assisting his grandmother.

As Pat approached, Jaynee saw her eyes turn glassy. She held out her arms as she approached Jaynee, "Oh, my Lord, honey," she exclaimed, embracing Jaynee in an unyielding squeeze. "You're gorgeous." She leaned back and inspected Jaynee thoughtfully. "Jordan, you could have told us you married a supermodel." Her southern drawl was stronger than Jordan's. Her words were slow, and each one had an inflection as though uttered in deep meaning.

Jaynee blushed, lowering her head. She could never be confused with a supermodel.

"Mom ..." Jordan complained. "You're embarrassing her." He took Jaynee's hand. "Mom, this is Jaynee. Jaynee — Pat Monroe."

"Oh, dear, please call me Mom ... if you're comfortable, that is."

Jaynee smiled shyly, still embarrassed. "It's nice to meet you." Could she call her *Mom?* She struggled for years to call her own mother *Mom.* Usually she didn't call her anything and just spoke directly to her, but she already felt an attraction to this wonderful woman. "Mom sounds nice; I'd like that."

Pat turned to Jordan and slapped his arm, but then wrapped her arms around his waist, pulling him into a tight hug. "You *could* have warned us, Jordan."

Jaynee wasn't sure if she was referring to the fact he planned to get married or her looks again ... maybe both.

Jordan stepped back toward his grandmother. "And this is Velma — everyone calls her Nanna, though." Velma was more reserved than Pat, but she shot Jordan an enthusiastic grin as if they shared a secret, probably this mysterious myth they called the *thunderbolt.*

Jaynee instantly liked both women and hoped the feelings would continue to the rest of the family.

Jordan escorted the ladies to the backyard, and Jaynee offered them something to drink. They both requested sweet tea. Luckily, Jordan had bought two gallons. Apparently, she was going to have to learn how to make the southern staple; she'd only made it in gigantic containers before and even then just followed instructions. She'd never been a tea drinker herself, couldn't stand the stuff. Diet coke and coffee had always been her poison. She wondered if Jordan wanted a beer. He hadn't drunk anything the entire week they were together except a few sips of champagne. Even the bartender where she'd worked had said that he'd ordered several beers, yet only drank a few sips of each, but he'd picked up a six-pack at the store.

Jaynee carried two glasses of iced tea to the ladies, then turned to Jordan. "Jordan, did you want a beer?"

Jordan's eyes shot up from the coals he was turning; he looked mystified by her question. His mother and grandmother looked to Jaynee and then to Jordan, their faces puzzled.

"No, darlin'," he said, composing his face. "The beer is for Ronny. I don't drink."

Her heart thundered in her chest. "Oh, I'm sorry ... I ... I don't know what to say." She struggled to compose herself. Mortification overtook her, and she thought she'd have a nervous breakdown. How childish she was behaving; she was overreacting. But when she'd seen the look on their faces, she'd panicked. Not wanting to create a scene, she turned to leave, hurrying to the kitchen to escape her gaffe. Why would they have reacted that way? She'd definitely have to ask him about it later.

Jordan caught up with her and shadowed her into the house. "Jaynee, it's okay." He smoothed her arms. "It's no big deal. I just don't drink," he whispered, nibbling on her ear in the process. "Not much anyway. Please *relax*, darlin'."

Now she really felt stupid. She needed to hide for a second to settle herself. "Tea then?" she asked, as if she didn't feel like crawling under the house. They probably thought she was stupid ... marrying a man she barely knew. Maybe they were right.

"That would be wonderful." She turned to walk away, but he grabbed her waist and followed her to the kitchen. "Jaynee ... *really* ... it's okay. My family, or at least most of them, doesn't drink. I'll explain later, but *please* don't be upset."

She let out a deep breath. "I feel stupid, Jordan. I should've known this already. I'm afraid they'll think I'm crazy, because I don't know you."

"No one thinks you're stupid *or* crazy; they know we just met. But you know something?" He tilted her head up, gazing into her eyes. "If anyone understands, it's those two women outside. They both married their husbands within weeks of meeting them. So think of this as a warm-up, okay?" He pressed his hand against her cheek.

She leaned into it, instantly comforted.

"The rest of the family will arrive in a few minutes. Are you okay?" he asked, smiling warmly.

"Yes," she said, still apprehensive. "I'm sorry. I'll be careful before blurting out things in the future."

"Don't be sorry, Jaynee; you didn't do anything wrong. Besides, I love you, and I don't think you're crazy. Isn't that all that matters?" She gave him a slow nod, and he kissed her forehead. "I just hope you're better, though, 'cause here comes Bobby, and he's obnoxious. But Melissa is the best … you'll love her."

She smiled and hugged him, then released him. She could pull herself together. She would for Jordan.

They walked together to answer the door, as a couple. His sister and brother-in-law were already making their way toward them.

Bobby was huge, at least six-foot-five, she guessed, knowing Jordan stood about six-foot, and the man probably weighed close to three hundred pounds. But she couldn't see any fat; he just looked like a giant bear. And all of a sudden, that bear grabbed her and swung her around. "We're so excited to meet you, Jaynee." Bobby's voice was ecstatic; he sounded sincere.

A woman almost as tall as Jordan grabbed Bobby by the arms and shoved him back. "Robert Brooks, put her down! You're gonna scare her half to death." She turned sympathetic eyes that mirrored Jordan's on her. "Sorry, Jaynee, he's very enthusiastic about you and Jordan. I've heard nothing but this since Saturday when Jordan called. I'm Melissa, but you can call me Sissy, everyone else does. And I'm happy to meet you too." Melissa gave her a warm hug that felt natural.

Jaynee hugged her back. "Hi, Sissy, it's good to meet you too. And thanks for the cookies and roses, everything."

Jordan lifted Jaynee's hand, squeezing it lightly. His eyes gave away the thrill he felt at the two of them getting along straight away.

Two beautiful children followed the couple, dashing straight into Jordan's arms calling, "Uncle Jordan" in unison. Jaynee saw the smile on Jordan's face and felt her own face lift in direct response to his delight. His affection for his niece and nephew was evident in the hugs and kisses he showered on them. Other than a little difference in height, the children could be twins. She guessed they were at most four and five and a half. And it was clear the little boy and girl returned his sentiments, since they hadn't let go of him.

Bobby knocked Jordan on the back with a hand that resembled a bear paw; the man was enormous. "C'mon, Jordan," Bobby belted out. "We got tons of food. Let the women folk get to yapping." Jordan followed obediently to his older brother-in-law's words, while Jaynee felt Melissa's hand circle around hers, drawing her toward the kitchen.

"I know tonight is not the best time," Melissa whispered. "But, you have to tell me everything. I'm so excited. I was afraid Jordan would never find someone. He was so sure of this enchantment that the Monroe men supposedly shared ... that it would happen eventually. I believe he wouldn't date a woman more than a couple of times to even give her an opportunity. Not to say that he's dated a lot, because he hasn't ... but he's always known that he hadn't met the *right* woman."

When Sissy finally took a breath, Jaynee stared at her incredulously before speaking. "He was waiting for me ... or rather for this to happen? Is that why no one is surprised at our marrying immediately?"

Melissa smiled so widely that Jaynee could barely see her eyes. "Well, that's not the only reason. Jordan has always been very — how should I say it — intelligent at making the right choices. He makes decisions quickly, but they are always correct." Melissa immediately started busying herself about the kitchen. "I'm sorry, Jaynee. I'm talking too much, and we have oodles of time for this later. Besides, here come the men with the food."

Bobby and Jordan unloaded two massive pans of ribs and chicken onto the kitchen island. The kids carried in containers of what looked like desserts.

Jaynee heard the door open again. Clearly, no one used a doorbell around here. It felt good, though; it reminded her of her uncle's house again. How everyone always came and went as they pleased. She wondered how long before she felt like part of the family. Maybe she could institute her own tradition, like Sunday brunches.

"Oh my goodness, Jordan," a squeal came from the doorway. Judging by the similar features, this had to be Rachael; all the Monroes' eyes were identical. The new woman rushed over to Jaynee, wrapping her arms around her as she patted her on the back and then leaned back to take a good look at her, right down to her toes. "You're absolutely adorable. Nothin' like Ronny and Bobby suggested."

Jordan glowered at his partners. "I never told them what she looked like; it was none of their business." But he said the words with a grin, letting them off.

Rachael pursed her lips. "Well, they fabricated their own ideas. Glad to see they didn't do you justice, honey. By the way ... love your pedicure. We'll have to go to the spa together someday ... what d'ya say?"

Try as she may, Jaynee couldn't gather the appropriate enthusiasm for her new sister-in-law. The hug that Rachael had given her hadn't felt as authentic as the embraces she'd received from Pat and Melissa. She smiled, but it felt shallow, so she was sure Rachael would sense it too. "That would be great. Though ... honestly ... I don't go often. It was a gift from Jordan."

Rachael winked at her brother, then raised an eyebrow. "You paid attention, little brother — for once. Good job." Her tone was smug.

A tall and thin, but extremely good-looking, man stepped in front of Jaynee. "Hi, I'm Ronny." He held out his hand. Jaynee took it awkwardly. It felt uncomfortable after the over-the-top welcoming from the rest of her new family.

Rachael snapped her fingers. "Ronny, get the kids to help you with all that food. Cody, Courtney, help your uncle."

Jordan stepped around the island, nudging Jaynee back into the laundry room, lowering his head to her ear. "A few hours, we'll be alone again." He kissed her on the neck then pulled back to absorb her appearance.

"Jordan, I'm fine. They're wonderful."

His face was skeptical. "I know you're lying, but thank you anyway."

She felt her defenses flare up at his remark. "I wouldn't lie. I do like them. It'll take a while to get comfortable with everyone, but they are very ... welcoming."

"Thank you," he said, kissing her again, this time on the mouth. His lips were soft and inviting; she almost forgot they had a houseful of people.

A deep clearing of a throat interrupted them.

"Go away, Bobby," Jordan hissed.

"Okay, if that's what you want," he said slyly. "I'm entirely capable of burning the ribs myself." He laughed and walked away whistling.

Jordan afforded Jaynee one more peck under her jaw, then charged after Bobby and the food. "Wait right there. You can't be trusted with grilling. I'm the master griller."

Jaynee entered the kitchen feeling embarrassed, but the glow on Melissa's face comforted her. She really was happy to see her brother married. Previously nervous, she now reveled in the emotions, as though she were already part of the family. At least with Pat and Melissa. She was sure Rachael and she would become friends, but couldn't suppress the feeling that Rachael wasn't completely genuine. "So, where do we begin? I'm sure you both know your way around the kitchen better than I do," Jaynee said, an anxious chuckle escaping.

Melissa reached in the kitchen drawer for utensils. "Most everything is hot, but why don't you put the oven on three-fifty, and we'll throw the food in there to keep warm?"

Rachael pulled the dishes out of the cooler — or warmer in this case — and set them on the island. Jaynee turned the

oven to three-fifty as instructed, and Melissa went to the
cupboards to get all the items she needed. Jaynee knew
where the glasses were, so she pulled out enough for the
remaining family who didn't have beverages.

"Do you both drink sweet tea?" Jaynee asked politely.

"Yes, for me and Bobby," Melissa responded.

"Diet Coke for me," Rachael offered. "And I'm sure
there's a Bud Light or two in there for Ronny."

Jaynee fixed the drinks and then delivered Bobby's and
Ronny's outside. A chance to move around the house felt
good; she wasn't ready to leap into a conversation with
either woman. Plus she figured as a good hostess she
should check on her new mother-in-law and grandmother.

Handing both gentlemen their drinks, Jaynee caught
Jordan's eye as he was turning the chicken. He was grinning
from ear to ear, and she couldn't help but wonder if she'd
missed a joke or if he was just that happy.

Both men thanked her, Bobby more ardently with a
"Thank you, darlin'!" What was it about southern men?
Why couldn't they just use a woman's name? She was
familiar with it from strangers in restaurants, and obviously
she didn't mind when Jordan used endearments. But it
sounded strange coming from Bobby, since she barely
knew him.

Jaynee turned toward Pat and Velma, but saw Jordan
punch Bobby out of the corner of her eye.

Bobby winced. "What?"

"Mine," Jordan hissed.

So, he didn't appreciate the *darling* comment either, or
maybe she'd heard wrong. Jordan certainly wasn't jealous of
his brother-in-law. He didn't seem like the jealous type, not
that she'd noticed.

Unable to verbalize the words *Mom* or *Pat*, Jaynee opted just to begin speaking as she approached the women. "Would you like more sweet tea?"

"No, honey, sit down and relax." Pat tapped the seat beside her. "The girls'll take care of everything. This is your wedding party after all; well, one of them anyway." She grinned conspiratorially.

Her new mother-in-law really was laid back. Jaynee wouldn't feel comfortable just sitting, but she sat down for a few minutes. Pat asked her simple things such as where she was born, siblings, parents ... her religious beliefs — all the normal first-time-you-meet-someone questions. They were all easy, non-threatening queries, but Jaynee was still relieved when Jordan called out, "Five minutes."

She excused herself to assist her new sisters.

When Jaynee stepped inside, everything was ready. Melissa and Rachael had obviously heard Jordan and already placed everything on the island.

Melissa looked up as Jaynee approached. "If it's okay, Jaynee, we put everything on the island and let everyone help themselves."

Jaynee couldn't believe she'd asked her if it was all right. She really did like Melissa. "That sounds like a great system. How often does the family get together?"

Rachael adjusted all the serving dishes so they lined up perfectly. "Usually once a month. If there's a birthday or holiday, we celebrate them all at once."

"That sounds wonderful." And Jaynee meant it. It should have sounded like work, but it didn't. It sounded like a family, a family she'd always coveted. "I think I'll enjoy that," she added thoughtfully.

The men walked inside at that moment carrying the grilled meat. "Enjoy what?" Jordan asked.

"We were just discussing our monthly cookouts ... which haven't felt too monthly lately," Melissa reminded him with a frown.

"You're right, Sis, we need to initiate them again," Jordan agreed, glancing in Jaynee's direction, confirming she approved of his assertion. She appreciated the thought and smiled, nodding in assent. "Well, dig in everyone. Cody, Court, you first." The two children had appeared from the living room where they'd been watching TV.

Jaynee stood and watched as everyone filled their plates and headed to the deck. There was such an understanding in this family, a peace in the way no one got in anyone's way or tried to be the center of attention; they all seemed to move in harmony.

When everyone was at the table, Pat looked up at Jordan. "Jordan, why don't you do the honors, honey?"

Without a moment's hesitation, Jordan broke into a beautiful prayer thanking God for all they had; family, food, health, his new wife, then ended the prayer in Jesus' name.

She'd seen him bow his head several times, but this was the first time she'd heard him pray aloud. It was beautiful. And he'd been right about his mother ... one of her queries had been if she was a Christian. She wondered if her mother-in-law would have gotten up and walked out right then, or if she would have tried to convert her. She giggled at the thought, thinking about how her grandfather would have. He was very religious.

The evening flashed by. It wasn't even ten and everyone began offering their good-byes. Jaynee wondered if that was usual or just their subtle way of giving them alone time. Pat and Velma, along with her new sisters, hugged her, and her new niece and nephew latched onto her legs. "Good night,

Aunt Jaynee," they said in unison, as they'd done with Jordan at the beginning of the evening.

The name took her by surprise; she didn't have siblings, so she'd never contemplated becoming an aunt. But as the idea blossomed, she found herself beaming.

Jaynee bent down and rubbed both of their heads. "Good night, guys."

Courtney bounced off, her tendrils flowing down her back, and Cody looked up at her with blazing red cheeks, then scurried after his sister.

"We'll see you tomorrow," Jordan called after the group.

Of course, Jaynee had already forgotten the reception tomorrow. That's why they hadn't stayed late. They stood on the porch, waving goodbye, Jordan's arm wrapped around her waist.

Jaynee watched the final vehicle drive away and then glanced up at Jordan. "They're all going to be there tomorrow?"

"Uh-huh," he said in his slow southern drawl, but there was something anomalous in his all-too-casual reply.

"That'll be nice ... knowing someone there."

"That was sort of the idea." A long pause elapsed as he pulled her closer, and then his eyes took on a look she recognized. "Now, what do you say we go practice making a motor for a tricycle?"

"A motor for a tricycle?" she burst out, understanding the gist of his comment. "As in a baby?" She laughed again, this time nervously, feeling a little apprehensive at his request. She'd thought she'd made it clear she wasn't ready.

He shrugged. "It was something my father always said. Thought he was being clever, I suppose, so when we were kids we wouldn't understand. I did say practice, though; I remember what you said..." His eyes held hers a fraction longer than necessary as if she may rethink her resolution.

"Let's go practice," she teased, but something gnawed at her. She needed to know why he and his mother reacted the way they had when she'd asked Jordan if he wanted a beer.

Chapter Twenty

Brushing their teeth as a couple in his-and-hers sinks felt bizarre. Had it only been a week ago she was about to brush her teeth and had said he was the man she was going to marry, and now she was standing in his master bath as his wife?

It felt like forever that they'd been together, as if she knew everything about the man standing beside her. Then, in other respects, he was a total stranger.

When they finished, Jordan approached her, wrapping his arms around her waist. "You were wonderful tonight, Jaynee. I'm at home and completely content now that you're here, but I was just thinking how strange it must be for you."

"It wasn't as difficult as I'd anticipated. I feel comfortable with your family. For the first time in my life, I feel as if I belong."

"That's because you do; you belong to me, and somehow it feels as though you always have."

Jaynee winced slightly at his words. But why should she? The way he'd said them, they didn't sound possessive. They sounded perfect. As though they did belong together, forever. She liked the idea of belonging to him, and the fact that meant that he belonged to her too.

She took his hand and led him to their bedroom. "I do have one question, though." Jaynee sat on the edge of the bed, pulling him down beside her. "Earlier tonight, when I asked if you wanted a beer, the look on your mother's face and your comment caught me off guard. I was wondering why you reacted that way?"

"Well, I guess it's only fair," he said, his face taking on a grave expression. "You shared your demons. It's only proper I share mine. My mother reacted that way because I promised her I'd never drink ... because of something that happened between my dad and me ..." He pulled her back deeper into the bed so they were against the headboard.

He took a deep breath. "My dad wanted me to enter the military, but I didn't want any part of that lifestyle. As a child, I hated moving every couple of years, never being able to establish lasting friendships. Only when I stayed with my grandparents here in North Carolina did I feel at home.

"As a teenager, I decided on a career in law enforcement, but knew I needed a degree to advance. So after high school, I enrolled at the University of Charlotte but lost focus. I started hanging out late, drinking and partying, standard college-kid foolishness. I managed to uphold my grades, but my father was furious, said I was throwing my life away, that I would never amount to anything."

Jordan took a breath. He glanced at her once, then stared at the wall. Jaynee wondered what he could have possibly done that would upset him so. Was there something he hadn't told her about his past? She'd always wondered why Jordan hadn't mentioned his father.

He finally just shook his head as if deciding it didn't matter. "I know he didn't mean it. He was just old school, but at the time, it seemed nothing I did pleased him. Then I came home late one night after drinking too much. If I drink excessively, I get feisty or frisky —" He stopped abruptly, turned to look at her, and placed both hands on her face. "Not that I have ever hurt anyone — well, no one who didn't deserve it anyway. But I would never hurt you, Jaynee. I'd never hurt any woman."

Unable to speak, she nodded her belief. But she wanted to hear the rest of what he had to say before she spoke.

His hands fell back to his side. "Anyway, as I said, I was extremely drunk, and my friend, John, had just dropped me off at the end of my driveway.

"My father — a God-fearing, passionate American, who'd raised his family to have upright morals and serve his fellow mankind — was standing on the porch when I stumbled up the front stoop. At that moment, I was an affront to everything he represented. All he saw was how I was wasting my life. When I tried to pass him, he pushed me off the steps and started yelling, infuriated by my actions. He thought every man should enlist. Not only to serve his country, but also to become a better individual. And according to my father, I was mocking the lifestyle he'd chosen.

"With great effort, I stood upright, brushed off the dirt, and attempted to walk around him. He grabbed me again. The second time, though, my instincts took over and I knocked *him* down. I sobered up immediately when my mother rushed toward us, but it was too late. I'd raised my hand against my father and in front of my mother no less.

"My father was tough, though. He scrambled to his feet, undeterred by my actions. Not trusting myself, I ran off. I listened to his insults, how I'd never amount to anything, and it strung a chord. I'd never wanted to disappoint my father.

"So the next day, I did the one thing I thought my father would consider a worthy accomplishment. In the vain hope of my father's acceptance and escaping him at the same time, I enlisted in the Army.

"I'd like to think we made amends over the next several years when I came home, but we never did completely. And then when my tour was up, Dad was dying, so I came home instead of re-enlisting. He died within months of my return.

"While I was in the military, I continued to drink, got in fights, and lived a life I was ashamed of." He sighed. "I don't know what was wrong with me. I was mad at God, mad at my father, mad at everyone. I didn't want anyone to tell me how to live. But the only thing that happened by living by my rules was that I almost got kicked out and would wake up feeling worthless.

"Since leaving the service, though, I quit drinking, roughhousing, and sleeping around. I promised my father I'd take care of my mother and sisters. And my mother ... though she says she knows everything wasn't my fault, she'd go ballistic if she ever saw me drink again. So, for her, I don't." Jordan turned to Jaynee and rested his hands on both sides of her face. "But honestly, Jaynee, I don't want you to assume I'm an alcoholic who goes off binge drinking and hurts the people he loves. I was just an ignorant kid."

Jaynee could see the pain in Jordan's eyes as he tried to assure her. "Jordan, I don't think that. You *were* a kid, and I've seen you drink ... even my bartender commented on how you took just a few sips then pushed it away; alcoholics don't do that. I'm not worried." She exhaled in relief. Almost giddy that that was the worst thing he'd thought he'd done. If he only knew *all* the things she'd witnessed her ex-boyfriend do. The drinking, the drugs, the fights ... and plenty of sleeping around. And of course, once she left him, he'd ended up in jail for armed robbery.

"I'd never hurt you, Jaynee; you're everything to me." He pulled her closer, holding her to his chest.

He made no attempt at making love, just held her close. Jaynee felt herself melt into his arms.

***

Jordan watched as Jaynee's eyes fluttered open. He loved watching her wake every morning, even if it meant staying in bed longer than he usually would have.

He brushed the hair back from her face so he could kiss her forehead. "Good morning, sleeping beauty."

How he loved looking into her eyes. He hated that in a couple of days he'd have to return to work, which meant getting out of bed before she woke up. He doubted she would want to wake at four in the morning. Who would?

He'd kept his hands to himself last night and this morning. He wanted to wait until this evening. Tonight would be special, he decided, like their wedding night all over again. He would enjoy the anticipation.

"Did you sleep well?" he asked.

She cleared her throat. "Of course, how could I not with you protecting me? Do you ever sleep?"

"Yes, but I enjoy watching you. You're so peaceful. Sometimes I can't even hear you breathe. I find myself holding my breath, listening for your breaths like a new parent. You must have been exhausted. One minute we were talking and the next I felt you go limp in my arms."

"I was," she admitted. "I guess the unwarranted stress I put on myself at the prospect of meeting your family wore me out. But I feel wide awake this morning; we never did get to practice." She moved her hands over his chest.

"No, we didn't, but we have tonight," he said casually, ignoring her innuendo.

"Oh ... okay ..." Dejection saturated her voice.

He tilted her head up at her distressed tone. "Jaynee ... I was merely suggesting if we waited until tonight ... after the reception ... it would be like our wedding night all over again. You don't think ... You couldn't possibly believe for a second I don't want you this very minute, could you?"

She laughed with relief. "Oh ..." She shook her head. "No, that makes sense. I understand ... anticipation, right?"

"Exactly ... but, if you *want* me to attack you, it wouldn't take much to convince me. We are married after all. I just figured since you fell asleep last night, we'd just wait. Anticipation sounds like fun ..." he trailed off, nuzzling her neck. "'Course, I could see if I could drive us both crazy with anticipation," he murmured.

***

Jaynee shivered as goosebumps traveled over her body. She could hear the smile in his voice. She knew he could stop; he'd stopped on several occasions.

She rolled over and adjusted the pillow and blanket as if she were going to get out of bed. "No ... no sense in tempting ourselves." She waited as the bait took hold, a couple of seconds, she assumed. She wanted to maintain a modicum of control. Within seconds, he pressed his body against hers.

"Where do you think you're running off to, Missy?" Jordan's voice was demanding, but playful.

"But, you said ..." He needed to swallow the entire bait, not just nibble around the edges.

"Forget what I said, maybe I still want to fool around."

Hook, line, and sinker, as her father used to say. Now, what was she going to do with her catch?

She turned over in his arms. "You're right, Jordan, it'll be good to wait. I'm actually looking forward to this evening." She buried her head under his chin.

"Really?" he mused, chuckling lightly, as if to a private joke.

"Yes, really. Your family is wonderful, and I'm sure your friends are great." She looked up at him. "By the way, what are we wearing?"

"Your wedding dress, naturally," he said, grinning.

He replied with such vehemence she didn't think there was a chance at arguing, but she did anyway. "Jordan ... won't that be awkward. Everyone knows we're already married."

"Not everyone, just the family. But even still, they wanted to experience all the traditions. Trust me; it'll be fun. Everyone knows it's formal; we won't be the only ones dressed up."

They rolled out of bed a little while later after cuddling and talking.

Jaynee still couldn't comprehend how she'd gotten so fortunate. One minute she was waiting tables, wondering how she was going to make her next grade, what she was going to do with her life, if she was ever going to find a man worthy of her love, and in strolls Jordan into her life.

From the second they'd met, she'd wanted him. Now he was hers ... and she planned to spoil him rotten so he'd always be happy. And at the moment, food was his second favorite thing, it seemed.

"How 'bout French toast for breakfast?" she shouted to the second floor, since he'd disappeared upstairs again.

"Sounds fantastic, darlin'. I'll be right down," he called.

He appeared a few minutes later, plopping down at the island, watching her move about the kitchen. She could feel his eyes follow her as she prepared breakfast. This was all she'd ever wanted. Of course, she still wanted to finish college. Without a college degree, she wouldn't advance as an author. Her professors had always loved her papers ... said she was a natural. But this here, with Jordan, was all she'd ever wanted in her personal life. She'd never enjoyed going out partying every night with different guys; she wanted what her grandparents and aunt and uncle had.

Her father had married so many times she'd been afraid of marriage, but she'd held out hope she could have what her grandparents had for almost sixty years. She couldn't see anything ever happening between Jordan and her. She loved him madly and believed he too was deeply in love, even if it'd only been a short time.

History had shown her many people who had fallen in love instantly and had married within weeks had made it. But she also understood marriages failed for ridiculous reasons. *He-said, she-said* discrepancies. They would always have to be honest with each other.

Jaynee set the plate of French toast in front of him. It was her own specialty, one she'd perfected since she was a teenager. She waited as he took a bite. Satisfaction lit up his face, as she'd known it would. Everyone liked her French toast. She battered it with a blend of pancake mix, eggs, and milk, then seasoned it with vanilla, cinnamon, and nutmeg.

"Wow," he said, swallowing between words. "This is incredible! You *are* an excellent cook. Did I tell you how much I love you today?"

"Several times, but you can remind me if you want." She took a bite from her own plate.

"Well, I do, and thank you for breakfast. This is nice." He motioned his hand at her and him sitting at the island together. "Other than cereal or a granola bar, I've not once had breakfast in my own house." He shook his head, contemplating his own statement it seemed. "Incidentally ... I have another surprise for you." He plopped another bite into his mouth before continuing.

"Jordan, you can't keep doing this; you're going to spoil me rotten."

"Well, I'm actually nervous about this one. I don't want you to be upset, so I'm not sure if I should tell you." He lowered his eyes to his plate and just moved the food around with his fork.

She decided to let him off easy. "If you did something you thought was a good idea, I promise not to be upset."

He looked up at her and his eyes widened. "You promise?"

"You sound like a little kid. What did you do? Did you decide to move us to another state, colder than this one? Other than that, I can't think of any reason I'd be upset."

He laughed once, a short burst as if he found what she'd said funny. "No, nothing that drastic. I just wanted you to know there *was* a surprise, and maybe that will take the edge off when you see it, tonight at the reception. And —"

She cut him off. "There's more?"

"I just wanted you to know my sisters are coming to pick you up this afternoon around three. I have to leave earlier."

"Uh ..." She swallowed her words, why bother. "Okay," she grumbled.

"It's for the best, I promise," he said, noticing her reaction, taking her in for a moment before speaking, as though he were unsure himself. "It won't be long, Jaynee. I just have a few things to look after, and then you'll have me all to yourself. Well, not exactly ... you'll have to share me for a few hours." He laughed. "You're so cute when you pout. You tend to jut out your bottom lip like a southern belle. I find it very disarming."

She smiled despite herself. "I don't pout." She crossed her arms over her chest, proving his point.

"Yes, you do, but it's adorable." Jordan stood up with his plate and carried it over to the sink. "Our delivery should be here any minute, and I need to break down the old to make way for the new."

"Okay. I'll clean up down here while you start upstairs," she offered.

He grabbed her in one of his unyielding embraces. "I do love you, Mrs. Monroe, and I'll miss you today."

"I'll miss you too," she admitted, pouting for his benefit. He kissed her again, effectively ending her pout, then bounded upstairs. Her stomach twisted at the thought of being alone with his sisters. Rachael didn't seem to like her, and Melissa was a talker.

The furniture delivery was punctual, and they worked together to set up everything. Their bed was colossal and delicate simultaneously. It looked ever so inviting with the down comforter and yards of gossamer flowing down over the canopy. Jordan promised they would go shopping for artwork and accessories tomorrow that would complement the room and make it their own private paradise.

He left afterward, just shy of two o'clock. She couldn't imagine what he needed to do that he would leave so early. The reception wasn't until six.

Melissa and Rachael arrived around three. "We're here to do whatever we can," Melissa replied as soon as Jaynee opened the door.

Both her new sisters felt it was their obligation to indulge and pamper her. Jaynee was self-conscious yet grateful, imagining if her cousins were here, they would have done the same.

Her cousins were the closest thing she had to siblings, and she missed them, wondering if it was right to have excluded them from an actual wedding. Then she thought of her mother and father. She'd always felt like an imposition to her parents. Although she was a trouble-free kid, never giving them a minute of difficulty, they'd been too busy with their own lives to be concerned about her.

Except for Gram, she was the exception. Jaynee knew indisputably that Gram would have wanted to give her a wedding. Heck, she would have flown to Vegas with them. But she'd made her decision and refused to let it upset her.

Melissa insisted on styling her hair, and Rachael informed Jaynee she would apply her makeup after she buffed her nails and touched up her pedicure. Both ladies had worked in salons, but had given it up when their husbands started working for Jordan. Evidently, the hours on your feet were agony according to Rachael, and Melissa had wanted to stay home with her children.

It was about four when they unanimously decided they were finished pawing over her. They turned her around in the chair for a look. Jaynee hardly recognized the woman in the mirror. There was a little more makeup than she normally applied, but it looked elegant. Her hair cascaded in delicate curls around her face and neck, a look she'd never been able to accomplish.

Overwhelmed by the attention these strangers had shown her, tears welled up in her eyes.

Melissa noticed and started fanning her. "Don't cry, honey, you'll ruin your makeup."

Jaynee found it hard to articulate a complete sentence; her throat felt desiccated. "Thank ... thank you so much, I ... I ... can't express how thankful I am," she choked out.

"We had as much fun doing it," Rachael admitted. Jaynee was surprised to notice she sounded sincere.

Melissa squeezed her shoulders and looked at her in the mirror. "I already think of you as another little sister, Jaynee, and I'm thrilled Jordan has finally found someone."

The genuineness in their words rung true for both women, and Jaynee fought to retain the tears again.

"Well, we better get going. Still more stuff to accomplish, and you know how Jordan can be a stickler." Melissa looked up at Rachael as she spoke. An understanding nod transpired between the women.

Melissa carried Jaynee's dress while Rachael carried the accompaniments, and they were off to the reception. She couldn't understand all the fuss for what was really a party but decided, as it seemed everyone else around her did, just to subscribe with what Jordan wanted.

Chapter Twenty-One

It took thirty minutes to reach their destination. It wasn't anything like Jaynee had imagined. She expected some hotel banquet room; instead, Melissa turned onto a road with a park-like setting.

The long driveway zigzagged through trees and gardens until they arrived in front of a building that looked more like a southern manor torn out of the pages of *Gone with the Wind* than a place for a party. Melissa ignored a jam-packed parking area off to the left and pulled alongside the mansion, directly below steps leading to an entry with a sign over top that read, *Bride's Room.*

The rear of the manor, completely canopied by magnolia trees, was breathtaking. Roses and countless other flowering shrubs, trees, and plants trimmed the grounds and walkways. A lake bordered the end of the property, and adjacent the bank stood a beautifully adorned gazebo with nearly a hundred chairs lined up in symmetrical rows, all embellished with garlands of pure white flowers and crisp satin bows, which people already occupied.

Melissa led her up the steps into a lovely chamber. "This is where we'll get ready." She hung Jaynee's dress on the back of the door. "I have to get my dress, Jaynee, and there's someone who wants to speak with you. I'll send him in if that's okay."

"Yes, of course," Jaynee said, wondering other than Jordan, who would want to talk with her.

An older gentleman walked in seconds later, as if he'd been waiting for her arrival. He was slight, only a few inches taller than she was and in decent shape for his age. He looked about seventy. He was dressed professionally in a dark suit with a crisp white shirt underneath, his tie a simple blue. But what she noticed clutched in his hand, confirmed her assessment of him — a Bible. He looked like a preacher.

He smiled as he shook her hand. "Hello, Jaynee, I'm Pastor Young. I know you're technically already married, but I needed to take a couple of minutes to speak with you. Is that okay?"

"Certainly, but I'm confused. Why exactly are you here?"

"Jordan wanted me to marry you as his pastor in front of your friends and family. I find I'm doing that more often as couples choose to elope, but then want to renew their vows more traditionally. I guess it takes down their stress level over the typical big wedding ceremony."

She wasn't sure about that. Suddenly she was extremely anxious. But she could also see his point ... wasn't she just thinking the identical thing about her family?

"Thank you, then, for providing us with your services," she said, returning his smile.

"I do have a couple of questions, though, because I'm a preacher, and it is my duty to serve God first. Generally, I counsel couples for a year before they marry, but that's obviously not possible. But, I do have one question." He paused a moment as she watched him. She knew what his question would be. "Jaynee, are you a Christian?"

"Yes, I am," she answered for the third time in two days. No wonder Jordan had asked. He obviously didn't want them to scare her. "I was saved by Christ when I was sixteen and baptized within a few weeks. I admit I haven't attended church in years. I've had some bad situations, but I pray regularly and truly believe Jordan is an answer to prayer. I love Jordan with all that is within me and want to spend the rest of my life with him." *There*, she thought. *That ought to answer all his questions*. It was the truth, of course, but she figured it'd be better to throw it all out at once.

"Well then." He seemed surprised by her candidness. "Those are the important issues, salvation and love. If anyone can make a marriage work, it's Jordan. He puts God first in his life and his decisions. If you put God in the center of your lives, you will have a successful marriage. Jordan's father and grandfather were just as quick to marry, and both of them lived long happy lives. Of course, no relationship is perfect. We all struggle. But as long as Christ is your foundation, you can weather any storm." He smiled at her again and then nodded. "I'll be happy to marry you — again." He stood, taking her hand in both of his. "Well, I won't keep you any longer, Jaynee. I'll see you under the gazebo."

Leave it to Jordan, she thought. He'd said a surprise, but then was nervous she might have been upset. Actually, it was rather romantic, and she was anxious to get outside to her husband.

Pastor Young left, and within seconds, Melissa was at the door again. "Jaynee ... please don't cry, but someone else wants to see you, and we don't have much time."

Melissa guarded the doorway like a sentry, shielding her from whoever was behind it. Would they allow Jordan to see her before the wedding? Was it unlucky when you were technically already married?

He was probably confirming she wasn't upset about his surprise. "Send him in," Jaynee said, excited to see Jordan.

Melissa allowed the door to open, and several people poured in at once. The first person — a man she'd recognize anywhere, even if dressed uncommonly in a black suit — was her Uncle Adam. Her grandmother followed right behind him. Her hands flew to her face as she took in the rest of her family. Melissa started fanning her eyes again, but it didn't help; the tears wouldn't stop. The last woman to enter was her mother; tears were already streaming down her mother's face.

"You didn't think you could keep us away, did you?" Gram spoke first, her voice cheerful and aggressive. Her eyes were dry; she was a strong woman. But her lack of tears did nothing to contain her emotions. She was clearly pleased with herself.

Jaynee flew to her feet. "Oh, Gram, Mom, everyone ... how did you?" The words caught in her throat from the tears. She felt as though she were gasping for air.

Gram pulled her into a hug. "Jordan and I have been working on this ever since you told me. I knew he wanted to marry you right away, but I couldn't stand to have my baby girl get married without me."

Jaynee's mother stepped closer, wrapping her arms carefully around her so as not to tarnish her dress. "Honey, Jordan picked me up at the airport. He's a wonderful man. I'm so proud of you." Unlike Gram, her mother's eyes were red and puffy as if she'd been crying for hours.

"He picked you up?" Jaynee reeled at this information. He'd not only had her family drive from Florida but had also arranged to have her mother fly in from New York. That was what he'd been worried about ... allowing her mother to come. Gram must have talked him into it, since she'd told him that the last time they'd seen each other they'd fought.

The man *was* incredible, and suddenly, all she could think about was getting to him.

Uncle Adam stepped around her mother and took Jaynee's hand in his. "Is it okay if your old uncle escorts you down the aisle, Cay?"

"Nothing would make me happier, Uncle Adam." And it was the truth. Her father wasn't here, but her aunt and uncle had been there her entire life, and she felt guilty she hadn't realized they'd want to be here. Thank goodness Jordan had realized she'd needed this. She wouldn't change this day now for anything.

Melissa fluttered her hands toward the group. "Okay, not to be a party-pooper, but we need to get going before Jordan comes looking. You'll see everyone at the reception afterward." Melissa hurried everyone out, requesting that Uncle Adam stay close, indicating they'd be out in a minute. "If it's okay, Jaynee, Rachael and I will stand up for you."

"Of course, Sissy, you've already made me feel so welcome. I can't begin to express how grateful I am."

"Then everything's settled. We're heading down the hall and out the rear doors. So follow us, and then we'll exit separately." She pulled in a deep breath. "Ready, Jaynee?"

"Yes, I am. Very much so, thank you again."

Both her new sisters smiled and left the room.

Jaynee held her position behind the doors while she heard the introduction of the traditional *Wagner's Wedding*

March. She knew her cue — every girl in the world knew her cue.

What surprised her was the nervousness she felt, as if she weren't already married. They had done this just a week ago, and amazingly, it felt brand new.

Both doors swung open as the music changed, and she stepped over the threshold with her arm latched around her uncle's arm.

The crowd stood. Then, uniformed sighs and gasps reached her, probably just shock at seeing the mystery woman. She wished they would sit … she just wanted to see Jordan's face.

She hardly noticed any of the faces staring at her. She was looking for her groom, and then she spotted him at the end of the aisle, waiting for her again. His smile was dazzling, and he was striking in his black tuxedo. The feelings that washed through her were unfamiliar. She'd loved him from their first night together, but now, the emotions that soared through her were overpowering; her heart pounded to the point of almost being painful. The love she felt at this moment seemed as if it could burn right through her skin, and he was staring at her in exactly the same way. His eyes were a little glassy as he accepted her hand from her uncle.

Their first wedding had been beautiful, but Jordan was right to have arranged this. She felt even more attached to him, as though being married by a preacher in front of their friends and family sealed their commitment. They repeated the typical marriage vows, and a feeling of utter peace coursed through her veins when Jordan spoke the two little words, "I do."

***

When the Pastor announced the words, "You may kiss the bride" Jordan felt as if he could barely contain himself. Jaynee was lovelier than ever.

He would have to think of something special to thank Lorraine and his sisters; they'd made this evening better than he'd imagined.

He'd thought that he was doing this for Jaynee's relatives and his own family. But now, he found he was even happier and felt even more of a connection, if that were possible.

He leaned down to Jaynee, pulling her chin up to meet his lips, but before kissing her, he whispered a promise, "I'll love you forever, Jaynee Monroe." Then her lips were warm and soft under his. A cheer went up in the crowd, but neither of them moved. They were lost in their own world. The clearing of throats broke them out of their solitude, and Jordan directed his bride down the aisle, his arm wrapped around her waist to the waiting reception.

***

Jaynee held onto Jordan's arm as he escorted her inside the building to a ballroom decorated even more elaborately than outside.

Everything was white, including large satin curtains that garlanded the windows and the rear of the room. Decorative squares, trim, and intricate moldings adorned every window and door leading up to a painted ceiling resembling a miniature Sistine Chapel. Just enough topiary and roses filled the room to break up all the white.

Jaynee glanced around the room, trying to decipher who was who in the crowd. She recognized Jordan's law enforcement co-workers by their stance and haircuts, but the remainder of the crowd seemed to be an eclectic collection of who's who in North Carolina. Besides the police officers, there were individuals who, even under their ties and occasional jackets, looked like construction workers, and others who were clearly businessmen. Other than a wedding, she couldn't imagine anywhere the group would coalesce. Everyone seemed to be getting along, but she could see the division of different social ranks forming at individual tables and loose-standing circles throughout the room.

As Jordan and Jaynee waited at the rear of the room, a line of well-wishers began to form. Jaynee noticed a woman approaching. She was a nice-looking woman, tall and thin with dark-blond straight hair cropped to her shoulders, framing her face. She had pale blue eyes set inside a tanned face with freckles dotting across her nose and cheeks, as if she worked outside. She wore a simple black dress and stilettos, which surprised Jaynee since she was already tall, almost as tall as Jordan with her heels.

Jordan leaned close to Jaynee's ear. "My secretary, Lorraine, chose the location and the decorations. She took care of everything after I gave her minimal instruction," he whispered.

"Where is she?" she asked softly, as the woman Jaynee noticed approached them with a half-smile.

Jordan nodded to the woman in front of her now. "Jaynee, this is Lorraine Condrey. Lorraine, I'm pleased to introduce my wife, Jaynee."

"Oh," Jaynee exclaimed, reaching out to hug the woman, but Lorraine took her hand instead. Confused by the cold greeting, but undeterred, Jaynee continued, "Thank you for everything. It's beautiful. Jordan said you took care of all the arrangements. I'm so delighted to meet you. Jordan explained how he wouldn't be able to function without you."

***

Lorraine sucked in a breath and held onto Jaynee's hand a moment longer than necessary. "Well, he managed to find a beautiful wife without my assistance."

She smiled, hoping they wouldn't see through her playful, but truthful, observation. After all, she'd meant every word.

She couldn't deny Jaynee was beautiful, and they looked perfect together. Lamenting, she realized Jaynee was the antithesis of her; they were polar opposites. No wonder Jordan had only treated her like a friend; she wasn't even remotely his type. This hurt, but also appeased her, knowing nothing she could have done would ever have altered that reality. She could change her hair, but she couldn't modify her complexion, shape, and height.

"I'm pleased to meet you, Jaynee, and I wish you both the best." She squeezed Jaynee's hand, then turned to embrace Jordan. "Congratulations, boss! It's about time I married you off. Maybe you won't require all those late evenings anymore."

Jordan frowned at her remark. "Um, as I recall, it's always you calling me after hours, asking about specific job sites." His cheeks lifted. "Nevertheless, I think you're right.

You might not see me at the office as much if I can help it."

Lorraine released Jordan, stepping back. It was as she suspected. She could only hope things didn't go haywire. She would do her utmost to keep everything working flawlessly. Her income depended on the success of the business too. She wouldn't allow Jaynee to take everything she'd worked so hard to get.

***

The next person in line was the gentleman who had stood next to Jordan at the altar as his best man, Jaynee noticed.

Jordan gestured to the dark-haired man. His best man was about the same height, but had a lankier build than Jordan's muscular frame. "Jaynee, this is Detective John Ramos, my mentor, business partner, and best friend. John, *my wife*, Jaynee."

John gave Jordan a smirk and raised one eyebrow. "Well-well, if I'd known all I had to do to marry off Jordan was to send him to Florida, I would have done it years ago. I thought I had a bachelor on my hands forever. Evidently none of the girls in North Carolina are good enough for you, huh, buddy?"

Jordan mock punched John's arm. "It wouldn't have made a difference what state I lived in. The second I saw Jaynee ... I knew. Now it's your turn, huh, old man? You always were jealous whenever I did something first."

John scowled at Jordan, then turned to Jaynee, a peculiar look in his eyes. The man exuded arrogance. The kind of guy she would walk the other way from if he approached.

He reached in to hug her, and on instinct, she tensed. He seemed to notice and pulled back, offering her an overconfident smile as he held onto her arms before releasing her. "It's very good to meet you, Jaynee," he said in a low voice.

A chill swept through her body. The guy gave her the creeps. She couldn't understand why Jordan would be his best friend; they acted nothing alike.

Finally, it was her family doing the well-wishing. Gram was in front along with her mother, followed by her Uncle Adam, Aunt Georgia, and her three cousins Kelly, Wilma, and Ashley. They hugged and kissed Jaynee and went on to embrace Jordan, thanking him for bringing them here.

Jaynee looked up at Jordan at their comment. "You brought them?"

"Well, I didn't bring them ... an airplane did." Jordan smiled, but it was a weak smile as if he thought she'd get upset, even though she'd promised him she wouldn't.

"You flew them here?"

Gram nudged Jaynee's arm conspiratorially. "And set us up in a fancy hotel ... with free breakfast and complimentary bottles of —"

Jaynee was aghast. "Gram, those aren't —" Jordan squeezed her hand slightly, shaking his head. "You did all of this, Jordan?"

Jordan's face fell; he knew how much she loathed him spending money on her.

Jaynee shook her head, but squeezed his arm at the same time. "I'm just having a difficult time getting accustomed to this, Jordan, but thank you."

"Surprise," he whispered.

The line finally ended, and Jaynee, hard pressed to remember everyone's name, just smiled at the people around her.

The DJ cut into the soft background music, announcing the new couple as his fingers roamed his CDs.

Jaynee recognized the classic he chose immediately — a song she'd heard her mother perform. She couldn't remember the artist but remembered the lyrics to *Can I Have This Dance*.

Tears formed again as Jordan took her hand. "Can I have this dance, Mrs. Monroe?"

He led her to the dance floor and then moved her around in a small circle. They danced alone for a minute, then others joined them. Her aunt and uncle twirled around elegantly. She'd always coveted a relationship like theirs. They'd been married almost forty years and looked as in love as Jaynee could imagine anyone could.

Jordan swept a lock of hair off her face. "What are you thinking about?" His words were a mere whisper.

"Us," she stated simply.

"What about *us* in particular?"

"I was watching my aunt and uncle. I hope we're dancing like them when we're sixty-something."

"We will, Jaynee. Forever, remember, I'm gonna love you forever."

She sighed and laid her head on his chest.

"Did anyone tell you how gorgeous you look tonight?" he asked after a few seconds.

"No."

"How is that possible? You're without a doubt the most beautiful woman in the room."

"I think you're biased, Jordan."

He squeezed her tighter. "Maybe, but I still have superior taste. And you, my love, are stunning. I didn't think it was possible, but I love you even more and desire you more than I did our first wedding night. I'm glad we did this; it feels right."

"Thank you, Jordan. You look rather dashing in your tuxedo too." She slid her hand under his lapel as she spoke. "I'm happy *you* did this. You couldn't have given me a better gift. I only wish I could offer something in return."

Jordan dipped his head to her ear. "I'm sure you can dream up something. I rather liked my surprise the other night. The only problem with you looking so appealing, though, is now I can't wait to get you home."

Jaynee felt a shiver travel down her spine as he said the words and kissed her below her ear. With Jordan, it seemed her exposed neck was the most erogenous part of her body. He made her blood race every time his warm breath caressed her neck and shoulders. She forgot about the surrounding assembly and wondered if she could feign a headache and leave her own wedding reception.

The song ended and another started. Her Uncle Adam approached, requesting a dance with the blushing bride. Jordan obliged and handed her off to her uncle. From her uncle, she danced with several other waiting arms, including Bobby and then John.

About a minute into the song, Jordan thankfully interrupted their dance by tapping on John's shoulder. She didn't know why, but John made her feel uncomfortable.

"Hey, man, you mind returning my wife?" he asked when John didn't let go of her.

"What? You want to monopolize the loveliest woman in the room?" John called over his shoulder, twirling Jaynee away from Jordan. "We just started dancing."

Jordan didn't move from the floor. Instead, he positioned himself with his arms crossed over his chest, a stern look on his face. "Actually, I do," he retorted, but his smile was light, and John twirled her back toward Jordan.

She wasn't good at confrontation, and she certainly didn't want to cause strife between Jordan and John. They probably always acted like this, though. Jordan had mentioned something about that earlier. Jordan wouldn't be jealous of his best friend; he wasn't insanely jealous like her ex. She chastised herself for even thinking of the two in one sentence. They were like day and night, good and evil.

Jordan smiled as he folded her into his arms. "Thought I was going to have to fight off the wolves; I warned you that you were stunning."

Jaynee tried to make her words light, but could only manage a wistful half-smile. "Are you jealous, Jordan?"

"Of John? Always. He's somewhat of a ladies' man. Always gets the girl ... always the most popular."

"Not this girl." She scowled. "He's your best man though ... why would you be jealous?"

"I'm not really jealous. I just couldn't stand seeing you in the arms of another man ... even my best friend, well okay, especially John," he clarified, laughing. "We may be best friends, but he's a player. He'd step over my dead body if he thought he had a chance at you."

Jaynee cringed. "Jordan, that's a terrible thing to say!"

He shrugged. "I know, but it's true. He's my friend, but I know how some men are. Shh, let's just dance. I'm not planning to let you go again anyway. You're mine; I don't intend to share. I'm kind of selfish in that respect." His eyes narrowed, and he growled in a protective but playful way.

"I think I need a respite after this dance anyway." She sighed and lowered her head to his chest, allowing him to move her around the floor. She wasn't going to have to fabricate a headache if she didn't get something to drink soon. She was exhausted from all the dancing and had yet to eat or drink anything.

All the standard traditions carried them through the night. They cut the wedding cake and took turns shoving too-large bites into each other's mouth. Jordan removed her garter again — not as seductive as the first time — and launched it directly at John. Hoping, she guessed, to marry him off quickly. Jaynee sent her bouquet up in the air aimed at Lorraine per Jordan's request. Lorraine caught it with a flourish.

As promised, Jordan didn't release her the entire evening. They took time to visit with all the guests, drifting from table to table.

After a while, they sat down with a table of his cop buddies who were discussing work, stories of the road no doubt. The conversation flowed comfortably, normal anecdotes of how some guy overreacted at getting a ticket, how some women tried to get out of them. Jordan seemed to turn on edge at the beginning of another story, though. Jaynee could see he wasn't trying to be rude, but noticed him try to make their escape.

Jordan placed his hand on John's shoulder, interrupting his story. "Hey, we gotta keep moving, guys."

"You're the champion of this one, man, hang on for a second." John continued with his story, "And then I come around the corner, and there's Jordan, taking on this behemoth of a man, who was obviously possessed or on something. He must have been six-eight and three hundred fifty-some pounds and get this ... butt naked." John held is hands up in front of him to emphasize something. "Jordan was fighting him alone, but it ended up taking six of us to arrest him."

Jaynee's eyes widened in horror. Fear rushed through her body. She'd never imagined ... she hadn't thought about Jordan's job being dangerous. She knew he was a police officer, but she just figured he wrote speeding tickets.

Jordan stood, pulling her with him. "I'll talk to you guys later," he said, whisking her across the room in seconds. "I'm sorry you had to hear that, Jaynee."

"What happened?"

"Nothing happened," he shrugged, "same thing that always happens happened. I get the bad guys, put them away, and within days they're set free again to terrorize the city. I don't see that kind of action anymore; that was on midnight shift. Morning shift is boring."

"But ... why was he naked?"

"God only knows," he grumbled, his face a mixture of pain and frustration.

"Jordan, have you ever been shot at?" Jaynee asked suddenly, finally realizing how dangerous his job was.

He sighed, looking deep into her eyes as he lowered her onto a nearby chair, kneeling in front of her. "I'm a cop, Jaynee. I work in Charlie-Two, the second worst district in Charlotte." A contemplative look washed over his face as he continued, "Yes, it's dangerous. But I'm a good cop; I don't make mistakes. And as I said, I'm on morning shift now. It isn't as dangerous."

She didn't miss the fact that he hadn't answered her question.

Jaynee's eyes filled with tears as she felt panic bubble up inside her. She knew something awful would happen. Something terrible always happened. She wasn't allowed happiness. Jordan was wonderful, which meant she'd lose him.

"Please don't cry, Jaynee." He wiped her cheeks. "Idiots!" he seethed. "This is why cops don't associate with civilians. They don't know how to interact with normal people."

Jaynee flinched at his words, unfamiliar with him raising his voice. The last time had been outside her work, after the men had attacked her.

He rubbed her arms to soothe her. "I'm sorry, but honestly, love, I'm careful." His voice had returned to its normal level.

"Jordan, things don't pan out for me like normal people. I've had a succession of misfortunes since I was born. And now, I'm wondering if this is some cruel joke the universe is playing on me ... letting me fall madly in love so I can be left heartbroken."

"Jaynee, as flattering as that is, that is the silliest thing I've ever heard." He covered his mouth to keep a laugh from escaping. "The *universe* is not out to get you."

"Feels that way," she mumbled.

"I know, darlin'. I'm sorry. But trust me ... nothing is going to happen under my watch. Besides, I'll be able to quit eventually. The business is doing superb, and I have a reason to be home now."

She gazed up at him. "Promise?"

"I promise to be extra vigilant, and I swear I won't allow anyone to hurt you ever again. Let's get some fresh air; maybe we can find someplace to hide."

He stood, offering her his hand. She took it, but then leaned against his side, allowing him to wrap his arm around her waist and lead her through the back doors to the lake below.

Chapter Twenty-Two

This morning ...

Today was the day Jordan had been waiting for. Dr. McMullen had explained that Jaynee's swelling was staying at the levels they wanted, and they were slowly going to bring her out of the drug-induced coma they'd kept her in since her arrival Saturday morning.

The doctor had also said that he felt optimistic about the fact the swelling had stayed down, but based on the exit point, he was concerned about her personality. Jaynee could wake up and not have any emotions, he explained.

That was impossible, Jordan thought. Jaynee was the most expressive person he knew. She cried when she saw things happy or tragic. She loved deeply, heart and soul, giving all of herself. She hated injustice with a passion and expressed her opinion, no matter what people thought of her, in any situation. To imagine Jaynee without a personality was absurd, but he took heed of the warning and knew he just needed to pray.

He was sure something had happened to Jaynee. She couldn't have fallen out of love with him; nothing could

thwart a love like theirs. If he hadn't been so foolish Friday
night and gone out drinking, he would have figured it out.
He'd been so lonely, night after night coming home and her
not wanting him. The day of the incident, he'd been angry
after their brief discussion the night before and a situation
earlier in the day. And like any brainless friend, John had
dragged him out of the office to go get drunk with him and
Ronny.

John and Ronny had insisted Jaynee was seeing someone
else and that Jordan should confront her. Once the idea
had planted itself, Jordan knocked back one too many
drinks and was ready to fight the world.

Lorraine had known he was upset earlier and had called
him to see if he was okay. He'd told her he wasn't, and
she'd picked him up, promising to have his truck retrieved
the following day.

When he crawled into Lorraine's car, too drunk even to
buckle up, she reached over him and clicked the seatbelt
into place. Though he'd been drunk, he remembered their
conversation.

"Why are you so good to me, Lorraine?" he asked,
slurring his words.

"Because I love you, Jordan," she answered
automatically.

Jordan knew it was the truth. She'd always taken care of
him, just like his sisters. She'd always told him the truth
about every woman he'd ever dated. She'd always been
there for him, taking care of the business. He sank back in
the seat as she drove, hoping to clear the buzz from his
head. The car felt as if it were spinning. It was a thirty-
minute drive back to his house, hopefully long enough he

could sober up before confronting Jaynee. He decided he would demand answers. No more of this walking-on-eggshells crud he'd been dealing with for the last two months.

When they pulled onto the long gravel road leading to his driveway, Lorraine stopped at the bottom of the hill. Although still drunk, he knew he wasn't in his driveway. His head lolled over, attempting to bring her face into focus. Then he saw something in her eyes as she leaned toward him, her face only inches from his. It could happen so easily. The anger in him transformed, as another emotion took its place. But it wasn't for Lorraine, even drunk he knew this.

He opened his mouth to speak, and she tried to stop him, but he pulled back, feeling very alert. "I love her, Lorraine. I love Jaynee. I always have, and I always will." He dropped his eyes from her poignant gaze. "I'm sorry. We shouldn't be here. Please, just take me home."

Lorraine jerked upright, obviously embarrassed. But she shifted the car back into drive and started up the road. She pulled up close to the house and let him out.

If only he'd talked to Jaynee, maybe this wouldn't have happened. He shouldn't have confronted her like that. He should have stuck to his original plan. Instead, he'd gone out drinking and then had charged into his house furiously.

***

Lorraine sat outside the hospital. Pat had called earlier, informing her they were going to bring Jaynee out of the drug-induced coma today.

What would Jaynee remember about Friday night? What would she tell Jordan? She should have told Jordan she was there the night Jaynee was shot, but she wasn't sure how. What would he think? Would he believe she was responsible for his wife's shooting? She needed to do something quickly.

***

Brian was in the main waiting area of the ER when he overheard the news.

Caycee's mother-in-law had ventured downstairs to make phone calls to other family members who weren't here, he suspected. He was wild with worry. He'd overheard discussions she might have brain damage. Would she be the same woman? What would Caycee remember about their conversation? Had she spoken to her husband about his visit?

***

The words blurred on the page. Unable to concentrate, he slammed the folder closed.

Pat had called everyone, requesting they pray for Jaynee. Evidently, they had some concern of whether she would awake with normal brain function. He needed to go there. His insides burned at the thought. Jordan remained with her around the clock; he never left her side. It wouldn't be possible to get into her room unnoticed. He could go there while Jordan was there; he'd appreciate it if he showed up. But that wouldn't accomplish anything. He needed to see her alone.

***

Jordan held Jaynee's hand tightly as though he could protect her just by holding her. He watched with anticipation as her eyes fluttered under her lids.

"Jaynee, love, I'm here." Tears welled up in his eyes again. "Please, Jaynee, come back to me. I love you so much." He couldn't stop the trail of salty tears streaming down his face. He didn't want her to see him like this if she woke up, but he couldn't impede them. And he'd always thought he was tough. He was, in all areas but one — Jaynee. He couldn't lose her; she had to be okay. He honestly didn't know how he could go on living without her. His chest felt as if a black hole had formed that if something were to happen to Jaynee, he would implode and cease to exist.

***

Jaynee could hear Jordan whispering in her ear, the way he always did to wake her in the morning.

He hated when she overslept; he was accustomed to getting up hours before her. It must be Sunday, the only day they had the morning together.

She tried to open her eyes, but they felt glued shut. Even if she could open them, she didn't know if she wanted to. She had a pounding headache. She needed to sleep a little longer. She tried to roll over, but she couldn't feel her body; it felt as if it were detached.

Then she remembered she'd wanted to tell Jordan something. He'd sidetracked her when he came home. He was upset, and she understood. She attempted to form the words. She knew it was important she explain everything. She concentrated on the words, trying to arrange them in her head. She felt as if she could, but then she was out of strength. She didn't know if she got anything out before she fell back into her dark abyss.

***

Jaynee's hand twitched in his, then she mumbled a few words. The only word that was decipherable, though, was *baby*.

"I'm here, Jaynee." His voice cracked at the overwhelming joy of hearing her voice. He rang for the nurse who came within seconds. "Jaynee spoke; she squeezed my hand. Get the doctor," he demanded. The nurse ran out of the room.

Jordan was thankful for such simple blessings but was confused. Why had she said *baby*? She never called him baby, and at the beginning of their marriage, she'd asked him not to call her by the endearment. He'd passed it off as not being important, but now he wondered. He pushed the thoughts out of his head. Jaynee loved him; he knew it with all his being. She'd heard his voice and responded.

The doctor entered the room and walked directly over to Jaynee. "Has there been anything else, Jordan?" The nurse hurried around the physician, proceeding to take his wife's vitals as Dr. McMullen checked her eyes and studied the monitors.

Jordan tried to push away the thoughts of whom she was calling out for. "No, she just squeezed my hand and muttered a couple of words. She called me baby, but that was all I could make out."

In his peripheral vision, Jordan saw a man in dark clothes walk slowly past the room. He knew it wasn't one of the hospital personnel. It looked like the man who'd been in the waiting area for the last few days, but he couldn't be sure. What had surprised him, though, was that it looked as though the man had been smiling, as if he'd just received good news.

Dr. McMullen patted Jordan's shoulder, slicing through his thoughts. "That's excellent." He nodded, seemingly satisfied with this news. "It will take time, she will sleep plenty. But the fact she has surfaced from the coma with us just lowering her medication is a marvelous sign indeed. Keep praying, son, I think we have a real miracle on our hands."

His eyes were bright with enthusiasm, but Jordan wasn't so sure. He wanted Jaynee back, more than anything. But the thought she could be calling out for another man drove him crazy. He knew who called her *baby*. Brian had called her baby, and she'd supposedly hated it. But maybe she just didn't want him to call her by the same endearment her past lover had.

***

Brian couldn't remain in the waiting area any longer. He had to see Caycee, even if he just walked by her room.

He walked by at the perfect time as it turned out. He heard her husband tell the doctor she'd spoken. She'd said *baby*. So she was thinking of him. He'd always called her *baby*. He liked the way it sounded, as though she were helpless without him, as she'd always been. She needed him. He could protect her better than her so-called husband could.

***

Jordan remained at Jaynee's side, unwilling to release even her hand. "Come back to me, Jaynee," he implored.

She'd heard him earlier and had responded. He couldn't be sure if she'd called out for Brian, but he didn't care. He just wanted his wife awake in his arms. He'd fight for her. No way would he ever give up without a fight.

He decided to make some promises. He'd told her before that when they had kids he'd quit the force. She'd always said how much she hated that he was a cop, only because she worried so much about him. He'd made her a deal. He'd told her that when they had children, he'd quit. She'd passed on his offer, telling him she wanted children, but not until she finished her degree. It was the only thing they really ever fought over in the last five years of their marriage.

It was time to end that fight. "I won't give up on you, Jaynee. I know I said I'd quit the force when you got pregnant, but I don't care anymore. I just want you back. If you wake up, I'll call right now. I'll put in my resignation at the force. Nothing matters to me but you."

Chapter Twenty-Three

Five years ago...

Happy Birthday, my love."

Jaynee smiled at Jordan's rough, yet seductive morning voice. He reminded her of a kitten she'd had growing up. At the crack of dawn, the frisky calico would be meowing for her to get up.

She didn't open her eyes. "Does this mean I get to sleep in?" She was exhausted from the late evening at their reception and the even longer, but incredible night once they'd returned home. Then a thought occurred to her. She opened her eyes and frowned. "How did you know it was my birthday? I purposely didn't tell you."

"I'm your husband. You don't think I noticed all the times I had to write down our information — to get married, the helicopter ride, and then again with the car. And naturally, your grandmother made a point of reminding me," he admitted, lifting her chin up to kiss her.

"Oh ... that makes sense. But I don't know yours?" She was embarrassed. Jordan took it upon himself to know everything. She hadn't even considered questioning when his birthday was.

He winked at her. "March twenty-fifth. You have plenty of time." He'd obviously noticed how contrite she felt. "Would you like your gift now or later?" he asked with a crooked grin.

"Jordan, haven't you spent enough," she complained, but then, sidetracked by the *later* comment, winced. "What's later?" she groaned. "Tell me you haven't planned any kind of party, please."

He shook his head and laughed. "I didn't. I couldn't bear sharing you today. I'm partied out myself anyway. I never was comfortable with excessive socializing."

"Thank God for that." She sighed with relief.

"So, now or later?" he pressed.

"Um ... what ... oh yeah, now would be as good of a time as any I suppose."

His eyebrows narrowed at her lack of interest. "You don't sound very enthusiastic."

"I'm sorry. I'm just tired, and we have to meet my family for breakfast and drive them to the airport. I'd rather just stay here. It's our last morning together, right?"

"Only a week ... not even a week. I'll go in late on Saturday, and ..." he drawled, his voice trailing off, "we still have plenty of alone time this morning. You actually woke before seven."

"No ..." She laughed. "You woke me before seven."

Jordan waved it off as if it weren't important, then produced a tiny box that he'd hidden under his pillow. He held it out for her to open.

Jaynee opened the lid, peering inside at the elegant gold cross. It was beautiful. The delicately etched cross contained one small diamond in the middle. It wasn't gaudy or too big; it was perfect. She remembered the cross her grandmother had given her a few years back that had disappeared from her jewelry box — at least that was the last place she'd left it.

She looked up at Jordan, and he grinned widely. "Do you like it?"

"I love it ... it's perfect. How did you? When did you? Never mind ..." She shook her head. He was always full of surprises.

His fingers lifted the little heart around her neck. "I noticed you only wear the same charm around your neck, and I wondered ..." He didn't continue with what he was saying, but she knew what he was suggesting. He *was* jealous.

"Jordan ... my stepsister gave me this. She wasn't my stepsister long; she was the daughter of one of my dad's passing marriages. You thought ... you actually thought I would wear something my ex had given me?"

He looked down sheepishly before speaking. "I wouldn't begrudge you, if that were the case. But yes, I did wonder. And yes ... I admit it ... I *am* insanely jealous, and I've never felt this way about anyone. I don't even like to imagine ... the thought of you —" He stopped talking as pain filled his eyes. He sighed, then continued, "When I think about you with someone else, I feel things I don't want to. When I even think of him or anyone else who has ever ... wounded you, it makes me want to hurt them, and I know that's not a Christian attitude, but —"

"Well then," she cut him off, "don't think about such things. I'm here with you, and I love you more than anyone else in the world." She rested her hands on his clenched fists.

His hands encircled hers. "So you're not angry that I'm ridiculous — *and jealous*." His eyes were concerned, as though he'd admitted a great weakness.

She pulled her hands away and reached behind her neck to unhook the latch of her necklace. "No, it's actually rather flattering. As long as it doesn't get out of control," she amended. "As long as you understand you have no *reason* to be jealous."

Noticing what she was doing, he moved to assist her, but she'd already unlatched the chain. He held out his hand for the necklace and removed the heart, placing it in her hand, then proceeded to put the cross on the chain. She threw the heart across the room as further proof that it meant nothing. She'd have to remember to find it later and dispose of it properly.

"Allow me," he said, draping the chain around her neck, fastening the latch and then straightening it until the catch was behind her neck and the cross rested in the center of her chest. "Perfect. Happy Birthday, my bride." He leaned forward to kiss her, but then pulled her down onto the bed and gathered her in his arms. "I love you too, more than you can imagine."

They held each other in silence; just their breaths filled the air. Her eyes filled with tears at the overwhelming emotions. Just lying next to her husband, she could feel the love he held for her and the love she undeniably felt for him. He was everything she'd ever hoped and dreamed of in a companion. She couldn't see her feelings ever changing and could only hope it was the same for him. Tomorrow, he'd return to his job as a police officer, and that made her anxious again, worried about his safety.

What would she do all day? College wouldn't start again for almost four months. She could write ... lengthen the story she'd been writing. She could add a love interest, something she hadn't contemplated before; it was a depressing story. There had only been the love between a divorced mother, her father, and her son. But now, she could envision it, there could be another character. A love interest who would accept her heroine for who she was, despite her preceding difficulties, a gentleman who could offer her character hope to love again. Yes, she could visualize it and knew exactly how she would write the new development into her story.

Jordan reached up and touched her face. "What are you thinking about?"

She rolled over on her side, facing him. "You ... always you." She traced patterns over his chest and down his side. With her fingers, she outlined the strong muscles of his lats and felt consumed with a hunger for him. "Make love to me, Jordan."

"I thought you'd never ask," he said casually, but then moved with indomitable speed as he flipped her to her back. She gasped at the suddenness of his attack, but felt overcome with excitement as she searched his eyes. They burned with desire. "You're mine, Jaynee, forever," he said with vehemence. "I cherish what I love, and I'll do everything in my power to prove that to you every day."

She thought that his words — rather, his claim — should annoy her. Instead, she felt engulfed by his statement, wanting only to drown in his fervor, but still she hoped his possessiveness wouldn't inundate her.

Chapter Twenty-Four

This morning ...

J ordan called his mother and asked her to come to
Jaynee's room. After the news from the doctor that
Jaynee had woken up — even if for only a couple
seconds — she'd been on the phone, telling everyone.

Dr. McMullen had explained to Jordan that the hospital
had to inform the detectives that Jaynee had woken up.

It was the perfect time then. Not that he wanted to leave
Jaynee's side, but he was a detective too, and it wasn't often
things slipped his notice. He'd been too distraught the last
couple of days to pay attention, but something had been
eating at him. Something he planned to resolve
permanently.

When Pat walked into the room, her eyes widened.
"What is it, Jordan? What happened?" She must have
discerned his look. She knew him well.

He shook his head. Now wasn't the time to calm down.
It was time to prepare. "Nothing, Mom. I just need a
moment, and I don't want to leave Jaynee alone. Do you
hear me; don't leave her side. I'll be back in a few minutes,"

he said, walking out of the room with determination. He looked first into the undersized waiting room designated for the ICU unit and then descended the stairs to the main waiting area when he didn't find the person he was looking for.

As he exited the stairwell, he saw him, leaning back in a chair, looking a little too composed, as if he'd just received good news.

He sucked in a deep breath and attempted to control his tone. "Hey, Brian!" he said, catching the loser off guard.

Brian's chin turned up instinctively. An expletive escaped his mouth. It was all Jordan needed. He crossed the floor in seconds, jerked him from the chair by his jacket, and dragged him outside as onlookers gawked in disbelief. Brian was taller than he was, by about four inches, but Jordan was larger and angry. He had the man by at least twenty pounds, he estimated, even with the difference in height.

It was cold, but Jordan couldn't feel anything but fire pump through his veins as he held the scumbag up. "Who the hell do you think you are, and why are you here?" Jordan exploded, not waiting for an answer. He gripped Brian by the collar with his left hand and cold-cocked him with his right. The degenerate struggled to stand erect while Jordan pounded another punch into his mouth. His face turned blood red under his hands.

"She doesn't belong to you! You had your chance, and you blew it. *She Belongs to Me!*" Jordan seethed. "Now you want to return, and take what's mine?" He punched him again, but then pulled back. "She almost died because of you." He released a breath. He needed answers, and a crowd had started to stream out of the hospital. Jordan released Brian's collar, allowing him to plummet to the concrete.

Brian gasped for air. "It's not what you think," he blurted out. "I just wanted to see her. I didn't hurt her. I would never hurt Caycee." He started to stand, but cowered under Jordan's glare. Brian lifted his hands to shield his face as Jordan pulled back to deliver another blow.

"How did you know she was here? How long have you been seeing each other?" Jordan's throat was raw with emotion. It was hard enough to believe something; it was another thing altogether to have his worst nightmare confirmed.

Brian didn't try to get up this time. "We weren't seeing each other, but I was there Friday night. I saw her —" His words broke off as Jordan launched again.

He could see nothing but red as he hurled his body at Brian. This sleaze ball had been at his house? How could she? A police siren wailed from behind him, but it didn't matter. Nothing mattered anymore.

"Listen!" Brian shrieked as Jordan encircled his throat with his hands, ready to squeeze the life out of him. "I wasn't with Caycee. I was watching her. I know it was wrong, but you have to listen ... there was someone else, a woman ..."

Jordan stopped, but he didn't release his hands from his throat. "You weren't having an affair?" He removed his hands from the man's throat, but grabbed a handful of his jacket with his fist.

"*I wish*," Brian snorted, but obviously witnessing the fierce look in Jordan's eyes, recoiled. "Sorry, dude, it's been a long time. I just wanted to talk, but she refused."

So they *had* talked. He knew something had been wrong, but was thankful it wasn't what he'd thought. It still irritated him, though, that Jaynee had withheld information. How could he protect her from losers like Brian if she didn't tell him about them.

A car screeched to a stop behind them. Jordan turned around, but continued to hold onto Brian, pulling him to his feet.

The officer jumped out of the patrol car, but crouched behind the door, gun drawn. "Hands over your heads," the officer yelled.

Jordan immediately let go of Brian and raised his hands, noticing Brian did the same. Brian was certainly accustomed to the familiar drill.

After assessing the situation, the officer straightened up and walked toward them. "What's going on here, gentlemen?"

"A misunderstanding, sir," Brian answered without a moment's hesitation.

Jordan let his eyes wander from the officer for a second, glowering at Brian. Why would he let him off? He'd just pummeled the guy. He should've wanted the officer to arrest him.

Another police car pulled up, this one an unmarked car. Out stepped two detectives: Nelson Williams and Len Powe.

"Mornin', Monroe, having troubles?" Detective Williams drawled, smiling.

The uniformed officer glanced at the detective, then jutting his chin toward Jordan, asked, "You know this guy?"

"Yeah, he's one of ours," Powe responded. "Is everything okay, Jordan? We heard your wife woke up."

Jordan lowered his hands after a glimpse to the uniformed officer. "Yeah, everything's cool, but we need to talk."

Detective Powe walked over to the uniformed officer. "Officer, my partner and I need to interview Jordan. Is it okay if he comes with us?"

"Unless this man wants to press charges for assault," the officer retorted, gesturing his chin at Brian.

"Like I said," Brian repeated. "It was a misunderstanding."

The officer turned and walked to his patrol car, shaking his head as he left. Jordan didn't know how he felt that Brian was giving him a pass, but again, he was grateful. Of course, now a discussion needed to occur between the four of them.

Brian rubbed his chin. "Man, dude, you got a mean blow," Brian complained as he followed them into the hospital. "I think you knocked my jaw loose."

Jordan couldn't suppress a grin. He'd been holding back, afraid to inflict too much damage and not retrieve answers. He'd always wanted to do that for Jaynee's sake anyway, so he was thankful to have gotten the opportunity. He now realized why Brian hadn't wanted to press charges. The loser was surely on parole. No matter who got the blame, it wouldn't look good to be in a fight. For that matter, he probably wasn't supposed to leave Florida, so Jordan could use that against Brian if necessary.

"Williams! Powe!" Jordan called ahead. They both turned. "Hey, take Brian to the cafeteria. He was at my house the night Jaynee was shot. I'll be there in a few minutes. I want to see if *my* wife is awake." Jordan glared at

Brian, then turned his back on the men, bounding up the stairs two at a time, the elevator too slow for him.

Jordan pushed through the heavy metal door, making his way back to his wife's room, hoping she'd not awoken while he was gone, but that she would wake up the instant he returned. He *was* selfish, he realized.

Pat was sitting by the bed, her nose buried in a novel, Jaynee's hand in hers. She scowled as he entered the room. His mother missed nothing.

He ignored his mother's glower. "Anything new happen?"

Pat shook her head and stood to let Jordan take her spot. He shot a glance at the monitor at the change in the rhythmic beeps. Jaynee's pulse had quickened at the sound of his voice. He felt triumphant. Jaynee had been upset, scared even, but she wasn't having an affair with Brian. He didn't know how long Brian had been harassing her, and for the life of him, he couldn't fathom why she wouldn't tell him about his stalking if she were aware of it.

He lowered his head to her ear and whispered into it the way he did when she'd oversleep and he wanted her to wake up. "Jaynee, I'm here. Please wake up." Familiar feelings soared through him, feelings he hadn't felt in months. She still loved him, he assured himself.

She'd been attempting to tell him about Brian when she whispered the word *baby*. Jaynee knew he would remember her request not to call her by that endearment and understand why she was frightened. He wondered whether he should mention it, but decided it wasn't important, and it might upset her.

Her hand moved in his. It wasn't a squeeze, merely a subtle movement. His eyes darted to hers in expectation. She was squinting, trying to open her eyes.

"Mom, turn off the light!" he demanded. She complied, and Jordan saw the most beautiful sight, Jaynee's hazel eyes, green and gold, sparkling again, staring at him. "Oh, God, Jaynee!" he cried out, not concerned by the tears swarming his eyes. He laid his head against her cheek. He wanted to kiss her, pull her up in his arms, but all he could do was be close to her. Wires still connected her to the bed. "Oh, God, Jaynee. I was so worried." He stared into her eyes again. She looked bewildered. "You're in the hospital, love. There was an accident, and you were shot." He shook his head. "It's not important." He turned to his mother. "Mom, get the doctor."

***

Jaynee struggled to make sense of everything. Jordan was here, and he was upset. Her head was throbbing, and she was extremely thirsty. She tried to speak, but nothing emerged.

Jordan saw this and reassured her. "It's okay. You don't have to speak. Nothing matters except that you're awake. It's been three days."

A doctor stepped in, and Pat and the nurse backed out of his way, but Jordan remained seated, an unmovable force.

The doctor held a device to each of her eyes. "She's responding well," he said with a smile aimed at Jordan. "I think you're going to be fine, Jaynee," he reassured her. "How do you feel? Can you talk?"

Jaynee opened her mouth; her throat felt like flames.

The doctor turned to the nurse. "Michelle, get some ice chips." He looked at Jordan. "Her throat is raw from the breathing tube and lack of liquid."

Jaynee was grateful for the doctor's understanding, but cautiously turned her head back to Jordan. She wanted to tell him something, but she couldn't remember what it was.

How had she ended up here? Jordan had said a shooting. *What had happened?*

Jordan had come home, and he was furious. He'd yelled at her, and he never yelled. She'd been waiting for him to come home. There was something very important. What was it? She was so frustrated that she couldn't remember; she knew it was important.

They'd made love. It'd been so long, she remembered. She'd gotten up after Jordan had fallen asleep. He always went to bed early. He had to get up before the break of dawn. She remembered walking downstairs.

Jordan took the Styrofoam cup of ice chips from the nurse and placed a small piece in Jaynee's mouth. It felt good. She opened her mouth for another, embarrassed that Jordan was waiting on her. She always took care of him; he never had to assist her. But here he was, this big strong man, delicately placing ice chips in her mouth. Red rimmed his beautiful blue eyes, and dark circles surrounded them; she ached to comfort him. But she was too weak even to turn her head and could feel the drowsiness threatening to take her away again.

Oh, God, she remembered ... "Lorraine," she garbled under her breath. "Where's Lorraine?" It was all she could get out. The darkness overtook her, and she felt herself plummet under the thick wool again. She couldn't find her way out from under the layer of darkness that descended on her.

***

Jordan stood as he watched Jaynee slip away again. "Why would she want Lorraine?"

He thought back to the night of the accident. Lorraine had dropped him off after he turned her down. Drunk or not, he knew there was only one woman for him. Had she returned? Had she been angry with Jaynee? Brian had said there was a woman with Jaynee. Could Lorraine have wanted to hurt her? No, it wasn't possible. He'd known Lorraine his entire life. He knew how she felt about him, but he only cared for her as a friend. Maybe it was wrong to have her working for him, relying on her so much. But murder? Never. He couldn't believe it.

Jordan looked at his mother. "Mom, can you stay with Jaynee again? I have to speak with the detectives. They're downstairs." And make a phone call, Jordan decided. But he needed to hear everything Brian had to say first.

Chapter Twenty-Five

Five years ago ...

The rest of Jaynee's birthday passed in a blur. Jordan and she had driven separately so they could take her family to breakfast and then afterward, drop them off at the airport. Tears and smiles overflowed as each of her family members hugged and kissed them before they left.

She was glad Jordan had arranged this. It wouldn't have been right to exclude her family from her wedding. Her relationship with her mother was sketchy, but she was trying, and Jaynee was her only child after all. Jaynee had always tried to make allowances for her mother. It really wasn't her fault. Her mother had endured a terrible childhood and didn't know how to deal with the stresses of life. Although Jaynee had never been like her mother, she tried to understand.

Jaynee had suffered one nightmare after another, and yet she still awoke every day with a positive outlook, always believing there was good in the world. It was just a matter of finding it, and she had. Jordan was her reward for being faithful no matter what life threw at her, and for her unceasing nightly prayers.

She fiddled with the cross at her neck. It was simple and beautiful. She didn't need fancy things. She hoped she could get that through to Jordan. She didn't want him always lavishing her with fancy gifts. The cross was a good start; it was perfect. She needed to explain she liked simple things. It wasn't because she didn't *have* jewelry that she didn't wear any. The truth of the matter was she didn't like jewelry. A necklace and ring were the extent of what she wore.

The drive to the house was long without Jordan, but she had to get used to it. After tomorrow, he'd return to work. Was the honeymoon over? The thought depressed her. She'd have to make sure that never happened.

Her cell phone rang, interrupting her thoughts. "Miss me already?" she said into the mouthpiece.

"Yes, of course, but that's not the reason I called. Do you want to get the artwork for the bedroom? I know a terrific gallery in Pineville, which is on our way home."

She didn't want to stop; she just wanted to return home. "Sure, whatever you want."

"You don't sound enthused," he teased.

"I am ... it'll be beautiful. I'm just tired." She stifled a yawn midsentence proving her point.

"We don't have to."

"Really, Jordan, this is the best time. Everything is so out of the way here. In Florida, everything was literally ten minutes away. Let's go now so we don't have to worry about it next weekend. I hate to shop." She frowned even though he couldn't see her expression.

Jordan let out a chuckle. "Well, that's a first, a woman who doesn't like to shop. I always knew you were unique. Okay, follow me; we'll make it snappy. We'll even order pizza, so we don't have to waste my last vacation day cooking. How does that sound? I love you, see you soon." He hung up.

The question was rhetorical. She was beginning to get used to his decision making. It was actually somewhat nice. For the first time in her life, she didn't need to worry about anything.

They managed to find several beautifully framed prints that would go perfectly in the bedroom. Jordan told her to shop for additional items she thought would complement their sanctuary at her leisure. He was evidently ready to return home also.

It was only three when they returned home, a benefit she realized of getting up earlier than she was accustomed.

Jordan hung all the frames, and he'd been correct. As always, the room was beautiful. Jaynee found herself feeling completely at home in her new quarters. They spent the remainder of the afternoon playing in the backyard with Boomer.

It was just turning dusk when their backyard filled with an incredible sound. At first, it was one lone chirp, promptly followed by millions echoing the same buzzing and clicking hum. She tilted her head at the resonance echo in the surrounding woods.

Jordan gestured his head to the woods that served as the backdrop of their backyard. "Cicadas," he said, apparently noticing her preoccupation. "The sound of summer in North Carolina," he continued, a warm smile lighting up his face. "Do you like it?"

She nodded. "It's beautiful, so peaceful. All I ever heard in Florida, where I lived anyway, were trucks and sirens."

He pulled her into his arms. "It's why I chose the country. Charlotte can be very distracting."

It was getting cooler; his arms felt nice around her. Jordan escorted her inside, and they snuggled on the couch and watched classic movies. She found they agreed on the same genres, except in the case of war movies ... she could never quite get into the battle scenes. But then, Jordan paused on a romantic comedy she loved even before she could get the words out that it was one of her favorites.

Underneath his cop demeanor, Jordan was a wonderfully romantic and sensitive man.

The next morning arrived too quickly, probably because Jaynee had been dreading it.

She vaguely remembered Jordan kissing her goodbye. But then she woke up, cold and alone, in their king-sized bed. She'd become familiar with waking up with his arms wrapped around her. Now she was going to have to get accustomed to him not being there.

She glanced at the clock; it wasn't even seven yet. Jordan had been trying to wake her earlier and earlier every morning; it looked as if he'd succeeded. She wrestled with the idea of trying to fall back asleep. After all, what reason did she have to get out of bed? There was no grandmother across the street, no classes to attend, no work schedule to keep, and worse, no Jordan.

Ridiculous, she wasn't needy. She couldn't have become so absorbed by Jordan that she couldn't find something else to fill her time. If she made an effort to get up early, it would give her more time on the weekends with him, she argued with herself, and that made her resolve. She'd get out of bed and start her new life in North Carolina. She would investigate the area, heading one direction today and another tomorrow. Only one main road connected the two nearby cities. She had two options — head toward Albemarle or Charlotte.

Jaynee made her way downstairs; she could hear Boomer in the garage, anxious for her to set him free. She stood back as he barreled through the doorway. Boomer took one look at her, then dashed around the house as if looking for something or someone. When he came back, he gave her a look like ... *Who are you, and why are you here without my master?* She bent down and ruffled his ears. It was all it took; his confusion melted away. He was suddenly interested in playing with her. Boomer ran to the patio door, so she let him outside to the fenced-in area of their property.

Jaynee stood in the large kitchen feeling misplaced. What did Jordan do with such a gigantic house? She brewed a pot of coffee, then booted up her laptop. First business of the day, she needed to decide where and when to start back to college.

After several hours of research on the Internet, she decided it was time to go exploring. She had her phone in her pocket waiting for Jordan to call. She wanted to call him, but was concerned she'd catch him in a dreadful situation. Her imagination got the best of her, and she envisioned him in a shadowy building, gun drawn, in quest of a suspect, then his phone going off and alerting the bad guy of his whereabouts. No wonder she wanted to be a writer; her imagination was entirely too vivid.

Hopping into her new Altima, she inhaled, luxuriating in the smell of the leather. Jordan had shown her how to use the navigation system, but she didn't understand. So he'd made sure she understood one important feature. No matter where she was, she could hit home, and the voice would direct her home. That made her feel more at ease as she set out to explore her new city.

She drove for miles before reaching the main road and then turned toward Charlotte. She passed a Wal-Mart — that would come in handy, and it wasn't too far — there weren't too many things in life you needed that you couldn't find at Wal-Mart. Now for a coffee shop with wireless Internet, that was a necessity. She'd decided after her research that correspondence school was going to be the way to finish her degree.

North Carolina had plenty of colleges, but the closest one was forty-five minutes away. The thought of driving almost two hours a day nauseated her. It would be nice, though, if Panera or Starbucks were nearby, heck, even McDonald's would suffice. It would give her an opportunity to get out of the house, yet still enable her to work online.

Upon reaching the Charlotte border, she realized that wasn't going to happen. She located what she was searching for, but it had taken her more than half an hour to get there. So it would be a wireless card then, and she'd have to find somewhere comfortable to study. She was sure Jordan wouldn't care; he probably already had the service for his company anyway.

Her cell phone rang, startling her. She peered down at the number and smiled. "Hey," she said.

"Hello, my bride. Did you miss me this morning?" he drawled. She could hear the smile in his voice.

She lowered her guard. "Yes! It was awful. I was so cold without you. But you'll be happy to know I woke up before seven."

"That's good. Maybe I won't have to be so persuasive on the weekends." His voice dripped with seduction. *How did he do that?*

She tried to imitate his seductive tone. "Oh, I don't mind. I rather enjoy your methods of coercion." Unfortunately, she didn't have that great southern drawl he did, so she was sure she fell short of sounding alluring.

He sighed into the phone. "You sidetracked me, Jaynee. I called you for a reason." His voice lost its seductive tone; actually, he sounded anxious, so maybe it worked a little. "Oh, I remember. I just finished work and was wondering if you would like to meet for lunch and then perhaps swing by my office afterward?"

She hadn't realized the time. She'd forgotten that he got off at one o'clock only to report to his construction business. "That would be wonderful. I'm actually exploring the area and was just thinking I needed to eat."

"Where are you?" He sounded excited to see her too.

"Um, I'm not sure," she mumbled, looking around at her surroundings.

"Jaynee," he teased, his tone taking on a sarcastic edge. "Just look at your navigation system."

She glanced down at the monitor. "Oh ... right ... I'm on Highway 74 approaching Harris Boulevard."

"Excellent! I'm about five minutes from you. There's a shopping center on your right with a great Mexican restaurant. You mentioned you liked southwestern food, so I'll just meet you there." He hung up.

He obviously remembered everything she told him. She thought his decisive character should irritate her, but somehow she felt awed and strangely comforted by his authoritative nature. He wasn't overpowering and never seemed severe. He just knew what he wanted and reacted to his wants.

She saw the restaurant he must have been referring to and pulled into the parking lot. She debated whether to go inside or wait outside until he arrived. Turning off the ignition, she remained inside the car, since she wasn't familiar with the area.

When his truck pulled in next to her, she couldn't help but leap out. She *had* missed him in these few short hours.

Jordan jumped down from his truck, dressed in jeans and a polo shirt, gorgeous as always. He must change out of his uniform at the station. With his long strides, he was in front of her in seconds. He picked her up as if she weighed nothing and pulled her face up to meet his. "God, how I missed you." He kissed her, then lowered her feet back down to the pavement. "It was maddening leaving you this morning. I almost called in sick."

A surge of pleasure soared through her, so it wasn't just her. She couldn't contain the smile that spread across her face. "Good. I missed you too." Her eyebrows shot up as she took in his face. She reached up and touched the side of his jaw. "What happened? I liked the beard. Not that you don't look good clean shaven, but wow ... it's kind of a shocker."

"I know, right? I was getting used to it. But it's not permissible as an officer." He lowered his head toward her, caressing his smooth face up the line of her jaw. "But there are benefits."

Her heart pounded wildly; she wondered if he would ever cease to affect her like this. He reached for her hand and pulled her gently to the restaurant.

They sat across from each other. His shoulders were too wide to sit next to him in a booth. Besides, she liked looking at him and in return, him looking at her.

He held her hand across the table, stroking the back of it seductively. "So, what did you do today?" His voice was nonchalant but interested.

"Well, I decided every college in this area is too far to drive to, so I did some research and found several distance-learning schools that look promising. What do you think?"

"I think that's a great idea; that's what I did. I received my undergrad through an external degree program, and I'm still deciding what to do for my graduate degree."

She cocked her head and smiled at him. "You didn't tell me you had your Bachelor's degree?" Of course, there were plenty of things she didn't know about him, she realized.

He pointed to himself. "Remember ... not a dumb hick?"

"Stop doing that." She slapped his hand with her free hand. "I told you before, I've never even for a second thought you weren't intelligent. And I like your southern accent, very much so ... it was the first thing I fell for."

He took hold of her other hand and smiled that crooked grin she loved. "Really ... what was the second?"

She guessed he'd forgotten the conversation about college.

"Your eyes, but it's a very close match. Heck, I guess there isn't much I didn't fall for. But that was just at first sight. Most of all, I fell for you — your personality, your generous nature." She squeezed his hand.

"My eyes?" He huffed in disbelief. "They're boring compared to yours."

She shook her head wildly in protest. "Oh no, they're not. They're strong and compelling, like you. And then there are your shoulders and chest — I think I'd better stop. We *are* in a public place." She giggled. She couldn't help it. The man drove her wild just looking at him, or rather, the way he looked at her, as though he wanted to gobble her up right here.

"Jaynee, you're making me blush, and we may not make it to my office if you don't stop." His eyes widened with anticipation.

"Is that a threat?" She attempted a seductive tone again. It seemed to work the first time.

"No, darlin', it's a promise," he retorted. And she couldn't tell if that meant he wouldn't go in if she asked him.

"A promise?" she asked in the sweetest voice she could muster.

"If you don't want me to go, I won't. They can manage without me another day."

She sucked in a breath. "But would that disrupt Saturday?" She could hear the defeat in her voice. She sounded pathetic. What would he think of her?

He shook his head. "Jaynee, I *own* the business. No one tells me when to come and go."

She decided to change the subject. She wouldn't push him to make any decisions he didn't want to, and she didn't want him to think she was needy. "So, tell me about your degree. What did you major in?"

He turned her hand in his and played with her wedding ring. "Criminal justice. The police department doesn't mind me taking time off, and they even paid for my courses, because it's the same field. But I'm probably going to get my master's degree in business, since it looks as though that is the best move at this point in my career." He shrugged as though it weren't important. "I like being a cop, but it's getting old." He'd been staring down at her hand, but he looked up, and his eyes were bright. "What I really want is to be a detective, maybe even enter SWAT."

She broke his gaze and looked around the room. She didn't like the sound of that. All she could imagine were those shows on TV, where some unknown rookie detective died every week. Suddenly, the thought of losing Jordan overwhelmed her again. She'd have to get over this; he wouldn't want her to worry.

Jordan tapped her hand as if he'd recognized her preoccupation. "So, I love the idea of you enrolling in a distance-learning program. I didn't like the idea of you driving so far every day and then walking around a large campus. College campuses aren't always the safest place for beautiful women."

A twinge of annoyance surged through her. "You drive forty-five minutes to work and deal with criminals *every* day," she snapped back. His eyes dropped, and she regretted the comment as soon as she said it.

He pulled out his cell phone. "I'll call Bobby and let him know I'm not coming in today. I think I'd rather spend the evening with you. It sounds as if we have to talk about a few things anyway." He pushed the number on his phone. "Hey, Bobby. I won't be in today."

Jaynee heard her brother-in-law's guffaws through the phone after he obviously made some ill-mannered remark. Jordan disconnected the phone, no comment.

Chapter Twenty-Six

Five years ago ... up until their fifth anniversary ...

The rest of their weekdays went much like the first. After a while though, they only met for lunch once a week, usually on Friday.

And Jaynee mostly kept her snide comments to herself. Jordan loved his job, and it wasn't right for her to give him a hard time about it.

The weekends were the best. Jordan would go to work early Saturday morning, have a meeting discussing what he expected of his employees the following week, do some paperwork, and then come home — often before noon.

Jaynee managed to experience more of North Carolina than most natives. Every Saturday, Jordan whisked her away to visit one mountain or another when the weather was nice. The first place he took her was Linville Gorge, which was spectacular, known as The Grand Canyon of the East.

The first set of falls was beautiful. It wound around a bend in an S-shape and then disappeared into the rocks below, cutting a deep gorge through the valley. Since they were located just about a half-mile off the road, there was no lack of tourists, though.

But Jordan, being an avid hiker, led her up several more paths to view the opposite side of the falls where they cascaded to the river below. Several spots along the trail opened up to fields of wild ferns, barely touched by the sunlight beneath the tall pines. It looked like a scene from a fairy tale. Jordan then proceeded to descend a path to the bottom of the gorge, which ended up being an all-day adventure. The trees closest to the river were already giving up their green, replaced by magnificent colors ranging from yellow to orange and deep red. And the scents were incredible, a mixture of moss and soil and rotting leaves gave off an unexpected sweet aroma.

Month after month, they spent their weekends exploring North Carolina and, as a result, each other. They spent hours hiking and talking. She'd never known there were so many waterfalls and mountains, and that one man could have so much depth. They talked about God and politics, their views thank goodness were the same. The only instances even close to arguments were when they discussed children and his job as an officer.

Jordan wanted children something awful and didn't want to wait. Jaynee wanted kids as well, but wanted to finish college first, which didn't make any sense to Jordan.

"If you study at home and plan to work out of the house anyway, what difference does it make when we have children?" he'd constantly ask.

On their first anniversary, Jordan took Jaynee on a cruise. It was a perfect opportunity to escape; everything was slow in September, especially the construction business. Kids were back in school after summer vacations, and families were broke and weren't moving into new houses or having major repairs done. Things picked up again in late October or November as preparations for Christmas started, Jordan had explained to her.

Jaynee had made the mistake of mentioning over dinner if they had children, they wouldn't be able to get away at any time of the year. That was all it had taken to ruin a perfectly good evening. They were on a weeklong cruise to the Eastern Caribbean, it was only the first night, and she'd managed to introduce something stupid. She could have kicked herself.

Jordan didn't say anything during dinner. But later, when they walked to the top deck to look out over the waves, he furrowed his brow as he always did when he was upset or didn't understand something. "Jaynee, I just don't understand why you would say something like that."

She feigned ignorance as if she didn't know what he was referring to, as it had been over an hour since the conversation, but they were good at this game. One of them would simply start talking about something they'd discussed hours or even days before, and the other would continue as if there had been no downtime.

He raised an eyebrow skeptically as if he wasn't buying her ignorance. "If you don't want children, why don't you say so instead of making up excuses?"

Jaynee had to watch herself. She had a terrible temper, one she tried never to let escape, because she would end up throwing things like an adolescent or end up hitting something and break her hand.

"I never implied I didn't want children," she said. "I merely suggested that if we had kids, we wouldn't have been able to escape like this. I adore children. I babysat my cousins' children since I was twelve years old. I just think we should wait. We've only been married a year." She pleaded with her eyes for him to drop this discussion.

He refused. "Are you sure it's not something else?"

"Such as ..." She felt her blood begin to boil.

"Well, I know how you feel about your mother and how she treated you —"

She cut him off sharply. "I'm nothing like my mother!" she fumed. "My grandmother raised me, and she had four children and tons of grandchildren and great-grandchildren too. Don't ever compare me to my mother!" She turned away, knowing she had tears in her eyes. She always cried when she was angry.

He turned her around then reached for her face, but pulled his hand back as she jerked away. "Jaynee, I know you're nothing like your mother. I wasn't implying —" He paused, sighing. "I just wondered if you thought children would come between us, as you think you did with your parents. I know you would never hurt a child." Despite her rejection to his touch, he wrapped his arms around her, refusing to let her go. "I'm sorry. It's just that I'm twenty-eight, and I don't want to wait until I'm over thirty to start a family, but I understand. I won't pressure you."

She relaxed in his embrace. "I'm sorry too, Jordan. I just think it's best. Besides, being a cop isn't the best occupation when deciding to raise children, either."

She couldn't see his face, but she felt his body tense. He was ready to end the fight, and she'd broached another sore spot. "I won't be an officer forever. Actually, I was waiting to tell you this as a surprise, but I have it on good authority they are going to offer me a detective's position. It's not the division I wanted, but at least my foot is in the door."

Jaynee wasn't sure this was good news, but she knew it was what Jordan wanted. At least he wouldn't be on the streets every day.

She did her best to sound enthusiastic. "That's great, Jordan. When? What division?"

"Auto-theft." His tone lacked the excitement she expected from his announcement. "I wanted rape or homicide, but I'll take it. Probably right after we return."

At least it didn't sound too dangerous. She wasn't certain what an auto-theft detective would do, but at least he wasn't working the streets in one of the worst neighborhoods in Charlotte.

She turned in his arms and looked at him. "Aren't you happy?"

He shrugged. "It'll be okay. It's just not what I envisioned when I joined the force. It's a lot of insurance fraud more than anything — teenagers stealing joyrides, junkies losing their vehicles in awry drug deals. And then, every so often, they make a big bust on a chop-shop." His eyes thrilled as he discussed the possibility. "Hard to imagine, but over six hundred vehicles are reported stolen every year in Charlotte. It's a big division. It's where John works, and he put in the recommendation."

"It sounds exciting," she added, hoping they were finished arguing.

Jordan pulled her closer, noticeably feeling similar emotions. Here they were under the stars with no appointments, no work in the morning, no reason to get out of bed if they didn't want to.

He kissed her gently and then with more fervor. "Not as exciting as you. Let's go back to the room." He stood and held his hand out for her. She took it gratefully, and then he pulled her against his side, effectively ending any further argument.

Jordan did achieve the detective's position, and no surprise, he was an excellent investigator.

His hours virtually remained the same, except the few times when he was on call. Fortunately, his captain didn't have a personal life and tended to take all the overtime calls. But often, when they detained a suspect and couldn't obtain a confession, they'd call in Jordan.

He was a natural; even criminals liked him. He had the ability of making everyone feel comfortable.

"They don't confess because they are pressured; they confess because they want to," Jordan had explained after one exciting situation.

Uniformed officers had apprehended suspects who supposedly raped a cocktail waitress. The detectives in the rape division couldn't seem to elicit a confession from the perpetrators and were standing in the hall frustrated. They knew the guys had committed the crime; several witnesses had seen them walk out after her, but it would make it incredibly easier if they could obtain a written statement. Jordan's captain, having overheard the detective's frustration, indifferently suggested sending Jordan in to speak with them, even though Jordan wasn't in rape.

The detectives allowed him, and it wasn't ten minutes and Jordan had one guy confessing to everything and consequently his friend felt compelled to do the same after hearing about his friend's admission of guilt.

Jordan never talked about police work, but that day, he'd called Jaynee all excited and continued the conversation when he came home. He loved being a detective, and she thought he would never quit.

Again, over the next few years, it was the only other cause of discord among them. Several times when they went to dinner with another couple, typically cops, she would hear stories. She would try to remain calm, not wanting to upset Jordan and start an argument. Luckily, they were usually only old stories about how some woman offered her body in exchange for a ticket.

They'd been married for almost five years, so she was getting used to the stories about fights, but she still hated to hear them. She tried to prepare herself for more of the same this evening, as they walked into a restaurant to meet some of Jordan's co-workers.

John, the only detective she knew, was there with his newest girl — who Jaynee had tried to strike up a conversation — but it was no use; the girl was dumber than a box of rocks. Patrick, she recognized the other man's name, worked with Jordan in auto-theft. His wife seemed nice, but uninterested in socializing. Two other detectives, Powe and Williams, worked in Homicide, according to Jordan. The men weren't married, and neither had chosen to bring a date.

Jaynee listened to the office politics and the *he-said, she-said* monologues, finding herself bored with the melodrama. The men were worse gossipers than the women she'd worked with in restaurants.

As if cued by their conversation, Powe raised his hand to break into an exchange she couldn't hear between John and Patrick. "So ... we heard we almost had a new case on our hands, and here we thought our jobs were exciting."

Jordan winced in his seat.

"Man! Can you believe that?" Patrick retorted in response. "Li should have been locked away years ago; instead, he's sporting an AK47 and taking potshots —"

"Excuse me," Jordan interrupted Patrick, tapping his pockets as he stood up in front of his chair. "I just realized I think I left my credit card in my jacket. Jaynee, do you have your purse?"

He knew she didn't. She always left it inside the vehicle when they were together. "Uh, no," she answered suspiciously. "It's in the truck."

Jordan reached for her hand, pulling her up at once beside him. "Let's go get it."

Jaynee sat back down. "That's okay, Jordan. You go. I'll wait here."

Patrick rested his hand on Jordan's arm. "Hey, hold on a minute, man. You're the hero in this one. If it weren't for you, we might all be dead."

Jaynee eyed Jordan contemptuously. "I'm interested, Jordan. I haven't heard this story."

Jordan sat back down in defeat, his jaw clenched. Apparently, this wasn't a story he wanted to share.

"So," Patrick began again, his face animated, "we've arrested Li many times for auto-theft, but the judge always releases him ... since it isn't a *violent crime*." He made quotes in the air, sneering at the judge's words. "To make a long story short ... Jordan and I were eating lunch when John calls. They'd just made an arrest in a string of *armed* carjackings, and this perp starts singing, giving them the head of their gang, who just so happens to be Li. As I said, we'd arrested Li repeatedly, but now we had him on multiple armed offenses and an informant.

"John told us to meet him at the suspect's mom's house; we were just supposed to bring him in for questioning.

When we got there, his mom answered the door and said loudly, 'he not here, go away!'" Patrick did a bad impression of an Asian accent. "So, we knew right away Li was there.

"John escorted the mother downstairs, and I called for Li to come out. Li shouted from behind a door right off the front room, 'Is my mom still here?' And this is where it gets exciting. I don't know how Jordan knew, but he told him 'yeah, she's right here.' Li must not have believed him, though, because the next thing I knew, Jordan pulled me to the floor, whispering frantically, 'He just racked a gun! Go now! Stay down!' I hadn't heard anything. And then, BAM!'"

Jaynee jumped when he clapped his hands in front of him.

Patrick made eye contact with her. "Sure enough, the rounds commenced. And y'all know the story from there ... four hundred eighty-six rounds later, SWAT, and a whole hell of a lot of paperwork ..."

Jaynee said nothing the entire dinner, and no surprise, Jordan did have a credit card with him. He requested their check as soon as he finished eating, apologizing to his co-workers that he needed to get up in the morning.

Jordan slid his arm around Jaynee as they left the table and directed her out of the restaurant, but she wriggled herself free as soon as they passed through the exit. She waited as he opened her door but refused assistance. Even with the running boards, it was difficult getting into his truck, but she could manage.

She waited until he climbed up in the truck and then let him have it. "You were shot at? With an AK — whatever it was." Jordan nodded, apparently embarrassed by his friend's blunder. "And you didn't tell me? You never tell me anything." Traitor tears formed in her eyes when all she wanted to do was be angry.

He rolled his eyes, sighing deeply, an attempt at downplaying the severity of the incident. "You don't want to hear it, Jaynee."

"Yes, I do."

"No, you don't, trust me."

She glared at him. "Was that the only time?"

"No," he admitted. He may have kept his police work from her, but he never lied when she asked a direct question.

She exhaled loudly, attempting to control her temper. "How many times, Jordan? How many times has someone attempted to take your life that you've failed to mention?"

He licked his lips, then looked out the window, evidently deciding whether to tell her the truth. "Three times with a gun," he said in a solemn voice. "But that was when I was on the road. Those situations don't occur now."

"But it did!" The tears ran free now. "When you discovered that ring of motorcycle thefts and located the warehouse where they were taking them apart...that I had to hear about on the news. What if they'd been ready when you busted in the door? What if they had machine guns, too?"

"It's not like television. Li was a freak incident, and I'm fine, obviously." His tone abruptly turned; it had an edge she rarely heard.

In the last four and a half years of marriage, she'd learned his moods. Knew when she'd pushed him too far, but she didn't care. She wanted to know, and she knew Jordan would never hurt her. "I want to know, Jordan. I hate not knowing what is bothering you. When you're melancholy and I wonder if I did something wrong ... I need to know."

He shook his head and huffed. "You don't know what you're asking."

"Yes, I do. I hate not knowing. I hate this!" she fumed.

Jordan turned to her then, his eyes bore into hers. "You don't want to know that I had to hold a two-year-old in my arms, trying to do CPR after he'd fallen into a pool and drowned because his mother was busy in her room having sex with some random man. Or, when I got into a fight at the scene of an accident where the motorcyclist was so drunk that he fought over his dead friend and actually threw his brains at me. Is that what you want to know? Is that what you want me to come home and discuss?" He hit the steering wheel in frustration.

Jaynee couldn't speak; she'd never seen him lose it and hit something.

"I warned you that you didn't want to know," he seethed.

She lowered her voice, hoping to calm him down, but she didn't want to drop the argument this time. "You're wrong, Jordan. I do want to know. I just don't want you to have to contend with it either." Before she could rethink her words, something she swore she'd never say burst out of her mouth, "I want you to quit, Jordan. We don't need the money ... your business does fine, and I can't endure this anymore."

The look in his eyes was shock at first, and then she watched as his face transformed into something else — indignation. "Fine!" he hissed. "I'll resign when you get pregnant! How's that for a compromise?"

She'd heard this before, but never in this context. He'd always said he'd quit and said he didn't want to be a cop when they had children, but he'd never used it as an ultimatum against her before now. So now what? If she still refused to get pregnant, did that mean she didn't care about Jordan? If she did get pregnant, only because he wanted her to, then how would she feel toward him? Would she always resent him, feeling as if he'd forced her into something she didn't want right now?

It wasn't that she didn't want children; she just wanted to be finished with school. And she'd said it so often that she felt as if she had to stick to her decision. She had less than a year to go. Really, she should be finished by fall and would be able to graduate with her master's degree by next spring. She'd taken so many classes, even through the summer, to finish at her five-year mark.

She hadn't answered him, and he glowered at her. "That's what I thought." He turned his head to look out the front window, threw the truck into drive, and pulled out of the parking lot too fast. The tires squealed in protest.

"Jordan ... I ..." she tried to speak, but her words hitched in her throat.

He turned to her, his face bright red. "What, Jaynee?"

She bit her lip to hold back the tears, but she felt the strain in her throat she always got when she cried. "Never mind ... I'm sorry."

"I'm sorry too," he retorted.

But his words didn't match his tone, and she wondered what he'd really meant. Was he sorry for falling in love with her? Was he sorry for marrying her? No matter how angry he was, she couldn't believe that.

Jaynee pulled up the center console as he used to and shifted her body closer to his, resting her head on his shoulder. Tears poured down her face, but she made every effort not to make a sound or wipe them away, so he wouldn't know.

He didn't push her away; instead, he rested his head on hers and stroked the side of her face. "I'm sorry, love, that was uncalled for. We'll work this out, and I promise I'll never keep anything from you again."

She pushed back the tears and the doubt. She wanted to believe him.

Chapter Twenty-Seven

Their fifth anniversary ...

For their fifth anniversary, Jordan surprised Jaynee with airplane tickets to Florida.

Since she'd moved to North Carolina, she'd returned to Florida twice a year, but never with Jordan. He'd always said she deserved the time alone with her family. And besides, with only so much vacation time, wouldn't she rather they spend their vacations in the mountains or on a cruise.

But this year, he rented a car and booked reservations on Clearwater Beach. That way, as he'd explained it, they could be together at night and spend some alone time on the beach, but they could still visit her grandmother who was having knee surgery. Gram was eighty-four and the surgeon didn't want to perform the surgery, but Gram insisted, saying she didn't want to live if she couldn't walk. Her doctor surrendered to her wishes, admitting she did have a healthy heart, and if anyone was going to survive surgery, she was. But just in case, Jaynee wanted to be there before she went under for fear it may be the last time she'd see her.

After checking into their hotel, they headed over to her grandmother's house to visit with her before she went to the hospital.

Jordan glanced at Jaynee briefly as he turned onto her grandmother's road. "So, do you suppose we might run into any of your old buddies while we're here?" he asked surreptitiously.

She narrowed her eyes. "I don't have any old friends. None in Florida anyway. I told you that Rainey, the girl I grew up with, moved to New York right out of college."

He sighed when she waved off his inquiry.

Then it occurred to her. It had been five years since Jordan and she had met. She'd told him her ex was in prison – for five years. Had that been weighing on his mind all these years? Could he be jealous? She ignored the implication; it wasn't even worth getting into it. How could she ever want anyone but Jordan? She couldn't understand why he would even consider such a thing, especially after all this time.

She wondered if he would accompany her every visit back to Florida now. Not that she cared; she loved having him here. Sometimes she got bored when she was alone. No ... he couldn't tolerate vacationing here twice a year. Certainly, he wouldn't forbid her from coming alone. She started to form her question, but then decided against it. She would wait and see what happened.

He never introduced the issue again, and they had a fantastic time. The days were temperate enough for sunbathing and swimming, and the evenings were perfect to stroll down the beach hand in hand.

One evening, Jaynee took Jordan to Pier 60. "When I lived here and felt like escaping, I would come down here at night. It always made me feel as if I were vacationing in some tropical locale." The beach at the end of Highway 60 was too crowded with tourists in the daytime to be relaxing, but at sunset, it turned into a festival.

Jordan had his arm latched around her waist. "It sort of reminds me of our first anniversary, the cruise to San Juan, only safer. I never felt comfortable there."

She laughed. "Exactly where do you feel comfortable?" She leaned back against his chest as they marveled at the street performers who painted and danced for money.

He tightened his grip around her and nuzzled her neck, laughing too. "That's true. When I have such a precious commodity that I'm in charge of protecting, how can I relax?"

"You're so silly, Jordan. I don't think anyone is going to try to run off with me."

He kissed the top of her head. "They'll be sorry if they try."

She sighed. She never had to worry when he was with her. Jordan would always protect her. She'd never fretted wherever they went, even Puerto Rico. She knew nobody would take him on.

They made their way over to the fire show, her favorite performance. She'd seen his act many times over the years.

Jaynee grabbed Jordan's arm and tried to pull him back. "Don't stand so close —" Her warning was belated; the entertainer signaled her out to assist in his presentation. Jaynee shook her head wildly.

Jordan nudged her forward, thrilled to impel her in the spotlight, knowing it was her least favorite position. "Go ahead, darlin'.'" He winked and smiled with obvious delight. "I'll enjoy watching this."

***

When they returned to North Carolina, Jaynee had made her decision on what she needed to do next in her life.

It would be difficult, but with finals coming up, she thought she could manage. It was October, and she just needed until December, early December at that. She had several school papers to complete, and of course, the time needed to finish her novel. She wanted to finish all her classes in the next two months and graduate in the spring. It would keep her occupied morning and night.

***

They'd been back from Florida for two weeks, and since Jaynee had been working frantically to finish her classes, Jordan had barely seen her.

At the normal time he went to bed, he waited by the stairs to see if she would follow as she usually did. Although she awoke two hours later, she usually came to bed with him, but she hadn't for the last few nights.

They'd had such a wonderful time in Florida; he'd even enjoyed the time they'd spent with her family. Then, there were the days they'd stayed on the beach, and the nights — they'd made love almost every night. He'd been a little worried they might encounter her ex, fearful he'd kill him if he ever met him. But she'd dismissed his question as immaterial. She'd understood what he was referring to when he'd asked about old buddies, but she obviously hadn't wanted to discuss it, which was probably a good idea, so he hadn't pressed her on the subject.

Now he was confused. He understood this was it for classes, but didn't she always have papers and finals due? It'd never made a difference before. "Goodnight," he called from the stairs.

Jaynee looked up and smiled. "Goodnight. I'll be up in a few."

She hadn't moved an inch from behind her computer, so he stomped upstairs like a scorned child.

By Sunday it was worse, it had been almost three weeks. The last two weeks she'd complained of PMS, which she never did. And then, it was that time. He was going insane. Not because they hadn't made love, but that she didn't want to be with him. He wanted her to come to bed, simply to feel her beside him. He didn't have to have sex. He'd gone without for several years before he met Jaynee. But the idea of her not wanting him caused him grief beyond words.

Sunday had always been their day. The only activity outside the two of them was church. He would wake her in the morning, the way she always liked, and then they would go to church. They'd have a light lunch afterward, and if the weather was nice, they'd do something outdoors. But if it was bad weather, they'd spend all day indoors watching old movies or reading, and those days were always the most enjoyable.

But this morning Jaynee wasn't in bed. Not once in five years had she awoken before him. He started downstairs, but saw light emanating from the door of their entertainment room.

Jordan stepped inside, and there, curled up on the sectional, an afghan draped over her midriff, was Jaynee.

He walked over to where she was curled up and lifted her to carry her back to their bed. Need and passion flared through him as he held her in his arms.

She started awake. "Jordan?" she said through half-opened eyes.

"Yes, love?"

"What are you doing?" Her voice sounded confused.

He smiled down at her. "I'm taking you back to bed."

She frowned. "What time is it?"

"It's still early ... there's no rush," he implied a little suggestively.

Her head whipped around as if she were looking for something — an escape. "I'm awake. I'm not tired. I have a few things I have to finish, and I'm starving. Are you hungry?" Her words rushed from her lips as if desperate to convey something.

He sighed and shook his head, then set her down in the hallway. "I'm not hungry," he grumbled. *Not for food*, he thought. He was ravenous for affection, but he guessed she wasn't willing to help him with that. Pride got the best of him, and he stormed off, leaving her standing alone.

He remained upstairs for the remainder of the morning, only coming down when it was time to leave for church.

He grabbed a muffin and coffee. "It's time to go Jaynee, or we'll be late."

After church, it was the identical situation. Jaynee found a million things to occupy her, and when it was time for bed, again she insisted she wasn't tired and would be up in a minute.

The weeks passed, and before long, it was Thanksgiving. As always, the entire family gathered at his mother's house.

The day dragged, and Jordan found he was in a bitter mood, snapping at the most minuscule reasons.

Jaynee kept herself busy in the kitchen, assisting his mother and sisters, but that wasn't abnormal, she'd always been comfortable at family get-togethers. She'd taken to his family as if they were her own, and that reflection brought on another wave of dejection.

Was it only him she was reacting icily to? The men congregated in the family room watching football while the women cooked and interacted. Jordan found himself scrutinizing everything Jaynee did. She looked happy. But how was that possible? She was never good at hiding her feelings. If she was upset, he could always tell. She'd always complained he could read her like a book. So why did she look so cheerful, when something was wrong? Unless it *was* just him. Maybe she'd grown so cold that she didn't even care. He shook his head at the notion. It couldn't be ... it wasn't possible.

"What's not?" Bobby's deep bass voice interrupted Jordan's thoughts.

Jordan turned to him in confusion, bothered that he'd interrupted his lamenting. "What, Bobby?"

"I don't know, man, you tell me. You shook your head and said, *not possible.*"

"Nothing, I don't know what I was thinking." He was going insane, that's what ... talking aloud to himself. He was losing his mind.

Jaynee and Jordan were the last stragglers. He'd been ready to leave hours earlier, but Jaynee kept talking with Pat.

When he couldn't stand another minute, he curtly interrupted their chatter. "I have to get up in the morning, Jaynee. Can we go?" The police department didn't give

Friday off because it was the day after Thanksgiving. In fact, the day after a holiday was very busy. Reports would've already started piling up on his desk from officers who *did* have to work on holidays, taking complaints and calls.

As soon as they arrived home, he went upstairs without saying a word. He knew the drill. He wouldn't solicit or insinuate anymore. When she was ready, she'd have to approach him.

The entire week passed, and Jordan wrestled with the idea of going home after work. Why bother? His wife obviously didn't want him.

He'd always looked forward to going home after marrying Jaynee. He'd rush from his office, regardless of what was happening or what papers he needed to sign. But lately, he didn't see any reason to hurry, as she was too busy with her schoolwork to pay him any attention these last two months.

Every night this week, however, even though he'd started coming home later and later, she had dinner waiting for him — and not just any dinner — his favorites. Meals he knew she didn't like, but he craved. Good old-fashioned recipes like Baked Macaroni and Cheese and Meatloaf. Homemade food you couldn't find in a restaurant. Jaynee preferred to create fancy, elaborate meals and plenty of southwestern dishes, which he enjoyed too. But whenever she wanted to do something special for him, she would prepare his favorite foods. Thursday night when he came home, later than usual, she had Chicken Marsala waiting. It was his favorite, and he knew it took a long time to prepare.

Jordan couldn't help but hope that whatever had been her problem, she was certainly over it. Though not touching, they sat together on the sofa watching a funny sitcom. He actually laughed; it was an uncomfortable feeling. He realized he hadn't laughed in weeks. She gazed up at him with those beautiful eyes of hers, and he was instantly lost in them. He wanted to ask what had been wrong, but decided not to push his luck. When it was respectfully late enough to retire, Jordan stood and held out his hand for Jaynee.

She took his hand and squeezed it once, but then quickly released it. "I'm not tired, Jordan. I'm going to stay up a little while longer. I didn't have time to read over my final paper I need to send tomorrow because I was busy all afternoon."

"Doing what?" he snapped, his voice unexpectedly harsh, but he didn't care. "What were you doing that's so important you couldn't get your school work finished before I come home, Jaynee?"

She didn't answer. She looked down as if not wanting to explain.

"I work two jobs, and I was able to finish college. I provide a substantial living for us, and I want you to finish your college, but the least you could do is *want* to be with me when I come home."

"Please don't do this, Jordan," she pleaded, her eyes already tearing up.

Well, it wasn't working this time. "Don't do what, Jaynee? What am *I* doing? You know what, never mind." He turned to leave.

"Jordan, it's not you — it's me. I'm sorry. Please, this is almost over...I'm almost finished."

She said the words, but made no attempt to follow him, so he continued walking.

The words rung truer than he could've ever imagined. It *was* almost over. Two months was too long for her to ignore him. He didn't turn around. Instead, he stormed upstairs, slamming the door behind him.

Chapter Twenty-Eight

Three days ago ...

Friday night again, another week, Jordan thought. He couldn't bear going home, seeing Jaynee, wanting her.

It was obvious she no longer cared after giving her, *it's not you, it's me* speech. But for the life of him, he couldn't fathom what had gone wrong. The last thing he remembered was Florida. It was a fantastic trip. They had a magnificent time and nothing anomalous had happened since. Had she been contemplating her ex? The idea drove him mad. Had she seen him the last couple of times she'd gone? Had he interrupted their rendezvous by accompanying her? Is that why she'd been so cold lately?

He gave Jaynee every part of himself. He didn't hang out with the guys every night as some men did. Ronny never went home. John and he would go out almost nightly. Rachael never seemed to notice; it was as if she didn't care. They had been married longer than Jaynee and him, and they didn't have children either. Jordan couldn't see Rachael with kids anyway; she wasn't like Melissa. She was always worried about breaking her nails.

It was no wonder Ronny never wanted to go home. Rachael always nagged at him about something or other, even in front of the family. Ronny was like a whipped dog, and he just accepted it for some reason.

John was another story. He went from one woman to the next, but never settled down. He preferred to spend all his time gambling. Many a day when he should have been working, Jordan noticed he was in Cherokee. Jordan never mentioned anything to John, because he was his best friend. But still, there was only one thing in Cherokee — gambling. And it worried Jordan. He would have to confront John soon before it became uncontrollable. He couldn't trust someone with gambling debt over his head. It would be too much of a liability to keep him on as an employee.

He and Jaynee were different from any couple he'd ever known. They genuinely cherished being together. On the rare occasion the guys forced him to go out for UFC night at Wild Wings or a friend's bachelor party, he couldn't wait to return home — to Jaynee.

She would always encourage these outings and then would send him seductive text messages until he arrived home, where she would be waiting, dressed in something frilly she'd purchased to surprise him, knowing how much he liked surprises.

They enjoyed everything together. She'd even learned to whitewater kayak because he enjoyed the sport so much. So for her to unexpectedly say it was almost over, confused him.

She'd been working diligently to finish school, and this was it, one of the stumbling blocks in their relationship.

She'd promised they would try to have a baby afterward. Now he wasn't certain if he even wanted a child, it would just make everything that much more complicated.

Especially after a day like today.

Normally after a horrible day, he would rush from his office to be with Jaynee. Obviously, he couldn't disclose his police work. It would just cause her grief and instigate their argument about how he should quit. But, he wanted to confide in her tonight. He wanted her to hold him and understand his anguish. After what he saw on a day-to-day basis, it was a wonder he even wanted children. It was foolish to want to bring an innocent child into this world.

When he arrived at the station this morning, he'd had a criminal waiting for interrogation. Not an unusual occurrence, and usually something he would have anticipated with enthusiasm. It was always an interesting challenge, breaking a person's will, having them confess their dirty deeds.

But this morning was different. When he entered the room where they'd detained the car thief, he saw nothing but a child. Uniformed officers had apprehended the barely twelve-year-old boy jacking the Cherokee his division had left as a ploy.

He worked the boy easily; the youngster knew nothing. He was only delivering vehicles to a specific location. From there, an older boy delivered them somewhere he wasn't privy to. For his part in the thievery, he received protection, and sometimes the older kid would throw him a few bucks. He knew neither the older boy's name nor where officers could locate him, and his vague description could be one of a thousand teenagers in Charlotte.

After an hour of talking with the minor, Jordan drove him home. No need to press charges, as it would only get him thrown in detention hall, and he would emerge worse than he'd entered. No, the wiser course was for Jordan to monitor the boy, befriend him, and try to talk some motivation into him.

When they arrived at the boy's house, Jordan followed him inside to speak with his mother, hoping she could provide him additional information for his paperwork and that she'd be concerned how her son spent his evenings.

The boy's mother was lounging on her sofa, watching Court TV when he entered. She didn't spare her son a fleeting glance but instead glared at the man in her doorway. "Who're you?" Her tone was indignant. Obviously, she didn't appreciate an officer entering her house.

"I'm Detective Jordan Monroe, ma'am. Your son —"

"What'd he get caught doin'?"

"Auto theft," he answered without emotion. "I have a few questions."

"Humph. What d'ya wanna know?" Her words held no concern, only irritation at him interrupting her show.

Jordan sighed. This was going to be fun. "Willie didn't know his middle name. Does he have one?"

The woman looked at her boy sitting, head lowered, in a tattered chair. "Willie, don'cha know your middle name?" Her face puckered as if it were her son's job to know his own name, not his mother's.

Willie shook his head as tears started rolling down his face.

The woman turned back to Jordan. "Don' know, can't 'member. Maybe I din't give 'em one."

At this juncture, Jordan was sure this woman was worthless as a parent. "How 'bout his date of birth?"

"No idea'r. Was summer. It was hot I 'member that."

Jordan sighed, exasperated. "His father's name ..."

The woman rolled her eyes and harrumphed. "No idea'r? Wouldn't matter if I did ... We through?" She turned away and clicked the volume up on the remote.

Jordan walked over to Willie and handed him his card with his number on it. "Willie, my man, you stay away from them other boys, ya hear me? Call me if they come 'round, and I got your back, K?" The boy nodded.

Jordan had wanted to strangle the woman, but he left the apartment without another word. His temper had been unmanageable lately. He needed to get a fix on himself. He couldn't deal with the scum he had to interact with daily with his current attitude. It wouldn't serve him well; he would end up in a fight.

His head fell to the desk. He needed to hold his wife; she was the one person who could soothe him. But he couldn't even confide in Jaynee. It would mean he would have to relive the conversation, and he just wanted to repress it.

"Dear Lord," he prayed. "Please help me. Help me be a better man. Help me understand what's happening. I love her. I want everything to be right again. Please show me what I need to do."

Instantaneously, he knew. He would go home. He would confront Jaynee with his love, the correct way. He would make her understand. He would talk to her, find out what was bothering her, and he would do whatever she wanted —

John stormed into the room without an inkling of apprehension for what Jordan may have been doing. "Come on, grumpy, let's go!"

"Go where?" Jordan grunted. He had no desire to go anywhere.

"We're going out! Ronny and I are taking you drinking."

Jordan shook his head and huffed. "You know I don't drink anymore, John."

"You do tonight!" John retorted, grabbing Jordan by the arm and pulling him out of his chair. John was a big guy, but he wasn't stronger than Jordan. He was tall, naturally lean and strong, a runner. But he didn't work out like Jordan and wasn't as proficient in martial arts. Jordan knew this because they'd sparred many times. Still, Jordan allowed John to haul him from his office anyway.

Ronny was waiting when they arrived at the wing house. He'd already ordered a pitcher and was working on his mug when John and Jordan approached.

It only took a few beers for Jordan to start rambling. He'd never before uttered a word about Jaynee to anyone, especially not John and Ronny. He suddenly wished Bobby had come, because here he sat, pouring out his heart to these men, who wouldn't know a relationship if it hit them upside the head. They continued to refill his mug, obviously excited at the prospect of him joining them in the misery of their pathetic lives.

From there, it only took a couple of shots of tequila John had ordered to incite Jordan to wanna fight. Anyone would suffice, and he didn't even care that he was so wasted he'd probably lose.

He could feel the misery and frustration aching for release. It didn't help matters that John insisted that if Jaynee wasn't getting any at home, she was getting it somewhere. Suddenly, John looked like an ideal outlet for his wrath, but Jordan's cell phone rang at the exact moment he was debating whether he'd pummel John here or drag him outside. Instead, he stared at the number, deciding whether to answer.

"Hi, Lor — raine." His words were sluggish and slurred; he never was a proficient drunk.

"Hey ... you okay? You seemed upset today. I just wanted to make sure everything was okay."

"No ... 'm not o — kay. I'm DRUNK! Would you come take me home?"

***

Lorraine didn't think twice. She'd been waiting for this for years. She knew Jordan wasn't suggesting her home, but possibly, she could persuade him.

Jordan was sitting on the bench outside the restaurant, leaning against the brick wall when Lorraine pulled up to the curbside. Knowing Jordan never drank, the scene infuriated her. He looked helpless, and Jordan never looked helpless. He was the strongest man she'd ever known.

As much as Lorraine had wanted to hate Jaynee, she never could; she was a very likable person and had always made Jordan happy. But tonight, hatred rushed through her veins for what she was doing to him.

Lorraine opened the passenger door for Jordan but then realized maybe she needed to assist him as he stumbled to the car. "Do you need help?"

"No, 'm ... fine." Jordan dipped his head to enter her car, which sat too low for him. He seemed to have a difficult time turning his shoulders just right to get through the door. He hadn't thought to open it wider. He slumped into the seat, his head falling back against the headrest, looking as if he'd already passed out.

Lorraine reached across his body to the seatbelt and locked it into place.

Jordan's head rolled to the side. "Why are you so good to me, Lorraine?" His words slurred again.

"Because I love you, Jordan," she answered honestly.

He had no response and said nothing the entire ride. It was a long thirty minutes. Lorraine wanted to ask him the questions in her head: Why was he putting up with Jaynee torturing him? Why couldn't he see she'd loved him since they were teenagers? She'd always been there, always given him advice. Why couldn't she enlighten him now?

She stopped at an empty driveway at the bottom of the gravel road. Jordan turned to look at her, clearly sober enough to know they weren't at his house. Lorraine shifted the car into park and then turned her body toward Jordan. He was staring at her, his expression indistinguishable, but she knew if she didn't at least try, she would always regret it.

Lorraine leaned in closer, feeling the heat of his breath wash over her face. And she felt something else, a longing, passions that needed to be filled. He wanted this too. She leaned closer, so their lips were only inches apart.

He opened his mouth to speak, and she shushed him.

He sat upright, alert. "I love her, Lorraine. I love Jaynee. I always have, and I always will. I'm sorry. We shouldn't be here. Please, just take me home."

Lorraine felt as if he'd slapped her, but she shifted the car into drive and drove up the long road, pulling into Jordan's drive. She pulled close to the front door, still concerned with his walking abilities, but offered no further help as he exited.

She'd needed to talk to Jordan about what she'd found, but he'd sidetracked her when she'd called earlier. Deciding Jaynee was the one she needed to speak with, she pulled out of the driveway but parked down the street. She figured Jordan would probably crash, so she'd wait for a while and then send Jaynee a text.

***

Jordan struggled with his keys, trying to unlock the deadbolt, but Jaynee opened the door.

She gasped as he stumbled through the entry. "Oh my heavens, Jordan, I've been so worried." She touched his arm, and he jerked away from her. "I've been calling you for the last hour."

Good, he thought, then remembered he hadn't received a call. He peered at his phone. It was dead. Lorraine must have been his last call. He tossed the phone on the coffee table.

Jaynee eyed the phone or maybe the way he'd tossed it. Then her eyes darted to his. "Are you drunk?"

He threw his head back. "What difference does it make? You don't care, and you know what, Jaynee, I don't either. You need to make a decision. If we're finished and you plan to leave, you need to do it now. I can't take this anymore. If I'm not what you want, release me and let me continue with my life. I can't handle coming home, you not wanting me —"

"Jordan," she exclaimed, cutting him off, approaching him, the closest she'd been to his face in weeks.

He couldn't find the strength to push her away again. She was dressed in his favorite threadbare t-shirt and smelled fantastic. He closed his eyes, attempting to suppress the feelings that rushed through his body.

She touched his arm again. "You don't know what you're saying."

He pulled away from her again and walked over to the sofa. His head was starting to spin. "I'm not that drunk," he barked. "You're almost finished college, so I guess you don't need me anymore." Despite his anger, his head dropped to his chest at his words and their revelation. "Just leave if that's what you want. I won't stop you. I'll survive ... I'll be okay." He willed the words to be true. He knew he wouldn't literally die, but he just didn't see how he could go on living without her. He slumped onto the loveseat in the front room they never used — it was just for looks — wasted space like his life.

She sat down beside him. "Oh, God, Jordan, how could you consider?" She didn't continue speaking; instead, she started kissing him. "Jordan, I love you. I've always loved you," she whispered under her kisses.

He didn't believe her, but he was unable to stop himself. He soaked up her kisses as a man would drink water in the desert — as if it were his lifeline. She kissed him, and he couldn't resist kissing her back. He pulled her body to his, savoring every feeling. He wasn't drunk anymore. He wanted her so much that he couldn't think of anything else. He stood, taking her hand, but didn't give her an alternative this time as he pulled her toward the stairs. She walked beside him willingly.

As soon as they entered their bedroom, he scooped her up and laid her on the bed. She still hadn't objected. In fact, her eyes burned with the same desire. He honestly just wanted to hold her, comforted by the fact she wanted him too. But she started undressing him, and he lost all control.

It was as though they'd never missed a beat, as if the last two months hadn't happened. And when it was over, she curled up beside him as she'd always done.

Exhausted from the mental stress and too much alcohol, his eyes began to close. He stayed awake as long as possible, breathing in her scent. She smelled like the familiar vanilla he loved, the lotion she always used. Amazing how he'd missed just being close enough to smell her. He hadn't thought such a trivial part would be so important, but the fact was … he'd missed everything about Jaynee. It was as if he couldn't breathe when she wasn't a part of him. She was as important to him as food and water. He heard her sigh. It was a sigh of contentment, and it made him happy.

He lowered his head to hers, kissing the top of her head and breathing in her scent again, as if starved too long. "I love you, Jaynee," he whispered. He didn't want to mention anything negative when everything felt right, so he just uttered the truth. "Please don't ever stop loving me."

"I won't, Jordan. I love you too," were the last words he heard before he crashed.

✳✳✳

Jaynee heard Jordan's breathing change to a steady rhythm, indicating he was deeply asleep.

She'd been stunned to see Jordan drunk, but understood the reason. She never would have interpreted her standoffishness would lead him to believe she didn't love him. It'd been important, but tonight was the night she'd been waiting for. She'd planned a romantic evening for them, and it'd surprised her when he didn't come home. She'd called him several times and then called Bobby, who had no clue where Jordan was either. She hadn't wanted to call John or Ronny; she'd never felt comfortable around his other partners. Ronny always looked as if he hated her. And John, well ... she didn't know what to think of him; she just didn't feel at ease around him.

So she'd waited by the door, looking for his arrival. Who was she kidding? It was her fault. She should have told him, but she hadn't been ready.

Jaynee watched Jordan sleep. She didn't want to get up, but all that food was downstairs. She hadn't been thinking about dinner when Jordan came home and started giving her ultimatums. She'd thought about nothing but him and how she could never live without him.

She'd been afraid he'd found out that Brian had contacted her, and that was why he'd been so upset. But when she realized what he was thinking, she couldn't force herself to be angry at his accusation. She'd just wanted to show him how much she loved him.

Jaynee knew she'd have to explain Brian's appearance at the coffee shop where she went to study. She'd always been a creature of habit. Jordan had told her repeatedly not to stick to the same routine.

She thought back to the encounter earlier this morning. Brian had been at the coffee shop reading the paper when she slid into the same booth she did every morning.

"You've always been predictable, baby," he said, his tone mocking.

She jumped as she recognized the voice, choking on her first sip of coffee. "How did you find me?"

"It wasn't difficult. I had Kenny checking your grandma's mail till he saw a letter from North Carolina. It really is amazing that not once did anyone question him. He'd been doing work for several of the neighbors, helping elderly people with their garbage, mail, and newspapers since he was in the area anyway doing handyman work. Or, at least that's what they thought. He even made a little money, so he didn't complain. You know Kenny; he's fairly simple-minded. He's grown rather fond of your grandmother. I wouldn't be surprised if he kept returning to help her."

"He'd better not hurt her," Jaynee hissed, not wanting to make conversation with Brian. Her eyes kept darting to the door. Jordan seemed to know everyone. She could imagine if it got back to him she was talking with a guy in their favorite coffee shop. Not that anything was happening. He was sitting at a separate table than she was, merely two acquaintances talking. So why did she feel so culpable?

Brian waved off her comment. "Relax, Kenny wouldn't hurt a fly."

"Oh yeah, well he didn't have any problem practically jerking my arm out of its socket then shoving me to the ground. If it weren't for Jordan, who knows what he would have done to me?"

Anger flared in Brian's eyes. Whether it was her comment about Kenny or Jordan, she wasn't sure. "It wasn't supposed to happen like that, Caycee. He was only supposed to warn you not to date anyone."

"Well, that's what happens when you order alcoholics to do your bidding. Please leave me alone." She turned her head away, ending the conversation.

He started to stand up, but sat back down. "I've changed, baby. Honest. I haven't had a drink or any type of drug in almost six years, and I'm not going to start again. We were good in the beginning, remember?"

She turned and glared at him. "Brian, I'm married — happily married. Jordan is the best thing that has ever happened to me, and I love him more than life itself."

"But you're mine, Caycee. You'll always be mine. I was your first, and you were mine. That has to count for something," he pressed.

Jaynee closed her computer, packing it into her satchel. This was ridiculous; she shouldn't be having this conversation. She stood up with everything in her arms.

He grabbed her arm. "Please don't go."

She jerked away from him. "Don't you *ever* touch me again; you have no right." She took a deep breath. "We had six months together, that's all. The remaining time we were together, you were drunk or high or sleeping with other women. I haven't loved you since I discovered your infidelity, and truthfully, I don't think I ever loved you. I was immature and needed to escape my life. As it turned out, I stepped out of the frying pan and into a bonfire. I wanted to help you, but you were beyond help. Please leave and don't ever come back. I love my husband." She turned to walk away but looked back. "And not that it matters ... but you weren't my first. My virginity was stolen from me."

After her outburst, she darted out of the restaurant. She would have to tell Jordan; she couldn't keep this from him. She'd promised never to keep anything from him. It was terrible enough what she'd been doing to him for the past two months.

She'd tell Jordan about Brian showing up at the coffee house tomorrow, she decided.

Chapter Twenty-Nine

Jaynee stood in the kitchen, feeling wonderful after making love with Jordan for the first time in two months.

She hated the thought of telling him about Brian, but she knew with the other news she had, he wouldn't dwell on him.

She packaged up all the food; she could reheat it tomorrow. She picked up her cell phone out of habit to see if she'd missed any calls. She always kept it on silent; she hated being disturbed when she was writing. Her novel had been just as long of a struggle as school had been. As she neared the end, she found her days eaten up with her need to finish. Jordan didn't know about the book or the sample chapters she'd sent in for review. She could imagine his surprise when he found out she hadn't even graduated, and someone was interested in publishing her book.

There was a text message from Lorraine requesting she call no matter how late. That was weird. Lorraine and she'd always gotten along, but they weren't what she would consider friends. There'd always seemed to be a strain in their relationship. She couldn't be certain, but she sensed Lorraine was interested in Jordan. Jaynee never felt threatened by their working relationship, though, because Jordan never appeared to have the same feelings. He looked at Lorraine as indifferently as he did his sisters.

Not wanting to wake Jordan, Jaynee picked up her mobile and walked out onto the porch to return Lorraine's call. Jordan had looked so tired this evening and still had to get up so early; she hoped he would quit soon.

As a last-second precaution, she picked up her gun she always left near the door. She hated walking outside at night without Boomer for protection, but he was upstairs with Jordan. They lived deep in the country. Not that there were very large animals, but there was no light in the country, and you never knew what type of two-legged predator could be prowling the neighborhood.

Standing on the back porch, directly outside the French doors, she called Lorraine. She didn't bother closing the door; the cool air felt nice.

Lorraine answered on the first ring; no pleasantries, she simply started speaking. "Jaynee, I need to talk to you. I'm down the street."

"Oh ... okay, Lorraine, come around back. I'm on the porch."

Jaynee looked out at the starlit sky; it was beautiful. What a strange request for Lorraine to ask to speak with her, especially at this hour.

Minutes later, Lorraine stepped onto the porch. She just stared at her for a second.

Oops ... Jaynee tucked the gun under her arm and gestured for Lorraine to sit on the bench. "Well, this is unusual," she started.

Lorraine sat down and sighed. "Yeah, but I have to ask you a question. I planned to ask Jordan but then realized you might know, and I had a second question anyway."

Thoroughly confused, Jaynee waited.

Lorraine turned to her. "Jaynee, you know I do the bookkeeping, so I'm privy to everything you spend, right?"

"Yeah, so ...?" Jaynee asked, already peeved. She did know that, and it had bothered her. She'd always asked Jordan to get a personal card, but he put everything through the business.

The woman fidgeted in her seat some more as if she wasn't sure. "Well, you've always spent the exact amount on your credit card, you visit the salon every other month, you go to the coffee shop almost every day, and you drive about the same distance every month. So I was surprised when your credit-card bill escalated."

Jaynee was miffed. One, that this woman knew everything she did or lack thereof, and two ... she was clearly accusing her of something. "What's your point, Lorraine?" She didn't have time to play games. She shouldn't even be here; she belonged upstairs with her husband.

"I'm going to skip to my second question first, because the first doesn't matter depending on what you answer to the second."

"You're not making any sense, Lorraine," Jaynee said brusquely.

"Oh, it will, Jaynee. Do you love Jordan?" she asked, no hesitation and with deep inference.

Jaynee's intuition flickered again. It was as she'd suspected all along. "I love Jordan more than life itself."

"Well, that's what I'm afraid of, and quite frankly, if I didn't believe you, I wouldn't even be relaying this. I would like nothing better than to see you out of the picture, but I know it would kill Jordan."

Jaynee stared at Lorraine, shocked by the candidness of her statement.

"Jaynee, I don't need to ask you. I know the charges aren't from you. They are automatic drafts against your credit card by one of our life insurance companies. It's a different policy but from the same company we use for our other policies, so it was sure to go unnoticed because Jordan would never question your statement. He authorized you to spend thousands a month, and your account barely reaches a few hundred. So, imagine my surprise when your bill suddenly increased." Lorraine paused a second then stared at her. "I thought I had you. I thought I could prove you were cheating on Jordan. Instead, I found something much more shocking."

Jaynee shook her head. "What does life insurance have to do with me?"

"I checked into it. Someone took out a huge policy for the business on both you and Jordan. Let me explain. We already have a partners' insurance policy on Jordan; it's a common practice. If something were to happen to Jordan, we'd all suffer ... the company would suffer. But every one of the partners has a policy that will go back to the business if something happens to them. This is a separate policy, though, and since no one knows about it, he — I say he, because it has to be one of his partners — could find a way to sift the money through the company if something happened to you or Jordan."

"Sorry, Lorraine, I'm afraid I'm still lost."

Lorraine exhaled, exasperated. "Jaynee, there's no other way to say this, except spit it out. I think someone might try

—" She took in a deep breath, and her eyes actually looked concerned. "I think you might be in danger. The only reason someone would take out that large a policy ... is if they planned to kill one of you. I know Jordan didn't do it; he doesn't do any paperwork without me looking over it. And if Jordan died before you, the company would automatically go to you, but if you died first ..."

"Then they would kill Jordan next, you think?" Jaynee finally understood what Lorraine was implying. "And why didn't you tell Jordan?" she asked incredulously, amazed at how calmly she could discuss the possibility of her own death. But the thought of someone trying to murder Jordan enraged her.

Lorraine released an awkward huff. "That's very interesting."

"What is?" Jaynee asked, feeling perturbed by Lorraine's insinuations, but then acting so lax.

"*You*. You said nothing about your own impending death, but the concept of something happening to Jordan infuriates you. I can see you do love him." Lorraine took a moment to collect her thoughts and then answered Jaynee's question. "The reason I didn't say anything is because I *wanted* you to leave. But I never wanted you to die. That's why I realized I was wrong in not telling Jordan the moment I discovered the policy. He loves you, Jaynee. I see the pain he's been in these last few weeks and truly wonder if I couldn't kill you myself." Lorraine chuckled nervously.

Jaynee nodded. "I feel the same way, Lorraine. But I made it right tonight, and I *will* explain everything to Jordan tomorrow. But he's fine, I assure you." She thought about his eyes when he kissed her earlier. She'd caused him so much pain. She didn't realize how much until last night. She should've just gone to him, but she'd wanted to make certain.

Lorraine stood. "That's all I want. I know Jordan could never love me." Lorraine took another deep breath and then her voice was a whisper. "I attempted to approach Jordan before dropping him off earlier. I'm sorry, but you should know ... even drunk he had no interest, and Jordan has never been a good drunk. He loves you, Jaynee, and I do want him to be happy."

Jaynee stood too. "I understand."

"Are we okay then, or are you going to have him fire me in the morning?" she asked straightforwardly.

"We're okay, Lorraine." She reached out to Lorraine, careful of the revolver still tucked under her arm. She couldn't bring herself to be angry with her when she knew Lorraine only wanted the best for Jordan. She wasn't sure how she'd feel tomorrow, however, when the shock registered.

Lorraine leaned back and smiled. "You know, Jaynee, I always liked you, despite the fact you took the man-of-my-dreams."

Jaynee crinkled her nose. "Thanks, I think."

Lorraine turned and walked toward the front porch, but turned back before she rounded the corner. "Call me in the morning and let me know if you change your mind. I'd rather Jordan not be involved with my leaving. I'll go if it is what you want, but only after we figure out this situation."

Jaynee nodded solemnly in reply. Could someone really be trying to kill her husband — or her? She would wait until morning, but then, Jordan and she needed to have a long conversation about numerous things. He would just have to call off work; they could handle a Saturday without him.

***

Brian saw the woman approach Caycee on the deck. Strange time of night to be making house calls, but who was he to judge?

He was camping out in her backyard, hoping to get an opportunity to talk again. He'd seen her cleaning up the kitchen and had hoped she'd come outside. She always stayed up later than her husband did, and sometimes she'd walked their dog. But then, the woman had walked around the side of the house so he would have to wait to talk with Caycee. He'd actually dozed off waiting for the woman to leave.

***

Lorraine was such a busybody. He would deal with her later. Right now, Jaynee was the important one. He'd come too far to stop now. Everything was in place.

Lorraine had stepped around the side of the house and down the front stairs when he crawled from under the deck and strolled up behind Jaynee before she entered the house.

His intention was to strangle her, a victim of her old boyfriend who'd been sniffing around. He'd seen them talking at the coffee shop earlier today ... everything had worked out perfectly. He knew she'd been up to something.

He startled her when he came up behind her, quickly pulling her in a headlock and proceeding to choke her. Her arms flailed as she struggled to escape, but he had a perfect grip, and the jacket he wore was plenty thick that her clawing hand gained no purchase. She was such a tiny thing. For a second, he felt a twinge of remorse, but he squashed those feelings. It had to be done; it was the only way to make everything right again. He hadn't seen the gun she was holding until it discharged. He dropped his grip as she collapsed. He bent over her to assess the damage. She'd ended up shooting herself. He couldn't have planned it any better.

Slinking back down the steps, he was careful not to tread in any of North Carolina's famous red clay. It would be like leaving behind a plastered footprint.

***

Brian jumped when he heard a gunshot but couldn't see anything unusual.

Caycee was gone and so was the woman. He waited, assuming the shot had come from somewhere else, but he was sure it'd been nearby. He wondered if he should check on her, confront her as he'd originally planned. But if it was a gunshot, her husband would hear and come out to investigate — he *was* a cop after all. How ironic that she would marry a cop. Brian decided he would wait until morning when her husband left. He would talk to her then, insist she listen to him, prove to her that he'd changed.

***

Lorraine jumped at the sound. Was it a gunshot?

Jaynee had been holding a pistol ... would she have done something stupid? She hadn't seemed too upset about the news.

It was probably some redneck neighbor shooting at squirrels. Gunfire wasn't uncommon in the country. She jumped into her car and drove off, hoping Jaynee wouldn't have Jordan dismiss her in the morning.

Chapter Thirty

Today ...

Jordan bounded downstairs again to the cafeteria. He needed to find out all Brian knew about the night someone shot his wife.

He could see Williams and Powe through the glass; Brian's back was to the window. They were all sitting there, leaning back as if they were old friends.

Jordan entered the room, smacking the door open so hard it hit the wall, threatening to slam back against him. "So, what's the story?"

"Well," Williams began, "it seems your wife's lover has turned into a regular stalker." Jordan glared at the detective, and he quickly substituted his words. "Sorry, ex-lover."

Powe must have discerned his countenance. "Uh ... Jordan ... why don't you sit down? Brian's been cooperating so far; he wants to expose who's responsible as much as you do."

Jordan seriously doubted that, but he pulled out a chair and sat down on it backward. "I'm listening."

Williams leaned back in the chair again and pulled his leg up on his knee. "Evidently Brian spoke to your wife on Friday morning, and according to him, she wouldn't give him the time of day. But he'd noticed she stayed up later than you and decided he would attempt to talk with her, convince her he'd changed — that kind of nonsense."

Jordan gripped the table in an effort to remain seated. He wanted to pummel the man, but was also irritated with Jaynee. For one, not telling him about her interaction with him and two ... how many times had he told her to close those damn blinds? It didn't matter that they lived in the country; perverts were everywhere. All they needed was an invitation as simple as an open window to delude them into thinking a woman was interested.

Williams eyed Jordan and continued, "According to Brian, Jaynee was on the phone and then a woman appeared on the porch and they talked awhile. He didn't hear anything they said and actually dozed off, but said he awoke the same way you did, when he heard a gunshot. Of course, we already knew Jaynee had spoken with someone — your secretary, Lorraine. Jaynee had received a text from her and had returned her call. We investigated, but her account checked out. She'd driven you home earlier in the evening and had just wanted to confirm you were okay. Lorraine had no motive to hurt Jaynee, so we didn't pursue her as a suspect.

Jordan rolled his eyes. "So, he didn't see a woman shoot Jaynee?" He shoved his chair back from the table.

"No," Brian interjected, "but who else could have ... she was the only person there. I didn't hurt her, and you certainly weren't there to protect her."

Jordan jumped up from his seat. It took everything he had not to punch Brian again. "Jaynee shot herself." His entire body seethed at this man's impudence. He'd sent someone to hurt her once, and he had the nerve to question him.

Brian chewed his bottom lip and shook his head. "I don't believe it. When I talked to her earlier, she told me how *happily* married she was." Brian said the words bitterly as he stared at Jordan in total disbelief.

Jordan was finished; this conversation was getting him nowhere. It was obvious from Brian's reactions that he hadn't caused Jaynee's shooting, so he needed to find out who had. "I didn't say she did it purposefully, just that it was by her own hand, and I need to get to the reasons why." He looked at the detectives. The detectives didn't need him; they'd already gotten his statement the night Jaynee had been shot. "If you guys don't have anything for me, I'll call you when my wife wakes up. I'm finished here." Jordan opened the door. "I need to see my wife."

Jordan had to catch his breath before walking into Jaynee's room; he felt lightheaded.

He hadn't eaten anything today, but had already been in a fight, interviewed a suspect, and had to cope with the knowledge his wife had kept something from him. Not to mention there still wasn't a hundred percent chance she would recover. He gripped the outside of the doorjamb to stabilize himself.

Jaynee was motionless. She'd only spoken twice and only to him. He didn't want to leave, but he needed to do something.

If Lorraine had been even remotely responsible, he would expose the truth. And if she were guilty, he'd arrest her himself. Nothing in him could perceive such an outcome. Lorraine couldn't have hurt Jaynee. She wouldn't, not if she really cared about him, and somehow he always knew she had, just not to the extent of murder. It wasn't possible.

Jordan leaned over Jaynee, kissing her forehead. His mother started to stand to let him sit, but he motioned for her to stay. "I have to handle something else." Jaynee's heartbeat increased. She knew he was here, and it made her heart race. Was that a good thing? Had she been frightened of Brian? Or, had she been calling out for him? The suggestion drove him insane. Brian had admitted that Jaynee'd said she was happily married. Why would he repeat her statement when the notion was repulsive to him? He could hear the mocking in his voice, even as he'd uttered the words.

He lowered his mouth to her ear. "I love you, Jaynee," he whispered, watching the monitor, noticing her pulse increase. This was good; she loved him too. Despite the confusion of the last couple of months, she still loved him.

Jordan rested his hand on his mother's shoulder. "Mom, I need to go somewhere. I'll be gone a couple of hours. Will you be okay?"

Pat looked up at him, her eyes wide. "What if she wakes again?" She clearly struggled with the idea he would leave Jaynee's side again. He hadn't moved in over three days, and now when she might wake up, he was leaving?

"I know, Mom, but I have to handle something. It's important, but I'll rush."

"Jordan, what aren't you telling me, baby?"

"I can't discuss it." He walked out the door. The faster he could get there, the better. He still didn't have his mobile. It had died the night of the accident, and he hadn't thought to ask anyone to bring the phone and charger to the hospital.

Picking up the courtesy phone, he dialed the number; the line connected before the first ring ended.

"We need to talk," Jordan said.

"I know. Meet me at the Coffee House. I need to return home first. But by the time I backtrack to my residence and head back to the restaurant, you should have arrived."

Jordan hung up without a response.

He darted down the stairs. He wouldn't go to the restaurant; he'd head straight to the house. He could probably arrive faster if he drove as he did when he was responding to a call. He should have asked to borrow the detective's car, but they would ask too many questions.

If a cop attempted to pull him over, he'd just have to follow him, which wouldn't be a bad thing.

***

From down the street, he watched Lorraine pull out of the construction trailer's driveway.

He'd follow her. He needed to stop her before she told anyone what had happened the night Jaynee was shot. He knew she wouldn't have wanted to admit she was with Jaynee the night of the shooting, admit that she too wished Jaynee were dead, as he did. She was probably hoping Jaynee would die, and then she would provide comfort. He watched as she made her turn away from town, heading toward her house.

He kept a safe distance, even though he could tell she wasn't paying attention. Everything would work out perfectly. He'd already decided how she would die, and she was playing directly into his hand.

Who would suspect foul play in this type of demise? It was one of the easiest ways people committed suicide. He'd thought about it himself when everything'd looked hopeless, until he'd decided what needed to be done instead.

He had what he needed in his vehicle. They were all normal items for him to have in his possession. Whenever they did a lot of sanding or painting on a job site, he would wear the mask.

He watched as Lorraine pulled into her driveway, and the garage door opened. She'd left the interior garage door unlocked so she could enter without a key. She didn't pull into the garage. What a shame, he'd have to assist her.

Parking his vehicle on the street, he grabbed the mask. He'd already donned his gloves. He approached her garage, thankful she'd left the door open and the car running as if she'd be right back out.

He jumped into the car and pulled it forward, then pushed the remote to close the garage door. She'd be out in a minute, and instead of being cautious, she'd be curious, wondering if she'd pulled into the garage. Surprise would be on his side.

Lorraine stepped through the door cautiously, glancing around in confusion, but as he'd suspected, she must've decided she was losing her mind. She stepped into her car, and as she started to push the garage door opener, he grabbed her from behind the seat, clamping down hard on her arms and then lifting the cloth to her face. It only took a second, and she was out. He lowered the windows in the car, grabbed the folder she'd placed on the passenger seat and then stepped out after pushing the garage door button again until it rose halfway, then pushed it once more so it would close as he raced underneath it.

Perfect. It would surface that she was the one with Jaynee Friday night and that she was distraught. Nobody would doubt her decision to commit suicide.

Now he needed to return to the hospital and finish what he'd started.

***

He sat in a corner booth staring at the headline.
WIFE OF CHARLOTTE-MECK DETECTIVE FOUND SHOT SATURDAY MORNING.

He turned to the local section to read the article, skipping through all the mumbo-jumbo, reading only the facts.

> Wife of Nine-year Charlotte-Meck detective Jordan Monroe was found shot in their Stanfield home early Saturday morning. Detective Monroe, a highly-decorated officer, recognized for saving lives when a warrant for the arrest of a habitual criminal went awry earlier this year, discovered his wife of five years, Jaynee Monroe, unconscious in their home from a gunshot wound to the head...There are no reports of foul play at this time.

He needed to see her. Folding the paper, he left a tip on the table and headed toward the hospital.

***

Jordan made it to Lorraine's house quickly. What should have taken forty-five minutes, took less than thirty as he ignored every traffic light and drove as fast as traffic would allow and not one cop.

He pulled onto Lorraine's driveway. Had she come and gone already? He didn't think it was possible. He calculated the time it would have taken her to drive from the office to her house. He didn't think she would have been able to come and go. If she had, he would have seen her leaving; he'd been watching the entire way.

He stepped out of his vehicle, walked to the entrance, and rang the bell. He waited, but there was no answer. He wished he had his cell phone. What a time not to have it. He knocked on the door, practically beating it down, nothing. He started to walk back to his car but heard something from the garage. Was her car running?

"Oh, God ... NO!" He reached for the handle, struggling to open the door. It wouldn't budge. The entrance was useless; he'd built this house. The front door was steel with a top-notch deadbolt. But the rear of the house — the patio doors.

He picked up a rock as he rounded the side of the house, hoping she'd set the alarm. He smashed the rock through the windowpane, reached in, and unlocked the door. The alarm instantly rang. He raced across the kitchen, already inhaling the fumes saturating the air. He opened the door and felt to the side for the garage door opener, pushing it once to allow fresh air inside.

Jordan skipped the steps, bounding to the driver's door, pulling Lorraine out in seconds. She was breathing, but barely. How could this be happening? Twice in three days, he was holding one of the women closest in his life, in fear of their death. He laid her on the ground and returned to the car; he needed her phone.

This couldn't be a coincidence; something was going on. Jaynee had said Lorraine's name, but not in a terrified manner, more as though she'd needed something from her. And then Lorraine knew they'd needed to talk. She'd sounded apprehensive about seeing him.

He could hear sirens; he didn't have to call 911. When the instant alarm went off, the security company would have notified the police. Lorraine would have a considerable headache, but she would live.

He dialed his mom's cell phone. It rang several times before she answered, probably at the bottom of her purse.

"Mom," he said frantically. "How's Jaynee? Did she wake up?"

"Not when I was in there, she —"

Jordan cut her off. "What do you mean? Where are you now?"

"Jordan, it's fine. I didn't leave her alone. But I needed to get something to eat. I've been trapped there all morning while you've been running around."

"Who's with her, Mom?" he demanded.

"John showed up to see how she was, said he'd watch over her while I took a break. I don't know why —"

Jordan didn't know why either but suddenly he knew something wasn't right. Lorraine was no accident. Jaynee's shooting wasn't an accident. And John had connections to both Jaynee and Lorraine.

"Mom, go to the waiting area now." He couldn't believe he was going to do this, but it was his only option. "Do you see a tall surfer-looking kind of guy, about 6'4, longer sandy-blond hair?"

"There's one fellow who looks something like that."

"Is he wearing a black jacket and black jeans?"

"Uh, yeah ..."

"Give him your phone."

"You want me to do what?" she shrieked.

"Mom, trust me. His name is Brian. Give him your phone."

Jordan heard her approach him, asking if his name was Brian. He must have nodded because he couldn't hear a response. He couldn't believe he was doing this, but if it meant Jaynee's life, he could swallow his pride. Brian may be many things, but it was clear from his tormented face, he really wasn't there to hurt Jaynee. And right now, an outsider was all he could trust.

"Hello?" he heard Brian's tentative tone filled with questions. From all his stalking, he certainly knew Pat was his mother, but Jordan had clearly caught him off guard.

"Brian, it's Jordan. Listen, something is going on. I think Jaynee might be in danger. You need to go up with my mother and make sure no one else is allowed in with Jaynee."

"Dude ... You *want* me to see your wife?" he asked, bemused.

"*No*, I want you to protect her. I think you're right; she may be in danger. Don't let anyone other than you and Pat in Jaynee's room. Do you hear me?"

"Yeah, man, I hear you. Not sure I understand ... but sure." He sounded excited by the prospect, and Jordan was suddenly nervous, but he had to trust his instincts. Brian hadn't hurt Jaynee, and he was confident Pat wouldn't let him touch her.

"Brian, there's a man in there now; he's a cop too, and I want him out."

"You want me to force a cop out, are you fu — freaking crazy?"

"Pat will explain, just support her. They won't allow more than two people in her room, so tell them you're her brother."

Jordan disconnected the phone. The police and medics had arrived. He'd have to explain and get out of there fast.

***

Brian relayed the conversation to Pat as Jordan explained, leaving out the "in danger" part. He was pretty sure she didn't know about what was happening.

Her eyes narrowed at him. "And you are?"

"I'm Brian. Jaynee's brother."

"But, I thought —"

"I'm her stepbrother. Listen, Pat, we don't have much time. You and I need to go to her room, and you have to tell that John guy to leave, so I can see my sister."

Chapter Thirty-One

John sat down next to Jaynee as soon as Pat exited the room. He glanced over his shoulder several times, figuring Pat would be a while, but he didn't want her to walk in on him.

"Hi, Jaynee, it's me. John." He waited for a response to his voice; there wasn't any so he continued. "It's going to be okay; everything will be better very soon." He sat for a second, not sure what to say or do; this could be his only chance. "You know something, Jaynee, I loved you from the second I saw you. When I saw you walking down the aisle, I imagined you were walking toward me. Then, when I held you when we danced, I imagined it was our first dance. Everything has always worked out for Jordan, and then he found you."

John stared at her face; even in a halfway comatose state, she was beautiful.

"I insinuated to Jordan you were cheating, but I knew you weren't. You're too wonderful. You would never leave him, would you?"

Jaynee's eyes flickered open, but what he saw terrified him. She was looking at him in fear. Her eyes filled with tears, and she looked as if she were going to scream.

***

Jaynee stirred at the sound of a new voice. Who was speaking? It wasn't Jordan. The moment she made visual contact, the conversation with Lorraine rushed to her consciousness. She stared up in trepidation. John was sitting beside her. Where was Jordan?

John's eyes widened and his hand moved to her face. "Jaynee, 'S okay there's no reason to be alarmed; I would never hurt you."

She tried to move, but it felt as if something held her strapped to the bed.

Tears filled her eyes. "Where's Jordan?" She struggled to get out the words ... they sounded like gibberish even in her own ears. She tried to scream, but nothing surfaced. Was John here to murder her?

Lorraine had told her she was in fear for her life. That someone from the company may be trying to murder her and Jordan. Someone had approached her on the porch. She thought it was Lorraine returning, but then she'd felt a strong arm circle her neck. When she tried to escape, the gun must have discharged. Oh, God, what had happened? She was in the hospital, her head hurt. Had she shot herself?

Someone else entered the room, but she couldn't turn her head to see who it was.

"You've upset her, John, you should leave. I'll take over watching her." It was another man's voice. Everything inside her felt clouded, she couldn't remember who the voice belonged to, but it sounded familiar.

John made eye contact with her again, his eyes pleaded with her as if she should understand something. "But I didn't do anything."

"Oh, didn't you?" the other voice sneered, suddenly cold and callous. "Leave. I'll stay with her until Jordan returns."

Jaynee couldn't see around John, and she felt herself slipping away again. *God, please help me*, she prayed as the room grew dark again.

***

John stood up with one fleeting look at Jaynee. He hadn't meant to frighten her, he didn't even think she'd heard him, but she did appear panicky.

He hoped this wouldn't get back to Jordan; he would definitely despise him. It's not as if he would have ever propositioned her. He knew how Jordan felt about her. But he couldn't resist telling her when he didn't think she'd hear. He just needed to get everything off his chest. He always felt so uncomfortable when she was around, as though she could interpret his feelings.

John headed for the elevator, but noticed it was still on the ground floor, so he opted for the stairs instead. Ashamed, his head fell low as he descended the steps.

Jordan would kill him when he found out.

***

Jordan explained the situation to the officers arriving on the scene, but told them he had to return to the hospital. That he feared for his wife's life.

He called 911, requesting that the operator transfer his call to Detective Williams or Powe. The dispatcher connected him to Len within seconds. He relayed what had happened with Lorraine and that she probably held information that would lead to an arrest.

Once again, he pushed the Altima to its limit on the highway. He raced toward the hospital, thankful for no cops on the streets. Not that he would have stopped anyway, but he couldn't afford anyone detaining him.

Jordan reached for the phone again, but it started vibrating. He clicked *answer*.

"Jordan, it's Powe. I'm sorry, man. Lorraine went into cardiac arrest en route to the hospital, and the paramedics weren't able to resuscitate her. I know she was a good friend."

Jordan snapped the phone shut, disconnecting the call. There was nothing further to say. He stomped on the accelerator even harder.

He pulled the car directly outside the emergency room when he arrived. Let them tow it; he didn't care. It was the fastest corridor to the elevator leading to ICU. In case someone wanted to move it, he threw the keys on the receptionist's counter. He walked directly to the locked doors of the ER. "Buzz me in," he demanded.

The receptionist recognized him this time and didn't falter.

***

Brian walked with Pat toward Jaynee's room. When they walked in, Brian saw a man standing over her.

"Ronny?" Pat's voice sounded confused as she walked through the doorway. "Where's John?"

"I have no idea ... I just came in and she was all alone."

Pat knew the man's name, but cocked her head at him as if he were a stranger. "What are you doing here?"

Ronny glared at Pat. "I'm allowed to visit my sister-in-law, aren't I? I *am* a member of this family." He scowled and gestured to Brian. "Who's this?"

Brian narrowed his eyes and smiled as patronizingly as he could muster, then extended his hand. "I'm Brian, Jaynee's brother."

Ronny eyed Brian with suspicion as he shook his hand, holding on to it a fraction too long as if he wanted to convey a message to him. "Does Jordan know you're here?"

"Of course, he requested I visit, and you? Does he know you're here? Jordan told me nobody was allowed in Cay's — I mean Jaynee's room but Pat and myself." It wasn't a big slip, he was her brother after all — hilarious thought that was. They had to know her first name was Caycee.

"He asked for *you* to be here — with Jaynee?" he sneered, his tone incredulous as he shook his head back and forth.

Brian wondered if Jaynee had something going on with this guy and had confessed to him about their conversation at the coffee shop.

Pat stared between both men, obviously as confused as he was. "Do you know each other?"

"Never saw him before in my life," Brian answered.

"No," Ronny said flatly.

Brian straightened to his full six-foot-four-inches and puffed out his chest as far as he could. "You need to leave, Ronny. I'm sure Jordan will call you when he returns." Maybe this guy was a cop too. He felt great finally being able to tell a cop what to do. The man certainly wouldn't try anything.

Pat nodded. "Unfortunately, Ronny, Brian's right. Only two people can be here, and Jordan requested that Brian stay with me and Jaynee."

Brian couldn't help but smirk at Caycee's mother-in-law's acceptance. He didn't know who this guy Ronny thought he was, but he didn't trust him. He'd hung out with enough bad dudes to know one when he saw one. The look in this man's eyes spelled danger.

***

Jordan ascended the stairs two at a time, anxious to return to Jaynee. He needed food but couldn't waste the time.

He pushed through the stairwell door, which felt even heavier than earlier. He rounded the corner to Jaynee's room and exhaled when he saw Pat sitting and Brian, his arms folded across his chest and legs crossed at the ankles, leaning against the wall.

Jaynee was still sleeping, but a modicum of color had returned to her face.

Jordan leaned against the doorway. "Mom, I think I'm gonna be sick. Can you get me something to eat?" He did feel nauseated, but also he needed to talk with Brian alone. He didn't want to get into explanations with his mother.

Pat got up at once. "Oh sure, hon. I'll be right back." His mom lovingly patted his arm as she walked past him, leaving the room.

Jordan took her vacant spot in the chair, letting his head gently fall onto Jaynee's arm. He didn't know how much longer he could go without sleep.

Brian said nothing. He had to notice how weak he was at this moment. He could feel him staring at him. Jordan looked up as he attempted to keep his head from spinning. His blood sugar had dropped, and he felt as though he would collapse at any moment.

"Thank you, Brian," he groaned.

Brian shook his head. "You look horrible. You really love her, don't you?"

He sighed and took in the man he wanted so desperately to hate, but was feeling oddly grateful he'd been here. "I do, and I can't thank you enough for watching over her." He wondered why he was even being civil. Was it only for Jaynee's sake?

"I didn't do anything. When we arrived, John had supposedly just left and your brother-in-law was safeguarding her. He didn't seem overjoyed to see me here. He looked angry ... acted as if he knew me."

Jordan cocked his head. "Bobby was here?" He'd spoken with him this morning; he had a large job in Lake Norman. No way could he have made it back already.

"I think your mother said his name was Ronny."

A chill swept through Jordan. "Ronny? Are you sure?" Ronny never showed up anywhere to help or check up on anyone in the family. Jordan and he got along okay at work, but he'd never felt like family. He'd always hovered on the outside, never happy with his lot. He would never come to family gatherings unless Rachael dragged him along. He hadn't visited Jaynee since the accident. Even on the first day, when everyone was here. So why would he show up today? He'd been in the office this morning when Jordan had called to talk to Bobby. He was just checking out the local projects they were working on, saying he'd be around all day, not to worry he'd take care of everything. Those had been his exact words.

Jordan looked back at Brian; he had to be sure. "What exactly did he say?"

Brian shrugged. "Nothing much. We walked in, and he was standing next to her. Your mother asked where John was, and he said he didn't know. Then he asked who I was and acted as if he didn't believe me when I said I was her brother. I thought I'd lied pretty convincingly."

Somehow, that didn't surprise Jordan. He shook off his feelings. "Then what happened?"

"Well ... I did what you asked. I told him he needed to leave, that you didn't want anyone here, but Pat and me." Brian smirked. "He wasn't pleased, especially when your mother agreed. He bolted after that."

Jordan turned back to Jaynee. "Jaynee, love, you have to wake up. You need to tell me what's going on." Jordan squeezed her hand, persuading her to wake up. He leaned in closer, whispering in her ear, "Jaynee, please wake up."

***

Jaynee could hear Jordan's voice. She struggled with the veil that hung over her eyes.

She knew she had to wake up. There was so much they needed to discuss. She couldn't continue to hold all the secrets she'd been keeping. She had to tell him about Brian showing up at the Coffee House. She'd promised when they married to never keep anything from him.

But more than anything, she had to warn him about what Lorraine had said. She had to warn him about John ... she couldn't believe John had tried to kill her. Or that he would try to kill Jordan ... he loved Jordan. He was like a brother to him.

***

Jordan watched as Jaynee's eyes slowly squinted open again.

"Jordan?" Jaynee's voice was raspy but more coherent.

"Thank you, God! Please stay with me, Jaynee. You need to tell me what's happening. Who hurt you?"

"Where's ... Lorraine?" She labored to get out the words.

"Lorraine isn't here, love." He couldn't tell her; he could barely believe it himself. "Why do you want Lorraine?"

Jaynee's eyes darted as if she expected someone to walk up. "She ... she said you're in danger."

Jordan held his hand against her face to soothe her. "Me? What danger am I in?"

"Your partner ... an insurance policy ... John, I think ... she said she had proof ..." She struggled to speak the words. Jordan could see she was on the edge of passing out again.

"John?" It was all making sense. Lorraine had known something. She had come to warn Jaynee Friday night. Then she'd tried to tell him today. Ronny was in the middle of something, not John ... he was certain. John was just a coincidence; he would never hurt Jaynee. He saw the way John looked at his wife, and he would never hurt Jordan; they'd been friends forever.

Ronny, on the other hand, had so many debts. Jordan had helped them out for his sister's sake, but Ronny was never satisfied with just enough. And he and Rachael had an unhappy marriage.

Ronny hated his life, and he'd never liked Jaynee. He'd felt threatened the moment Jordan had brought her here. He'd told Rachael she was going to ruin the business and probably have Ronny fired. Rachael had confided in Jordan after they first married. Jordan had told Rachael how ridiculous that was. Jaynee wasn't even interested in the business, and she definitely wasn't interested in money. He had to beg her to spend anything on herself. The woman hardly spent a few hundred dollars a month, no matter how much he bugged her.

Jordan could hear Jaynee struggling to speak again. "It's okay, Jaynee, you can sleep. I'll be right here."

"Jordan," she mumbled. "How long ... have I been here? My baby ..."

Jordan looked up at Brian, who was still leaning against the wall, listening to their exchange. He pushed his body forward from the wall to come nearer.

Jordan winced at her words. "What is it, Jaynee?" But nothing mattered as long as she was safe and alive. If she wanted to leave him for Brian, so be it. It'd hurt, he wasn't sure he'd live through it, but he couldn't bear to see her in pain either. "Brian's here, Jaynee, did you want to speak to him?"

Jaynee's eyes opened more. She looked so tired; it was obviously a task even to open her eyes. But the look of shock that crossed over her face was anything but enjoyment at seeing her former lover standing over her. As weak as she was, Jaynee looked angry, Jordan thought, as if she were going to jump out of bed. She didn't look like the fragile woman who'd been lying there for almost four days.

Then her eyes darted back at Jordan with confusion, or was it guilt?

"Why ... why ... is he here?" Her eyes narrowed, the confusion replaced by anger again.

Jordan was baffled, and Brian looked discouraged. "Didn't you ask for him?" He tried to mask his pain from showing.

She shook her head, but then winced when she realized the movement hurt.

Brian shrunk away from the bed. "I'd better leave you two alone. I'll be downstairs if you need me, Jordan." Brian left the room with a final glance at Jaynee.

She had no desire to see him, even on her deathbed. Jordan couldn't help but feel satisfaction, even as he read the torment spelled out across Brian's face.

Jaynee looked befuddled again. Her eyes flicked between the men as Brian exited the room. "You know each other?" she asked, gazing at Jordan for an explanation.

"You said *baby*, Jaynee, isn't that what he used to call you? You said it the other day, just the one word and fell back to sleep. I figured it out then, what you were keeping from me, but I don't care what has been happening for the last couple of months. I just want you to know I love you and never want you to leave. But I'll let you go if that's what you want."

"Jordan," she said, shocked by his statement, sounding even stronger.

He looked down at her, embarrassed by his whimpering. He must look like a bloody fool, what she must think of him.

"Jordan ... I planned it. I quit the ... pill ... but we had to wait until it was safe. I wanted it to be a surprise ... for us to try for a baby ... I took a test ... I was ovulating. I never imagined ..." The words flowed easier, her strength was returning. "I hoped by Christmas. Wanted to surprise *you* for a change." Tears started welling in her eyes. Jordan couldn't say anything; now he was in shock. "But for you to think ... for you to assume I didn't love you? That I'd want —"

Jordan reached over and cupped her face gently, breaking off her words. "Jaynee, what are you saying — are you — you might be pregnant?"

She nodded slowly. "I hope so."

"Oh, Jaynee. I'm so sorry. I was just ... I couldn't understand." Jordan sighed in relief after the pain of the last two months fell away to nothing but a misunderstanding. "We had such a wonderful time in Florida, and then we came home and I understood the first few weeks, but then I went insane." He considered the situation for a second. "Jaynee, thank you, thank you, but please don't ever surprise me like that again. My heart can't take it, love." And he'd always thought he liked surprises.

Jaynee did her best to smile.

"So we're going to have a baby?" he exclaimed despite himself, and the fact they were in the hospital, and he'd just lost a good friend, and someone was still trying to kill them. At that moment, the only thing that mattered was that his wife loved him, and they were going to have a baby. If not now, at least someday.

Pat stepped in the room the moment of his announcement, her eyes drifting to Jaynee. "Is it true? Are you pregnant? Wouldn't the hospital have known if you were pregnant?"

Jaynee smiled, though it was weak.

"Not if it happened the night she was admitted," Jordan answered, smiling sheepishly, grabbing his mother up into a bear hug. "But it doesn't matter, Mom. Jaynee is awake." He looked back at Jaynee; her eyes were closing. He could still see the smile playing on her lips. "Well, she *was* awake. But she loves me, and it looks as if she's going to be fine, and we *are* going to have a baby."

***

Brian was in the hall waiting for the elevator when he heard Jaynee's confession and Jordan's overwhelming cry of joy, which should have been his.

He stepped into the elevator and pressed the lobby button. He had to come to terms it was over. The girl he'd loved for almost ten years, the woman he'd given away for drugs and alcohol, was no longer his. She belonged to someone else. He needed to escape this place, return to Florida. He didn't know what he would do when he got there; he just had to leave.

Chapter Thirty-Two

J ordan barely had a chance to grasp the entire situation
that his wife may be pregnant and that someone had
definitely tried to kill her, when Lorraine's phone
vibrated in his pocket, reminding him that she was gone.

Lorraine, *dead*? God, it couldn't be true.

He stood from his chair next to Jaynee's bed and walked
out of the room so as not to wake her. As soon as he was
outside the glassed-in room, he clicked *answer*. "Hello?"
What if it was Lorraine's mother? What would he tell her?

"Jordan, it's Powe." The detective sounded out of
breath. "I haven't had a chance to call. You must be going
insane with grief."

Of course he was grief-stricken, and he had to tell
Jaynee. It'd devastate her to know that inadvertently she'd
been the cause of Lorraine's death.

"Are you there, Jordan? Did I lose you?"

Jordan sighed. "I'm here." He wished he wasn't, wished
he could get his hands on Ronny. But he couldn't leave
Jaynee's side. *What if Ronny came back to finish what he'd
started?*

Powe's end of the line was noisy, voices echoed in the
background. "Anyway, as I said, I've been too busy to call,

but Lorraine's alive. She went into cardiac arrest in the ambulance, but the ER docs were able to resuscitate her. We're waiting to see her now. Attendees said she's awake, but weak."

"Thank God!" Jordan felt relief, but it was fleeting, marred by what he had to say next. "You don't need to speak with her. I know who tried to kill Lorraine and was probably there the night Jaynee was shot."

This time, Len's end of the connection was silent. "Who? And how do you know?" the detective finally asked.

"Hang on a sec." Jordan walked back into the room. His mom had moved to sit beside Jaynee. "Mom, I'll be back in a minute, please don't move from her side." He leaned over his wife. "Jaynee, my love, I'll return shortly." He kissed her forehead, confident she could hear him, even if only subconsciously.

His mother nodded. "I won't leave her side, Jordan, I promise."

Jordan walked down the hall, just out of listening range. "My brother-in-law Ronald Duncan," he spat out the words, disgusted at the thought. *How could he?*

"How do you know, Jordan? What proof do you have?" Len demanded.

"Jaynee ... she woke up," he blurted out the words. "The night Jaynee was shot Lorraine had come to see her. She told Jaynee about some information she found and believed one of my partners wanted Jaynee and me dead to collect on an insurance policy."

"But how do you know it's Ronny? What about Bobby, or God forbid, John?" It was apparent Len didn't want to believe a fellow officer could be responsible, but cops were human too.

Jordan paced the hallway. "John came here after I went looking for Lorraine, offering to watch over Jaynee while my mother got something to eat. But then Ronny showed up. He never does anything for the family. When Brian and Pat returned to the room —" Jordan took a deep breath, as he comprehended the danger that had almost befallen his wife. "He was standing over her, Len ... he was going to murder her, God knows how, right here under our watch."

He wanted to capture Ronny himself and bring him in, but he knew he couldn't. He had to stay with Jaynee, keep her secure, and he knew if he did get Ronny alone, he'd probably kill him with his bare hands. He couldn't do that to Jaynee or Rachael. What would Rachael even think? Would she believe that Ronny was even capable of such atrocities? "Len, I need you to go to my office and get my laptop, and then I'll be able to tell you exactly where Ronny is."

"Tell me you have a tracking device on your company vehicles, please."

"Yep ... something my car saleswoman suggested. I can tell you where all of my vehicles are located, where they stop, and how long they've been there. And it was one of the only things I didn't share with any of my employees or partners." He hung up the phone.

The last thing he wanted was to wait for Len to get his laptop and come to the hospital, but he wasn't leaving Jaynee's side for anything.

He needed to make a couple more calls before returning to Jaynee's room. He just hoped they wouldn't ask a lot of questions. He could see the room from where he stood, so he knew Jaynee was safe.

"Yeah?" his sister answered, sounding out of breath as if she'd been running or upset.

"Hi, Rachael."

"Jordan? Is everything all right? Mom told me Jaynee was coming outta the coma. Is she okay?"

Her genuine concern surprised him. She'd never been close to Jaynee or even him for that matter, but he knew she loved him. She was just spoiled, always had been. Nothing was ever enough. Not that that was any excuse for what Ronny did. "Rachael, I can't talk but a second, but yes, Jaynee seems to be doing better. She's awake and talking, though very weak. But the reason I called is not about Jaynee; I need you to do something."

"Anything, Jordan," she said.

Again, this was all new to him. She was being extremely altruistic. "I need you to go over to Melissa's house, and whatever you do," he paused, knowing she wouldn't just comply without questioning him, "do not answer if Ronny calls or comes by, but I doubt he will."

"What the heck are you talking about?"

That sounded more like the sister he knew. "Rachael, for once in your life, will you trust me? Have I ever let you down?" he asked, truly upset now. He gave her everything, and she gave him nothing but heartache, and now her husband —

"No ... but he's my husband."

"I know, but I'm your brother. For the love of all that is holy, would you trust me and do what I request for once?"

"Okay, Jordan."

He hung up the phone and called Bobby. Bobby needed no explanation. Jordan told him to get home, keep Ronny away, and most importantly protect the women. Bobby didn't hesitate, just said, "Whatever you say, Jordan."

His final call was to John. Somehow, John managed to answer the phone on the first ring. "Hey, Lorraine."

"John, it's —"

"Jordan, I'm sorry, man, I'm so sorry, I didn't mean it."

Why was John apologizing? *Had he gotten it wrong?* It couldn't be — not John. Jordan waited without saying anything, not wanting to tip his hand. The person who talked first always lost. He knew this with a business deal or a confession. He utilized the same techniques to close a sale as he did to prompt a confession.

"Ronny called you, didn't he?" John blurted the question. "You have to know, Jordan, I would have never acted on anything. I just wanted to talk to Jaynee while she was unconscious. I thought if I could get it off my chest, it would help somehow."

Jordan squeezed the phone in his hand. "Talk to her? You almost murdered her!" He couldn't contain himself and was suddenly ashamed for assuming it was Ronny. How could he have been so wrong, how could John? He'd known him practically his entire life. He'd been more of a brother to him than Ronny ever had. "Where are you, you no good —"

"Whoa ... wait ... what? I would never — I love Jaynee. I could never hurt her."

"But you just said you would never have acted and you were trying to get it off your chest while she was unconscious."

"What exactly did Ronny tell you?"

"Ronny didn't tell me anything. You did. You were there the night Jaynee was shot, weren't you? And then — did Ronny stop you from finishing the job today, John?" His voice seethed with emotion. It was a good thing he wasn't in front of John. He didn't know if he could keep himself from killing him.

"So Ronny hasn't spoken to you?"

"No, he hasn't." Jordan couldn't believe he was having this conversation when he only wanted to slaughter him.

"Crap! If I'm not the largest moron, I don't know who is." John exhaled through the phone. "Ronny walked in when I was talking to Jaynee. Admitting to her why I'm always so cold to her. I might as well tell you because Ronny will anyway. I love her, Jordan. I know you don't want to hear this, but I've loved her from the first moment I saw her. I'm sorry, and I swear, man, I never would have come on to her. I just wanted to talk to her. And I would never try to murder her."

As ridiculous as it sounded, Jordan was relieved. He'd always known how John was, he knew he would step over his dead body to get to Jaynee; he'd even told her that once. He also knew John didn't love Jaynee; he only wanted whatever Jordan had. Just like when they were kids.

A chuckle actually slipped out over the thought of his friend's libido. "You *are* a moron, but not a murderer. I knew better. You and I will deal with this later. Right now there are other more important issues." Jordan wondered how many men he'd have to battle for his wife. She seemed to bring out the worst in men. He thought about Brian's defeated look and a smile washed over his face. Jaynee didn't want any of them; she loved him.

Jordan explained to John what had happened with Ronny.

"Wow," John said, understanding the confusion. "I'm sure thankful I wasn't standing in front of you when I made my stupid confession. You would have certainly killed me."

Jordan sighed. No doubt there. *Later*, he thought. They had more important business to discuss. "John, I need a favor."

"Anything. Name it."

"I need you to go stay with Lorraine. She's at the hospital in Concord. Ronny may end up there, trying to finish what he started. He knows I won't let Jaynee out of my sight. I tipped my hat earlier when I had Brian throw him out of Jaynee's room."

"Brian? Who's Brian?"

"Long story ... get to Lorraine now." Jordan paused before hanging up. "Oh, and, John ... I'm gonna kick your ass when I see you again."

"I know ... I deserve it," he said, hanging up.

Of course, it couldn't have worked out that both women would be at the same hospital. Lorraine was in Concord whereas Jaynee was in Pineville, and it wasn't very convenient at the moment. Jordan had done everything he could. Now, he just had to wait for Len and his computer. Anxious for every minute now, he rushed back to Jaynee's room.

When he walked back inside the room, Jaynee was still asleep. His mother stood, offering him the seat beside his wife.

"Mom, why don't you go home?" He really didn't like the idea of Nanna being home alone either. "I'm not going anywhere else today."

"Are you sure, honey? What's been going on? Why did Brian leave? He looked devastated. I thought maybe something had happened to Jaynee when I saw his face, but then I heard your announcement."

"It's a long story, Mom." He rested his hands on her shoulders. "There's just one thing you need to know, and I know it's going to sound strange, but you have to trust me."

Her face was serious, worried at once, but she reined it in. "Of course."

It went without saying; he knew she trusted him completely. "Don't let Ronny anywhere near your house or speak to him. If he shows up, get your gun, and then call 911."

Her eyes revealed that she clearly didn't understand, but she trusted him. "Okay, Jordan. Please call me if anything changes with Jaynee. I'll be back tomorrow morning." She kissed him goodbye and left the room.

Jordan sat down and took Jaynee's free hand in both of his. As much as he wanted to talk to her, he knew she needed to sleep, especially if she might be pregnant. He wondered how long it would be before they'd know for sure. He hoped the fact that she'd been medicated wouldn't have any effect on a baby that was days old.

He chastised himself. How could he feel so much joy at a time when there was so much pain? But then he remembered, Lorraine was going to be okay. Jaynee had been awake several times, each time stronger than the last. He was going to be a father, if not now, someday. But more than anything, Jaynee's love had him wanting to jump for joy. His life had felt over when he thought for even a moment that she could have wanted Brian.

Brian. He felt bad for him. He'd probably saved her life. Who knows what Ronny would have talked his mother into if she'd come alone? He would have to find a way to thank him. But not today. He wasn't ready to leave Jaynee's side again. The hospital walls would have to be falling down first, and even then, he wouldn't leave without her. He wouldn't leave until he could talk to her again, thank her, and apologize for his assumption. He felt like a schmuck.

Thinking back over the last two months with renewed eyes, he realized she hadn't been cold. She'd just done everything she could to keep them from having sex. But not one time had she ever uttered a cruel word. She smiled at him constantly, made his favorite meals, and socialized with the family.

How could he have misjudged this? Even when she'd said, *This is almost over.* He should have known she'd meant school or something else. He would never doubt her again. It wasn't fair for him to have jumped to a conclusion when she'd never done anything to deserve it. Of course, it wasn't as if he didn't trust her. He'd never once before this time thought she would have ever been up to anything.

Even when he was jealous, he never blamed her. It wasn't her fault she looked so darned good. She didn't even dress to elicit attention. Rachael dressed like a teenager, always wearing clothes that were low-cut and too short, another thing Ronny used to complain about but didn't even bother mentioning anymore.

The phone in his pocket buzzed, bringing him out of his thoughts. He pulled it out and looked at the number, John again. He hesitated, not sure if he wanted to answer it. It wasn't long enough that he could have left the house, let alone retrieved anything new about Lorraine. He must be trying to apologize again. Jordan vacillated, then decided what the heck, he'd let him beg for mercy a little — not that it was going to change anything — he was gonna kick the everlasting crap out of him when this was over. The grief must be eating him up. He clicked the green button and waited for the pleading to begin.

***

John had been pulling on his shoes and jacket when he heard a rap on the front door.

He didn't bother checking to see who was at the door. He was in a hurry to get to Lorraine, frantic in his need to see her and make sure she was safe. Opening the door, he saw Ronny standing there, a strange look on his face.

He concealed his shock and opened the door wider. "Hey, what's up?" He made a conscious effort to smile.

"Business," Ronny said solemnly, stepping into John's house.

John closed the door, shoved his hands in his jacket pocket, and curled his hand around his cell phone. Nothing good could come of Ronny showing up here. His fingers deftly found the recall button. He knew where it was, had practiced many times. He hit the send button, knowing it would call the last number called or received — which would be Jordan.

He raised his chin at Ronny, who just stood in his foyer, his hands also in his jacket pockets. "Did something go wrong today?"

"Everything," Ronny muttered in an irritated voice.

Ronny's one-word answers were starting to unnerve John. He wished he'd already grabbed his gun. It was resting behind him on the credenza. He wondered if he should make an advance for it.

"But, I think I can make it right," Ronny continued.

"What are you talking about, Ronny? I was just leaving. Can we talk about this later?" John's voice elevated an octave, exposing his frustration.

"No!" The one word was menacing and sounded foreign coming out of Ronny's mouth.

John stepped back within inches of his gun; unfortunately, a second too late, Ronny had already drawn his pistol.

Ronny sneered. "Don't bother, John. Step away or I'll shoot you where you stand. I may not be a *cop*; they never accepted me at the academy, but you know I'm a crack shot."

John did know this; they'd gone to the range and hunted together many times over the years. He also now understood why the academy hadn't accepted him into law enforcement. His psyche profile must have indicated instability. "Why are you doing this, Ronny?"

A mocking smile lifted his face. "Whatever do you mean, John? I'm not doing anything ... this is you and Lorraine. Lorraine has pined over Jordan for years, and you're in love with Jaynee. You both recognize they'll never leave each other, and you have a gambling problem." With the gun, Ronny motioned for John to sit at the table. "While consoling each other, you have fallen in love and concocted the perfect scheme to get rid of them, Jaynee by suicide and Jordan by an accidental police shooting. But everything went awry, and your treachery revealed itself. So Lorraine committed suicide and now so will you — just like Romeo and Juliet, how romantic."

John watched as Ronny's face transformed into a fierce scowl. He pulled out a prescription bottle with his gloved hand; the label was missing. A wild smirk crossed his face at the look of confusion in John's eyes.

"Rachael's sleeping pills. I've been heisting a few out of the bottle for months. Of course, they call them sleeping pills, but they're actually numb pills. You won't feel a thing ... heck you'll probably even pull the trigger yourself. Amazing stuff really. *My wife*," he spat the words, "will even have sex with me when she's on them. Obviously, she never remembers and thinks she's still holding out. Her power trip over me, as if breaking me financially wasn't enough. She had to take everything. It's not as if I can't get sex elsewhere, but it's sort of fun taking advantage of her when she doesn't know — a little payback for all the misery."

John shook his head in disbelief. "You're sick, Ronny, but it's not too late." He questioned whether he should tell him Lorraine was still alive. He figured it was the only way. He hoped Jordan was listening and hadn't just let the call go to voicemail. "Listen, Ronny, it's not too late. No one is dead; you can still get out of this with minimal jail time. Jaynee's awake, and Lorraine has pulled through. They'll both know it was you. You won't be able to get to them before Jordan takes you down."

A half-laugh half-huff burst out of Ronny's mouth. "They won't consider me a suspect. Everyone knows it's you, John. Don't you remember Jaynee's face as you confessed your feelings?"

John winced at the memory, but he knew Jordan knew differently.

Ronny's lips were in a straight line as he shook his head. "And you call me sick? You're supposed to be his best friend, and yet, you coveted his wife and tried to get him drunk and make him believe she was cheating on him. If that didn't beat all ... calling Lorraine and letting her know he was drunk and telling her to call him. And you say I'm sick?"

John's chin dropped to his chest; he was sick. What had he been thinking? How could he have done that to Jordan? Now he wondered if he did want him to be listening. Jordan hadn't realized he was the one who'd told Lorraine to call after he'd gotten him drunk.

"You're right, Ronny, I *am* sick, more like delusional, both of us are. Jordan has been nothing but generous to both of us, and I coveted his wife, and you tried to murder her. I don't need your help ... I *should* want to kill myself. Do you mind if I have a drink? I don't need sleeping pills."

Ronny smiled at this revelation. "Go ahead. I'll have one too if you don't mind."

How amiably they were discussing murder and suicide over a drink. John just hoped it would be enough time. He knew Ronny would want him to use his own gun. If he could talk Ronny into letting him get drunk first, maybe he could buy some time until Jordan could send help.

Chapter Thirty-Three

J ordan heard nothing but silence on the other line.
John must have hit the recall button by accident. This
should be interesting. It would give him something to do
while he waited for Jaynee to wake up again. He hoped
John talked to himself, as he did when he was in the car
sometimes.

It was hard to make out anything from John's line,
mostly just muffled sounds of John's voice, but then he
realized there were two voices.

He turned up the cell phone volume the highest it would
go and heard Ronny's voice, "Have a seat, John!"

Jordan burst out of his chair, sprinting from the room to
the waiting area with the courtesy phone. He didn't know
Len's number. He'd been connected to him on the first call,
and though Len returned his call, he wasn't about to hang
up and redial. He pressed the mute button on the cell
phone, picked up the courtesy phone, and dialed 911. He
had to argue with the operator this time that not only did
she need to send police to John's house, but she also
needed to connect him with Detective Powe. Jordan gave
her his badge number and position as before and held the

line for what seemed like forever. He heard Ronny's confession, how he planned to take care of everything.

Finally, Len came on the line. "What's up, Jordan? I just got to your office. No one was here, so I —"

"He's at John's place," Jordan burst out, interrupting him. "I only heard part of what was going on, but Ronny said something about John would want to pull the trigger himself. I wasn't thinking straight, Len. I told the dispatcher to send black and whites; no telling what he'll do if he hears 'em."

"I'll call and have them standing by. I've got John's address in my computer. He still off Albemarle Road?"

"Yeah. I'm right behind you," Jordan blurted out before Len could hang up.

"No, Jordan! This is not your division, and I don't need you going off on either of them. Move from there and I'll have you arrested myself."

As much as Jordan didn't want to concede, he knew he had to follow his order. Besides, how could he ever face Rachael if things turned badly, and he was the one to pull the trigger?

Jordan darted back to Jaynee's room, plopped down, and dropped his head back against the cool vinyl chair. Would this day ever end?

He listened to John's request for a drink. They were just gonna sit there like old friends. John was smart; he knew Ronny would want to make his death look as if he'd gotten wasted and committed suicide. He'd be willing to draw it out. John hadn't tipped his hand entirely. Now Jordan would have to wait and listen, and pray he didn't hear something he didn't want to.

No conversation could be heard, only the echo of glasses clinking. Were they toasting? How deranged. Lorraine's phone chimed the melody Jordan knew would come eventually. It was dying; he'd been on it all morning.

How long would Ronny wait, Jordan wondered? Quiet muffles and chuckling filled the background. Were they telling stories? John was trying to sidetrack him as long as possible, it seemed.

"Jordan?" Jaynee's voice, barely a whisper, broke him from concentrating on their conversation.

His gaze leveled on her. "Yes, love?" He took her hand in his as moisture filled his eyes again.

As bad as this day was, in some ways it was also the happiest day of his life. Jaynee was going to be okay, he was sure. And nothing was more important to him now or ever. It was irrelevant if she was pregnant or if she ever became pregnant or if she ever stopped loving him — not that that seemed likely. All that mattered or would ever matter was that she was safe, and he would never stop loving her. He heard the final chord of the phone as it died. He groaned. There was nothing he could do.

Her eyebrows pulled together, and she winced at the pain. "Is everything okay? Are you all right?"

Jordan reached to her face, soothing her forehead.

"Everything is now, Jaynee. I love you so much. Can I kiss you, or will that hurt?"

"Please," she whispered.

He leaned over her and kissed her as delicately as if she were spun glass, his lips moving softly over her cheekbones. "Oh, God, I love you," he murmured through kisses. "I missed you so much." His lips continued along her jaw. "And then this happened. I truly believed I was going to die. I would have — if something had happened to you — you're my life, Jaynee."

"I'm sorry," she mumbled.

"Don't apologize. I'm the one who jumped to horrible conclusions. I feel awful, how could I — what was I thinking? You didn't do anything." He choked on the awful feelings. How could he have been so ignorant? "You never did anything, and I yelled at you. I got drunk ... and almost ..." he trailed off, hanging his head, not wanting to admit his weakness.

"Shh, Jordan, it's going to be okay," she whispered, trying to comfort him. He didn't deserve to be comforted.

"Jaynee, I have to tell you something. Nothing happened but still I have to confess. I'd want to know." He looked deep into her eyes, ashamed. "The night *it* happened," he couldn't bring himself to mention her shooting herself and almost dying, "I *was* drunk, and I'm sorry. Lorraine called, and I asked her to drive me home. She made a pass at me. I swear nothing happened, but ... I ... it could have ... I was so stupid."

"I know. Lorraine told me."

Jordan's eyes widened. "She told you?"

"Yes ... I know you didn't do anything — even drunk."

"No ... I didn't," he admitted. "I love you, Jaynee, only you. And I want only you, forever."

"Forever," she agreed, smiling, but then her hands went to her head.

"Does it hurt? Do you want me to call the nurse?"

"Yes, but no. I want to stay awake. I just realized that my hair ..." She whimpered, and her eyes glazed over as the realization hit her fully.

Jordan understood what she was thinking. It was the first thing he'd noticed when he saw her after surgery. Her long beautiful hair was gone, but he'd gotten used to it over the last few days.

"Don't cry. It'll hurt." He soothed her forehead with his hands again, tracing her features with his fingers.

"But I'll be ugly."

"No, you won't," he offered with a chuckle. "You'll be my G.I. Jaynee."

Jaynee laughed in spite of herself; it obviously hurt her head and she moaned in reaction.

"You should rest, Jaynee. I'll call the nurse for more medication."

"No, Jordan, please. I want to stay awake a little while longer. There was something else I wanted to say."

His stomach flipped. Though the last one was a good one, he wasn't sure if he wanted any more surprises. He didn't want to hear about her meeting with Brian, knowing the conversation would have to turn around to him eventually. He still wasn't thrilled that she hadn't told him. He hoped he could keep his jealousy intact when she mentioned his name. The idea was ridiculous, he knew. He had no reason to be jealous ... heck, even Brian admitted that.

She smiled fractionally. "You look worried."

He shook his head, attempting a smile, but knew it was shallow, so she'd see right through him.

"Don't be. I just wanted to explain the question you asked the other day. What was keeping me so busy that I didn't have time for my husband," she repeated his question, looking up at his response as he blanched at her words, ashamed.

"I'm sorry —"

She cut him off. "Don't be ... I *was* trying to keep myself unavailable. Everything I read said you should use alternate protection for two months after going off the pill, but I wanted to surprise you. *But* ... I really was busy too. I finished my novel, Jordan."

He looked at her bewildered, then. She hadn't told him that she'd been writing a book, only that she wanted to.

"I began writing the story that I told you about when I started college, and as I neared the end, I couldn't stop. An agent requested my manuscript after receiving my initial query. And ..."

"Yes ..."

"She's interested, and she wants to represent my book. So, that is what has been keeping me so busy."

"That's fantastic," he exclaimed, holding her head gently between his hands as he kissed her again lightly. "I'm so proud of you and happy you're going to get everything you ever wanted."

She moved her head slowly back and forth. "I already have everything I ever wanted, Jordan. This is just icing." She moved her free hand to her stomach. "And now, you'll have everything you ever wanted too."

He covered her hand with his. "I already had everything I wanted; I just didn't realize it. But thank you, this will definitely be icing."

She smiled, and her eyelids drooped as the darkness threatened to take her again. "Jordan," she murmured through half-shuttered eyes. "You need to get some rest. No offense ... but, you look awful. Although, I do like the start of the beard. It reminds me ..."

He watched as her eyes closed completely. He was sure she was right about how bad he looked. He'd probably lost ten pounds in the last few days. But he wasn't going anywhere. He laid his head beside hers on the bed and caressed her arms until he was confident she was deep asleep. Then he rested back in the recliner, thinking he could sleep for the first time in days. Len would call him. No news is good news.

Jordan jumped when he was shaken awake. His eyes darted around the room expecting danger, but instead he saw Bobby standing over him.

"Hey," Jordan said confused. "You were supposed to stay with the girls."

"It's over, Jordan." Bobby released a heavy breath. "John called me from the station to pick him up. The detectives demanded he go down and sign an affidavit before releasing him." He paused for Jordan to reflect on his words. "John gave me the complete story on the ride back. What the heck was Ronny thinking?" He lifted his large hands in the air. "Who would have thought he was capable?"

Jordan caught up with Bobby's words, relieved to hear that at least John was safe but wasn't sure what happened or what he wanted to have happened to Ronny. He didn't know how he'd ever face Rachael again.

"What about Ronny ..." Jordan asked.

Bobby released a puff of air through his nose. "He's probably still too drunk to know what's going on. John explained how he called you when he was trying to stall Ronny. He'd asked him if he could have a drink and then offered him one. Before he knew it, Ronny was talking about Rachael, practically crying over her according to John. He kept refilling Ronny's glass, and he kept accepting. John always could drink anyone under the table.

Not that you or I were ever competition for him even when we did drink."

Jordan nodded. "True."

Bobby paced around the room. He always looked like a trapped bear. "John said he saw the police surround the house through the back window, but Ronny was too far gone by then to notice. John made eye contact with Len and lifted his glass to explain. Len just laughed according to John. When all was said and done, all John did was open the back door for Len to step inside." Bobby released a nervous laugh.

Jordan knew what he was thinking. He too wondered how they could have worked and lived beside Ronny and not have known he was capable of such atrocious acts. If Jordan had thought to question him once, he was sure he would have seen through him. But he would never have thought to question his own brother-in-law.

"Does Rachael know?" Jordan asked, wondering how she was coping with the news.

"Yeah ... I called her on the way over. I almost feel sorry for Ronny."

Jordan glowered at Bobby.

"Not for what he's done," he quickly explained. "Because of Rachael. She didn't even care; she was embarrassed more than anything. Not once did she ask if he was okay. How's that possible? I'd like to think that no matter what I did, no matter how repulsive, Melissa would still have some vestige of concern. And to think, John said he was crying over Rachael."

Jordan nodded. "I guess that makes sense." He reflected back on how he'd felt when he thought Jaynee had cheated on him or had attempted suicide and still, his largest concern was only her safety. He hadn't cared about what she'd done as much as he'd worried about her wellbeing, even if it meant losing her. "Still ... I could kill him."

"Me too," Bobby agreed.

"So ... *where's John?*" Jordan hissed.

Jordan watched the confusion crease Bobby's forehead, unmistakably noticing the sneer in his tone. Apparently, John hadn't told him everything.

"He had me drop him off at his house; he was in a hurry to get to Lorraine. I wanted to go too, but he asked me to come here instead and let you know what happened. He assured me that he'd let us know if anything changed in her condition."

This news surprised Jordan. If Ronny was in custody, then there was no reason for John to be anxious to see Lorraine. Maybe he was just trying to appease him, lessen the beating he was going to get.

Bobby rested his bearlike hand on Jordan's shoulder. "Why don't you get cleaned up, eat some real food, and get some sleep? Jaynee looks as if she's gonna be out for a while, but I'll sit with her all night if you want."

Jordan didn't like the idea of going home alone and leaving Jaynee. But Bobby was right, and Jaynee had told him he looked awful. It wouldn't do any good for them to both be sick.

"Okay," he acquiesced, standing. "But, can I go to your house instead? It's a lot closer, and I don't want to return home alone." He thought of the mess he probably had to clean up and grimaced. He leaned over Jaynee to kiss her goodnight and then turned to walk out of the room.

"Sure, bro. I'll call Melissa and tell her you're on your way." He paused for a second. "Oh, and, Jordan ..." Jordan looked over his shoulder at his giant but gentle brother-in-law. "It's safe to go home. When Melissa picked up Boomer, she took care of everything."

"Thanks, Bobby. You're the best brother a man could have." Jordan walked out of the hospital room. Exhausted as he was, he still couldn't help but feel incredible. His wife was going to be okay, and hopefully soon, he'd be a father. It'd been a rough two months, but in the end, life was good.

Of course, he still had to deal with John. He'd look forward to that little bit of aggression release.

Epilogue

Two weeks after the accident — as Jordan liked to refer to it — Jaynee was out of the hospital, but not before taking a pregnancy test. She was right, of course; she was pregnant. Once again, Jordan felt as though he were the happiest man in the world.

He kept his promise and gave his captain his two-week resignation to quit the police force. Not willing to leave her side during her recovery, though, he took advantage of his comp and vacation days and only showed up on the last morning for a going-away breakfast, consisting of bagels and doughnuts, thrown by his coworkers. Money wasn't an issue. His construction company was booming, Jaynee had a book deal, which would bring in a little money, and she never let him spend money on her anyway, so they had more than enough savings.

Convicted on two accounts of attempted murder and one account of conspiracy to commit murder, Ronny received the maximum sentence of twenty years in prison, which meant he'd be out in seven to ten. Jordan figured there was no concern, though. He knew Ronny didn't hold a grudge against him or Jaynee. He hated Rachael. Jordan was sure when he got released, he'd hightail it out of the area faster than he could beat a stick. He probably figured Jordan would seek revenge for his crimes against them.

Jordan decided, as sick as it sounded, if Ronny attempted repentance, he'd set him up in another state with enough money to start his own business. Jaynee, obviously, thought he was crazy ... maybe he was. But he figured if his Savior could forgive, then so should he.

Jordan also located Brian in Florida through information he received from Len Powe and offered him a deal as well because of his gratitude for protecting Jaynee.

Brian scoffed at Jordan. "I don't need a handout," he protested, but listened when Jordan assured him he wasn't about to hand over anything; instead, he would offer him an opportunity he'd never received.

Brian had been a latchkey kid because his mother worked two jobs to support them, and he'd grown up around drug users and the worst society could offer. He'd been in and out of detention homes since he was thirteen. Although Jordan felt there was no excuse for choosing to lead a criminal or immoral life, no matter your circumstances, he decided to give Brian a chance to prove, if given the opportunity, he could make something of himself.

Jordan explained to Brian he wouldn't give him money, but would pay for his college if he chose to finish.

Reluctantly, Brian agreed; he was shocked but grateful. Jordan never told Jaynee what he did for Brian and was relieved that other than a couple of phone calls of thanks, Brian had not attempted to contact either of them. His last call had been when he was at his four-year mark.

Brian informed Jordan how he'd met a girl — "Get this," he'd explained to Jordan on the phone, his voice ecstatic. "She's a preacher's daughter ... she helped me make Christ the center of my life, and we're planning to get married right after I graduate in the spring."

Jordan, thrilled by his conversion, but apathetic about Brian's insistence that Jaynee and he come to his wedding, promised to consider it objectively. Brian understood and thanked him again for giving him a chance, telling Jordan he now understood the power of forgiveness and why Jordan had offered him this gift.

Because of the time John spent with Lorraine while she was recovering, Jordan never did get an opportunity to deliver the beating he'd intended.

Then when John confessed his feelings about Lorraine, Jordan couldn't mess up his face. Instead, the next time they sparred, he held back nothing, and even through the pads John wore, he knew he'd have bruises for weeks.

Lorraine's near-death experience enabled John to realize how he'd always felt about her. Lorraine, however, took a little convincing. She couldn't comprehend how John would ever stop his womanizing. He'd assured her he could be patient and would prove his love. They'd celebrate their third wedding anniversary in two months, and their son's first birthday in three.

And today was, as always, Jordan's favorite day of the week. Now that he wasn't a detective anymore, he could sleep in any day. It was Jaynee who woke up at the crack of dawn, but only because she insisted on doing everything.

She spoiled him. So he decided she deserved a little spoiling this morning. He brushed her hair back off her neck and planted tiny kisses down her throat.

"Mmm," Jaynee murmured.

"Good morning, my love ... did you want to sleep in, or can I interest you —"

A tiny knock and then a whimper behind their bedroom door broke off his words. "Mommy ..." Justin whined. "Johanna won't share."

Unfortunately, their four-year-old twins had other ideas for Sunday mornings.

Jaynee tilted her head up toward the door to hear her son. "What is it, Justin ... what won't Johanna share?"

"The remote to the TV," the little voice answered.

"For the love of —" Jordan started, but Jaynee placed her fingertips over his lips. He continued anyway, "There are three televisions in this house. Don't make me come out there," he shouted playfully. They both heard giggling and scampering as the two retreated from their door.

"See," Jaynee teased. "You can't say I didn't warn you."

He nuzzled his head between her jaw and shoulder. "I know," he said between kisses.

She giggled as his breath tickled her neck. "But they're worth it."

Jordan shrugged and continued his trail of seductive kisses. "Most of the time," he whispered. "When they don't interrupt my attempts to spoil you. Where was I?"

***

Almost ten years and Jaynee still felt the familiar thrill soar through her body. "I think you were here." She pulled his hand around her waist.

"We probably don't have very long," he groaned.

"That's okay. We'll wear out the kids today, and then you can take your time tonight," she suggested.

Jordan's eyes widened, and his breathing accelerated. "That's all I needed to hear, Mrs. Monroe." He pulled her closer, tightening his grip around her. "I love you," he crooned.

"I love you too, Jordan, forever." She kissed him back fervently then pulled back. "Oh, incidentally," she said, "I was thinking."

Jordan pulled back a few inches, narrowed his eyebrows, and gazed into her eyes warily. It was unusual for her to stop him when he kissed her. She laughed at his expression.

He held his breath. "Yes, what is it, Jaynee?"

She waited, allowing him to reflect for a moment.

"You're killing me; you know how I hate —" he grumbled.

She smiled and wiggled herself under his body to get exactly where she wanted. "Well, it's the office. I don't think we need it anymore, since I can't do any work in there and leave the twins alone downstairs to their own devices. And it takes up the entire back of the house. So I was thinking maybe we could remodel it into two rooms instead."

"Two rooms? What in the world would we do with two additional rooms if we don't need an office?" He shook his head in confusion. "Why would you want —" He stopped mid sentence.

He bolted upright, staring at her, waiting. They hadn't been trying, but they hadn't been not trying to get pregnant either, and they were starting to get worried. She was thirty-two, he was thirty-seven, and they both really wanted more children.

"Jaynee, are you saying? Are you pregnant? Are you positive? How far along are you?" His face went from a curious countenance to a thrilled expression in a matter of seconds.

She grinned widely, delighted by his excitement. "Yes, yes, and yes, and about six weeks. You always were a top-notch detective, Mr. Monroe."

He jumped out of bed with a hoot and a holler.

"Hey, where do you think you're going? I wasn't finished yet."

"Oh, sorry," he said, jumping back beside her even more enthused than before. He kissed her hands, her neck, and then her belly. Lightly touching the soft flesh, he stopped ... "Two rooms?" he asked. "Twins again?"

She nodded.

Jordan sighed, and a glorious look washed over his face. He rolled over on his side and pulled her with him. He cupped her face as he kissed her, then his hand moved to caress her hair down her back.

Jaynee could tell he wasn't going to go any farther this morning. So she curled up in his arms. She could wait until tonight. She sighed with complete contentment as he automatically pulled her closer.

"Happily ever after, love," he whispered, kissing her softly again.

And they ... lived ...
Life isn't always happily-ever-after, rather, loving forever, regardless.
— Carmen DeSousa

Sneak Peek

Book Description

Split Decisions is a follow-up story to *She Belongs to Me*, a *what if* type of story that explores the questions we often ask ourselves about our life and the choices we've made. Since you've read Jaynee's story, you know she had many doors that she could have gone through in her life, and each one had the potential to cause her harm or bring her happiness.

While doing my final read-through of *She Belongs to Me*, I saw many of the doors that Jaynee could have chosen ... and a few things I hadn't even realized were there. If you've ever spoken with authors, you will have heard that sometimes when we write, we get lost in our writing ... and we look back later, and think, "Did I write that? I don't remember writing that."

Well, that's what happened, so get ready... *Split Decisions* is not your normal romantic-suspense ... this is romantic-suspense with a twist, by twist I mean it has an element of Magical Realism. If you don't like books that step a tiny bit out of the realm of what seems possible, please skip *Split Decisions*. You can jump right to *Land of the Noonday Sun*, which technically was the next book in the collection.

If you like your reality dipped in a little *what if*, though, please turns the page for a sneak peek.

Split Decisions

Prologue

A Week Before Jaynee's Fortieth Birthday ...

Jaynee awoke with a start, salty tears streaming down her cheeks, burning her already chapped lips.

She attempted to swallow, but didn't have enough saliva to moisten her mouth. It'd just been a nightmare. The nightmare she used to have nightly after her father committed suicide. Though, she hadn't had it in years. Not since Jordan had taken her away from her previous life, providing a stable home, love, and strong arms to shield her from the demons that haunted her.

Unfortunately, Jordan wasn't here, and her surroundings were all too real. Pinpricks of sunlight streaked through the corners of the shaded windows, illuminating the dust motes dancing in the air.

The room was still dark in most spots, but she could almost make out her surroundings. It looked like a cabin of some sort. The walls were a dingy off-white or possibly just stained from years of exposure, but the ceiling and trim were dark wood along with the slatted floors. A musty scent permeated the area, irritating her sinuses, but she couldn't even scratch her nose.

Cuffs still secured her to the four bedposts. *What kind of sicko would do such a thing?* Her arms and legs ached from the position they'd been in all night, and she had to go to the bathroom something awful.

When she opened her mouth to speak, nothing but a croak escaped, leaving a trail of lava in her parched throat. "Hel-lo?" Though her voice had cracked, she attempted to sound friendly. Screaming or sobbing wouldn't do any good. Not that she had the strength or vocal cords anyway.

She wasn't in the city; only the country would be as dark as it'd been last night when her assailant had brought her here. Even if she screamed her head off, no one would hear. "Please," she tried again. "I really have to use the bathroom."

The door finally opened, the hinges protesting in a lengthy screech, begging for oil. Her captor entered the room, still wearing a black ski mask, gloves, and the same dark jeans and thick overcoat he'd worn the previous evening. He wasn't too tall or heavy. If given the chance, she could probably take him. Jordan had taught her a few things. But as long as he had the gun trained on her, she'd have to be submissive.

His gauntleted hand unlocked just one of her wrists. Then placing the key in her hand, he stepped back. Obviously she was to unlock her other restraints. She didn't waste any time. She unlatched her left hand, then both of her ankles. After rubbing them to increase circulation, she jumped out of the bed on the opposite side of her detainer. He motioned with the gun that she should move to the door on the far side of the room. She did as instructed, opening the door to a small bathroom with just a sink and toilet. No window. She quickly relieved herself. It felt incredible; she'd actually been in pain.

When finished, she opened the medicine cabinet and cubbyhole under the sink, finding nothing usable as a weapon. Both rooms were completely barren, stripped of everything. The abduction had not been a coincidence ... but premeditated.

And it was her fault. If she hadn't been searching...

Thank you for reading this sneak peek. I hope you'll look for *Split Decisions* and my other stories.

You can find all my books on my website:
www.CarmenDeSousaBooks.com.

Acknowledgements

My journey as a writer has been a long one. Although *She Belongs to Me* took two years to write and publish, the story took twenty-five years to compile, as life tends to get in the way of dreams.

If it weren't for my wonderful, supportive husband of twenty-four years, my writing would not be possible. He truly made me believe in a happily-ever-after. Without my husband and two wonderful sons, there would be no reason to write.

I would also like to thank a friend who has cheered me on from the beginning, Jamie Rush. Jamie's books were an inspiration, but more so, her words of encouragement kept me going.

A big thank you to my best friend and cousin, who endured the first drafts of this story and provided much-needed feedback. Without their insight, this novel would never have seen the light of day.

Many thanks to Bernadette Soehner — a great friend and publisher — not a day has gone by that she hasn't communicated with me as we worked feverishly to put together this novel.

And lastly a thank you to my biggest fan — my youngest son — he has stood by me longer than any other person, championing me constantly through every rough turn in the road.

I love you all.

About the Author

I love writing. As far back as I can remember I created stories — no, not to my parents — with my best friend. We would sit for hours playing with Barbie dolls, creating new adventures with the iconic toy. Then when I was eight, I actually wrote my first story. A horror story about gigantic fleas of all things; I guess I had a fear of fleas. Who knew I'd grow up to be a romantic-suspense writer?

When I was in college, I wrote my first novella. My professor wanted something that entailed drinking and fishing — he was a huge Hemingway fan. Well, he sure received a surprise when he read my short story. It entailed drinking and fishing all right, but there was nothing funny about it. It was sad; it was real life. Luckily, he enjoyed it, even admitted I was the first student who'd ever made him cry and that I had potential.

Unfortunately, it wasn't in my future at the time. After all, I needed a roof over my head and food on my plate. At seventeen, I was on my own and a career as an author just wasn't feasible at that juncture in my life. At that time, if you didn't live in the Mecca — aka New York — you didn't stand a chance, or at least that is what my peers insisted. So, I shelved my dreams and set out for a career. I spent the next twenty-five years in the business world, rising to the top of a Fortune 500 company.

Now I'm back, seeking my dream. And guess what, it's a new world where dreams really do come true. My first novel, *She Belongs to Me*, was first published in December 2011. Since then, I've shared many of the stories I'd been writing ... fourteen as of 2015, and I have many more to come. I waited twenty-five years to share my love of the written word, so I hope you will want to read all of my stories.

Until next time, happy reading!

Carmen

Before You Go ...

Dear friend, I hope you enjoyed my first novel, *She Belongs to Me*. Jordan and Jaynee will return in *Split Decisions*, and then you will also see them in the seventh book in my Southern Romantic Suspense Collection.

All of the books in my Southern Romantic Suspense Collection have slight connections, and then in book seven — there are five right now — all the connections will come full circle.

All of the novels are stand-alone stories — NO CLIFFHANGERS — but a couple of them should be read before the follow-up novels, so as not to run into spoilers. They can be read in any order, as long as you read Charlotte 1 before Charlotte 2 and Nantahala 1 before Nantahala 2.

In order by release date:
She Belongs to Me (Charlotte 1)
Land of the Noonday Sun (Nantahala 1)
Entangled Dreams (Florida)
When Noonday Ends (Nantahala 2)
Split Decisions (Charlotte 2)

New Women's Fiction/ Chick Lit
Some Lucky Woman
Down on Her Luck

Although all of my stories have a common thread —
learning to live and love again after betrayal, loss, or tragedy
— some of my books have a supernatural edge. If you like
your romantic suspense dipped in a little paranormal, please
look for The Creatus Series and my Mystery Series with a
Ghostly Edge.

The Creatus Series
Creatus
Creatus Rogue
Creatus Eidolon
Creatus Animus

Paranormal Mystery Collection
The Pit Stop (This Stop Might be Life of Death)
The Depot (When Life and Death Cross Tracks)
The Library (Where Life Checks Out)

The Watermen Series
A Solstice with Jacky Waterman

You can find all my books on my website:
www.CarmenDeSousaBooks.com.

Please ... please ... please ... if you enjoyed *She Belongs to Me*,
leave a review. It doesn't have to be fancy, just a few words
to let other readers know if they should download it too. It

means so much to an author to hear what readers loved —
even didn't love — about a book. It's how we grow and
learn what you want to read next time ... and in the case of
a series, which characters you want to see more of in the
next books or which ones we should knock off. :)

Thank you again!

Carmen